# KULTI

MARIANA ZAPATA

Book Cover Design by Jasmine Green

*To my dad.*
*My friend, my playmate,*
*my champion, my co-conspirator, and*
*my backup any and every time I've ever needed you.*
*Any father I try to write would be*
*a poor replica of you.*
*I love you, dude.*

# 1

I blinked. Then, I blinked some more. "What did you just say?"

The man sitting across the desk from me repeated himself.

Still, I stared at him. I heard him correctly the first time. He was loud and clear. No problems. But my brain couldn't wrap itself around the sentence that had come out of his mouth. I understood all the individual words in the sentence, but putting them together in that moment was the equivalent of telling a blind person you wanted them to see something real quick.

Basically, it wasn't going to happen.

"I need you, Sal," Coach Gardner, the man who was asking the impossible of me, insisted.

I sat back against the chair in his office and took in the silvering hair on his head, his smooth, unlined face and the Houston Pipers polo shirt he had on. For being in his late forties, he was still a looker. Demented and out-of-his-freaking mind, but handsome nonetheless.

Then again, Jeffrey Dahmer had been attractive, so good

looks weren't exactly the best scale of measurement for an individual's mental health.

*Calm down, take a deep breath, and get it together, Sal. Focus.* I needed to focus on something else to relax. I chose his office walls.

A neat line of diplomas hung to his right. On either side were pictures with his son and a few framed photographs of the Pipers on the field over the years—my favorite was a shot of the team last year when we'd won the Women's Professional League championship. He was in the middle of the group with the league trophy, this three-foot monstrosity, held high above his head. I was right next to him holding the game soccer ball under one arm with my other around Jenny, our team's goalie. I had the same picture in my apartment, a constant reminder of twenty years' worth of hard work paying off. Plus, it was my motivation on the mornings when I sat on the edge of my bed looking and feeling more dead than alive, to get up and go on my daily five-mile run.

"Sal," the head coach of the team said my name again. "You've never let me down before. Come on," he chastised me in a low, playful voice that gave the impression he was giving me a choice.

He wasn't.

Just thinking about what he wanted me to do sent my heart pounding. My nervous system had slowed the minute he said the words 'you' and 'press conference' in the same sentence just a minute before. Then, when he said the word 'today,' my brain wished me good luck and shut down. I didn't know what to do besides stare at him blankly.

Me. Press conference. Today.

I would rather get a root canal, donate my kidney and be constipated. Seriously.

I hadn't given much thought into Gardner calling me the night before. I didn't think twice when he asked me to come to his office at the Pipers headquarters because there was something he wanted to talk about in person. I should have pleaded a case of food poisoning or bad cramps to get out of it, but obviously it was too late now.

I'd walked right into his trap, physically and emotionally.

Cameras. So many cameras.

Oh God, I was going to puke just thinking about it.

My initial thought was: No. Please, *no*. Some people were scared of heights, the dark, clowns, spiders, snakes... I never made fun of anyone when they were scared of things. But this horrible fear I had of speaking in front of a camera with a group of people watching had gotten me called a wimp at least a hundred times, mostly by my brother, but that still counts.

"You're going to tell me you can't do it?" Coach Gardner raised an eyebrow, cementing the fact that he wasn't giving me a choice, while also baiting me with words he knew I wouldn't back down from. I was in his office at ten in the morning because he wanted *me* to be, not anyone else.

Son of a bitch.

If I were a lesser person, my lower lip would have started trembling. I might have even blinked and batted my eyes so that I wouldn't cry because we were both well aware of the fact I couldn't tell him no. I wouldn't tell him no.

Even if it killed me, I'd do what he wanted. He was banking on it, too. Because I was that idiot that didn't back down from a taunt. A broken arm after someone said I couldn't climb up this massive tree when I was eleven, should have taught me that backing down every once in a while was the right thing to do, but it didn't.

I mentally stepped into my Big Girl Socks—the equivalent I'd been given as a kid instead of Big Girl Panties because my dad thought that was a creepy expression.

"I'll do it." I grimaced, more than likely looking like I was getting an enema. "But... G, why isn't Grace doing it? Or Jenny?

You know they usually do all of the interviews and stuff." Because I sure as hell avoided them, at least the ones in front of a camera.

"I didn't ask Grace because I think it'd be a good idea for you to do it," he explained, referring to the team's veteran captain. "And Jenny isn't arriving until Sunday."

I blinked some more at him, on the verge of puking and shitting myself at the same time. My leg had already begun shaking and I palmed it, trying to get it to stop.

Gardner smiled tenderly, leaning across his big glass desk, hands clasped. "You haven't even asked me what the conference is for."

Like I freaking cared. It could have been because someone had found a cure for cancer, and it wouldn't matter. I'd be trying not to lose it all the same. My heart just started beating faster at the mention of the 'c' word, but I forced myself to look like I wasn't fighting back a panic attack. "All right, what's it for?" I asked slowly.

Our soccer team's preseason training started in a week and a half, so I guess I'd subconsciously assumed that was it.

But the question had barely left the head coach's mouth when he started smiling, his brown eyes wide. He leaned forward and said something that was just as bad, if not worse, than asking me to do a press conference. Sixteen words that I hadn't been braced to hear. Sixteen words that I had no clue were about to change my life.

"We just got confirmation that Reiner Kulti is taking the team's assistant coach position this season," Gardner explained, his tone implying 'this is the best thing to ever happen.'

My face said 'no, it's freaking not.'

It took a minute for his smile to fall and a confused look to take over, but it happened. It fell like a Jenga tower, slowly and surely.

He gave me a look. "Why are you making that face?"

* * *

I WAS seven years old the first time I saw Reiner Kulti on television. I can remember the exact moment he came on the screen. It was the semi-final for the Altus Cup—the tournament that happened every three years and included every national soccer team in the world eliminating each other left and right over qualifying rounds. It was the most highly televised sporting event in the world.

Why wouldn't it be? Soccer, also known as the 'real' football or *futbol*, was the most widely played sport across the inhabited continents. It didn't discriminate. You could be tall, short, skinny, poor or rich. All you needed was a ball that was at least sort of inflated, and something to make a goal, which could be anything. Coffee cans. Coke cans. Trash cans. Anything. You could be a girl or a boy. Have a uniform, not have a uniform. And as my dad said, you didn't even need shoes if you really wanted to get technical.

Because my brother played it and loved it—and for some reason back then I thought my brother was the coolest person ever—I made my parents put me on a team when I was around six. My mom on the other hand, was slightly horrified and enrolled me in karate and swimming as well. But a small part of me had always known I liked soccer more than I liked anything else.

On my dad's side, I came from a long line of soccer fanatics. The Casillas didn't play much, but they were big fans. With the exception of my older brother, who had supposedly showed an interest and a talent for it from the moment he was old enough to walk, everyone else just watched.

But as I remember, and from the hundred times Dad retold the story, my brother and my father had been talking about whether Spain was going to wipe the floor with Germany or not, before the game started. A little after halftime, most of the players on the German team had to be substituted because of one injury or another.

Eric, my brother, had already said, "Germany's done," and my dad had argued there was still time left for either team to score a point.

Clear as day, I can visualize in my head the fresh-faced, nineteen-year-old who made his way onto the field. He was the last player on the team that could possibly be put in, the guy's first time playing on the international scene. With light brown hair that seemed even lighter because of our static-y old television, a face that was hairless and a body that was long and thin... oh man, he'd been the cutest, youngest player I'd ever seen on the Altus Cup so far.

Truthfully, Germany should have been done. The odds were against them. Hell, their own fans were probably against them by that point.

Yet, no one had seemed to have given the team the message.

At some point between the forty-five-minute marker that started the second half of the game, and the ninety-minute mark that ended normal regulation time, that skinny boy with the cute face who couldn't have been that much older than me, but he was, managed to steal the ball from a Spanish forward attacking the German goal and ran. He ran, and ran, and ran and by some miracle avoided every opposing player that went after him.

He scored the most beautiful, ruthless goal in the top right corner of the net. The ball seemed to sail through the air with a one-way ticket to the record books.

My dad screamed. Eric yelled. The freaking stadium and the announcers lost it. This guy who had never played on such a platform had done what no one expected of him.

It was one of those moments that lifts a person's spirit up. Sure, it wasn't you that did anything special, but it made you feel like you had. It gave you the impression that you could do anything because this other person did.

It reminded you that anything was possible.

I know that I stood there screaming right along with my dad because he was yelling and it seemed the most appropriate thing to do. But mostly, I know I thought that this Kulti on the German national team who looked barely old enough to drive, was the most amazing player in the world that year.

To do what no one believed you could do...

Jesus. Now, as an adult, I can look back and understand why he had such an effect on me. It makes total sense. People still talk about that goal when they bring up the best moments in Altus Cup history.

What was the turning point when I decided to follow this dream of turf, two goals, and a single, checkered white and black ball? That moment. That goal changed everything. It was the moment I decided I wanted to be like that guy—the hero.

I dedicated my life, my time and my body to the sport all because of the player I would grow to follow and support and love with all my little heart, my patron saint of soccer—Reiner Kulti. For him, it was the moment that changed his career. He became Germany's savior, their star. Over the next twenty years of his career, he became the best, the most popular and the most hated.

Then there was the whole, I-had-posters-of-him-all-over-my-walls until I was seventeen, and the whole me-telling-everyone-I-was-going-to-marry-him thing.

Before the posters and the marriage announcements, there had been the letters I remembered writing him as a kid. 'I'm your #1 fan,' written on construction paper with markers and crayons. They never got a response.

But I kept that crap to myself.

Plus, it had been ten years since I'd torn down the posters in a fit of rage, when the man who had grown to become known as Reiner 'The King' Kulti by his fans for being one of the most explosive and creative players in the sport, got married.

I mean, hadn't he known we were supposed to get married and have soccer-playing-super-babies together? That he was supposed to sit next to me on an airplane one day and instantly fall in love with me? Yeah, apparently he hadn't gotten the memo, and he married some actress with boobs that seemed to defy gravity.

And then less than a year later, he did other things that I couldn't forgive.

Gardner had no idea about any of this.

* * *

I SAT up straight in the chair across from the same head coach I'd been working with for the last four years and shrugged. *Why was I looking like that?* Like I wasn't excited at all? "G, you know what happened between him and my brother, right?"

At that point, I guess I was expecting him to not know, because he'd been way too excited to tell me about Reiner Kulti getting hired.

But Gardner nodded and shrugged, his face still a canvas of confusion. "Of course I know. That's why you're the perfect person to do this conference, Sal. Besides Jenny and Grace, you're the most well-known and well-liked player on the team. What do they call you, 'the home-state sweetheart?'"

Home-state sweetheart. Gross. It made me feel like I was back in high school running for homecoming queen instead of the kid that skipped every homecoming because she usually had a game.

"Kulti broke—"

"I know what he did. PR already brought up what happened with Kulti and Eric during our meeting last night when they told us he was hired. No one wants this season to be a soap opera. You going on camera and smiling and giving everyone that Sal-smile is exactly what the team needs. This isn't a big deal, and everyone needs to get on board so that the focus is on the team and not drama from years ago. It'll be ten, maybe twenty minutes, maximum. You, me and him. You'll answer a few questions and that's it. I won't put you through this again, I swear."

My initial thought was simple: this was all Eric's tibia and fibula's fault.

I wanted to bang my head against the desk that separated me from Gardner, but I managed not to. Instead, dread pooled a bloody lake in my belly. It made me cramp, and I had to press a hand over it like that would help ease my suffering. Then I sighed again and accepted the reality behind Gardner's words.

The league was all about family values, morals and everything wholesome. I learned that lesson the hard way, and the last thing I needed to do was ignore what had to be done to uphold that façade. Realistically, there were girls out there who would slit my throat for my position. And maybe meeting Kulti right before a press conference was exactly what I needed.

Just get it done, get it over with and move on with my life. I hadn't really followed his career in the last decade, and he'd retired from the European League two years ago. Since then, he'd fallen off the celebrity wagon he'd been adopted into with all of his endorsements. At one point, you couldn't go to the mall without seeing his face on an ad for something.

"I get it," I moaned and dropped my head back to stare at the ceiling. "I'll do it."

"That's my girl."

I only just barely won the fight to not call him a sadistic asshole for making me do something that almost made me break out in hives. "I can't promise that I won't stutter my way through the entire interview or throw up on the first row, but I'll do my best."

Then I was going to punch Eric in the fucking kidney the first chance I got, damn it.

* * *

*You can do this, Sal. You can do it.*

When I was little and my dad would ask me to do something I didn't want to, which usually only happened if it was something I was horrified by—example, trying to kill those gigantic flying roaches that snuck into our house—he'd point his finger at me and tell me in Spanish, "*Si puedes!*" You can. Then, even if I cried as I went into the room housing the creature from the bowels of hell with a shoe as a weapon, I did whatever it was that I didn't want to.

'I can and I will,' had been the motto I held closest to my heart at all times. I didn't like people telling me I couldn't do something, even if I didn't want to do it. This was how Coach Gardner had gotten me to say I'd do the interview.

I could do it. I could be in the same room as Reiner Kulti. Sit a couple seats down from him for the first time ever in front of several television networks. No biggie.

On the inside, I crumpled into a ball like a dead spider and asked myself to please dissolve into dust sooner than later. This terror, this phobia of mine, was that unreasonable. No one ever says that fear is logical, because it isn't. It's stupid and irrational and on a scale of one to ten it sucked about a fifty.

"You ready?" Coach Gardner asked as we waited for the beginning of the press conference. The journalists and reporters were so loud in the other room it was making me sick. How the hell had this even happened? I was usually third down the chain of players that got requested for these publicity events, and that was for a reason.

I could play in front of thousands of people, but the instant cameras got within ten feet of me, I just shut down. I was like the Ricky Bobby of the WPL. I was sure there was a video of me making awful hand gestures throughout an interview somewhere. The three S's came down to make me look like an idiot —stuttering, sweating and shaking. All at once.

My hands felt like I'd just rubbed them all over my lower back after a long run, my armpits were sweaty... and my leg was shaking. Both my legs were shaking. I knew shit was about to get real when my leg shook.

But instead of admitting that I was nervous, I stuck my hands in my pockets, thanked the lord above that the sweat pants I'd put on that morning were baggy enough so that no one could tell my legs had a mind of their own, and forced a smile on my face. "Ready," I lied through my teeth.

And unfortunately, he knew me well enough to recognize the fact I was lying out of my ass because Gardner laughed loud. A hand came down on my shoulder and he gave me a shake. "You're a wreck. It'll be fine."

One of the public relations people for the organization peeped around the corner of the hallway and frowned for a second before disappearing again.

I couldn't do this.

*I could do this.*

One hacking cough later, I told myself: I could do this. I really could.

My leg only shook harder as someone came over a microphone in the other room, "We need a minute, please."

Oh God.

"I think I just threw up in my mouth a little," I muttered more to myself than to Gardner.

"It'll be fine," he assured me with a sympathetic smile.

I cleared my throat and nodded at him, begging myself to calm down. I took a couple of quick inhales and exhales before sucking in one deep breath and holding it, like I did when I was too amped up before a game.

Yeah, it didn't help.

My stomach swelled with nausea and I had to swallow back bile.

"Where is he, anyway?" I asked.

Gardner actually looked around like the question surprised him. "You know, I have no clue. I guess they put him in a different room?"

We got our answer a second later when the same PR rep who had just made an appearance was back, the corners of her mouth twisted downward. "We have a problem."

# 2

"Sal, *no*."

"Yes."

"Sal, I'm not kidding. Not even a little bit. Please. *Please*. Tell me you're joking."

I laid my head back against the headboard and closed my eyes, giving myself a grim smile of defeat. All was lost. This afternoon had been real, and there was no escaping it. So I told Jenny the truth, "Oh, it happened."

She groaned.

Jenny was a true friend, like one that felt the worst of your pain for you, suffering right along with you; she let out a groan that I could feel from over a thousand miles away. My humiliation was her humiliation. Jenny Milton and I had been friends from the moment we met each other at camp for the United States national team—the 'best' players in the country—five years ago. "*No*," she groaned, she choked. "*No*."

Oh, yes.

I sighed and relived the twenty minutes in front of the cameras that afternoon. I wanted to die. I wouldn't go as far as to say it was the worst thing that had ever happened to me, but it was definitely one of those few moments that I wished I could go back and redo differently. Or at least go all *Eternal Sunshine of the Spotless Mind* and pretend they never happened. "I'm going to dye my hair, change my name and go live in Brazil," I told her evenly.

What did she do? She laughed. She laughed and then snorted, and then laughed a little more.

The fact that she didn't try to tell me everything was okay meant that I wasn't overreacting to the events that had transpired hours before.

"What do you think my chances are that no one ever sees the entire thing?"

Jenny made a noise that gave the impression she was actually putting some thought behind the question. "I would say you're out of luck. I'm sorry."

My head hung and my chest puffed out in a suffering laugh-slash-dry cry. "On a scale of one to ten, how screwed?"

There wasn't a response until there was, and it was sharp and tight. A high laugh that let me know Jenny was feeling it down to her toes. She was laughing like she did every other time I'd done something incredibly embarrassing. Like waving back at a stranger that I thought had been waving at me—he wasn't, there'd been someone behind me. Or the time I skid across a freshly mopped floor and busted my ass.

I shouldn't expect any different.

"Sal, did you really…?'

"Yes."

"In front of everyone?"

I grunted. I could barely think about it without tossing my cookies and wanting to find myself a cave and hibernate forever. It was over and life would go on. Ten years from now no one would remember, but…

I would. I'd remember.

And Jenny, Jenny would remember especially if she ever

found the footage. And she would, I knew she would. She was probably already trolling websites looking for Sal Casillas's entry into those video compilations people did for Fail of the Week.

"Would you stop laughing?" I snapped into the receiver when she couldn't stop cracking up.

She laughed even harder. "One day!"

"I'm hanging up on you now, bitch."

There was a loud snicker, followed by another, and then one more piercing gut-laugh. "Give... me... a... minute," she wheezed.

"You know, I called you because you're the nicest person I know. I thought *who isn't going to give me shit*? Jenny, Jenny won't. Thanks a lot."

She gasped, and then she laughed even more. There was no doubt in my mind she was reliving the events of my day in her head and finally enjoying the humor in them—the humor anyone could have when it wasn't them that had embarrassed themselves in front of the media.

I pulled my phone away from my face and held my finger over the red button, imagining myself hanging up the call.

"Okay, okay. I'm fine now." She did these weird breathing exercises to calm down before finally getting it together. "Okay, *okay*." A weird wheezing noise came out of her nose, but it only lasted a split second. "Okay. So, he didn't show up? Did they say why?"

Kulti. The entire afternoon had been his fault. All right, that was a lie. It'd been my fault. "No. They said he had some travelling issues or something. That's why they made Gardner and I do the conference by ourselves."

Cue my imaginary sob.

"That sounds pretty fishy," Jenny noted, almost sounding normal. *Almost*. I could already envision her pinching her nose and holding the phone away from her face as she cracked up.

Asshole. "I bet he was eating brunch and looking at ads of himself online."

"Or looking up old footage and criticizing himself."

"Counting his collection of watches—" He'd had a watch endorsement for as long as I could remember.

"He was probably sitting in a hyperbaric chamber reading about himself."

"That's a good one," I laughed, stopping only when the phone clicked twice. A long digit number with fifty-two at the beginning flashed across the display and it only took a second for me to realize who was calling. "Hey, I need to let you go, but I'll see you at practice on Monday; your best friend is calling."

Jenny laughed. "Okay, tell him I said hi."

"I will."

"Bye, Sal."

I rolled my eyes and smiled. "See ya. Have a safe trip," I said, right before clicking over to answer the incoming call.

I didn't even get a chance to say a word before the male voice on the other line said "Salomé."

Oh God. He was being serious. It was the way he said it, more choked rather than enunciated, all *Salo-meh,* instead of his usual "*Sal!*" that burst out of his mouth like I'd broken something irreplaceable. No one ever called me by my first name, much less my dad. I think the only times he ever had were when he meant business... as in the business of him trying to kick my ass when my mom thought I did something spectacularly dumb and wanted him to do something about it. There was the time I got into a fight during a game when I was fifteen and got thrown out. He never actually went through with any sort of real punishment. His idea of discipline was chores—lots and lots of chores as he secretly praised my jab when my mom wasn't around.

So when Dad continued by saying, "Is this a dream? Am I dreaming?" I couldn't help but laugh.

I pulled the covers down and away from my face to speak with him. The first thing I said to him was, "No. You're just crazy."

He was crazy. Crazy in love, Mom joked. As a total soccer snob, my dad was like most foreigners—he wasn't a fan of U.S. soccer if it didn't have me or my brother in the equation. Or Reiner Kulti, also branded as 'The King' by his fans and 'the *Führer'* by those that hated his guts. Dad liked to say he couldn't help liking him. Kulti was too good, too talented, and he'd played on my dad's favorite team for most of his career, with the exception of a two-year stint he had with the Chicago Tigers at one point. So there was that, too. The man owned four different types of jerseys: the Mexican national team jersey, each club or team Eric had played for, mine, and Kulti's. It went without saying he wore Kulti's way more often than someone with two kids who played professional soccer should, but I didn't take it too personally.

The three of us—my mom and little sister excluded—had spent hours on top of hours watching all of Kulti's games. We'd record the ones we couldn't watch in person on the VCR and later on, through DVR. I'd been young enough for the six-foot-two German national to make the biggest impact possible on my life. Sure, Eric had been playing soccer for as long as I could remember, but Kulti's influence had been different. It had been this magnetic force that drew me to the field day after day, making me tag along with Eric every chance I got because he was the best player I knew.

It just happened that Dad had gone along on the ride with me, fueling my hero worship.

"I was sitting here eating, when your cousin runs into the house," my parents were visiting my aunt in Mexico, "and tells me to turn on the news."

It was coming...

"*Why didn't you tell me?*"

"I couldn't! We couldn't tell anyone until it was official, and I found out right before they made me do the press conference."

There was a pause, a choke on his end. He said something that sounded like *Dios mio* under his breath. In a low whisper he asked, "You did a press conference?" He couldn't believe it.

He hadn't seen it. Thank you, Jesus. "It went just as bad as you're imagining it did," I warned him.

Dad paused again, absorbing and analyzing what I was telling him. Apparently he decided to let the news of my stupidity in front of the camera go for the time being before asking, "It's true? He's your new coach?" He asked the question so hesitantly, so slow, if it was possible for me to love my dad even more—it wasn't, that was a fact—I would have.

For some strange reason I had the mental flashback of having Kulti's late-twenties face on my sophomore math binder. Bah. "Yeah, it's true. He's going to be our new assistant since Marcy left."

In a weird rattling exhale, my dad muttered, "I'm going to faint."

I burst out laughing even harder at the same time a yawn tried to climb out of me. I'd stayed up watching a Netflix marathon of British comedies until I found the mental strength to call Jenny with my story. I knew it was close to midnight, which was way past my usual old-lady bedtime of ten, or eleven if I was feeling really crazy. But I knew she was still in Iowa for two more days and she'd be up. "You're such a drama queen."

"Your sister's the drama queen," he griped.

He had me there.

"You're not lying?" He kept speaking in Spanish, and by speaking, I really meant he was more like panting at that point.

I groaned, shoving the sheets further down my waist. "No, Dad. Jeez. It's true. Mr. Cordero—our general manager, that idiot I told you about—sent out an email to the team right afterward," I explained.

Dad was quiet for a moment; the only sound coming through the speaker was his breathing. I was dying a little bit inside at his reaction. I mean, I wasn't surprised he was having his own version of a shit attack. I'd think there was something wrong with him if he wasn't acting like this might be one of the single greatest moments of his life. "I feel light-headed—"

This man was ridiculous.

There was a pause, and in a tiny voice that was so at odds with the man that could usually be heard screaming *GGGGGGGGOOOOOOOOLLLLLLLLLLL* down the block, my dad croaked, "My hands—my hands are shaking—" he switched back to English, his voice choppy.

My entire body was shaking with laughter. "Quit it."

"Sal." His tone turned thin, too thin for a man whose voice only had two volumes: loud and louder. "*Voy a llorar*. You're going to be on the same field as him."

I had to let it go. My stomach started cramping from how hard my dad was making me laugh. I didn't bring up Eric, it wasn't like any of us would forget his experience, but that was true love for you—blind and unconditional. "Dad, stop." I couldn't quit laughing because knowing him, he was being totally honest.

He wasn't much of a crier. He'd cried when I'd been called to the U-17 team, the national team for girls under seventeen, and again when I moved up to the U-20 team. The only other time I could remember seeing him with tears in his eyes was the day his father died. By the time I got drafted into the professional league, he'd just beamed, more comfortable in my position than I was. I'm pretty sure I was so nervous I had sweat stains on my butt.

"He's going to be your coach," he squeaked, and I mean really squeaked.

"*I know*." I laughed that time. "I've gotten like ten emails from people I know asking me to confirm. You're all insane."

Dad simply repeated himself, "He's going to be your coach."

That time, I pinched the bridge of my nose to keep from making a sound. "I'll tell you when the open practice will be so you can meet him."

Then he did it, he crossed the line again. "Sal—Sal, don't tell anyone, but you're my favorite."

Oh my God. "Dad—"

There was a shout in the background that sounded suspiciously like my younger sister and was followed by what I could only assume was Dad holding the phone away from his face as he yelled back, "*I was joking!...You told me you hated me yesterday, te acuerdas? Why are you going to be my favorite when you say you wish I wasn't your dad?*" Then he started yelling some more. Eventually he came back on the line with a resigned sigh. "That girl, *mija*. I don't know what to do with her."

"I'm sorry." I was, at least partially. I couldn't imagine how hard it was for my little sister to be so different from Eric and I. She didn't like the same things we did—sports—but mostly, she didn't seem to really like anything. My parents had tried putting her in different activities, but she never lasted and never put in any effort. Like I'd told my parents, she needed to figure things out for herself.

"*Ay*. I guess I can't complain too much. Hold on a second—Ceci, *que quieres*?" And then he was off, yelling at my sister a little more.

I just sat there with the phone still to my face, lying in my bed two hundred miles away from where I'd grown up, soaking in the idea that Reiner Kulti—*the* Reiner Kulti—was going to be my coach. I swallowed the nerves and anticipation down.

No big deal.

*Right.*

What I needed to do was get it together and focus on making it through preseason training to ensure my spot as a starter. I'd have to fuck up royally to not start the season, but sometimes the unexpected was known to happen. I didn't like to play around with chance anyway.

And with that thought, I finished up my conversation with my dad, lay in bed, and talked myself out of going for a late, last-minute, five-mile run. My body needed the rest. It only took me ten minutes of staring off blankly at the wall, to really decide I could save a run for the morning and it would be fine.

One of my favorite coaches when I was younger would always say when motivating us to practice: *To be prepared for war is one of the most effective means of preserving peace.*

There'd be no peace in my life if I didn't do well when practices began, with or without The King being there.

# 3

"The meeting is on the fifth floor today, Sal, conference room 3C." The guard winked at me as he slid my visitor's pass across the granite desk.

"Thanks. See you later." I flashed him a big grin and nodded, eyeing the huge mural on the wall behind him. It was a mixed media piece, multicolored and vibrant, with dozens of snapshots of Pipers players and Wreckers, the Houston men's professional club. We were their expansion team, created and managed by the same ownership group. Or as I fondly thought of it, we were the adopted kids, the ones that had come years after a successful track record for the men while the owners had hopes and dreams in their eyes for our potential. Why they named the team the Pipers, I had no idea. It was probably the worst name I'd ever heard, all it made me think of was a boner for some reason.

One of the players in the piece was me, right in the middle, my arms thrown over my head after I'd scored a goal two seasons ago. I'd have to tell my dad about the mural, I told myself, taking in the new artwork they'd added to the lobby since I hadn't really been paying attention when I'd come to see Coach Gardner days before. Headquarters for the Wreckers and Pipers was an impressive building, only a couple years old and located in a developing neighborhood just outside of the downtown area.

It'd been three days since the press conference, and so far I hadn't heard anything from a single person regarding the huge idiot I made of myself. Nothing. Not a phone call or a text or an email from anyone telling me they saw what happened. I was used to being the butt end of a joke, or being teased for the things I liked or the way I dressed, so I was prepared for it.

But still.

I dreaded the day the video would leak, but I shoved the worry to the back of my head for another time. Priorities. I had priorities, like today.

The staff and the team were scheduled for an introductory meeting before practices began. It was mainly to get the new people acquainted with schedules, rules and a whole bunch of other details that usually went in one ear and out the other.

The conference room was easy to find. There were only a few people already waiting, and I took a seat halfway into the room after waving to and greeting the girls closest to me. I watched a couple of the other assistant coaches and Coach Gardner, who had given me a hug after the press conference as he tried hard not to laugh, talked in one corner of the room.

Someone squealed.

"Sal!" It was Jenny, my favorite goalkeeper in the world. She was half-Japanese, half a bunch of other European nationalities, had the best skin I'd ever seen, was tall, pretty and had a great attitude. I used to hate her guts—in a friendly way—because she'd blocked way too many of my shots when we were on opposing teams. It was sort of horseshit in the world of fairness when someone was good at everything, and then smart and pretty on top of it. But she was such a nice, kind person that my hatred had lasted about twenty seconds.

"Jen-Jen." I waved at her. She pointed at the chair right next to her and urged me forward. I waved at a few of the other players nearby that I knew, most were looking around suspiciously. Oh lord. I took another quick glance at the coaches to make sure Kulti wasn't hiding between them.

He wasn't.

*Stop it, Sal. Focus.*

Jenny sat up straight to give me a hug. "I'm so happy to see you," she said. Most of the players didn't live in Houston year-round and she was one of them, heading back to her home state of Iowa when the season was over. This would be our third year on the team together. Though I wasn't exactly far from my parents—it was only a three-hour drive more or less to San Antonio—I didn't mind living in Houston, despite the humidity.

Everyone in the conference room seemed to be buzzing around. The players were all keeping an eye out, an air of expectancy saturating everything. I had to remind myself a couple more times to quit doing it too. I caught Jenny glancing around as she dug in her purse for a tube of lipstick, and she blushed when she noticed that I saw what she was doing.

"I really don't think this is that big of a deal," she said, and I believed her. "But... you know, I'm half-expecting him to come here with Hermes wings on his shoes and a halo over his head since everyone thinks he's some kind of god." Jenny paused for a moment before quickly adding, "On the soccer field, I mean."

I winked and nodded. Adding, "Uh-huh, whatever you say," just to mess with her. I was familiar with her type and it wasn't brown-haired men who played soccer. Her boyfriend of two years was a six-foot-two beast, a sprinter who had won a bronze and a silver medal at the last Olympics and had quads the size of my ribcage. Show-off.

Jenny frowned. "Don't make me bring up those pictures I saw."

Damn it. She had me, and from the smirk on her face, she knew it. My mom had busted out the pictures of me in my younger days during a visit Jenny had taken back home with me. In several of them, my Kulti obsession was well-documented. I think it was the three birthday cakes in a row with his face on them that really sealed the deal.

"Hi, Jenny," a familiar voice said from above my head. Almost immediately, two hands grabbed my face from behind and squished my cheeks together. Then two brown eyes appeared over the top of my head. "Hi, Sally."

I poked at the space between the two brown eyes. Her dark blonde hair was trimmed short like always, in a style that would be called a pixie-cut on any other person in the world but her. "Harlow, I missed you," I told the best defender in the country.

Harlow Williams really was the best and for good reason. She was a little scary. Incredibly nice off the field, but on it, those ancient survival instincts every being is born with begged you to run the other away when she was barreling toward you.

We called her The Beast for a reason.

Her reply was in the form of pinching my nostrils together with one hand, cutting off my air supply. "I missed your face too. You got any food on you?" she asked, still peeping over the top of my head.

Of course I had food on me. I pulled three Kind bars out of my purse and handed her the peanut butter one, her favorite.

"That's why I always have your back," she said with a satisfied sigh. "Thanks, Sal. I'll harass you later so you can tell me what you've been up to."

"You got it."

Harlow patted the top of my head a little too hard before taking her seat down the side of the table. She leaned over the edge and waggled her fingers at us as she bit into the bar. Jenny and I made faces at each other. The three of us had played on the national team together back when I was still on it, so more than anyone else we knew each other the best.

"She's a nut."

Jenny nodded. "Yeah, she is. Remember that time she clotheslined you during practice?"

My shoulder throbbed thinking about it. It was Harlow's fault I had chronic pain in it. "I couldn't play for three weeks afterward. Of course I remember." She'd dislocated it when I tried to sneak a ball around her. Never again. While I didn't usually run from an aggressive player, Harlow was in a league of her own.

Coach Gardner clapped his hands once everyone had shown up and welcomed us all to preparation for this season's training. Nearly everyone in the room looked around, surprised that he was starting when someone was so obviously missing. Either Coach Gardner didn't realize no one was really paying attention or he didn't care, because he jumped right into it.

If anyone else thought it was strange that the man who had played through games with the flu and fractured bones wasn't around for our first team meeting, no one said a thing. His attendance record had always been impeccable. It would have taken a force of nature to keep him off the field.

"Coach Marcy took a position with the University of Mobile this summer, so upper management reached out to a few different people to fill in the assistant position she left us open with. We were lucky enough to get a commitment a few days ago. Reiner Kulti—who we all know needs no introduction—will be taking over assistant coach duties."

There was a small collective of sucked-in breaths before Gardner continued. Were these people not checking their emails or at least watching some television? "Although I know you ladies are all professionals, I'm going to say it anyway: this is Coach Kulti. Not Reiner, not *King,* and if I hear any of you calling him *Führer*, you're out of here. Understood? Sheena from PR will be in here to talk about what you can and can't post on social media a little later, but please exercise sound judgment."

I'd never call Kulti *Führer* to begin with, but with that threat, I didn't even want to think about him just to be on the safe side. From the awkward silence that came over the group for the remaining speech, it was obvious everyone felt the same way. We were professionals. I'd never met a group of more competitive people in my life other than when I'd played on the national team.

It was like we were a class of kindergarteners, all sitting there staring absently and nodding as Gardner warned us of our possible demise.

Getting benched? For the season? Or even traded? Yeah, no. That sure as hell wasn't happening.

I caught the tail end of his spiel as he pointed out the six newest additions to the team and then stated his expectations for what he hoped to accomplish—to find a winning combination of talent to take the team to the top for another year in a row. Something about access to the local college's gym and a list of expectations when we were off the field were passed around. It was the same talk I'd heard every other time a new season started.

Except I'd never been threatened with getting kicked off a team for talking badly about a coach who made more money in a year that most of us would make in our entire lives.

I'd worked too hard and too long to let something so dumb ruin my career for me.

No, thank you and fuck that.

Gardner went on for a little while longer about what they would be focusing on during the six weeks between the start of training and the beginning of the season. He introduced the rest of the staff and eventually Sheena, the public relations person who had stood by while I made an ass of myself, took over.

It was all Kulti, Kulti and more Kulti.

"...presence is going to bring more attention to the team. We need to use the momentum of the press and public's excitement to turn it around and focus in on our organization. It's positive and it's a valuable tool to keep the league growing..."

I knew it! I'd known they'd brought him in mainly for the publicity.

"...if you're approached, turn it around and bring attention to the team or the league. Be excited..."

Be excited?

"...Mr. Kulti should be here tomorrow..."

Jenny kicked me beneath the table.

* * *

THEY WEREN'T KIDDING when they said the team would be getting more attention because of the retired German player. What was usually a quiet low-key event with players getting dropped off in minivans, was now an event saturated by rental cars and a few news vans. Freaking news vans. A small group of people were scattered through the lot as I pulled in. I recognized some of the girls as players, but the rest were strangers: journalists, reporters, bloggers and possibly even Kulti fans. At least I hoped it was more fans, but I wasn't optimistic.

This wasn't even the start of practice; it was our yearly fitness assessment before real training began just to see how everyone was doing. No big deal, yet there were so many people...

Anxiety seared my stomach, and I took a deep breath to make the feeling go away.

It didn't really work.

One more deep breath, then another and by the third, I was parked. Thankfully my nerves had settled enough for me to get out of the car without looking like I was battling morning sickness. About five seconds after I got my bag out of the trunk, I heard it. "Casillas!"

Fuck my life.

"Sal Casillas! You got a minute for me?" the masculine voice called out.

I slung the bag over my shoulder and glanced around to find a man breaking away from the group of strangers. He waved, and I felt my stomach sink even as I plastered a smile on my face and waved back. It wasn't anyone's fault that I got all awkward and anxious in front of a video camera.

"Sure," I answered convincingly. Our assessment didn't start for another twenty minutes, but I still had to get ready.

"How you doin'? Steven Cooper with *Sports Daily*," the man greeted me with a handshake. "I just have a few questions if that's fine."

I nodded. "Shoot."

"I'll be recording this for documentation purposes." Showing me the recording device in his hand, he hit the button to start. "What are you looking forward to the most this season?" he asked.

"I'm really looking forward to just starting it. We have some new players and staff on the team, and I'm excited to see how well we all do together." The fact I sounded like a well-adjusted human being instead of one that was about to shit her pants made me proud.

"How do you feel about Reiner Kulti being hired as the Pipers' assistant coach?"

It was the same exact question I'd answered during the press conference from hell days before. "It's still pretty surreal. I'm excited. I think it's great that we're having someone with so much experience coming in to help us out."

"He's an unlikely choice for a coach, don't you think?"

I shoved my hands in my pockets when I felt them start to get clammy. Most of the time these things were fine, but every once in a while they turned into ticking time bombs. I'd put my foot in my mouth more times than I could count, which didn't help my fear with doing these interviews.

"It's different but there's nothing wrong with it. He's been named World Player of the Year more times than anyone else for a reason. He knows what it takes to be the best, and that's something every player strives for. Plus, I think it's unfair to discredit him before we even give him a chance to prove himself," I told him.

He gave me a disbelieving look, like he thought I was full of shit, but he didn't argue with me about it. "All right. What's your prediction for this season? Are the Pipers going to the finals again?"

"That's the plan." I smiled at him. "I need to get going, unless you have one more question?"

"Okay. One more: do you have any plans on joining the national team again soon?"

I opened my mouth and left it open for a second before closing it. I rocked forward on my heels as I rubbed my palms down the front of my shorts. "I'm not planning on it anytime soon. I want to focus on our regular season for now." I swallowed hard and thrust my hand out for him. A second later, I was marching toward the field, watching a few of the other girls get corralled into conversations with other reporters. Two other journalists called out for me, but I declined with an apology. I had to warm up before our assessment began.

Today pretty much consisted of running sprints for an hour, upper body endurance in the form of a push-up-palooza, and endless squats from the third circle of hell, among other forms of torture that the old biddy fitness coach developed recently. Some people really dreaded it, but I wasn't totally opposed to our fitness stuff. Was it fun? No. But I worked out a lot, hard, all year so that I wouldn't be the one huffing and puffing during the first half of a game, and I liked being the fastest. So sue me.

I worked harder than just about anyone for a reason. I was fast, but I wasn't getting any younger, and my bad ankle wasn't getting any better either. Then there was my knee, which had been a problem for the last decade. You had to make up for stuff like that by never getting soft, putting your well-being first, and not taking things for granted.

I'd just finished dropping my things on the side of the field when it finally happened.

It was the "*Oh. My. Godddd*" out of one of the girls I wasn't familiar with that suddenly snapped me into paying attention.

I spotted him. He was there. *There.*

Oh hell. I was dead.

All six-feet-arguably-two inches of brown hair, five-time World Player of the Year, was *right there* talking to the team's fitness coach, a mean old woman who had no pity on anyone.

*Oh snap*. I reached up to make sure my hair hadn't frizzed up in the five minutes I'd been out of my car and then stopped. What the hell was I doing? I dropped my hands immediately. I'd never cared what I looked like when I was playing. Well, I rarely cared what I looked like period. As long as my hair wasn't in my face and my armpits and legs were shaved, I was good. I plucked my eyebrows a couple times a week and I had an addiction to homemade face masks, but that was usually as much effort as I put into myself. People asked me why I was dressing up if I wore jeans, it was that bad.

I'd worn lip balm and a headband on my last date, and here I was fixing my hair. Sheesh.

For the record and for the sake of my pride, I don't think I'd ever fan-girled outwardly in my life. There were a few soccer players I think I'd gotten a little red-faced over and there was that one time when I was fourteen at a JT concert, he'd touched my hand and I'd swooned a little bit... but that was the extent of it. But seeing the master of ball control standing out on the side of the soccer field in a blue and white soccer training jersey and track pants was just... too much.

Way. Too. Much.

Reiner Kulti nodded at something the old, sadistic demon said, and I felt... weird.

To my absolute horror, my inner thirteen-year-old, the one that had planned on marrying this guy and having soccer-playing super-babies with him, peeked in and reminded me she'd been around once. I'd swear on my life that my heart clenched up and my armpits started sweating simultaneously. The best term to describe what was going on with me: star struck. Totally star struck.

Because... *Reiner Kulti.*

The King.

The best player to come out of Europe in...

All right. This wasn't going to work, not at all, not even a little bit. Rationally, I knew that mooning over him was stupid. I was too old for this crap, and I'd gotten over my crush on him a decade ago when I said 'screw you' to the man who had married someone else, and then nearly ended my brother's career right after it started. Kulti was just a man. I closed my eyes and thought of the first thing that could get me out of my *holyshitit'sKultistandingrightthere.*

Poop.

*He poops.*

He poops.

Right. That was all I needed to snap out of it. I pictured an image of him sitting on the porcelain throne to remind me he was just a normal man with needs like everyone. I knew this—I'd known this for the longest. He was just a man with parents that pooped and peed and slept like the rest of us. Poop, poop, *poop, poop, poop*.

Right.

I was good. I was really fine.

Until Jenny tapped her elbow against my lower ribs unexpectedly, her face getting up in mine while she did these huge goofy eyes, barely tipping her head in Kulti's direction. It was the universal friend sign for *there's that guy you like. Do you see him?*

This bitch. I made my own eyes go wide and mouthed 'shut the hell up' to her, moving my lips the least amount possible.

Like any good friend, she didn't do what was asked. She kept elbowing me and giving me that crazy, stupid look and strained head-tipping, trying to be inconspicuous and failing miserably. I didn't look at him for very long, just that first initial glance from more than fifty feet away, and then another quick look right afterward.

Poop. Remember: poop. Right.

The silence on the field said more than enough about what everyone was thinking but couldn't actually say out loud.

But dumb Jenny knocked her foot against mine while we put on sunscreen, grinning when she caught my eye, which I was purposely trying to ignore because she made me laugh. I knew in my gut that I was never going to hear the end of this. Never. I'd gotten over my crush-slash-infatuation when I was seventeen, when I finally accepted the fact that I didn't have a single shot of ever playing against him—obviously—and... there was no chance in hell that he'd ever be interested in me, the Argentinian-Mexican-American tomboy thirteen years younger than him. There wouldn't be a marriage in my future or soccer-playing super-babies.

It was the worst non-break-up ever in the history of imaginary relationships with a man who didn't even know I existed.

My poor, innocent heart hadn't been able to handle the only love I'd ever known marrying someone else—Reiner Kulti hadn't known he was supposed to fall head over heels in love with me one day.

But like every unrequited first love, I got over it. Life moved on. And then all the shit with Eric happened shortly after that, and the posters on my wall had turned into an even bigger betrayal to the guy in my life who had always let me tag along for impromptu soccer games with his friends.

"Keep it up, bitch," I whispered to Jenny while she rubbed sunscreen on the parts of my back I couldn't reach.

She snorted and hip-bumped me as we walked toward our designated stretching area. There was already a small group waiting, their voices still a lot lower than they would be normally. Sure enough, Kulti was standing nearby with Coach Gardner and Grace, our team captain and a veteran defender who had been playing professionally since I was still in middle school. She'd been with the Pipers four years at the beginning of this season, just like me.

"He's taller than I'd thought he'd be," Jen muttered just loud enough for me to hear.

I looked out of the corner of my eye at where the coaches and Grace were standing without being completely obvious. With only twenty feet of distance between us, we were closer than I ever could have expected, and I nodded because she was right. He was spectacularly tall compared to a lot of the male forwards—also called strikers by some, or in the way my sister described the position: 'the people that hung out by the other team's goal and tried to score.' The best forwards tended to be a lot shorter, not six-two or six-three depending on what analyst or know-it-all you asked. Considering how unparalleled his footwork was, it was a—

*Stop. Stop, Sal.*

Right.

Poop.

I could look at him without fan-girling, I could be unbiased.

So I tried my best to do just that. He looked bulkier than he'd been a couple of years ago when he'd stepped out of the spotlight. Like most players, he'd been muscular but extra lean and long from all the endless running. Now, he looked a bit heavier, his face was more filled out, his neck looked a little thicker and his arms—

Poop. Fart. Peeing in a urinal. *Right.*

All right.

The guy was more muscular. A hint of his tattoo peeked out from beneath the sleeve of his shirt and he still had that even flawless skin tone that was somewhere between a creamy white and a perfect light tan.

His hair was that same perfect brown as it'd always been and if it hadn't been for the touches of gray at his temples, that familiar aspect would have been the same. Basically, it was obvious he'd gotten older and he wasn't on his feet as much as he'd been for the largest chunk of his life. His build had become more gym-rat than swimmer, and there was not a single thing wrong with that.

But when I zeroed in his face, something just seemed... off. He'd always been good-looking, really good-looking, in his own untraditional way. Kulti didn't have the symmetrical high-boned features that companies usually looked for when they endorsed athletes. His facial structure was more raw, smart-assedness oozing from the fullness of his mouth and from the bright color of his eyes. He was such a supreme athlete it had never mattered during his career that he didn't have a patrician face. His confidence was blinding. Clean-shaven for once, the sharp bones of his jaw and cheeks that made his profile so masculine were on all-out display. A few more lines creased out from the corners of his hazel-green eyes than had been there before.

I forgot he was turning forty this year.

The puzzle pieces were all there, but it was like they weren't put together properly. I knew it wasn't anything different outward about him. Being in stealth mode, I couldn't figure out what it was, and it bothered me. My gut recognized a difference in him, but my eyes couldn't. What was it?

"Will someone pass me a band?" a girl nearby asked, snapping me out of the human Rubik's cube I was playing.

Realizing I was the closest person to the mini-bands we used for stretching, I grabbed one and passed it to my teammate.

"Everyone circle around!" Gardner called us, like a shepherd calling his sheep.

Which I don't think any of us really appreciated but all right. Like zombies, the group flocked to him silently, hesitantly. We were bugs being called to the bug zapper, the shiny bright thing that could potentially kill us, only with a man as the attraction. Gardner and Kulti stood together along with the fitness coach and a few other staff members shaking hands and greeting each other.

I fought the urge to swallow because I knew one of the idiots around me would see, and I didn't need to give Jenny any more room to give me shit about my former Kulti obsession.

"Ladies, I'm pleased to introduce your new assistant coach for the season, Reiner Kulti. Let's break the ice real quick before we start. If you could go around and introduce yourselves and tell him what position you're playing..." Gardner trailed off with an eyebrow that dared us all to tell him how stupid and elementary school this was. I hated it then and I wasn't a fan now.

Without missing a beat, one of the girls closest to Gardner started off the circle of introductions.

I watched him, his face and his reactions. He blinked and tipped his head down each time a player finished talking. One after another, half the group went, and I realized I was near the middle of the semi-circle when Jenny piped in.

"I'm Jenny Milton," she grinned in that way that always had me grinning back no matter what kind of mood I was in. "Goalkeeper. Nice to meet you."

I didn't miss the way his cheek hiked up a millimeter more in reaction to her greeting. You'd have to be the freaking Grinch to not appreciate Jenny. She was one of those people who woke up in an excellent mood and went to sleep with a smile on her face. But when she was mad, I wouldn't hold murder past her.

Then it was my turn and when those light-colored eyes landed on my face expectantly, I thought *poop*. Lots of poop. Clog-the-toilet amount of poop.

Like a pro, I amazed myself by not squeaking or stuttering. Those green-brown orbs that were said to be the windows of a person's soul were right on me. "Hi, I'm Sal Casillas. I'm a forward." More like a winger, but what was the point in being specific?

"Sal did your press conference," Sheena, the public relations employee, commented.

I cringed on the inside, and I didn't miss the tiny snort that escaped Jenny. I ignored it. Bitch.

By the time I looked back at where he was I'd been dismissed. His attention had gone right on to the girl next to me without a moment to spare.

Well. Okay.

I guess I should have been glad I cancelled our wedding preparations years ago.

I gave Jenny a look out of the corner of my eye. "Shut up."

She waited until the next player stopped talking before replying. "I didn't say a word."

"You were thinking about it."

"I haven't stopped thinking about it," she admitted in a whisper that was way too close to a laugh.

My eye twitched on its own. Neither had I.

* * *

I HAD JUST LAID down on my bed after dinner when my phone rang. My legs ached after my morning run, our fitness test and then the landscaping job I helped Marc with most of the afternoon. Considering it was eight at night and I had a tiny number of friends that actually called me occasionally, I had a pretty good idea of who it was. Sure enough, a foreign area code and number showed up on the screen.

"Hi, Dad," I answered, sliding my cell into the crook between my shoulder and ear.

The man didn't even beat around the bush. In a quick rush he blurted out, "How was it?"

How was it?

How could I tell my dad, a die-hard Kulti fan despite the fact that he had no business still calling himself a fan, that the day had been one big whooping disappointment?

A disappointment. I could only blame myself. No one had ever given me the impression that Reiner Kulti was going to blow our minds with tricks and tips we hadn't even thought of —especially not during a day set aside for fitness tests—also known as cardio-all-day-until-you-were-on-the-verge-of-puking. Or maybe I'd anticipated that that infamous temper that had gotten him red-carded—ejected out of games—more times than necessary, would come out? There was a reason he'd been called the *Führer* back when he played, and it was part of the reason why people both liked him and disliked him so much.

Today though, he hadn't been an asshole or greedy or condescending. All the characteristics I'd ever heard of from people who had played with him were nonexistent. This was the same person that had gotten suspended from ten games for head-butting the hell out of another player during a friendly game—a game that didn't even count for anything. Then there was the time he'd gotten into an altercation with a player who had blatantly tried to kick him in the back of the knee. He was the train wreck you wanted to watch happen and keep happening... at least he had been.

Instead, he'd just stood there while we introduced ourselves and then afterward, watched us when he wasn't talking to Coach Gardner. I don't even think he touched a ball. Not that I was looking that much.

The single thing that I'm pretty sure any of us had heard him say had been "Good morning." Good morning. This simple greeting from the same man that had gotten in trouble for bellowing "Fuck you!" during an Altus Cup on major television.

What the hell was wrong with me that I'd be complaining about Kulti being so distant? So nice?

Yeah, there was something wrong with me.

I coughed into the phone. "It was fine. He didn't really talk to us or anything." And by 'didn't really' I really meant 'at all'. I wasn't going to tell Dad that though.

"Oh." His disappointment was evident in the way he dropped the consonant so harshly.

Well I felt like an asshole.

"I'm sure he's just trying to warm up to us." Maybe. Right?

"*Alomejor*." Maybe, Dad said in that same sort of tone he used when I was a kid and I'd ask him for something he knew damn well he wasn't going to give me. "Nothing happened, then?"

I didn't even need to close my eyes and think back on what had happened that day. Not a single thing. Kulti had just stood back and watched us run around executing a variety of exercises to make sure we were all in shape. He hadn't even rolled his eyes, much less call us a group of incompetent idiots—another thing he'd been known to call his teammates when they weren't playing to the level he expected.

"Nothing," and that was the truth. Maybe he'd gotten shy over the years?

Yeah, not likely, but I could tell myself that. Or at least tell Dad that so that he wouldn't sound so disheartened after he'd been so over-the-moon when he'd first found out Kulti would be our coach.

"But hey, I had the best times during each sprint," I added.

His laugh was soft and possibly a little disappointed. "That's my girl. Running every morning?"

"Every morning and I've been swimming more." I stopped talking when I heard a voice in the background.

All I heard was my dad mumbling, *"It's Sal... you wanna talk to her?... Okay...* Sal, your mom says hi."

"Tell her I said hi back."

*"My daughter says hi... no, she's mine. The other one is yours... Ha! No!...* Sal are you mine or your mom's?" he asked me.

"I'm the milkman's."

"I knew it!" He finally laughed with a deep pleased sigh.

I was smiling like a total fool. "I love you too, old man."

"I know you do, but I love you more," he chuckled.

"Yeah, yeah. Call me tomorrow? I'm pretty tired, and I want to ice my foot for a little bit."

A ragged sigh came out from him, but I knew he wouldn't say anything. His sigh said it all and more; it was a gentle wordless reminder that I needed to take care of myself. We'd gone over this a hundred times in person. Dad and I understood each other in a different way. If it had been my brother saying something about needing ice, I probably would have asked him if he thought he'd live and Dad would have told him to suck it up. It was the beauty of being my father's daughter, I guess. Well it was the beauty of being me and not my baby sister, who he constantly fought with.

"Okay, tomorrow. Sleep good, *mija*."

"You too, Dad. Night."

He bid me another goodbye and we hung up. Sitting up on my bed in the garage apartment that I'd been renting for the last two years, I let myself think of Kulti and how he'd just stood there like a golden gargoyle, watching, watching and watching.

It was then that I reminded myself about him pooping again.

# 4

The next few days went by uneventfully and yet as eventful as they normally were. We had to get our physicals for the team one day and the next day we got measured for our uniforms. After each small chunk of a morning, I'd go to work afterward where I'd be harassed by Marc about whether I'd gotten Kulti's autograph for him yet. Then each evening, I'd practice yoga or go swimming or do some weight training, depending on how tired I was. Then I'd get home and talk to my dad or watch television.

Everyone wanted to know what Reiner Kulti was like, and I had nothing to give them. He showed up to whatever we were doing and stood in whatever corner was available, and watched. He didn't really talk or interact with anyone. He didn't do *anything*.

So... that was kind of disappointing for everyone who asked.

A small part of me was surprised the vultures hadn't descended on his unmoving ass. If he ever needed the money, he could work as one of those living statues that painted their bodies in metallic colors and hung out in Times Square, letting people pay them tips to take pictures with them. His apathy was that bad.

But no one said anything about the press conference from hell, or brought up stuff about Eric and Kulti, and there weren't any more questions about me rejoining the national team. Overall, there was nothing really for me to complain about. I could act like a normal human being with some dignity, not a stuttering idiot that a decade ago had a crush on the man that everyone was talking about.

So really, what was there to complain about?

* * *

ON THE MORNING of our individual photo shoots, I should have known how the interview was going to go when the first thing out of the journalist's mouth was a mispronounced "Salome!" Suh-lome. Then even after I corrected him he still said it the wrong way. Which wasn't a big deal; I was used to having someone butcher it. It happened all the time.

Suh-lome. Saah-lome. Sah-lowmee. Salami. Salamander. Salmon. Sal-men. Saul. Sally. Samantha.

Or, in the case of my brother: Stupid.

In the case of my little sister: Bitch.

Regardless, when someone continuously messes up your name even after you correct them... it's a sign. In this case, it was a sign that I should have known this guy was a moron.

I had tried to get away from him. Usually I tried to sneak away, but lately there were so many of them, it was impossible. The minute I spotted the group of television reporters and journalists by the field where the photographs were set to be taken, my gut churned. I didn't have a problem walking around in my sports bra in front of everyone and anyone. I could play games just fine in front of thousands of people, but the instant a camera came around when I wasn't doing those things...

No. No, no, no.

So as soon as I spotted them, I started to circle my way as far from their location as possible. Let them get the other girls first. The furthest group from the entrance stopped Grace, the captain and veteran on the team. Thank you, Jesus. Then I saw another group swoop in on Harlow, and I felt a bolt of relief go through my stomach.

Fifteen more feet to go. Fifteen more feet and I'd be clear. My heart started beating that much faster and I made sure to keep my eyes forward. No eye contact.

Ten feet. Baby Jesus, please—

"Salome!"

Fuck.

I looked over and breathed a sigh of relief when the reporter shouting didn't have a camera or a cameraman with him. He was a blogger. I could have kissed him.

The first few questions were normal. How my off-season had gone. How training was going. Who I thought were going to be our biggest competitors.

It was right around the time that I was finishing his last question, preparing myself to tell him that I needed to go, when I heard the reporters I'd bypassed start chattering loudly. Again it was no big deal. The journalist's eyes started darting to the area behind me even as I spoke, watching and waiting for his next victim. There weren't usually reporters or journalists waiting around before practice unless it was playoff time. At least that's what it had been like before the former German superstar showed up.

Now apparently, they all had bottle vision whenever he was nearby. And from the look on the journalist's face when he saw his next subject, I knew who had caught his attention.

Two eyes swung from whatever the journalist was looking at behind me... to me and then back again.

A strain of dread-like anger saturated my belly when Kulti

walked by, waving off the three media people that were trying to get his attention by asking questions and shoving their cameras and recording devices in his face.

He could get away with being antisocial, but I couldn't?

"Isn't your brother a pro too?" the journalist asked slowly.

I swallowed and forced myself to hope that this wasn't going the way it seemed to be. And yet, I knew it was. "Yeah. He's a center back," or as I called him, a center bitch. "He plays for Sacramento normally, but he's on loan to a team in Europe right now." This was the only reason I was sure he hadn't called me to complain about Kulti yet. Did he know? He had to. But he was cheap and wasn't going to call until our standing phone-date every other Sunday.

The man's eyes swung back over to me, so low-lidded I knew I was screwed. "Wasn't his leg broken years ago?"

It was his left tibia and fibula to be exact. Just thinking about it made my own shins hurt, but I settled for a nod in reply. The less I spoke, the smaller my chances were of incriminating myself by saying something stupid. "Ten years ago."

"Did it happen during a game?" he was asking, but we both were well aware he knew the answer.

Asshole.

Did I look that dumb? I wasn't about to let him steer me into looking like an idiot. When I was in college, they made athletes for every sport take a class in public speaking. Sure I'd barely passed, but they had taught me one thing I hadn't forgotten: how important it was for you to keep the interview under control. "Yep. Ten years ago, he went in for a loose ball during a game against the Tigers and was hit in the leg by an opposing player." The journalist's eyes twitched. "He was out for six months."

"The player got yellow-carded, didn't he?"

And... there it was. Since when were sports bloggers sneaky little shits looking for drama when it was uncalled for?

I plastered a smile on my face, giving him this look that said *yeah, I know exactly what you're doing, dingle-berry.* "Yes, but he's perfectly fine now. It wasn't a big deal." Well that was a lie, but whatever. My smile grew even wider and I took a step back. Being an asshole didn't come naturally to me. I didn't like it, but I wasn't about to roll onto my back and show someone my belly. Coach Gardner had already made it painfully clear to me that I needed to keep attention on the team and not Kulti, especially not Eric and Kulti. "I need to get going. You have anything else you need to ask about training, though?"

The reporter's eyes slid over in the direction Kulti and his followers had gone. "We're all done. Thanks."

"Anytime." Not.

I took another step back, snatched my bag off the ground and started walking in the direction of the field. I still had to collect the uniform they wanted us to wear for our profile shots and put it on. Someone with the organization had set up two tents on the outskirt of the field, one with long flaps to provide some modesty for changing, and the other more basic, without flaps, where the uniforms could be found.

"Sal! Come get your stuff!" someone yelled from beneath the smaller tent.

I made my way over there, looking around to see who had survived the gauntlet, aka the media, and waved at the players and staff members who made eye contact with me. There were only a few people under the uniform tent where we needed to go before our player photos—two management employees handing out uniforms, two players and three staff members.

One of the staff members was Kulti.

*Poop.*

Okay, I was fine.

"Good morning," I said as I came up to the group in the tent, rubbing my hands down the front of my pants.

Poop, poop, poop, poop, poop.

A chorus of "good morning" greetings came back to me, even from the ancient demoness known as our fitness coach who was yet again standing by the former German superstar.

It was the same German super-athlete who was now only about five feet away.

I went to the Louvre once years ago, and I remember looking at the Mona Lisa after standing outside of the famous museum for hours trying to get in and being disappointed. The painting was smaller than I'd thought it would be. Honestly, it was just a painting. There was nothing about it that made it so much better than any other painting ever at least to my untrained eye. It was famous and it was old, and that was it.

Simply standing mere feet away from the man that had led his teams to championship after championship... seemed weird. It was like this was a dream, a very weird dream.

It was a dream with a man who looked better than any thirty-nine-year-old ever should.

"Casillas? It's your turn, honey. I got your uniform right here," one of the women working behind the tables called out to me with a smile.

I blinked and then smiled back at her, embarrassed that she caught me daydreaming. "Sorry." Walking around the coaches, I took the plastic-wrapped bundle she handed me. "Need me to sign anything?"

She handed me a clipboard with a shake of her head. "What size shoe do you wear? I can't read whether it's an eight or a nine."

"Eight," I said, signing the area to the side of my name.

"Give me a second to find your socks." She turned her back to me and started rifling through an organized container behind her.

"Mr. Kulti, I have you down for a medium shirt and large bottoms, does that sound right?" the other employee who wasn't busy asked, her voice sounding a little high, a little breathless. Her hands were folded and pressed to her chest, her eyes only just barely holding that glint of nervous excitement in them.

"Yes," was the simple answer that rumbled out deeply; his enunciation was sharp with just the slightest hint of an accent that had been watered down from living in so many different countries over the years.

I felt his tone right between my shoulder blades. I could remember hearing him talk about whatever game he'd just finished playing dozens of times. *Poop, fart, hemorrhoids. Sal. Get it together.*

I swallowed hard, unable to get over how different he looked. Back when I'd been a fan, he'd gone through every hair style from dyed tips to a mohawk. Now standing there, his hair was shaved short and his arms were loose at his sides, his spine rigid. A hint of his cross pattée tattoo—a cross with arms that narrowed toward the center—appeared beneath the hem of his T-shirt sleeve. It wasn't huge from what I remembered, maybe five inches high and five across and he'd had it for a long time. When I was younger, I thought it was kind of neat. Now... meh. I liked tattoos on men, but I liked big pieces, not a collection of random little ones.

But whatever, it wasn't like anyone was asking me for my opinion.

"Here you go, Sal, I got 'em," the staff member said, hanging me another sealed packet out of the corner of my eye. "We'll have the rest of your gear later."

"All right. Thanks, Shelly." Holding the uniform under one arm, I took another glance at Kulti, who was steadfast keeping his attention forward and fought the anticipation that pooled in my chest. My feet wouldn't move, and my stupid eyes wouldn't move either. At no point in my childhood had I ever really expected to be so close to this man. Never. Not once.

But after a second of standing there awkwardly, hoping for

a look or possibly a word? I realized he wasn't going to give me either. He was making a point to keep his eyes forward, lost in his own thoughts; maybe he wanted to be left alone, or might have purposely not wanted to waste his time speaking to me.

That thought went like a mortal blow straight to my chest. I felt like a preteen girl that wanted the older guy to pay attention to her when he didn't even know she existed. The hope, the expectancy and the following disappointment sucked. It just sucked.

He wasn't going to acknowledge me. That much was clear.

All righty, then. While I wasn't exactly a Jenny who made friends with everyone, I liked being friendly with people. Obviously this guy wasn't going to win a Mr. Congeniality award anytime soon, since he wouldn't even bother looking at me standing there two feet away.

So... that didn't sting at all. My heart didn't feel funny either.

Then I remembered the crap with the journalist outside and the effect that kind of attention could have on me. I tried my best to keep under the radar. I just wanted to play soccer, that was it.

With another quick glance at the man who was standing, oblivious to everything around him, I took my crap and went to change. I didn't need Reiner Kulti to talk to me. I hadn't needed him before and I wouldn't need him in the future.

* * *

IF I THOUGHT for a second that things would get less hectic as the days passed and Kulti's presence slowly became old news, I would have been sorely mistaken.

It didn't.

Everyday there were at least half a dozen reporters outside of the field or headquarters. Wherever we'd be that day, they would be there. I'd scratched the skin on my neck nearly raw from how much I was scratching at it on my walks toward wherever we were meeting.

I tried to stay as far away from them as I could.

It was just like I tried to stay away from the team's new coach.

To be fair, he made it easy. The German stayed in the corner of the universe he had dug out for himself—a lonely little corner that included him and him only. Apparently only Gardner, the mean bat known as the fitness coach and Grace got invitations every so often. He stood and watched; then he moved a little to the side and kept right on watching.

"I feel like we're in the lion exhibit at the zoo," Jenny whispered to me when we were taking a break during our last meeting. We were in that bathroom alone after having just sat through two hours of scheduling details, and I was on the verge of wanting to stab myself in the eye with my pen. I was restless sitting in the chair doing nothing.

My prayers had been answered when they gave us ten minutes to use the bathroom and get a drink.

I looked at her in the reflection of the bathroom mirror and made my eyes go big. I guess I wasn't the only one who noticed the wordless man who went through the meeting with his back against the wall and his arms crossed over his chest. "It does feel like that, huh?"

She nodded like she was glum about it. "He hasn't said anything, Sal. I mean, isn't that weird? Even Phyllis," the mean old fitness coach, "talks every once in a while." She hunched her shoulders up high. "Weird."

"Very weird," I agreed with her. "But we can't say—"

The door opened, and three of the newer girls on the team walked in, joking around with each other.

Jenny shot me a look in the mirror's reflection because what was more obvious than immediately stopping a conversation when other people walked by? I might as well have the word guilty tattooed on my forehead. So I spouted out the first thing that came to mind, "—that you didn't ask for onions on your burger without sounding like an asshole..."

One of the girls smiled at me before going into the stall, the other two ignored us.

Jenny visibly bit her lip as the newcomers went into the bathroom stalls. "Yeah, you can't complain about that...?" She mouthed, 'what was that' the second they were in.

'It was the first thing I thought of!' I mouthed back to her with a shrug.

Jenny pinched her nostrils together as her face went red.

"I know, right?" I held my arms out at my sides in a 'what was I supposed to say' gesture even though she was too busy trying not to burst out laughing, to see me in the mirror. God, she was no help in our made-up conversation. "I clearly asked for no onions but whatever. I guess. It's not like I'm allergic to them."

By that point, Jenny had her forehead to the bathroom counter and her back was arching with repressed laughs.

I kicked her in the back of the knee lightly just as one of the toilets flushed. She looked up and I mouthed 'stop it' to her. Did she? No. Not even close.

Yeah, she was too far gone to keep going with the charade. One look and the other girls would see Jenny losing it over onions. God, I really was a horrible liar.

I shoved her out of the bathroom just as one of the latches turned.

* * *

"THERE'S a rumor going around that you're going to be rejoining the national team soon, any word on that?"

It was the first official day of practice and my feet were itching. After nearly six months of playing soccer with friends and family, while training and conditioning on my own, I was ready.

And of course I'd gotten waved down by a writer for Training, Inc., a popular e-magazine.

So far, two questions in, it was going fine.

That still didn't mean that I was going to open my big mouth up and tell him all my deepest secrets. *Vague, Sal. Don't ever confirm or deny anything.* "I don't think so. My ankle still isn't back to where it needs to be, and I'm busy with other priorities."

Okay, that wasn't too bad.

"Oh?" He raised an eyebrow. "Like what?"

"I'm working with youth camps." I left out the other small parts of my life, the parts that weren't glamorous and had nothing to do with soccer. No one wanted to hear about our miserable paychecks and how most of us had to supplement our incomes by getting second jobs. That didn't go with the image most people had of professional players in any sport.

And no one especially wanted to hear that I did landscaping when I wasn't busy with the Pipers. It didn't embarrass me, not at all. I liked doing it, and I had a degree in Landscape Architecture. It wasn't glossy or pretty, but I'd be damned if I ever let anyone give what I did a bad name. My dad had supported our family being the 'the lawn guy' or 'the gardener' and any and all other things that could put food on our table. There was no shame in hard work, he and my mom had taught me from a very early age when I had cared what other people thought. People would laugh and crack jokes when Dad would pick me up from school with a lawnmower and other tools in the back of his beat-up truck, with his goofy hat and sweat-stained clothes that had seen better decades.

But how could I ever give my dad a hard time about picking me up from school so he could take me to soccer practice? Or he'd pick me up, take me to a job or two with him, and then he'd take me to practice. He loved us and he sacrificed so that Eric and I could be on those teams with their expensive fees and uniforms. We got where we were today, because he worked his ass off.

As I got older, people just found more things to pick on me about and laugh. I'd been called a priss, stuck-up, a bitch, and a lesbian more times than I could count. All because I loved playing soccer and took it seriously.

Eventually one of my U-20 coaches pulled me aside after some of my teammates had gotten an attitude with me. I'd declined an invitation to go out so I could go home and get some rest. He'd said, "people are going to judge you regardless of what you do, Sal. Don't listen to what they have to say because at the end of the day, you're the one that has to live with your choices and where they take you. No one else is going to live your life for you." Most times it was easier said than done, but here I was. I'd gotten what I had worked so hard for, so it hadn't been in vain.

There were going to be a hundred parties I could go to when I was older and past my athletic prime, but I only had the first half of my life to do what I loved for a living. I'd been fortunate enough to find something that I enjoyed and that I could work toward. I wasn't going to blow this chance I'd been given.

Sometimes though I didn't feel like having to defend what I liked doing, or why I made sure to sleep so much, or why I didn't eat that greasy meal that would give me indigestion on a run later or why I didn't like to hang around smokers. This guy was one of those people I'd rather save my breath on. So I didn't elaborate.

The blogger's eyebrows went up to nearly his hairline. "How are your soccer camps going?"

"Great."

"How do you feel about critics saying that the Pipers should have gotten a coach with better qualifications than Reiner Kulti?"

I knew exactly how the little sister on the Brady Bunch felt. Kulti, Kulti, Kulti. Holy shit. Honestly, part of me was surprised I wasn't dreaming about him. But could I ever say that? Absolutely not. "I've been told I was too short to be a good soccer player. You can do anything you *want* to do as long as you care enough." Maybe that was a bad thing to say when Kulti didn't actually seem to care a little bit about us, but the words were already out of my mouth and I couldn't take them back. So...

"Kulti's notorious for being a one-man show," he stated, matter-of-factly.

I just looked at him but didn't say a word. If there was a way for me to answer that, I didn't know how.

"He also broke your brother's leg." At least this guy wasn't pretending to have amnesia when bringing up Eric, unlike the last guy I'd talked to.

"It happens." I shrugged because it was the truth. "Harlow Williams dislocated my shoulder once. Another friend of mine broke my arm when I was a teenager. It's not unheard of for stuff like that to happen." And then there were the dozen other injuries my brother had caused me over the years.

Was I full of shit? Only about half. While it was true that Harlow had dislocated my shoulder and that a teammate had hit me so hard during a scrimmage game that I got a hairline fracture, they had been accidents. What happened between Eric and Kulti... not so much, and that was the problem. Kulti had played dirty—real dirty—and all he got was a yellow card. A yellow card in that situation was pretty much a warning after you'd hit someone with your car, backed up to hit them a second time and driven off afterward. It was insulting.

He had almost ruined my brother's career, and all he got was a miserable yellow card. It was the biggest bullshit call of the last century. People had gone nuts over it, claiming that he'd been forgiven because of his status and popularity. It wasn't the first time a superstar had gotten away with something, and it wouldn't be the last.

But could I say that on record? Nope.

"I really need to start warming up," I said carefully before he had a chance to ask anything else.

"Thanks for your time." The writer for Training, Inc. smiled as he extended his hand out for me to shake.

"No problem. Have a nice day."

This guy had done enough in my life.

* * *

"WHAT'S GOING ON WITH YOU?" Jenny asked me while we were off to the sidelines, waiting for the rest of the team to finish their ball-touch drills.

I pulled my shirt up to use the bottom to wipe my upper lip and mouth off. The temperatures and humidity were out of this world in Houston—no surprise. The tension headache I'd been rocking all morning didn't help any either; the conversation with the reporter kept picking at my nerves. "I'm fine," I told her before snatching a bottle of water off the floor.

She raised a single eyebrow, her cheeks puffing out as a disbelieving smirk crossed her face. Who was I trying to fool? Regardless of whether we'd been friends for five years or fifteen, she still knew me better than almost anyone. "You know you can talk to me about anything."

She gave the worst guilt trips because she was so nice about it, but still. Sometimes I didn't want to talk about things. "I'm fine."

"You're not fine."

"I'm *fine*."

"Sal, you're not fine."

I squeezed another mouthful of water out as a few more

players made their way around to wait where we were. "I really am all right," I insisted in a lower voice so only she could hear me.

She didn't believe me and for good reason.

I was a little bit pissed and a little bit annoyed.

I wanted to play, not have people digging up stuff from the past. I didn't want the world. The most I'd ever gotten out of playing was a deal with a major athletic clothing company that basically just took pictures of me playing and paid me for it. But that was it. Kulti's presence could potentially put me at risk when the past wasn't even my fault.

He'd hurt my brother seriously and that was that. I could learn to put it behind me for the time being, especially when he didn't seem to either know or care about who I was related to.

With that thought I accidentally looked over to where Mr.-Silent-Superstar stood, arms crossed over his impressively sized chest, looking at the players on the field with a plain expression. It was the same unemotional demeanor he'd been portraying since he arrived. He annoyed me, but I was also annoyed with myself for letting his attitude bother me. All I needed was to focus on getting through preseason training.

I wasn't totally surprised when Jenny blinked slowly. "You're bitch-facing out there. You only bitch-face when someone pisses you off during a game."

She had a point. I could feel myself bitch-facing. Smiling and smirking were two expressions my facial muscles were used to. Scowling was newer territory. I took a deep breath and tried to relax my face by stretching my jaw and mouth. Sure enough tension eased its way out of those small muscles, going even all the way up above my eyebrows.

"Told you so." Jenny smiled gently at me. "You looked like you had during the Cleveland game last year, remember that?"

How could I forget? A defender on Cleveland had twisted the hell out of my nipple when I'd landed on top of her after a play and hadn't gotten caught. That bitch. I didn't get her back during that first half, but I sure as hell did in the second when I scored two goals on her team. I couldn't wear a bra for a week without being in pain, but at least we won.

"My nip still hurts," I said to Jenny with a small worn-out smile on my face.

She raised an eyebrow. "Is your ankle bothering you?" she asked, looking around once more to make sure other players weren't around. Injuries were like shark bait. On one hand we were all teammates with the same objective, but I didn't for a second think someone wouldn't try to exploit an injury for their own benefit. Competitive people were like that.

I wiped at my face again and took another sip of water. "A little bit," I told her honestly because it was true, just not the whole truth.

Jenny grimaced. "Sal, you need to be careful."

This was the difference between venting to Harlow and venting to Jenny. Harlow would have slapped me on the back and told me to walk it off. Jenny worried, she stressed. From now on she'd keep an eye on me, and that was part of the reason why I cared about her so much.

I scrubbed at my face with the back of my hand. "I'm all right."

She eyed me a little critically before asking, "What else is up?"

Jenny wasn't going to leave me alone about it. I scratched at the tip of my nose and made sure no one was close enough to hear me. "This morning some writer brought up the Kulti-Eric thing." Frustration bubbled in my throat. "I'm a little worried about it."

My friend let out a low whistle, completely aware of the situation.

"Yeah," I agreed to her wince.

"Why? That's old news."

I shrugged. Yeah, it was. "I know, right?"

She nodded in agreement.

"I'm just a little grumpy about it, I guess."

"Take a breather," she demanded easily. "We're only allowed one person to have looking like a serial killer on the field."

At the same time our eyes swung around to search out Harlow. When we looked back at each other, we smirked. Harlow was awesome but... she really did look like a murderer. I could have easily imagined her as a Viking princess, raiding villages and mounting people's heads on spikes.

"Who's ready for some three-on-three drills?" Coach Gardner yelled.

High-intensity drills, my favorite.

I must have smiled or something because I heard Jenny clearly murmur, "You're a monster," under her breath.

I pushed my ankle, The King and Eric out of my head, and smacked Jenny on the butt cheek right before I took off toward the coaches. "You coming?"

She sighed and shook her head before taking off behind me.

We arranged three different mini-fields for our games. I went into the first group to play a five-minute game. The game finished a blink of an eye later and the groups switched places, the girls off the field replacing the ones who just played.

I spotted Harlow walking toward the sidelines and started to make my way toward her, bypassing Kulti and Coach Gardner standing together. The other man held out his fist for me to bump the side of mine against. "Have you been working on your left foot?"

I grinned at him. I'd worked on it a lot. *A lot.* It was the result of hours and hours spent running with the ball during our offseason. It had always been pretty good, but I wanted it to be better. “I have. Thanks, G.” I bumped my fist against his once more and honestly, I’m not positive why I paused afterward.

What was I expecting? Maybe a compliment from The King or at least a look, a tiny fraction of acknowledgment? Any of the above would be nice. But it was just a blip of a second too long, long enough to be noticeable, for Gardner to glance at the German out of the corner of his eye like he was expecting him to say something too.

But he didn’t.

Those almost-hazel eyes, like a murky pond, didn’t even *look* at me.

Embarrassment bled through my insides, my belly and my throat specifically. What could have been acid or just overactive nerves in my cheeks made them feel weird as I forced an easy-going smile on my face that told Gardner it was fine that I’d just been ignored. But really, I was seething and dying a little inside.

I knew better. Damn it, *I knew better.* Hadn’t he done the same thing to me before?

I couldn’t remember the last time anyone had just looked right past me like I didn’t fucking exist, and I didn’t mean that in some vain pretentious way. Most people I met were friendly, and if they were shy at least they’d look me in the eye before looking away. Most assholes were at least dismissive after a quick glance. But this ass-wipe hadn’t even spared the calories he could have burned turning his neck in my direction.

Nothing, he’d done nothing.

I smiled at Gardner a little tighter and gave him another quick nod before striding toward Harlow, this ugly feeling clenching my gut.

“What’s wrong, Sally?” Har asked me in a concerned voice the minute I made it to where she was waiting.

Was I that obvious? I guess so.

# 5

Two weeks went by in the blink of an eye, just like I knew they would. Days became a repetition of each other. They were a steady, reliable daily battle that had to be perfectly planned.

6:15 a.m. -- A run.

7:00 a.m. -- Breakfast.

7:20 a.m. – Make lunch.

7:45 a.m. – Attempt to dodge the media/if I failed: talk for ten minutes

8 a.m. -- Pipers practice followed by a protein shake.

11:30 a.m. – Lunch in the car.

12 p.m. – Wait for Marc to pick me up so we could go to an afternoon appointment(s)

6 p.m. -- Yoga/weightlifting/gardening/maybe a swim/anything else.

7 p.m. – Dinner.

8 p.m. -- A shower.

8:30 p.m. -- A snack/television/reading time.

10 p.m. -- Bedtime.

If you really wanted to get down to specifics during practice, you could add: make sure I won daily sprints, fart around with Harlow, have Jenny mother me, help out the younger girls and stare at the mute that stood in the corner every once in a while. I mean, *every once in a while*. No one had time to do it all practice, every practice.

I mean, come on.

Then off to burn under the sun, despite wearing shirts and a hat designed to protect against UV rays. The one shower a night was probably the reason I was still single, but what was the point in showering twice if I knew I was just going to get sweaty from practice and work? Nothing said sexy like long jeans, a long-sleeved shirt and work boots. During work, Marc would harass me about Kulti and if I had any gossip to share with him. Needless to say, he was disappointed I didn't have anything to complain about.

The man everyone was so curious about hadn't said a single word to me. Whomp, whomp, whomp.

In between all of the ways The King had saturated my life, was the annoying conversation I finally had with Eric, my brother, that went along the lines of "blah, blah, blah, that guy is a fucking asshole, blah, blah, blah, don't listen to a goddamn thing he has to say to you—" I didn't even get a chance to tell him that Kulti had forgotten how to speak "—blah, blah, blah, no one here can believe he decided to coach for the WPL. Someone told me he got offered an eight-figure contract to coach for one of the Spanish teams—" more blah and a little more wah.

On top of everything else I didn't get to tell him, he didn't find out during that biweekly conversation that I'd begun getting passive-aggressive messages from Kulti fans… all because of him and his damn leg.

* * *

"...AN IDIOT." I looked up at Gardner and noted, "He is an idiot. I'm not going to argue that." Then I continued reading the email I'd gotten the night before. "*Casillas had it coming to him. I'm tired of Kulti getting blamed when he was doing what he needed to be doing. You seem like a sensible lady, so I really hope for your sake you don't start talking a bunch of shit about The King and learn to regret it.*"

Gardner sat back in his chair with a shake of his head. "Jesus, Sal. I'm sorry." He blinked a few times. "Let's get someone in here so we can come up with a strategy to get this crap figured out because I'm really over my head here."

"I'm sorry too, G. I hate to bother you with this crap, but I don't know if there's something I should do, or if I should keep ignoring the messages."

He waved me off with one hand, already dialing numbers on the conference phone on his desk. "Don't think twice about it... Sheena? Can you come down to my office? I have Sal Casillas in here. She's been getting some strange emails regarding Kulti, and I'm not sure what the best route to take is." A second later, the phone was back on its cradle, and he raised both eyebrows up to his hairline. "She'll be over in a second."

I nodded and smiled at him. "All right."

Gardner gave me the gentle smile that always reassured me. "How's your family doing?"

"Good. How's your fam—" *and* I'd forgotten I'd heard through the grapevine that his divorce had been finalized in January, "—kiddo?"

"Great. Twelve going on eighteen," he answered with an easy smile. "You? Planning on taking some time off to have some of your own?"

I stared at him. Then I stared at him a little longer.

*The fuck?*

"I'm messing with you, Sal," Gardner laughed dryly.

"I really thought you were serious," I said slowly. Jeez. Not that you need a boyfriend to have a baby but... My eyebrows went up. "Yeah. No." I hadn't had a date in.... a year? And I hadn't had sex in...? A long, long time. Not that I didn't want to —because I did—but because I had a vibrator, and a vibrator never left you hanging. Or had a wife or a girlfriend you didn't know about. *Anyway*.

He snorted. "I'm just messing around. You're still young."

I thought about the other girls on the team and winced a little. Not that long ago, I was one of the new girls, the really young ones that had just finished college and been drafted. Now I was one of the girls that the other ones looked up to. I rolled my ankle and let the stiffness in it answer back, reminding me how precarious its health was.

Someone knocked on the door, and Gardner welcomed them in.

Sheena peeked her head through the cracked door. "Hi." The door swung open and a second later, I spotted the head that appeared above hers.

My stupid, stupid, stupid traitorous heart remembered what it was like to be thirteen.

My brain, apparently the only logical organ in my body, said to all of its brothers and sisters: Get your shit together and calm down.

I put my Big Girl Socks on, took a deep steadying breath, and managed to smile at the two people who made their way into the office, right toward the chairs next to mine. I swallowed and said, "Hi, Sheena, hi, Coach Kulti." All right, that came out a lot dumber than I would have liked. My cheeks decided right then that they were going to get hot, real hot.

Damn it. *Get it together, Sal!*

"Hello, Sal," Sheena greeted me as she took the seat right next to mine, glancing over her shoulder for a moment to say, "I asked Mr. Kulti—"

*Mr.* Kulti? Really?

"—to come along."

I blinked at the same time my bones froze.

The short-haired man, who resembled someone in a branch of the military, shook his head, still silent.

My knees felt stiff and traitorous as I planted my feet solidly on the ground and got to my feet, thrusting a surprisingly steady hand toward the man that had shaken hands with—

Poop. Poop, poop, poop.

Why should I care who he'd shaken hands with? I didn't.

With a slow quiet breath through my nose, I tipped my chin up higher, like that would help me keep my dignity intact more. And like that wasn't enough, I blurted out another "Hi, I'm Sal Casillas, one of the forwards...?"

Was it time to shut up? Yes. Definitely.

A large, warm masculine hand gripped mine almost immediately, and I filled my lungs with another steadying breath, smiling at the man standing on the other side of Sheena. It was a normal handshake; he wasn't limp-fishing it, but he wasn't trying to break my hand either. He was just a man. He was just a normal man with interesting eyes and a serious face.

"Can you tell me a little about the emails you've been getting?"

Drawing back the hand that had just touched Reiner Kulti, I settled my gaze on the woman next to me and nodded. I summarized the messages I'd been getting. Insults aimed at my brother, warnings that I should do everything I could to learn as much as possible from the German, and a bunch of other crap that stressed me out a whole lot.

Sheena's cheek hitched up high, and it was easy to see on her clear dark skin that she was thinking. Then she nodded sharply. "Okay. I've got it—"

"Your brother was that imbecile?"

'That imbecile' had been the fourteen-year-old to my seven-year-old who held my hand when I crossed the street, let me tag along when he'd go play soccer with his friends even though he grumbled, kicked the ball back and forth with me in the backyard before he would go out, and he was the same person that would be on his feet in the stands, yelling at the top of his lungs when I had a bullshit call made against me. I *loved* my brother. Was he an arrogant jackass who thought he was gifted with a talent straight from heaven? Yes.

But he was the one that had held on to my shoulder when I'd made a horrible play in my younger years that cost my team a championship and told me that it wasn't the end of the world. While I looked at Kulti as the type of badass I wanted to aspire to be one day, Eric had been the one to assure me I could be better.

When Kulti had broken my brother's leg, I made my choice.

I would choose my brother every single time.

Except as my lips formed the shape it took to enunciate the letter 'b' for bitch, I *remembered.*

I remembered what Gardner had warned us of two weeks ago during our first Pipers meeting. *If I hear any of you call him Führer, you're out of here.* Fuck me.

Calling him a bitch wasn't better, was it?

A bag of dicks wasn't much better either.

My lips sealed themselves together and in response my nostrils flared.

"He isn't an imbecile, but Eric *is* my brother," I answered him carefully. My eye was starting to twitch.

From ten feet away, someone's green-brown eyes narrowed. "What else would you call someone—"

My eye went full speed twitching and before I thought twice, I cut him off. "That purposely swept an opponent's leg harder than necessary?" I shrugged. "You tell me."

My throat clogged instantly and the twitching in my eyelid got worse once the words were out. I'd done it. Jesus Christ. I'd insinuated he was an imbecile but hinting at it wasn't the same thing as outright calling him one, right?

Sheena let out a low, ringing laugh that had 'awkward' written all over it. "Okay, I'm sure we can avoid the name-calling, yes?" She didn't wait for an answer from either one of us before going on. "I have an idea, and I don't see why it wouldn't work to calm things down a little. I spoke to Mr. Kulti's publicist a week ago and he made it clear to me that his party has been receiving some similar messages, but we were hoping things would calm down eventually. Since they're not, let's do this: Sal, we'll release your part of the press conference we had a few weeks ago—"

My jaw dropped and I'm pretty positive that my heart skipped a single beat. I choked, loud and clear on my saliva.

The PR employee shot me a look. She'd been there. She'd seen what an ass I made of myself. "I'll make sure it's edited. We have videographers coming in to film some of the practices for the website, and I'm sure they can catch some footage of the two of you getting along. There are also some promo shots coming up, and with some easy placement," she grinned and waggled her fingers like she hadn't just spouted out one of the worst ideas I'd ever heard, "problem solved for both of you."

I chewed on my thoughts for a minute, glancing at the German sitting four feet away. Mouthing and discarding the curse words that ran through a loop in my head.

The press conference video? No. Hell no.

The filming? I glanced at Kulti again and almost snorted, remembering how he had yet to speak to anyone that wasn't on staff besides Grace. So the likelihood of that happening? Ha.

The pictures? Those were doable.

But...

The press conference. A shiver used its spindly legs to crawl up the length of my spine. I made a hocking noise in my throat.

"Sheena," I said steadily, hoping that I wasn't going to

sound like a bitch. She was trying; I knew and appreciated the effort she was putting in. "That video..." I tried to remember the words I was capable of, but all I could do was settle for a shake of my head. Then, just to make sure she really got my point, I shook my head really quickly, too adamantly maybe. "Maybe not the best idea, don't you think?"

Gardner didn't even bother to try and mute his laugh. He just went for it.

"It will be fine. I won't let them use any of the parts you're worried about. I promise."

Taking my silence for exactly what it was—wariness and distrust—Sheena said, "I promise, Sal. It'll be fine. Trust me."

Trust her? I had this rule about trusting people until they gave me a reason not to. When you play soccer with strangers on a regular basis, leaving your health and safety in the hands of others out of need, being too cynical doesn't work for anyone. Was it a little intimidating? Yes. But in the words of my sister, 'you only live once.'

"All right," I ground out, though some part of my consciousness called me an idiot for not fighting harder.

The smile she gave me in response was wide and bright.

I smiled back at her. *Idiot, idiot, idiot.*

"Mr. Kulti are you onboard too?" the nice woman asked.

Eventually he nodded. His lightly tanned face didn't exactly look like he was jumping for joy, but he didn't tell her to fuck-off like I would have bet my life on him doing years ago. I wasn't sure whether to be disappointed or not.

"We'll get this all sorted out in no time, Sal. No need to worry," Sheena added.

What she didn't know was that telling me not to worry was like telling me not to breathe.

* * *

I HAD BEEN asleep for at least an hour when my phone rang. For a couple of rings, I considered not answering it. Because, really? Who the hell would be calling at almost midnight during the week? It was pretty common knowledge that I had an early bedtime.

Marc's name flashed across the screen and I narrowed my sleepy eyes. He wasn't usually a drunk-dialer, so what if it was an emergency?

"Salamander?" This man that was more my friend than my boss spoke. We'd grown up together. He'd been friends with Eric for as long as I could remember and somehow transitioned from being his friend, to being a brother figure and a great friend to me. He'd moved to Houston to get his doctorate, and once I moved too, he'd said, 'Why don't we start our own business?' For two people with insane schedules and my degree and experience to help us out, it worked as an easy way to make our own money and not have a boss who didn't understand we had other things that came first.

I yawned. "Hey, everything all right?" I answered tentatively.

"Salami," he hissed, sounding just a little drunk while the sound of loud voices filled the background, making it really hard to hear what he was saying.

"Hey, it's me. What's going on?"

There were more sounds in the background, people laughing, what might have been glasses clinking together. "I don't know what to do."

Immediately I sat up in bed and threw my legs over the edge. Marc didn't know what to do? My gut said he wasn't calling me for shits and giggles. "It's all right. Are you okay? What do you need?"

"Oh? Me? I'm good. Sorry. I was actually calling because... hold on one sec, I'm trying to get into the bathroom real quick..." All of a sudden the background noise cut out completely and my friend's voice became clear over the line. "Hey, he's here."

Rubbing at my eyes with the back of my hand, I yawned. "Who's where?" Then it hit me. "Shouldn't you be in bed?" He had class at eight in the morning.

"My professor isn't coming in."

"Okay..."

"I'm at that bar by my house. You know which one I'm talking about?" He didn't give me a chance to respond, but I knew where he was referring to. We'd gone there together a few times in the offseason. Marc continued, "Kulti's here. Been here. The bartender cut him off a while ago, but I think he's asleep. The bartender's been asking if anyone knows him, but I guess I'm the only one."

He breathed loud, continuing. "This is some shit, Sal. I thought about taking a picture of him to sell it, but that's kinda fucked up. Imagine if anybody recognized him."

I could imagine and I cringed a little. The WPL's focus on morals and family values flashed through my head. If it got out our brand-new superstar of an assistant coach was passed out drunk at a bar before the season even started... it'd be a disaster.

"I figured you'd know what I should do," Marc finally ended.

Jeez. What a mess. A small part of me didn't want to get involved. He wasn't my friend, and it wasn't like he'd been particularly friendly or kind in any way. But the point was he was a member of my team. That part of me that battled between being a dick and saying he wasn't my problem lost to the bigger part of me that made me do the right thing. My mom would be horrified if I was an asshole. I wouldn't want to give her another reason to be disappointed in me.

I bit back a groan and stood up with a sigh, already looking through my dresser for a pair of pants. "Can you call him a cab?" Please, Jesus. Please.

"I asked the bartender who checked his ID, and he said it wasn't a Texas driver's license. He either wasn't paying attention or doesn't care who he is," Marc explained. "I don't think he has any car keys on him either."

If I was drunk, famous and what seemed like mainly alone in a foreign country, would I want someone looking through my pockets? Or, I don't know, videotaping me when I wasn't at my best? Definitely not.

Pulling my pants up, I sighed. "I'll be there in fifteen."

* * *

I SHOVED my phone back into my pocket with a tired and slightly frustrated sigh. Sheena hadn't answered her phone and neither had Gardner; then again, what had I been expecting? It was almost one in the morning, and apparently I was the only idiot that left their ringer on overnight.

The warm yellow lights from inside of the bar made me sigh again. What the hell was I doing? A man I hardly knew was sitting inside, drunk and possibly on the verge of making an ass of himself if people realized who he was. I wasn't naïve enough to believe that if he were recognized, people would brush it off. That wasn't how people worked. I could already envision the videos being uploaded and going viral and all the hell that would come from it.

Was it totally unfair? Of course it was. Most people had too much to drink at some point or another, and no one ever thought twice about it.

Shit.

I sighed and threw the door open, not thinking about the fact I was in gray six-dollar sweatpants and an old, stained sweatshirt that I'd thrown on over the baggy shirt I usually slept in. Marc must have been keeping an eye out for my car because he was waiting at the door for me. In a T-shirt and jeans, he looked like a cleaned-up version of the man I spent nearly every afternoon with. He was showered, his hair was styled, and he had his nice set of glasses on, so that was pretty fancy. He had a striking resemblance to Ricky Martin when he wasn't dressed in his work clothes. Dark hair, dark eyes, tan skin and he was just... well, pretty.

"Over here," he said, waving me toward a booth in the back.

The figure hunched over the table was unmistakable, at least to me. That shade of short brown hair was the same I'd been seeing in person for the last two weeks. It was definitely Kulti. The fact he didn't have on any team-related clothing like the polo shirt he had on earlier in the day was a small blessing, I guess. His beanie was slouched pretty low on his head, another bonus.

For the first time I thought, what the hell was he doing getting drunk at a bar in Oak Forest? This side of town was predominantly a middle-class neighborhood that had slowly been getting taken over by the upper middle-class with small houses being demolished and bigger, near-mansion-like homes taking over. It was a family neighborhood, not one you'd expect a rich single man living in.

"I'm sorry," Marc said over his shoulder.

"No, it's okay. You did the right thing calling me." Well I still wasn't convinced that was true but... if it were Harlow calling me because she needed a ride home after drinking too much, I would have gotten her without thinking twice about it. Hell, if any of the girls on the team felt desperate enough to call me for a ride home, I would have been there. We were a team. That's what you did. When you played on a team with people who held grudges against each other, it was a lot harder than it needed to be.

*Sigh.*

"All right." I eyed Kulti and tried to guess how much he weighed. If I could throw him over my shoulder I could probably carry him out, but that wouldn't exactly be inconspicuous. I tapped on his arm, then I tapped on his arm some more. Nothing. Next, I shook his arm. *Nada*. "Hey you, wake up," I said, shaking him some more.

And still nothing.

I sighed. "Help me carry him out to the car."

Marc didn't even blink; he just nodded.

For a moment I thought about whether his tab was open or not, and then I decided he could figure it out in the morning when he was sober.

"Ready?"

Marc and I dragged my coach across the seat and got him to the end of the bench. Squatting down, I peeled the arm that was plastered to the table and lifted the heavy weight to put it over my shoulders. Over the top of Kulti's head, I watched Marc do the same thing.

How did I always let myself get dragged into this crap?

"Ready?"

At the count of three, we stood up. Well, Marc and I stood up, and Jesus Christ. I was used to people jumping on top of me, but it was never deadweight. It was also never someone almost a foot taller leaning up against me.

I huffed and I heard Marc make a light grunting sound. He was used to lugging around bags of soil, grass seed and mulch, so that said something. Somehow we managed to circle around and slowly make our way toward the door. I ignored the patrons that were watching us, interested and disapproving at the same time. Whatever. Keeping my eyes forward, I focused on making sure to take as much of Kulti's weight as I could to save Marc the hassle. My rear passenger door was unlocked and we slowly finagled the big man into the seat, letting him slump over onto his side.

Good enough.

I rubbed at my eyebrow with the back of my hand, closing the door with my hip at the same time. "I tried to call Coach Gardner, but he hasn't answered, so I'm not sure whether to take him back to my place or take him to a hotel, I guess."

He gave me this look that said 'good point.' "Are you going to stay with him?"

Stay with him? I glanced in the backseat and shrugged. "I don't know. You think I should?"

Marc lifted his shoulders too, looking into the car as well. "If it was you I was picking up, I'd say yes because it's you. If it was Simon, I'd pretend I dropped the call because he's a grown man that shouldn't have gotten messed up."

I understood his point. He'd heard me tell him day after day that I hadn't spoken much with my coach. "I'll figure it out, I guess."

"You need any help?"

He didn't go out often, and I realized he'd already gone above and beyond by calling me. I shook my head. "Don't worry about it. I can get him in somewhere."

"Call me if you need me though, okay?" he asked.

I reached forward and pulled at his shirt cuff. "I will. I'll see you tomorrow."

He grinned, taking a step back. "See you."

"Goodnight," I called after him before getting in my car and watching him go back inside the bar.

A single rough snore from the backseat reminded me of the treasure I had there. What in the hell was I going to do with him? Take him home?

It didn't even take me five seconds to decide that was a shitty idea.

I didn't know him. He wasn't my friend. How weird would that be for him to wake up on my sofa in an apartment of a player he'd spoken to once?

One quick search on my phone later and the input of my credit card information, and I was driving down the dark dead streets toward the closest hotel. It took five minutes to get to the chain hotel, another fifteen minutes to check in because my discount reservation hadn't gone through yet, and then I was back at the car, eyeing what had to be close to two hundred pounds sprawled out on my backseat.

Thank God for squats and deadlifts.

It took a whole bunch of huffing and puffing, breaking out into a sweat, slapping at his cheek in hopes of reviving him futilely, and dropping the F-word every five seconds before I had his arm over my shoulders, my arm around his waist, and a barely conscious man trudging along besides me.

"Come on," I pleaded with him as we hit the stairs what felt like thirty minutes later.

I was dying. *Dying.* And that had to say something because I had full-sized women who jumped on top of me, and had me helicopter them around.

Fuck me.

Every other time I'd ever done this, I always had help.

By some miracle, the room assigned was right by the stairs.

His sleepy face was shuttered, and I slowly let him slide down the length of my side to sit on the floor. I opened the door, held it cracked open the back of my foot and snuck my arms under his armpits to drag him in.

I sure as hell did drag him in, his long legs and feet extended out in front of him. Three huffs and a rough hoist later, I pulled him onto the bed and set him on his side with one knee cocked up and his top arm extended across the length of the mattress. I peeled one eyelid open to make sure, what? I wasn't sure. I stuck a finger under his nose to make sure he was breathing evenly. And then I watched him for a solid thirty minutes, sitting in the chair just to the side of the bed. I'd been around enough over-drinkers in my life, and he wasn't giving me the impression he was going to puke up blood or anything.

Now what?

The idea of staying with him didn't seem like a good one. I wasn't sure how he'd react in the morning and, frankly, a part of me didn't want to find out. I took a breath and searched for one of those complementary notepads some hotels provided. Sure enough, across from the bed, bingo.

*Dear Kulti,*

I tore it up.

*Kulti,*

I tore it up again.

Fuck it. I scribbled a message that was longer than I expected, pulled the forty bucks I had stuffed into my bra out, and set the note and the money on the nightstand next to him.

Then I looked back at the armchair with resignation. I wasn't going home tonight and I damn well knew it. If I left, I'd stay up worried the whole night. Obviously, I only had one choice: stay in the hotel room for at least a few hours and then get the hell out of there before he knew I was there.

My conscience said it was the right thing to do, but my gut said to get the hell out.

Damn it.

# 6

"You look like crap."

I snorted at Harlow's observation and nodded my agreement. There were individuals who were morning people and could wake up after a couple hours rest and be happy to be alive.

Then there were people like me. I had to get up early so I did it, but that was only after I lay in bed for approximately seven minutes, and then followed that up by sitting on the edge of my bed and staring absently forward for at least another five. Then, if it was a good day, I wouldn't say anything for another two hours because my morning routine kept me away from humanity. If it was a bad day, someone would force me to talk to them within an hour because things hadn't worked out as I planned.

So, add up the fact I hadn't gotten rest the night before, wasn't a morning person, and my morning run turned into more of a leisurely jog that I yawned through. Needless to say, I was overly anxious about Kulti. I'd looked at my phone at least a dozen times expecting him to call or text me, but he hadn't.

He also hadn't shown up yet, and practice was supposed to

start in five minutes. He'd been sleeping soundly when I left around six this morning, my neck hurting from how I'd slept in the uncomfortable chair and my body stiff from lugging his ass around. I knew he was alive.

So...

"Are you sick?" Harlow asked as she continued to rub sunscreen onto her shoulders.

I gave her a lazy blink and shook my head as I slowly lowered myself onto my butt with a muffled groan. My back hurt like a son of a bitch. "I didn't get enough sleep last night." I sat up too straight and it sent a super-sharp pain across my lower back. "Mother fuck," I hissed before gulping and looking back at Harlow, who had an eyebrow raised. "I strained my back."

"Doing...?"

I looked her right in the eye, because I didn't want to seem like I was hiding something. "I got stuck dragging a drunk person around."

She made a noise deep in her nose. "Should've left them there, Sally."

How I wish I could have.

A moment later, the defender shoved two painkillers in my direction. "Here."

"Thanks," I said, taking the pills from her and dry-swallowing them before chasing them with a swig from my bottle of water.

Someone groped the messy knot I'd thrown my hair up into. "You okay?" Jenny's clear chipper voice asked.

She knew me too well. "Fine. I got some back pain."

A furrow formed between her eyebrows; she was just as confused by my predicament as Harlow was, and for good reason. We were all so particular about taking care of ourselves that it seemed weird I'd do something dumb like hurt myself off the field.

"You want me to rub you down later?" she asked, dropping her stuff right by Harlow.

Harlow and I glanced at each other in a single split second. Without even thinking twice about it, I answered, "That's okay, Jenny. Thanks, though."

"Are you sure?"

Was I sure I didn't want to get manhandled by Jenny's freakishly strong hands? Yes. I was no stranger to massages or the soreness that accompanied them afterward, but what Jenny was capable of was beyond that. The CIA could have used her Hercules-like strength to torture answers out of people.

So... yeah. *No.*

"I'm sure," I said carefully so that I wouldn't hurt her feelings. "I'll be fine once we start warming up."

She shrugged. "Okay."

"Where is he?" I heard one of the new girls ask as they walked by.

He.

I wasn't about to look around when I knew damn well who the only missing 'he' was. I'd definitely set the alarm clock on the nightstand for seven. It was more than enough time for him to get here.

I glanced at my phone again and checked to see if I had a missed call. Still nothing.

Oh well.

Our workout started a few minutes later, and I had to push Kulti and his absence to the back of my brain. Then Gardner waved me over immediately after we ran sprints.

"Is everything okay?" he asked as we stood off to the side of the field while equipment was being moved around. "I was asleep when you called."

Ahh shit.

"Oh, yeah. Sorry about that. I called you by accident." Vague, right? That was good enough?

Gardner didn't think twice about it; he simply shrugged. "I figured as much."

Before I could ask him what he meant by that, I spotted someone lumbering across the field.

Kulti.

I swallowed, scratched at my eyebrow and then pointed behind me. "I should get back."

My longtime coach nodded in agreement.

I got the heck out of there.

At least I tried to, but as I walked toward the group of women standing together, I made the mistake of looking over my shoulder.

Those amber-moss eyes that I'd seen from across my bedroom walls for thousands of days in my childhood, were on me. On. Me. Not looking through me, not over me. But directly on me.

Though there wasn't a slice of an expression on his features, there was no missing the intensity behind his gaze. I'd seen the intent before. Many, many times before when he played.

When he played and he was about three seconds away from losing his shit.

And... *poop*.

Pushing my shoulders back and taking a deep breath, I looked right back at him with a neutral face.

Had I done anything wrong? No.

I picked up a near complete stranger that was drunk, paid for a hotel room for him to stay at, drove him there, left cab money and a note. What else did he want? I hadn't told anyone what happened, and I wouldn't. Not even Jenny.

Okay, so I guess he didn't know I wouldn't tell anyone.

Sliding my gaze forward, I reminded myself that I hadn't done anything wrong. I did the best I could. It also wasn't my fault he hadn't woken up on time. Either way, it wasn't like I could go back in time anyway. Maybe I should have called in the morning to check on him, but obviously he was fine.

*Head in the game, Sal. Keep your head in the game. Worry about things when they happen instead of wasting your time anticipating.*

Right.

I focused.

Practice was fine until two hours later, when it happened. I was out of breath and grinning like an idiot as I high-fived the two girls I'd just finished playing with. It'd been a three-on-three mini-game that lasted five minutes. We'd won and after a cool down, our practice was over.

I made it so far as to grab my stuff, walk back to my car, stash my bag in the trunk, and put my hands up over my head to stretch my shoulders when a hand gripped my elbow out of nowhere.

The last thing I expected was to look over my shoulder and see a tall figure with brown hair and lightly tanned skin. Kulti. It was so much Kulti up close again. The night before had been such a blur the only thing I'd focused on was the size of his body and his weight, nothing else. Unlike today. In a sky blue and what I'd heard was officially called 'snow mint'—it was really just a soft, calming green—training jersey, the famous pooping German had the fingers of his left hand clasped around my elbow, and he was looking down at me.

I swallowed.

I freaked. Just a little but more than enough, even if I managed to contain it all inside.

This was no big deal. None. Poop, poop, poop.

"Say a word about yesterday and I will make you regret it," the low hard-edged accent whispered the declaration so low that if I hadn't been staring at him, I wouldn't have thought his lips moved. But they had.

Reiner Kulti was standing by my in-desperate-need-of-a-carwash Honda, saying.... *What?*

"Umm...excuse me?" I asked slowly, carefully. I didn't usually imagine hearing things.

"If you," his tone sounded a little too 'you're-stupid' for my tastes, "tell anyone about yesterday, I'll make sure you're watching the season from the bench."

I could count on my hand the number of times I'd gotten in trouble for something that wasn't me playing too roughly on the field.

Once when I was in second grade, I got caught copying my friend's homework.

Twice I lied to my parents about where I was going.

Then there was that thing when I was on the national team, which was me being plain *stupid* rather than really trying to deceive anyone.

The point was I didn't like to do bad things or disappoint anyone. Honestly, it made me feel about two inches tall and that was the absolute worst. It was for me at least. Throughout my life, most people had called me a goody two-shoes because I didn't like to do things that would get me into trouble. I had better things to do, anyway. Pushing around a few players didn't count because they gave as good as they got.

So it seemed absurd to me that he would think I'd do something like that.

Immediately after I got over how surprised I was that he'd assume that, I got pissed. Really fucking pissed. Bench me?

Indignation, a blast of anger that rivaled freaking Krakatoa and disbelief made my heart start pounding and my chest get tight.

I was panting. Was I panting?

My face got all hot and a knot formed in my throat.

For one half of a split second, I forgot who was in front of me.

It was just long enough for me to ball up my fists, rage making me jut out my chin, and say "You—," I don't know what

I was about to call him because I was so pissed off—*so pissed off*—I couldn't think straight. But just as my hand began to make its journey toward the German's face, I caught Gardner and a couple of the players that hadn't left yet just behind him, walking toward their cars.

And common sense mixed with that little voice in my head that kept me going when I felt like quitting this dream, reminded me to think about what I was doing.

The air went out of my lungs like I'd just been punched. A vein in my temple throbbed in response. *Don't do it. Don't you do it.* The hair on my arms prickled up.

Slowly, I let my hand drop to my side and made my mouth close itself.

This dipshit wasn't going to be the reason I had to sit out a season.

He wasn't.

The urge to open my mouth and tell him to go suck a cock was *right there*, but I reeled it in slowly and steadily like it was a barracuda fighting for its life. But I did. I kept it deep in my chest, in my heart and locked it up.

He wasn't going to take this away from me.

In what was probably one of the hardest things I'd ever done, I kept my middle fingers tucked in, my knee straight and away from the general vicinity of where a groin on a six-foot-two man would be, and pivoted around before sliding into my car. I closed the door without saying anything, made sure I wasn't going to run over anyone, and backed out of the spot I was in.

I didn't look in my rearview mirror once. I was too pissed.

I made it as far as the light before one single tear came out of my eye. Just one. How could he threaten me after what I'd done? I couldn't understand. I took a deep, ragged breath and told myself that I wasn't going to waste my tears on him. Whether it was humiliation or being insulted or plain being angry, it didn't matter. His stupid-ass opinion didn't matter to me. I knew who I was and what I was.

He could go suck a big dick.

And I hoped he gagged on it.

* * *

"ARE YOU OKAY?"

I tied the knot on the big black bag I'd just finished dumping the grass catcher into. I nodded at Marc and gave him a tired smile. "I'm okay. Are you?"

He pulled his hat off his head and ran a hand over his short black hair. "A little hung-over, but I've been through worse." He fidgeted with the duffel bag he had thrown across his body before following after me. "Was, uh, everything okay last night?"

"Yeah. He made it to practice this morning." I said that so casually I thought I deserved a gold star. "Thanks again for calling me."

He shrugged off my thanks and picked up the edger waiting on the driveway. "What the hell do you think he was doing there anyway?" He asked the question quietly.

"I have no clue." He hadn't said anything besides threaten me. Fantastic. "It seems pretty stupid to me, but at least we got him out of there."

Slamming the tailgate closed once we had all of our equipment back in the truck bed, Marc turned to look at me. "You did the right thing. Don't worry about it."

The sudden urge to tell him that Kulti threatened my season loomed in my mouth, but I kept it there. All it had been was a threat. I told myself that I wasn't going to give that cyst power over me.

Plus, I had a nagging suspicion that I would never, ever acknowledge that I might still let out a tear or two if I repeated his words aloud. It was only because I didn't have anything in my hand that I could afford to break that I didn't throw it onto the floor.

Wanting to throw something just wasn't like me. I wasn't this person. I couldn't believe he was capable of bringing these emotions out of me. I wasn't hot-tempered or emotional. Not anymore, at least.

It was his fault. It was all Kulti's fault.

* * *

"Salomé! Salomé Casillas!"

I had been purposely hanging my head low so that the journalists hanging around the training field wouldn't see me behind the group of players I was heading to the field with.

Damn it.

"Sal!"

Jenny snorted when I stopped, and she kept walking right on past me. Traitor. Forcing a polite smile on my face, I looked around at the female voice calling my name. She hurried over, recorder in hand, a smile so big I really wasn't sure whether it was authentic or not. You could never really tell anymore.

"Hi," I greeted her.

"Hey, thanks so much for stopping," she said, brushing her long hair out of her face. "Do you have a couple minutes for me?"

The "sure" that came out of my mouth sounded strangely convincing. Honestly, it was nothing against anyone in the media, it was just me being awkward and antisocial, knowing that my words could be documented and held against me. Maybe.

She slid me a grin, holding up her recorder. "I'm going to record this, if you can approve it for me." I did. "Okay, thanks again. My name is Clarissa Owens and I work for Social Jane."

A website I'd heard of. Okay, that wasn't too bad.

"What's it like working with one of the world's sexiest men?"

Andddddd it was the Hindenburg all over again. Crashing and burning, and then crashing and burning once more.

I blinked at her. "You meant Coach Kulti?" It wasn't like most women would find Gardner attractive; he was, at least in my opinion, just in an unconventional way. I liked his graying hair, his face was classic, he was in good shape, and he had a perfectly round booty.

But...

Clarissa Owens let out a really feminine laugh. "Oh you know who I'm talking about, silly. Reiner Kulti. What's it like being coached by one of the sexiest athletes in the world?"

It took everything inside of me not to look up at the sky and ask for divine intervention. My mouth opened and closed multiple times, like it was trying to make words magically appear in the place of complete silence. "Umm... well. He's our assistant coach and he was one of the greatest players in our sport, so that's pretty exciting."

"I'm sure," she said. "Tell us, does he wear boxers or briefs?"

How the hell was I supposed to know? Instead I said, "I... have no idea, but I hope he has something on under his uniform."

"What kind of interests does he have?"

"The only thing he's interested in is winning, I think."

Ms. Owens gave me an exasperated look. "Is he single?"

I blinked at her some more and finally looked over my shoulder to make sure no one was fucking with me. When I looked back at her, I blinked again. "Is this a joke?"

"No."

"Are you sure?"

"Yes."

It took a moment before I managed to get myself together.

"Kulti is my coach. He's the best soccer player to ever play in Houston, in Texas more than likely, and we're unbelievably lucky to have him here—" even if he didn't do anything, but why kill the illusion? "I respect him and so does the rest of the team because he's a great athlete. His personal life is his business and I have no idea what he does when he's not here, I'm sorry."

"Oh. Okay... Can you tell me anything else about him that you think the public doesn't know?"

That he was just as much of a bastard as he'd been made out to be? Or that he occasionally drank too much at bars and had to be picked up, without ever issuing a thank you in exchange? I made sure none of those ideas crossed my face as I shrugged at the woman who really was just doing her job. It wasn't her fault that people really would want to know things like that.

"I'm sorry. I really don't. I saw him wearing purple socks one day. That's as much as I know," I offered her the miserable piece of knowledge. He'd been wearing royal purple socks, that was a fact.

She gave me a look that said that wasn't what she was looking for, but realized that was as good as she was getting from me. Unfortunately for her, she didn't know that most of us were unable to give her any juicy gossip. No one knew anything about the German, except maybe Grace. *Maybe.* She was the only one on the team he seemed to ever speak to, but Grace was too professional to ever spill the beans anyway.

We quickly said goodbye to each other and went our own way.

But I couldn't shake off the annoyance at being asked stuff like that. More than likely, I just couldn't shake off the fact that they were questions about such a fucking asshole.

*I will make you regret it.*

Okay, Scarface. Cheese and fucking crackers. Jeez.

I had to tamp down the inner scream that went on inside of me.

Did he have any idea what he'd meant to me when I was younger? Of course he didn't. But that was beside the point. I was where I was because I thought he hung the moon when I was a kid. Because I thought he was the greatest player ever and I wanted to be him—okay, and be with him, but whatever. I used to get into arguments with people who talked badly about him.

That's what it was like. Even now, I defended his skills like an objective unbiased player because you couldn't argue the statistics. He had been amazing and there was nothing emotional behind that statement.

He'd been an incredible player above the layer of assholery he wrapped himself in.

Freaking jackass.

"How'd that go?" Jenny asked with a smile when I sat down next to her.

I didn't bother to hide how I rolled my eyes. "They asked me if he was single."

She snorted.

"I should have said, 'no, I met his life partner a few days ago. He's great.'" I gave her a little smile as I pulled my things out of my bag. "Maybe one day."

"Yesterday I had one of them ask me if I thought he was preparing for a comeback. Then, I was getting my mail when my neighbor asked, 'Hi, Jennifer, do you think you could get me tickets to your next game?' *I don't even know his name!*" she exclaimed. "The day before that, my aunt asked me if there was any way for her to drop by during practice. She doesn't even like soccer."

Jenny wasn't one to ever complain, so for her to mention it said something.

I settled just for nodding at her. I didn't trust the words that could potentially come out of my mouth.

"Genevieve told me that her boss said he'd give her a raise if she brought him back something that belonged to you-know-who."

Not surprising. On the other hand, I was sure that if I gave Marc Kulti's underwear, he'd probably tell me to take a week off and still pay me my half. "I heard Harlow tell a reporter this morning that she came to play, not talk about her coach."

We both snorted.

"But what are we going to do? Complain about all of the attention? I already told them about the weird emails I've been getting about Eric, and they're trying to turn everything around to work out positively. Eric told me Kulti was offered some huge deal from a European team, and he turned it down. They aren't going to want to risk losing him." I thought of the night at the bar again and his threat, and felt that familiar bolt of frustration streak down my back before I pushed it away. "Oh well."

She nodded in resignation. "I hope everyone calms down as the season goes on."

"Me too."

# 7

Practices and life just went on for the next few days.

There'd been at least a couple of reporters by the field every morning. It was usually the same ones for a couple of days before the rotation changed and other people showed up. Gardner led practices with the assistance of the fitness coach and one of the other assistants while the infamous *frankfurter* did what he always did: a whole bunch of nothing.

Eventually after a couple of days, I stopped giving a shit about the German—I had other things to worry about—and ignoring him became second nature, even when he was *right there.*

Like the day of the team photo.

Safely nestled in the front row with the rest of the under-five-foot-seven players, I had a midfielder on one side and a defender on the other, courtesy of the assistant photographer's manhandling. Had I forgotten that Sheena had said I should stand by Kulti? Nope. Was I about to say anything to fix what was going on? No way, Jose.

The sun had taken its punishing nature to the next level,

the humidity making me sweat in places most people never would, and all I wanted was the water under a canopy too far away to reach in a quick sprint. Standing there defenselessly huddled together was about a hundred times worse than running around having practice before the heat got too bad. Way worse.

"Is this almost over?" the player to my right sighed. She was one of the new additions to the Pipers.

"I think so," Genevieve, a girl in the row directly behind me, answered. This was only her second season playing in the WPL.

I glanced over my shoulder to see the assistant rearranging the women in the top row. Harlow was standing off to the side, scowling at whatever the woman was saying, and it made me smile. "They're almost done with the big broads up there, then it should start and it'll be another twenty minutes tops."

There was a collective groan from the six people around.

"Casillas!"

Oh hell. No. *No*. "Casillas! You're in the wrong place!" the photographer yelled from her spot right next to the Pipers' public relations employee.

"See you later, guys," I muttered.

It took everything in me to not hang my head and drag my feet toward Sheena, who had appeared out of nowhere. I'd been keeping an eye out for her. Bah. I understood that she was watching out for me, doing me a favor by helping me out of the predicament that the past had gotten me into simply by association. But as I thought about those emails that went unread in my inbox, I decided it was probably worth it to just keep my mouth closed and do what I needed to.

Apparently, none of that mattered. I swallowed, put my Big Girl Socks on and took a deep breath as I walked like a normal sane human in the direction I was being pointed.

"Sal, squeeze in right there one row below Mr. Kulti, next to

Miss Phyllis." Miss Phyllis, the fitness coach who resurrected herself year after year to make sure the team was in shape. It also happened that we were around the same height, so Sheena's thinking made sense. If you didn't take into consideration that the human Berlin Wall was at least six inches taller than the player standing next to him.

I threw my shoulders back and pretended like I didn't notice the way he ignored everything and everyone around him even when I stood less than a foot away.

But I took it like a champ, not letting him get to me.

Much.

Unfortunately just because I knew better than to try and engage him, didn't mean everyone else was on the same page. I'd barely been standing there two minutes when I overheard the player standing somewhere behind me ask, "Could you tell me what time it is?"

Anyone who knew even a little bit about Kulti was well aware of the fact that he had a watch endorsement. He always wore one.

We'd all been instructed to leave our cell phones in our bags, so I wasn't surprised that no one had a watch on. I'd played with one a long time ago, but didn't want to risk breaking the face.

"No one knows what time it is?" the player asked again.

Nothing.

Not a single response from the man who was paid to wear a watch.

Jeez. I finally turned around and said, "I don't have a watch on me, Vivian. Sorry." Because I hated when I asked something and no one responded. It was rude and awkward.

But what was more rude and awkward was being able to give an appropriate answer and not do so. From the look on the player's face, she knew he could have answered.

And he'd chosen not to. Classy.

I kept my face forward after that and smiled at the camera when the time came.

* * *

THINGS DIDN'T GET any better when the videographers showed up two days later to film practice. Sheena kept waving me over in the general direction of where the coaches were standing. "Go on," she whispered to me when I got close enough. "Just a few shots."

It was just a few shots with a man who had said three sentences to me in a month.

Bah.

I picked up my pride, shook it off and placed it around my shoulders before gradually easing my way toward the coaches who happened to be standing together.

I made a point to make conversation with Gardner, while Kulti stood nearby with those fantastic flexed biceps crossed over his chest, and his attention elsewhere. Every time I looked at him, he reminded me more and more of a soldier in some branch of the military with his crew cut and blank face. Meanwhile, in my head, I flicked him off with both hands at the same time. Maturity was definitely a personal strength of mine.

Not.

But I did what I had to do. Always. That's what put a smile on my face and made me talk to people I was actually fond of while the videographers walked around. It had to be good enough.

I brushed off thinking about the German ignoring life itself and paid attention to the girls standing around me; Gardner began speaking to someone else.

"I'm ready to get this over with. Anyone know what we're doing tomorrow?" I overheard Genevieve ask.

Another girl responded, "I think we're meeting at the offices tomorrow to pick up the rest of our uniforms, aren't we?"

We were, but I hated always being the one who knew what was going on and piping in.

Someone else agreed. "Yeah. Anyone want to go out for happy hour tomorrow?"

Go to happy hour the day before a game? I made a face to myself but kept my gaze forward and my mouth shut. But I still listened as two people agreed and another one said no.

Either way, it wasn't like they invited me or asked for my opinion. Most people had given up on inviting me places after so many no-shows, and that was my fault. I *was* busy. Sometimes it seemed like I had to schedule bathroom visits into my day. So while they were all going out for happy hour, I was going to finally be starting a new project with Marc for a customer that we'd fondly called a "Southwest Oasis." Fifteen years ago, I never would have thought I'd be excited about special-ordering rocks and cacti.

Was it glamorous or fun in a traditional way? No. But it was my life and I didn't care.

"I can't wait," another girl admitted. "This week has s-u-c-k-e-d. I could use a couple margaritas."

A couple? I winced.

"Girl, me too—"

"What you all need is some discipline, not drinks the day before a game."

Honest to God, I stopped breathing at the sound of the foreign voice speaking. I didn't need to turn around to know who had just spoken. You'd have to be an idiot not to know.

Of all the times, he'd chosen to speak up...

"But it's just a preseason—"

I wasn't sure who was dumb enough to even bother justifying that it was 'just' a preseason game. I partially understood that it technically didn't count, but still. Who liked to lose? I sure as hell didn't; I didn't even like losing at air hockey.

Regardless.

That coming from him? What a damn hypocrite.

"No game is 'just' anything," was the sharp, no-nonsense reply that came out of the *sauerkraut*'s mouth.

"Hey, why don't we—" Gardner quickly jumped in with some random topic to distract the newcomer.

I sure as hell wasn't going to turn around and look at him for using such an ugly tone or for being a massive phony. Maybe if I hadn't just dragged his drunk butt into a hotel room days before, I'd feel different.

But the damage had already been done.

Even *I* felt the burn of his words. No one else said anything. But the second I made eye contact with Jenny, she mouthed, 'what the heck was that?'

I gave her bug eyes and mouthed back, 'I have no idea.'

* * *

A FEW MINUTES LATER, Grace approached him. The conversation had to have lasted all of three minutes, if that, but in those three minutes I was positive that every member of the Pipers team watched. We watched Grace march up to him, say something in that way she'd talked to us all before when her captain pants were on, then we saw him respond in a short sentence. Two minutes later, one of the most collected, professional players I'd ever met had anger painted all over every feature of her body.

Grace was *pissed*. Grace. She was the type of person that always took the higher road. In the five years we'd played together, even back on the national team, she had never played dirty. Cool as a cucumber, determined and smart, Grace was the epitome of a pro.

She didn't lose her shit.

And she just had. Over what, I had no idea, but a small part of me was dying to know.

Had she said something to Kulti about how he'd snapped at the girls? Knowing her and how seriously she took her role of captain, more than likely. Every other time I'd seen them together, they seemed like friends... well, friendly. Friendly-ish. Yeah.

The scene left me a little worried.

What had happened?

* * *

"SAL, is that sexy-ass brother of yours coming to our opener?"

I stuck my tongue out and over-exaggerated some retching, earning a laugh from a couple of girls who knew how much I hated that they imagined dirty things with my brother every time he dropped by. Desperate, slumming sluts. Finally, I grinned at the girl who asked and shook my head. "No, he's not. My sexy-ass little sister is coming and so are my parents. They're actually here today."

"Aww, really?"

Joy and pleasure sparked through my chest. A lot of the players didn't have family that lived close enough to occasionally come to games... or didn't bother. My family, on the other hand, usually showed up to most home games, doing the three-hour drive and spending the day after to see me. I knew that I was lucky, and I was grateful they were so supportive.

Even if my sister, Cecilia, spent the entire game on her phone sending text messages and browsing Instagram. But, whatever. She was there even after she called me ugly names and made up horrible ideas in her head of what I thought about her. It wasn't like my mom would have chosen this life for me either, but she showed up and cheered anyway, even if it cost her. But that was love, wasn't it?

Today was our open practice before the preseason games began against the local college teams. This practice was a gesture that the league did for season ticket holders, friends and family of players, and winners of various contests. After practice we hung around and took pictures, and if there were little kids, we kicked the ball around with them for a while.

"Yup. I'm not sure if Eric will be able to come by this year since he's still overseas." Thankfully. I could easily picture him in the stands glowering at the bench, and by 'the bench,' I meant Reiner Kulti.

"Let me know in advance so I can put some make-up on that day," the girl laughed.

I snickered and waved her off, pulling my socks on over my shin guards since we were already finished warming up. Getting to my feet, I looked at the hundred or so people that were in the bleachers in a small, sectioned-off part of where we practiced. In the matter of just a couple of minutes, I spotted my dad's receding hairline, my mom's new bright red hair color and Ceci's big head covered by a cowboy hat. Throwing both hands into the air, I waved at my family and whoever else assumed I was waving at them; I smiled big. Instantly, Mom and Dad waved back, and so did a few other people I didn't know.

"Come on, ladies. If everyone is ready, let's get started," Gardner called out.

The next two hours flew by without a trace of the awkwardness that had been blanketing the team since Kulti decided to take his bastard-ness to the next level. We all seemed to block that out of our heads for the time being at least. I snuck glances at the bleachers throughout the exhibition. I had always been one of those kids that liked having her family around for games. There were people who didn't, but I wasn't one of them.

I played better when they were in the stands, or at least I took it even more seriously—if that was possible. My parents knew more than enough about soccer to catch everything and still make suggestions to me about things that could be worked on.

The sun seemed extra hot and my ankle was only bothering me a little bit, but overall it went really well. Except every time I looked in my dad's direction he was busy staring at Kulti like a total creeper. I loved him even if he had horrible taste in men.

We wouldn't even bring up that I'd been just like him many years before.

As soon as we'd cooled down and stretched, a few of the Houston's men's team employees—our team was owned by the same people—led the onlookers off the stands and onto the field. It'd been more than a month since the last time I'd seen my family, and I'd missed them. I watched my dad looking around the field for the only person that really mattered. I knew it wasn't me, ha.

"Ma." I held out my arm for my mom who quickly glanced at my sweaty training jersey, made a face and hugged me anyway.

"*Mija*," she replied, squeezing me tight.

Next, I grabbed my little sister by the brim of her cap and pulled her toward me as she squealed, "No, Sal! You're all sweaty! Sal, I'm not kidding. *Sal! Shit!*"

Did I know she didn't like sweaty hugs? Hell yeah. Did I care? Nope. I hadn't forgotten she'd called me a bitch the last time we'd been in the same room together, even if she was going to act like no such words had come out of her mouth. I hugged her to me even harder, feeling her smacking me on the back pretty damn hard as my mom said, "*Hija de tu madre*, watch your mouth" to deaf ears.

"I've missed you, Ceci," I said, peppering kisses all over my baby sister's cheeks as she tried to pull away, saying something about her make-up getting smudged.

She was seventeen. She would get over it. We were both almost the same height, had brown hair, although mine was a bit lighter, taking after our Argentinian grandma, and the same light-brown eyes. But that was about it as far as our similarities went. Physically, I had about twenty pounds on her. Personality-wise, we were as different as could be. By the time she was fifteen she had mastered wearing heels, while I thought putting on a real bra was fancy, and that was only the tip of the iceberg. But I loved the crap out of her, even when she was a little snobby and whiny… and sometimes she was a little bit mean.

When I finally let her go, I snorted in my dad's direction. He had his back to us and was busy looking around the field. "Hey, Dad? Give me a hug before you never want to wash your hand again."

With a startled jump, he turned around and flashed a toothy smile at me. He'd had a receding hairline for as long as I could remember, his facial hair cut short and his green eyes—inherited from a Spanish grandmother—were bright. "I was looking for you!"

"Oh, whatever, liar," I laughed. We gave each other a big hug as he gave me some commentary on the scissor kicks I'd done during the practice. It was a move that required you to throw yourself in the air and kick the ball over your head or to the side, whatever worked.

"I'm so proud of you," he said, still hugging me. "You get better every time I see you."

"I think your vision might be getting worse."

He shook his head and finally pulled away, keeping his hands on my shoulders. He wasn't very tall, only about five-nine according to his license, though I thought he was more five-seven. "*Alomejor.*"

There was a tapping at the side of my leg and when I looked down, I found a little girl and boy standing there with my player profile photograph from last season in their hands.

I talked to them for a little while, signed their pictures and then posed for a few with them when their mom asked. Immediately following them, another three sets of families—most of the time it was little girls with their moms—came over and we did the same. Between the photographs, I asked them questions and passed out hugs because they were the world's cheapest and most effective currency. I hated talking to the press because it made me nervous and uncomfortable, these strangers, these people made me incredibly happy, especially when the kids were excited. I lost track of my parents but didn't worry about it too much; they knew how these types of things worked.

What must have been thirty minutes later, once I was done signing a teenage girl's ball and telling her she wasn't too old if she wanted to play professionally one day, I looked around, trying to find my family. Off by one of the goals we'd used during practice, I spotted my dad and mom speaking to Gardner and Grace, the veteran. They'd met both repeatedly throughout the years.

By the time I made it over to them, I flung an arm around my dad's side and smiled up at him. But what faced me was a borderline grim faintly sad smile that tried its best to not look that way. It immediately put me on alert. "*Que tienes?*" I whispered.

"*Estoy bien,*" he whispered back, kissing my cheek. He didn't seem fine to me. "Coach was telling us how good you've all been playing together."

I watched his face really carefully, taking in the sun and age lines from years of working outside, most of the time with a hat and sometimes without it, and I knew that there was something bothering him. He was just being stubborn, which was where I'd gotten it from—him. But if he didn't want to say anything in that instant I wasn't going to force him to. I cleared my throat and tried to catch my mom's eye, but she seemed fine. "I hope we do. I don't see why not, right, Grace?"

The slightly older woman, turning thirty-five this year, smiled cheerfully back. Completely unlike the look on her face when she'd said who-knew-what to Kulti. "Definitely."

When Gardner and Grace were gone and it was just the three of us—Ceci was over talking to Harlow about God knows what—I elbowed my dad in the arm and asked, "What's wrong? Really."

He shook his head like I knew he would. "I'm okay, Sal. What's wrong with you?"

Deflection was a talent in the Casillas family. "What happened?" I insisted, because that was another Casillas family trait.

"*Nada*."

This man. I could shake him sometimes. "Will you tell me later? Please?"

With two pats to the top of my head, he shook his head once more. "Everything is okay. I'm happy to see you, and I'm happy we'll get to see the season opener in a couple of weeks."

He was so full of shit, but I knew it was pointless to argue with him, so I let it go.

A few minutes later, my family left and promised to see me in the evening. My mom and Ceci wanted to go shopping while they were in town, and we made plans to meet up once I was done working. There were still a few fans around; all the players were still on the field getting their stuff together if they weren't busy. I had just grabbed my water bottle to take a swig when Harlow came over and gave me a grave look. Two looks like that in one day were way too much.

"What's going on?" I asked her, stuffing the bottle under my armpit.

Her lower jaw moved a little. "I didn't say anything because I know you would want to do the honors."

I blinked. "Of doing what?"

Harlow planted her hands behind her back, the faintest trait of irritation crossing the planes in her cheeks. This was a facial feature of hers I was familiar with. She was trying to rein in that explosive temper. "Mr. Casillas didn't say anything to you?"

I blinked, suspicious. "No. About what?"

Har cleared her throat, another giveaway that something had made her angry—which wasn't saying much. She wasn't known for her patience. "I think he went up to you-know-who and asked him for an autograph." She cleared her throat once more. "I'm not sure, Sally. All I know is that your dad walked away and it looked like he'd gotten nut-punched."

*Patience, Sal.*

I took a deep breath. "You think..." I was speaking about a word a minute so that I wouldn't burst a capillary in my eye from how strained I felt on the inside. "He was mean to my dad?" *My dad?*

"I think that he was," she responded nearly as slowly. "I've never seen your dad look like that. Especially not after he had Valentine's Day in his eyes right before, and then didn't afterward."

*P-a-t-i-e-n-c-e. Be calm. Count to ten.*

I opened and closed my mouth to try and release the tension in my jaw, and nothing happened. The next thing I knew, my arms were shaking as I remembered the look on my dad's face.

Fuck it.

I tried. I could live with the fact that I really did try to not get so pissed. I put in the effort. Then again, there were very few times that I'd ever gotten so mad so fast. I was usually calm, and if I wasn't, I understood there was a time and a place to be angry.

Most of the time.

I took a step forward. "I can't—"

Like a good friend, Harlow understood that there was no talking me off of the ledge I'd set myself on. She herself was protective and knew that you didn't ever hurt a person's loved ones, so she let me go. Later on, if I ever really thought about it, I'd remember that she'd said she was going to let me do the honors despite the fact she'd had the urge to stand up for my daddy's pride, too.

"Just don't hit him in front of everyone!" Harlow ordered me as I marched toward... well, I didn't know where exactly. I only knew my destination and that was wherever the hell that German bitch was.

In the time it took me to find and speed-walk toward him, I calmed down enough to tell myself that I couldn't punch him. I also couldn't and shouldn't call him *Führer* or anything else that could potentially get me in trouble. Fortunately for me, I thought well on my feet.

My goal: ripping him a new asshole without getting in trouble.

I took my mental Big Girl Socks off and threw them on the floor. Fuck this motherfucker. If I would have had earrings on, I'd be taking those off and handing them to Harlow, too.

My shaking arms and pounding heart egged me on.

I found him.

He was just there, minding his own business looking over some notes in a binder. Tall and solemn and completely oblivious to the fact that he'd hurt the most important man in my life's feelings.

I didn't think or bother to look around me to check and see who the potential audience was going to be because I didn't give a single shit.

*Don't talk outright crap to him.*

*Don't call him a curse word or Führer.*

In that moment, I didn't give a crap who this man was or

who he had been. He was just some asshole with an attitude problem that had done the unthinkable. It was one thing to be an ass to me or my teammates. But he'd hurt my *papi's* feelings, and that shit just didn't fly.

"Hey," I snapped the minute I was close enough.

He didn't look up.

"Hey, you German bratwurst." Did that just come out of my mouth?

When the German bratwurst in question looked up, I figured out I'd actually said that out loud. Well I guess I could have said something a lot worse, and it wasn't like I could back out at that point.

"You're talking to me?" he asked.

I focused on how my forearms were tensed, on the anger that had flamed to life in my chest and I let the words out. "Yes you. Maybe you don't give a crap about helping the team out and that's fine. I get it, big man. Want to talk shit to us, *when you know you're in no position to say anything about what people should and shouldn't be doing*?" I shot him a look that said I wanted him to remember what exactly I'd done for him.

Hypocritical ass.

"We'll all get over you being rude with us, trust me. I won't be losing any sleep over you, but we don't treat our fans like crap here. I'm not sure what it was like for you back where you played, but here, we're grateful and we treat everyone kindly. It doesn't matter if someone asks you for an autograph or to sign their ass cheek, you do it with a smile.

"And you especially aren't allowed to be an asshole to my dad. He thought you were the greatest thing since frozen meals. He's one of your biggest fans, and you're going to be rude to him? Jesus Christ. Everyone knows you were a terror to play against, but I didn't think you were mean to people that have been supportive of your career."

Someone was panting, and I was pretty sure it was me. "All

he wanted to do was meet you and, I don't know, maybe get a picture so he could brag about it to his friends. He's the best man I know, and he's been talking about seeing you for weeks. Now my dad left here upset and probably disillusioned, so thank you for that, you German Chocolate Cake. I hope the next time someone approaches you, you think about how two minutes of your time could make one person's entire year."

You fucking *sauerkraut*.

Okay, I didn't say that, but I thought it.

I also thought about flicking him off with both my hands, but I didn't do that either.

My fingers flexed on their own and my molars started to grind together as we stared at each other in silence. I'd thought I was done, but when he blinked those eyes that reminded me of playing in New Hampshire once in late fall, I felt my inner thirteen-year-old come to life, the girl who had held this man on a pedestal and thought the world of him.

I felt her come to life and die in a split second. Just that quickly, this version of me who understood that people changed over the years was reborn from the ashes of teenage Sal. The grown up version of me didn't give a single fuck about Reiner Kulti. He hadn't been the one who sat through my practices, my games. He wasn't the one that stressed about my injuries and teased me through my recuperation periods. I had a list of people that I loved and respected, people that had earned their way into my heart and deserved my loyalty.

Reiner Kulti wasn't anyone special in the ways that really mattered. He'd been my inspiration a very long time ago, but he hadn't been the one to help me make it happen.

"I get that you're the greatest thing to ever come onto this field, *Mister* Kulti." Yeah, I said the 'mister' as sarcastically as I could. "But to me, my dad is one of the greatest people in the world. And the next person whose feelings you hurt by not caring to meet them is someone else's dad or brother or mom or sister or daughter or son. So think about that."

Goddamn *frankfurter*.

Luckily, I wasn't really expecting him to reply and, in the end, it was probably a good thing that he didn't because I seriously doubted something sincere or apologetic could have come out of such an indifferent apathetic mouth.

Hours later when I was hauling rocks around on a wheelbarrow and my shoulders were on the verge of sprouting tear ducts because they hurt so much, I couldn't help but still feel rattled, pissed. If I hadn't already taken them down almost ten years ago, I would have ripped the Kulti posters off my wall with a scream that would have made Xena proud. No one had stopped me as I grabbed my shit and left. Gardner had just stood there as I passed by him with what I recognized as an impressed look on his face.

So there was that, at least. I couldn't get kicked off the team if Gardner looked pleased with what I'd said.

At least that's what I hoped, but either way, I couldn't find it in me to regret what I had done. If I couldn't stand up for what I believed in, then I wasn't the person I strived to be.

* * *

I GOT three voicemails that evening while I snuck in a run before meeting up with my parents.

The first was from Jenny, who said, "Sal, I can't believe you said that to him, but I think it was the nicest things I've ever heard come out of anyone's mouth. I'm proud of you, and I love you."

The second was from one of the defenders on the team that I wasn't particularly close to, who laughed so hard she sounded like she was dying. "German Chocolate Cake! Oh my god, I thought I pissed my pants."

The third was from Harlow. "Sal, I always knew you had balls of steel in that puny little body, but goddamn, I almost cried. You let me know when you wanna go out to celebrate you giving Kulti the reaming of a lifetime."

Overall, I was pretty pleased with myself.

I didn't say anything to my dad that night when we all went out to eat, but I gave him a hug twice as hard as usual that left him gasping for breath.

* * *

If I was worried that the staff would be pissed about what I'd said the day before, it had been a waste of mental and emotional effort. A couple of the newer girls gave me discreet low-fives when I showed up, but it was the hard pat on my back that Gardner gave me that finally relaxed me. Nothing would come of it.

I held my head up high and didn't put in any extra effort to pretend not to look at Kulti. If I glanced in his direction, I kept on looking. The one time our gazes met, I let my eyes linger for a second before looking elsewhere. They say not to make eye contact with dangerous animals so that they don't perceive you as a threat, but I said screw it; I was no one's bitch, especially not Kulti's.

I hadn't done anything wrong, and I sure as hell wasn't going to stand by and let this German tank make the best dad in the world feel dejected. He'd been acting normal when we had dinner at the restaurant by their hotel but... still. My gut knew that his feelings had been hurt and that was not going to fly on my radar, ever.

When I happened to get knocked to the ground during a particularly competitive game of three-on-three, right at Kulti's feet, I hopped back up, brushed my thighs off as I looked him right in the eye, and then went right back to what I was doing.

Was it the smartest thing to do?

Maybe not, but all I had to do was think of my dad and I knew I'd done the right thing, the only thing, really. Though Grace and I never talked about what had gone down between her and Kulti, the look she gave me after that fateful day had me convinced she'd said something about how he'd talked to the other Pipers. While I hadn't found the balls to say anything to defend the girls he'd chastised, I'd stood up for my dad and also, maybe in a way, for every person he brushed off.

Which was all of us—sort of. Only it'd taken me a lot longer than it had Grace. Maybe if it had been Jenny or Harlow, I would have handled it differently. The point was no one deserved that treatment.

Nothing in his actions had changed at all. We were all tiptoeing, watching our backs and our words. Did it suck? Absolutely. There was only so much you could think about it, though.

With our first preseason game coming up—and five others following within a two-week span—I had to settle for keeping my thoughts on the game and not on the dumb man people had called 'The King'. Sure. He was 'The King' of every full-of-shit bastard on the planet.

# 8

"....Does anyone have any other questions?"

You could take a bite out of the tension in the room. No one except Grace had said a word over the last two hours. We all just sat there, listening to the coaching staff go over last-minute details regarding the upcoming season. Awkward and uncertain, every player sitting around the conference room simply watched and nodded. Spending so much time listening to others talk instead of actually playing was painful enough.

The culprit behind the team's weird behavior was the assistant coach standing in the corner of the room by the projection screen with his arms at his sides. No one had to confirm it, but we knew. We all definitely knew.

It was his fault.

When no one else responded to Gardner's question, I shook my head and answered. "Nope."

A frown indented the crease between the head coach's eyebrows as he looked around the room, waiting for someone to say something else.

Fresh words never came, and I could tell by the way his

cheeks tightened that he didn't understand why, either. For one thing, no one exactly lacked confidence. Secondly, if anyone had an issue, they usually didn't have a problem voicing it.

Except this time, the main problem had two arms and legs.

Dun, dun, dun.

No one was about to give anything away.

"No one?" Gardner asked again, his tone disbelieving.

Nothing.

"Okay. If no one has anything to say, I guess you're all free to go. We're meeting up here tomorrow at eight, and we'll all ride to the field together," he announced to a collective of nods before the team got up.

I stayed a few minutes longer talking to Genevieve about running trails nearby and had just grabbed my stuff when I heard, "Sal, you got time to come to my office?"

My instinct said I knew exactly what conversation was about to go down. I'd seen Gardner's face and my gut was well aware that he knew something was up.

Unfortunately, I also knew I'd be the first and more than likely the only one he'd come to with his questions.

Blah. It was the curse of being a well-known shitty liar.

"Sure," I told him, even though the last thing I wanted was to talk about it.

He grinned at me and beckoned me forward. "Come on, then."

Damn it. Slinging my bag over my shoulder, I followed. Within a couple minutes, we were turning down a hallway I was all too familiar with and heading into his office.

Gardner pulled the curtains up in the small window that separated his desk from the hall—it was procedure—and took a seat behind his desk, his smile friendly and his eyebrows halfway up to his hairline. "You know I'm not going to beat around the bush with you. Tell me what's going on."

And bingo was his name-o.

Where exactly did I start?

It wasn't like I wanted to bring up anyone's issues, much less my own conundrum—again—in front of a man that I trusted and respected but ultimately realized was using me as an informant. Okay, more of a snitch. It was the same thing, damn it. Sliding into the chair with my bag at my feet, I raised my eyebrows up at Gardner. I immediately decided to play the dumb card as long as possible.

"With us?"

"You all. The team. What's going on?"

"G, I have no idea what you're talking about."

"Sal." He blinked like he knew I was playing dumb. I was, but he didn't know that for sure. "Everyone is acting strange. No one's chatty. I don't see anyone playing around like usual. It looks like it's the first time everyone is playing together. I want to understand what's going on, that's all."

Once I really thought about it, I realized I shouldn't be surprised he noticed the differences. Of course he would. He noticed because he cared. I complained because Gardner cared and then complained because Kulti didn't. There was no winning, was there? I needed to embrace the fact Gardner was still around and noticed.

While practices were usually pretty serious, there had always been a playful aspect to our warm-ups and cool downs. We all got along with each other pretty well for the most part, and I think that's why we worked so well together. No one was a superstar or had a hot-air-balloon-sized ego. We played as a unit.

Of course that didn't mean some players didn't wish other players didn't twist an ankle from time to time, but that's just the way it was.

And yeah, practices had been pretty subdued and had gotten more and more quiet with each passing day. It didn't take a genius to figure out that it wasn't the fault of the new players to the team. They were great.

It was the German. If even Harlow was wary of opening up her mouth to complain about him not being active, then there was obviously a problem. I don't think Har had ever thought twice about the repercussions of speaking up. She was that good and that honest. Yet I'd seen her stand back and shake her head while the *frankfurter* in question paced around the outskirts of practices, silent.

Plus, there was my crap with him.

I leaned forward to rest my elbows on my knees and lifted up my shoulders in a lazy shrug.

"Tell me what to do," the coach said, seriously. "I trust your word, and I need to know where to start."

The t-word, goddammit. Trust was my kryptonite.

I suddenly felt my resolve give way and let my head hang down in surrender.

"Well." I scratched my cheek and gave him a steady look. "What exactly can I say that won't get me into trouble?"

"What?"

"What will get me in trouble? I don't want to say something that will get me benched," I told him carefully, like I hadn't called the German a bratwurst days before.

The look he gave me was incredulous. Gardner looked as if I'd spit in his face. "Is this Kulti-related?"

Given the fact that I hadn't been given parameters yet as to what would get me in trouble, I settled for a nod. I could always say I didn't vocalize anything with his name in it, right?

"You're messing with me."

I shrugged.

"Explain. You know how much I respect you as a person. I'm not going to rat you out or get you in trouble for being honest with me, give me a break." He really did look offended that I didn't want to come out and say something to him.

And yet...

"Sal, I know you're aware that I'm not blind or stupid. Tell me the truth. I only caught half of what you told him a few days ago. I know he wasn't friendly to your dad, but I thought that was it. I want to help, and I can tell that this isn't working the way it's supposed to be. Every time we're out on the field, everyone's acting tense; no one wants to say anything during our meetings. That's not like you all," Gardner said. "Usually someone's arguing about how inflated the soccer ball is, for Christ's sake."

I wanted to slump back in my chair and let my head fall back so that I could stare at the ceiling, but I wouldn't. Instead, I tugged my Big Girl Socks on a little higher and dealt with what he was saying. "I'm not disagreeing with you. Things are tense and it sucks, G. But you know we have that 'no whining' rule, so no one is going to complain."

"Then tell me what it is. Is it me?"

"Why do you always do this to me?" I groaned.

He laughed. "Because you're not going to BS me." Master manipulator, he was a master manipulator. "I want things to get back to the way they should be, so tell me what needs to be fixed."

Didn't he understand? You didn't threaten a career that had been made up of so much sacrifice for nothing. Each and every single one of us had given up birthdays, anniversaries, a social life, relationships, time with our families and more for what we had. It was precious to me, and I'd be a moron to give it away freely. Every other girl on the team had to feel the same way to some extent. "I know, G, but you know we're all going to be careful. What do you expect? We were warned from the beginning to watch what we say about Kulti, and then we show up to practice or go to the grocery store and get bombarded with him constantly."

The sigh that came out of him reminded me of a punctured

balloon. He still couldn't believe it. There were people in life that cared about fixing what was broken and there were people who waited for someone else to resolve their problems. Usually, I liked to think that I went for the things that I wanted, but that didn't mean I wanted to be the one to say something, especially not in this case.

I suddenly felt a little bad that I'd been holding back from telling the truth, just a little bit. Until I remembered the very real threat that the German had given me after I'd helped him out, and then indignation and anger washed over everything. "All right." I took a deep breath. "I think everyone is just a little unsure of his presence here, G. *I think*. I can only speak for myself. No one says anything because we're all probably too scared to put our feet in our mouths and get in trouble. And it doesn't help that he isn't exactly Mr. Rogers."

A smile cracked across the coach's face.

"I'm serious. I think at some point everyone has had that nightmare coach that calls you a worthless piece of shit who should have quit playing soccer years ago. But somehow, it's worse to be with someone at this stage that doesn't seem to care. He doesn't say anything; he doesn't do anything. He's just there." There was the incident at the photo shoot. And he'd threatened me when all I'd done was try to help him, but I kept that crap to myself. Not because of what he'd said, but just because I wasn't that type of person.

It was a fact. Kulti didn't do *anything*. He didn't say anything. He didn't share his knowledge or his anger except that one time, or even his vocabulary.

"Jesus." Gardner nodded and ran a hand over his head. "I get it."

Had I said too much? Maybe.

Puffing my cheeks like a blowfish I started yammering. "Look, he's a great player. I'm not saying he's not, obviously. But shouldn't he be coaching us? Bitching? Telling us when we're doing something good or at least doing something spectacularly bad? Something? I figured maybe he was just getting used to being around girls, but it's been long enough now. Don't you think?"

"I understand what you're saying. It makes sense." He rubbed a hand over his head and glanced up at the ceiling. "I don't know why I didn't think about that before. Huh." He nodded at himself before looking over at me. "At least now I know where I need to start."

Fidgeting in the chair for a moment, I sat up and nodded at him. "That's about it."

Gardner made a few faces as he thought about what I said but finally gave me a curt nod. "I appreciate you talking to me. I'll make sure we get this sorted out," he said finally, my cue to get the hell out of there.

"All right, then. I should get going. See you tomorrow," I said, grabbing my belongings and getting up.

He gave me a funny look. "Let me know if there's anything I can do for you too. Don't think I haven't noticed you look like you're ready to bite someone's head off. "

So apparently I needed to work on keeping my game face on a little better. I could do that. I smiled and nodded at the man sitting across the table. "I'm fine, G. Thanks, though."

His features eased a bit and an emotion I wasn't sure I recognized crossed his face as I took a step back. "I'm proud of you Sal, for standing up to him. Especially now that I know how you all are feeling about his presence here... I want you to know that. You're a good girl."

Gardner's words made me feel nice at the same time they made me feel guilty. I gave him a little smile and shrugged. "I should have said something to you earlier about the girls, G."

"It's fine. You said something now and that's all that matters."

Was it?

We said bye to each other one more time and then I was out of there.

Bag over my shoulder, I slowly made my way out, thinking. Had I done the right thing? I wasn't positive, but what else was I supposed to do? I could painfully go through another five months of tiptoeing around this German dingle-berry, but it was different if I wasn't the only one being affected by his presence.

The trek back was old and familiar. Down two hallways and head to the elevator. I knew it by memory. I rocked back and forth on my heels as I waited for the elevator.

It was the soft squeak of a foreign pair of tennis shoes on the linoleum floor that had me glancing over. The sound wasn't anything special in this building; mostly everyone wore tennis shoes unless it was game day or if it was a woman wearing heels. But when I saw a pair of special edition RK running shoes, black with lime-green stitching, my shoulders tensed up.

And I looked.

Of course it was the ass-gobbler I'd just been talking about.

Subconsciously, I started to reach back and make sure my hair was tucked up neatly beneath my headband, but I stopped before I got there. Poop. Plus, what did it matter if my hair was messed up? It shouldn't.

I cleared my throat when he stopped a yard or so away from me and our eyes met. His eye color was clearer that I'd thought it would be. It was a perfect mix of a honey-brown with a fitting blend of murky green. Bright, sharp and incredibly, unbelievably observant from the weight of the stare it was capable of.

Holy bejesus he was tall. His forearms were big beneath the sky blue training polo he had on. Then I glanced back up at his eyes to see them still locked on me. He was watching me check him out.

Fuck.

*Poop, Sal.* Poop.

Pee. *Stop it. Stopitrightnow.*

*You dragged him out of a bar and into a hotel room without a single thank you in return. Not even a smile. All you got out of it was a threat.*

And suddenly with that, I felt fine.

I swallowed and smiled my sugar-sweet asshole smile, using the only half of my face capable of moving. "Hi," I said before adding quickly, "Coach."

That heavy gaze flicked down to the number printed on my chest for a moment before moving its way back up to look at my face. The blink he did was slow and lazy.

I tipped my chin up and blinked right back at him, forcing a smug and closed-mouth smile on my face.

The elevator dinged open as he said in a low tone which sounded like it cost him ten years off his life to use on such a lowly faithless creature like myself, "Hello."

We looked each other right in the eye for a split second before I raised my eyebrows up and headed inside the small space. I turned to face the doors and watched him follow in after me, taking the spot against the corner furthest away.

Did he say anything else? No.

Did I? No.

I kept my eyes forward, and lived through the most awkward thirty seconds of my life.

* * *

THE PROBLEM WITH MEN, or males in general, that I'd discovered over the course of my life, was that they had huge mouths. I mean a whale shark has nothing on the average man with a couple of friends. Honestly.

But you know, it was my fault. Really, it was. I should have known better.

My dad, brother and his friends had taught me the reality

behind male friendships and yet I'd forgotten everything that I'd learned.

So I couldn't blame anyone else but myself for trusting Gardner.

Already more than halfway through that morning's practice, I had just finished my own one-on-one game against a defender. I went to take my place away from where the sessions were happening, and I wasn't really paying attention. I was thinking about what I could have done differently to get the ball into the goal quicker when someone stepped right in the middle of my path.

It was a simple side-step that landed the body bigger than mine just a foot away.

I knew it wasn't Gardner. Gardner had been on the other side of the field when I'd been playing, and there were only three other men on staff it could have been. Except two of them were too nice to do something so confrontational.

The German. It was the damn king of jerk-offs. Of course it was.

The instant I made eye-to-eye contact with him, I knew.

I knew Gardner was a caring, overly blunt bastard who had mentioned my name to the German.

My heart felt like it started to pound in my throat.

He didn't have to say 'I know what you said' because the passive look on his face said it all. If he'd stood through me ranting about my dad without making a face, then I knew whatever it was he'd heard had hit a nerve. A person like him didn't appreciate being criticized because he already thought he was perfect, hello.

It wasn't like I'd called him a worthless piece of retired Euro-trash—which was horribly rude. Or said he was an awful player and that he didn't deserve the job. Nothing remotely similar to that had come out of my mouth, but I put myself into his situation, thought of myself having an ego ten times the size of the one I currently had and asked myself how I'd feel.

I'd feel pretty damn pissed if some kid started saying what I needed to do differently.

But it was the truth, and I'd stand by it. I hadn't called him *Führer* or a dick or anything. What was I going to do? Apologize to someone who didn't deserve it? Nope.

I did what I needed to do. I stayed right where I'd stopped when he first got in my way, and I wrangled my heart into not beating so fast. *Calm down, calm down, calm down. Poop. Pee. Poop, poop.*

Big Girl Socks? On.

Voice? In check.

Steeling myself, I pushed my shoulders down and looked at him dead-on. "Yes?"

"Sprint time!" someone yelled.

My bravery only went so far because the next thing I did was turn around and run toward the line where sprints began. A whole nice round of conditioning, meaning running sprints at increasing amounts of distances, was my love-hate relationship. I was fast, but that didn't mean I really loved running them.

I lined up between two of the younger girls who were always trying to run faster than me. The player on my right bumped her fist against mine right before we took off. "I feel like today is the day, Sal," she smiled.

I wiggled my ankle around and slowly rested the weight on the ball of my foot. "I don't know, I'm feeling pretty good today, but bring it on."

One more fist bump and the whistle sounded.

Ten yards, back and forth. Twenty, back and forth, Forty, back and forth. Midfield, back and forth. Then the whole field and back.

My lungs seized up a little by the end of it, but I sucked it up and pushed forward on the last leg. I finished up with enough distance between myself and the next person to sleep okay that night. I thought about how good it was that I always tried to push myself on my own runs a little harder each day.

Rubbing my hands up and down on my upper thighs while I caught my breath, I smiled at the girl who had challenged me at the beginning when she made it. She looked a little annoyed but managed to keep a smile on.

"I don't know how the hell you do it," Sandy panted.

I panted right back. "I run. A lot." When she gave me this expression that said 'no-shit-Sherlock,' I snorted. "I do the bike trails at Memorial at six-thirty every day before coming here. You're welcome to come with me if you get up early enough. I'm not the greatest company to talk to that early in the morning, but it's better than running alone, right?"

"Really?" she asked a little too incredulously.

"Yeah."

She wiped at her forehead and gave me this funny look. "Okay. Sure. That sounds great."

I rattled off where I parked my car in case she really did want to go and wasn't just saying she did. By the time we finished talking, everyone else had finished their sprints too, even the slower players. Not that anyone was slow exactly, but slow*er*.

Practice finished soon after that, so I finished getting my stuff together, keeping an eye to see where Gardner was so I could give him a tiny piece of my mind. Regular shoes on, a clean pair of ankle socks beneath them, I made my way toward the head coach busy counting balls to make sure they were all there.

"Are you ready for the game?" he greeted me first thing.

"I'm ready," I agreed, watching his sneaky face for any sign that he felt remorse for taking advantage of my trust.

"Everything okay?" he asked, straightening up when I didn't move from where I'd been.

Glancing around to make sure that no one was too close, I turned my attention back to the male Gossip Girl and scowled. "Did you tell Kulti what I said?"

The old bastard had the decency to look just a little sheepish. "I had a talk with him this morning on the way here. I figured it was time," he neither agreed nor denied.

"Did you tell him it was me who said something?"

His brown eyes were careful and consistent. "He must have guessed it was you since you're the only one that's ripped him a new one."

He didn't deny it. I'd also been the one he saw coming from the offices too. It wasn't like the cookie trail hadn't been left behind. On top of that, I had laid into him for being a piece of horse crap to my dad. Once again, it was my fault.

It was done, and there was no point in dwelling on it.

"You can tell me if there's a problem," he stated in a careful honest tone that I couldn't help but believe.

What was I going to do? Tell him *oh, he gave me the stare down?* Nope. Or worse, tell him about me picking him up from a bar? Yeah, no.

Instead I gave him a reassuring smile that I didn't necessarily feel. "Everything's fine, I was just... curious if you said something or not. No big deal."

"No. I didn't say anything."

"Great, thanks G. I'll see you later then," I sighed, turning around to walk toward the bathroom, feeling the weight of the world on my shoulders.

I sighed to myself.

The last thing I wanted was to bring negative attention to myself, especially where Kulti was concerned. The team had a lot banking on him, and though I was considered one of the hometown favorites because I was from Texas—and I was the leading scorer for the team—I understood priorities. One of us was a lot more popular than the other, even if it was only me playing, and one of us got paid a lot more.

I would lose every time.

Patting my phone over the material of my bag, I thought about calling my dad to rant but then thought better of it. The bratwurst had already done enough. I didn't want to bring him up unless I had to. My mom? Jenny? No and no. Plus, I'd have to explain everything for my predicament to make sense, and I wasn't all about that either.

So I weighed my options and accepted again that keeping it all to myself was the best way to go about dealing with everything.

# 9

There's that saying some people use: Be careful what you wish for.

My first coach when I started playing club, a select group of players that wanted more than what their local school or rec center offered, told us almost daily, "A dream is just a wish without a plan." After you hear it enough times, it grows on you and the older you get, the more you realize how true the words are. So it wasn't that I didn't take wishes seriously, I just didn't put much weight into them. There weren't a lot of things I wanted, but I knew that if I wanted something expensive, I had to save for it by cutting out other expenses in my life.

The point was: I'd wanted to play soccer professionally most of my life, so I learned what I needed to do to make that happen. I had to practice, commit, practice some more and sacrifice in no particular order. Usually, I tried to apply that to every aspect of my life.

But once upon a time, a young Salomé Casillas had spent three birthday wishes in a row on the same thing: that one day Reiner 'The King' Kulti would know that I was alive... and marry me. Third on my list of wishes was that he'd teach me how to be the best.

I would have given just about anything for that to happen. *Anything.* I would have died of joy if he'd ever touched my freaking hand when I was twelve.

At twenty-seven, knowing what I knew about him at this point, I would have been happy living the rest of my life inconspicuously.

But sometimes fate was fickle and immature, because just a couple of days after telling Gardner about how everyone was being affected by the ex-superstar's lack of attention, my preteen prayers were answered out of nowhere.

He must have either been brainwashed or had his body snatched by an alien because a new man showed up to the field after that. A man with a rigid line to his shoulders, a rod of iron through his spine, and a voice that couldn't be misinterpreted.

How many times had I thought about how much I wanted Kulti to be the kind of coach that a player of his caliber had the potential to be? It wasn't a secret that great players didn't always make great coaches. But my gut, or maybe it was my inner thirteen-year-old, believed that he'd be an exception. That he could do or be whatever he wanted to.

Except I hadn't anticipated the fact that what I thought of as 'coach' he apparently interpreted as 'Gestapo.'

Those next two days were the most strenuous of my life, both mentally and physically.

Part of it was because the pressure to be perfect was right in my peripheral, pushing, pushing, pushing, and making its presence well-known, zt least to me. The main part though, was Kulti. He showed up to practice with an angry tick in his jaw and hard eyes that seemed to suddenly assess everything.

The first time he yelled, the drill most of the team had been busy executing had come to a sudden pause. I mean, it stopped. For all of two seconds, the players that had been maneuvering around obstacle courses stopped in their tracks and looked up. I was one of them. It was like the voice of God had suddenly come down on us and told a prophecy or something.

"Faster!"

One word. One word had caught us all off guard.

And then Gardner's, "What are you doing? Come on!" brought everyone back into their right minds.

Jenny, who was busy practicing with the goalkeepers, met my eyes from across the field. And telepathically we communicated the same three words: What the hell?

We kept going.

So did he. His voice was borderline angry, determined and strong, lilting and strangely fascinating with multiple accents curbing it as he kept hurling things at the group. My stomach churned each time I heard him.

This was exactly what I'd asked for—what I'd wished for.

When I was panting with my hands on my knees because he kept yelling about how we could go faster, I smiled because I'd pushed myself.

And because this is exactly what a younger version of me would have sold ten years of her life for.

Sure, he was a dick. Sure he'd been pressured into caring by me complaining to the head coach. But when I looked around and everyone else was busting their ass on a whole new level, I figured it was worth having the bratwurst hate me.

* * *

EVENTUALLY I STARTED to regret ever thinking that Kulti caring was a good thing, because another segment of what I'd always dreamed of came into play and it wasn't the magnificence I'd anticipated.

I got the attention I'd wanted. Only it wasn't as fantastic as my dreams had told me they'd be.

"Twenty-three!"

It took me a second to react to my number being called—the day of Dad's birthday. Eric's birthday had been my national team number and my sister's had been my number back when I played club soccer. I'd been using twenty-three for years, but no one ever called me by it.

"Twenty-three, what kind of a slow pass is that? Are you even trying?" he belted.

The hair on the back of my neck prickled up and my mouth might have dropped open just a little.

But I pushed.

He kept going. "Twenty-three, *this*." "Twenty-three, *that*." Twenty-three, twenty-three, twenty-three...

Shoot me in the face, twenty-three.

There wasn't affection in his tone, much less pride.

Every single time I looked at him when he called my number, his face was set in a rough expression. Glowering. He was glowering at me. That handsome, handsome face was staring at me with an expression that was definitely not very nice.

Good God.

I stood up straight, wiped my sweat off and just glared right back at him. I could deal with this jack-off that had been mean to my dad. At least that's what my bones said.

* * *

"He has the worst batting skills I've ever seen. No joke. He looks like a lumberjack out there with his bat six feet high and his ass in a different zip code than the rest of his body," Marc said with a shake of his head as he steered the vehicle onto the freeway. We were on the way to our next jobs—two big houses in a neighborhood called the Heights.

"Worse than Eric?" I asked because as fantastic as he was at kicking a ball and chasing after it, he was pretty shitty at most other sports.

The grave nod Marc gave in response said it all. If the softball player he was talking about was worse than my brother, God help everyone on their team. "Jeez."

"Yeah, Sal. It's that bad. He isn't scared of balls coming at him—"

We both looked at each other the second the two words were used together and we burst out laughing.

"Not that kind of ball," my friend laughed loudly. "There's no excuse for being that bad."

"It happens," I noted.

He shrugged in reluctant agreement and continued with his story about the new player that had recently joined in on their weekly recreational softball games. "I don't know how to tell him he's terrible. Simon said he'd say something, but he wimped out, and most of the time there's barely enough people to split into two teams," he said, eyeing me.

So subtle.

I'd played on and off with him for the last two years when I could. While I couldn't play soccer officially or not-so-officially in any team way besides with the Pipers during the season, no one said I couldn't join in on the occasional softball game, as long as it wasn't 'official.' That was the keyword I could twist and distort from my contract.

Right as I started to say that I could join in on a few games, my phone rang. On the screen, 'Dad' flashed.

Holding my phone up, I told Marc who was calling and answered. "Hey, Pa."

"*Hola*. Are you busy?" he replied.

"On my way to a job with Marco Antonio," I said, using my family's nickname for him. "*Y tu?*"

"Okay, I was just calling you quick. I'm going to pick up Ceci from school; she has early dismissal. I wanted to know though, do you think you can get us two more tickets for the opening game? Your *tio* is going to be in town that day and he wants to go," he said slowly.

My uncle wanted to go to a game, but he just didn't want to pay. What was new?

"I'm sure I can get two, but I won't be positive until later today, okay?"

"Yeah, yeah. That's fine. If you can't, don't worry about it. He can afford two tickets. Cheapskate. Call me later when you're off and tell Marco I said he's buying me a beer at the game."

I snorted and smiled, and an instant later I realized I hadn't brought up the incident with the German. My face flushed and my neck got hot. "Dad, hey. I'm sorry about the open house. If I had known he'd be such an asshole, I would have warned you. I'm really sorry—"

He hissed on the other line, and I didn't miss the perplexed look Marc shot my way from the other side of the truck's cab. "*Mija*, you have no idea how many times someone's been that way with me. I'm fine. I'm over it now. People are like that because they don't know any better, but I do."

"He had no right to act like that. I was so mad, I went up to him and called him a bratwurst," I admitted aloud for the first time since the incident.

Two howls went up. One was from my dad and the other from Marc. "No!" he cracked up on the phone.

"Yeah. I lost it. I think he hates my guts now. I'll have to tell you later the kind of crap he's been telling me on the field," I said with a big grin aimed at my boss, who was shaking his shoulders with laughter.

Dad kept laughing. "Yeah, I want to hear about it," he said before pausing. "*Pero* Salomé, *acuérdate de lo que te he dicho*. Kill them with kindness, *si*?"

I groaned.

"*Si*. Forgive him for not knowing better, okay?"

Forgive him for not knowing better? "I can try but what about Eric? You want me to be nice to the person that hurt him?" The recent memory of Kulti calling him an imbecile was still fresh, but I didn't tell my dad about it.

"*Pues si.* It was a long time ago and remember Eric broke that player from Los Angeles's arm? It happens. You know your brother. He kicks up a fit because he likes to hear himself talk."

"I don't know. It doesn't feel right. I feel like I'm cheating on Eric."

"It's okay. You aren't. I would tell you if you were."

I wanted to roll my eyes at the thought, but I managed not to; instead I sighed and agreed with him. "Fine. I'll think about it." Boo. "I'll call you later then. Love you."

"Love you too."

The second I hung up the call, Marc angled his body against the seat since we were at a red light and blinked at me. "Bitch, you've been holding out on me. Tell me everything."

* * *

"WELL THAT'S FUCKIN' awkward," Harlow whispered.

It was. It really was.

For the last five minutes, the team had stood by the curb outside of the Pipers' office building waiting for the vans that would take us to the location of our first preseason game about an hour outside of the city.

While we waited for the vans that happened to be running late, we'd all been watching Kulti arguing on the phone saying things in his native language that just sounded... *ugly*.

Whoo.

"What do you think he's saying?"

"His coffee was probably too hot this morning and he's complaining about it."

"He's threatening to make a coat out of their skin."

"Or use their stem cells to lengthen his life."

That one had me cracking up.

"He's probably just saying 'good morning, I'm having a great day' and it sounds that bad," Jenny suggested.

I shot her a smile. "You guys figure it out while I go to the restroom real quick."

I took off speed-walking toward the restroom on the first floor. No one was there, so I was able to get in and out in just a couple of minutes after relieving my bladder. By the time I made it back out, three white vans had appeared alongside the street.

Two of them were already filled from what it looked like when multiple sets of hands hit the glass windows as I walked by them, freaking zombie-wannabes.

"Come on girl, we've been waiting on you!" Phyllis huffed, standing outside of the first van with two other staff members.

I nodded and jumped into the van, instinctively going for the seat the furthest away from the door.

There was only one seat open besides the front bench, and that was in the very back row with Kulti. Kulti and a mesh bag of soccer balls. Fantastic. Absolutely fantastic.

Fighting back a groan and an eye roll that was totally over the top, I kept my gaze even and climbed all the way into the back to take the one and only empty seat right next to him. Thigh to thigh.

I could do this. I could be a mature adult. *Right.*

I had a pep talk with myself yesterday as I drove home after work. I could be an adult and set my pride aside to do what my dad had suggested. Was it going to be easy? Not exactly. But I was sure as hell going to try. I could put aside the fact this ass thought I was a snitch with no morals, and I could put my personal stuff aside and at least try to be cordial.

No one could take away me calling him a bitch in my head at least.

So I took a calming breath and said to myself, *patience. Patience, Sal.* Kill 'em with kindness, I'd been told. I could be a bigger person. Easy.

Right?

I pulled my bag onto my lap and watched the last staff member get in the van. The second that everyone started making a lot of noise, I braced myself, put my Big Girl Socks on and whispered, like someone who hadn't had her career threatened or her father insulted, "Can we call a truce?"

He actually responded. "What did you say?" the man sitting next to me asked in a voice just as low as mine had been.

He was talking to me. *Me.*

And: poop.

I was fine.

"Can we call a truce?" I kept my gaze forward and made sure not to move my mouth more than was necessary just in case someone turned around. They wouldn't be able to tell I was talking to The King. "I want things to get back to normal. I don't like drama, and I can't keep doing these hate-eyes with you. It won't be long before someone catches on.

"I would never say anything to anyone about you-know-what. I promise." The urge to say *I swore* was on the tip of my tongue, but I held it in. "I won't. It doesn't matter how much you might make me angry, that's between you and you. If I wanted to be an asshole, I would have taken pictures of you with my phone and sold them right after it happened, don't you think?"

Nothing. I kept going.

"I can also get over the fact that you called my brother an imbecile and that you were a jerk to my dad, I think. But if you think I'm going to apologize for what I said to Gardner, it's not going to happen. You should know that now. You weren't being helpful or nice and it wasn't helping the team. If it matters any, I didn't say anything rude about you as a person—" though I wanted to. "I don't want to feel awkward every time I'm around you for the next few months either. So, can we go back to pretending each other doesn't exist?" I asked finally.

Fair enough, wasn't it?

At least I thought so.

He didn't respond. A minute passed, and still there was no reply.

I blinked facing forward and then slowly, slowly, slowly just like those creepy possessed dolls in scary movies, turned to look at him.

He was staring at me directly, one hundred percent intense and focused on my face. Those warm-colored eyes were zeroed in on me like I was the first person he'd seen in ages...and wasn't really sure what to think. So I stared at him right back, right in the eyes, not at the small cleft in his chin or the scar that sliced through his right eyebrow from an elbow he'd taken to the face during his eighth season in the European League.

I kept my gaze steady. "I'm trying really hard here," I told him carefully.

Still, he stared.

Yet I wasn't a quitter and didn't plan on becoming one anytime soon. "I'm not asking you to be my friend or even to talk to me. I could care less if you like me," that was mostly true, "because it isn't like I'm fond of you either, but maybe we can just set this crap aside, all right? Whatever happened between you and my brother was a long time ago. Done. What happened at the bar is none of my business. If you want to pay me back for the hotel room, go for it. And yeah, I did say something to Gardner about you kind of sucking at being a coach, but it's the truth; if you were in my shoes, I'm sure whatever would have come out of your mouth would have been worse than what I said. Isn't that right?"

It was, it totally was. For one split second, I let myself imagine the Kulti I'd grown up in love with. The one that thought he owned every field he stepped out on, and I could imagine the way he would have erupted at being doubted.

Then I reminded myself that this wasn't the same man. For whatever reason, he just wasn't. People changed over time. I got that, so I wasn't going to think about it too much. This was the version of Reiner Kulti I'd been given, and this was the one I'd have to deal with for the next few months. It was like when I craved something sweet. I had a bite to get it out of my system and moved on.

Another minute passed and he still hadn't responded. I could play the staring game as good as anyone. Even if it made my throat feel weird and I had to tell myself not to blush or worry about whether I should have put some concealer on that morning.

I blinked.

He blinked.

Okay, I'd struck out twice. What was once more in the name of peace? In a careful, controlled voice I said, "I was a fan of yours for a very long time. That game about twenty years ago at the Altus Cup, when you scored the winning goal, changed my life. I've respected you as an athlete for as long as I can remember. I know that I'm no one to you, but I'm here, and I'm going to still be here until the season is over. If there's any part of you that's still that man I admired, I'd appreciate it if we could just... make it through the season without killing each other."

All right. I'd said more than I had planned on. Whether he was worried or alarmed by it, I had no idea, but screw it, it was the truth. You couldn't build a friendship or... a lasting whatever, on lies. My crush on him was just extra information that wasn't exactly relevant for this conversation... or any other.

Another minute dragged itself out and *nada*. Nothing.

Well, I wasn't going to beg anyone to be fucking nice to me. All I wanted was for him to be a decent asshole who wasn't stepping into my path during practice when he was mad over something I did. Zeroing in on me during practice? Bring it on.

Still, he was silent.

Well, I had tried.

*Universe, I tried and you know it.* Screw it.

* * *

"YOU KILLED IT," Harlow yelled about two feet away from me as she rushed up and grabbed my face, squishing the cheeks together, following my goal at the absolute last minute. "Fuck yeah, Sally!"

My face hurt a little. But I managed to mold out some sort of deformed smile while it was in the hands of the baddest defender in the Southwest. "You did all the work."

"You sure as hell know I did. We can't lose to these toddlers," her thirty-three-year-old butt scoffed. Harlow had played only two years of college soccer. She'd gotten recruited for the European Women's League early on and went to play overseas where she was molded into the crazy-ass she was with the WPL today.

The next thing I knew, she gave my cheeks a pinch and turned around to yell, "Jenny!" and then congratulate her on her excellent blocking by spanking her ass.

We had won seven to one, and I had scored two goals in the first half and a third in the last minute of the second. Could we have played a little better? Yes. Could I have played a little better? Yes. But it was done and I could think about it later when I was in bed. All I wanted to do was go home to ice my ankle for a minute.

On my way to the vans for our ride back to headquarters, I was completely distracted when my phone started to ring.

"Hey, Daddy," I answered first thing.

There was a strange panting sound on the other end.

"Dad?"

"Sal," he gasped.

"Yeah? Are you all right?" I asked hesitantly.

"Sal," he gasped again. "You're never going to believe what came in the mail." Was he wheezing? I couldn't be sure.

"What?" I asked slowly, expecting the worst.

He was definitely wheezing. "I don't know what you said or did but..." Wait, was he *crying*? "I got home from work today and there were two things on the porch—"

"Okay..."

"There was a note in one of the boxes that said 'My deepest apologies for being a real prick.' There was a jersey in there, a limited edition one that's a size too big, but *ME VALE!*" I could care less, he whooped. "And it was signed, Sal. Sal! It was signed by him!"

I stopped walking.

"There was a poster from when Kulti played with FC Berlin in the other package!" he continued on.

A small knot formed in my throat at the pure joy that resonated from my dad's voice at the unexpected gesture. Days had passed since the incident, and I would have hardly expected Kulti to remember or care enough to apologize for being an ass. The fact that he hadn't made a big deal about it...

I swallowed and felt my nose sting a bit.

"That's great," I found myself saying, still standing in place.

"*Si, verdad?* This is great. I'm going to show it to Manuel, he's going to be so jealous..." He said something that I barely caught. "Tell him thank you and that there's no hard feelings, would you Sal? There's no return address on here."

"You got it."

"*Oooh!* This is great! I want to look at it again, and I can't with the phone in my hand. Call me later."

"Okay."

We quickly said goodbye to each other as I just stood there, nose stinging, relief pecking at my throat. I licked my lips for a second and then decided to be an adult about this. The next thing I knew, I'd turned around and started walking back to where I'd come from, searching.

Sure I could have waited to see if he rode next to me in the van, but I wasn't betting on it.

When I spotted him, I wiped at my nose with my shoulder and kept on going. This time he must have seen me out of his peripheral vision because when he glanced up, he kept watching me make my approach. He was rummaging through his bag on a propped-up knee.

I stopped in front of him, licked my lips and took a deep breath. He was so much taller than me I had to tip my head back to look at his face, my own duffel dangling from my hand. His amber-colored eyes were clear and focused, and I suddenly hoped that he wasn't automatically expecting the worst from me.

"Thank you for doing that for my dad," I said to him in a voice that was a lot softer and breathier than usual. Was it embarrassment that was making my voice that way because of what I'd said before? Possibly. But he'd done something unexpectedly nice that made my dad happy before I approached him about calling a truce. "I wish I could tell you how much I appreciate it. So... thank you. You made his month and I'm very grateful." I swallowed. "And he said to tell you that there are no hard feelings from either of us."

Was he perfect? Absolutely not. Did I think he was a good person? That was debatable, but he'd done something nice that could make me put aside that he'd been a jerk to me. But what did I know? Maybe there was a reason for it, or maybe he was just a prick. Whatever.

Before I even realized what I was doing, I thrust my hand out to him.

The silence that stretched between us and those two feet of

physical space seemed eternal and infinite. It took two seconds from the moment in which I put my hand in the air for his hand, warm and made up of long fingers and a broad palm, to connect with mine.

I looked at his jaw while we shook on… whatever it was we were shaking on.

It seemed like everything was okay, or at least it would be.

But I guess things always seem fine until they suddenly weren't.

My phone rang the instant I got out of the van after we'd made our return to the team's offices. A number I didn't recognize flashed across the screen, but I answered it anyway.

"Hello?"

"Miss Casillas?"

"Yes?"

"I'm calling from Mr. Cordero's office," the woman introduced herself. Her name was Mrs. Brokawski. "Would you be able to come by the office within the hour?"

It doesn't take a genius to figure out that a meeting with your general manager isn't a good thing. Especially not when you and said general manager don't have the best relationship in the world. But what could I say? No thanks?

"I can drop by there in about ten," I agreed making a face.

"Great, we'll see you soon."

"Great," I said, on the verge of banging my phone against my face as I hung up. If there was one person I hated speaking to, it was Mr. Carlos Cordero, the Pipers' general manager and a major asshole.

Fantastic.

* * *

"He'll see you now," Mrs. Brokawski said, ushering me into the office I'd only been in three times over the years.

I smiled at her more to be polite than because I wanted to—she wasn't exactly the friendliest person in the world—and went into what had to be at least a four-hundred-square-foot office with furniture that cost more than I made in a year. Behind the massive mahogany desk was the fifty-something-year-old Argentinian who reminded me of a 1950s mob boss with his pompadour haircut and tailored suit.

To me, he looked like a weasel. He was a weasel that could do pretty much whatever he wanted with my career.

"Good afternoon, Mr. Cordero," I said, standing in front of the seat closest to the door after his assistant had closed it.

The older man leaned across his desk and shook my hand, eyeing the team sweatpants I'd pulled on over my uniform. "Miss Casillas," he said, finally taking his seat again and gesturing for me to take one as well.

There was no point in wasting time, was there? Hands on my thighs, I asked, "What can I do for you?"

He flicked up a groomed eyebrow—I swear he waxed them regularly—and tapped his nails on the desk's surface. "You can tell me why I heard that you got into an argument with your assistant coach."

The gavel fell.

Seriously? It'd been more than long enough since that had happened and he was bringing it up now? Damn it. "It wasn't much of an argument. I was upset with him and I let him know that he had acted inappropriately, that's all."

"That's interesting." He fidgeted and moved to rest his arms on the sides of his chair. "I was told you called him a bratwurst, I believe."

I don't think I'd ever wanted to smile more, but I managed not to. I had no business lying to him. I'd said what I said and I wasn't going to take it back. "Yes."

"Do you think that's appropriate language to use on the staff?" he asked.

"I think it's appropriate when someone decides to be ungracious with his supporters."

"You do understand how important his involvement with the team is?" The jackass was giving me this look that said exactly how stupid he thought I was, and I could feel anger bubbling up in my gut, leaving a sour taste in my mouth.

"I completely understand, Mr. Cordero, but I also understand how important it is to have the support of our fans. The WPL expects a lot from their players, don't they? Some of us live with host families; we depend on word of mouth from the people that come to our games. Coach Kulti wasn't very gracious, and all I did was let him know without using bad words or body language. I didn't disrespect him." Well, I didn't disrespect him *that much*.

For as long as I'd known him, the team's general manager was the type of person who wanted things done his way when he said he wanted them done. He didn't like back-talk and he always insisted he was right.

He wasn't.

So I knew that this conversation was going down the drain fast, and I wasn't about to back down from it, as much as my common sense begged me to. I hadn't done anything wrong and if I could go back in time, I would do the exact same thing again.

"Miss Casillas, I would be careful with what you believe to be right or wrong; are we on the same page?"

This fucker.

"The Pipers are a team, and this isn't the first time you haven't been on board with doing what's best for the whole."

Was he ever going to drop it? Each time I'd been in his office, except for this once, it had always been for the same damn thing. *Let us tell everyone*. And every time I had told him the same thing: *No—I'm not involving my family*. He had yet to forgive me for it and from how it seemed, he never would.

"I want you to apologize," he continued, ignoring the look of death I was giving him.

"There's nothing for me to apologize for," I told him in a calm steady voice.

He leaned forward and hit a button on his phone. "I beg to differ... Mrs. Brokawski? We're ready."

We're ready? For what?

My silent question was answered a minute later when the office door swung open and a beaming Mrs. Brokawski stepped in, holding it open for none other than the bratwurst we'd been talking about. Kulti entered, his expression that cool remote one, his eyes going from me on the chair to Mr. Cordero standing up.

"Come in, Coach." The general manager looked like a different man, smiling and jovial. The freaking rat. "Take a seat. You know Miss Casillas."

I didn't even bother forcing or faking a smile on my face; I just looked at him. I realized that he more than likely had nothing to do with this conversation, but I was too frustrated to forgive him for coming into the office at the wrong time.

The German took the chair next to mine, sitting upright and stiff. He was still in the same clothes he'd had on at the game.

"Thank you for coming in," Mr. Cordero told him, grinning. "I'm sorry it has to be under these circumstances."

To give him credit, Kulti glanced at me one more time before ignoring the fake gestures and words coming out of the man sitting across from us. "What is this about?"

A low whistle came out of his mouth, and I felt my jaw tightening.

"It has come to my attention that you and Miss Casillas had a small incident regarding a fan, and I would like to apologize for her behavior." His dark eyes swung to me, imploring me, demanding me to say what he wanted me to say.

I pursed my lips together and fought the great big breath caught in my throat. I was being treated like a dumb little kid who got caught stealing and had to take the goods back to where he'd taken them from. It was embarrassing.

"Miss Casillas, isn't there something you want to say?"

No.

"There is nothing to apologize for," that great deep voice next to me claimed, literally shocking the hell out of me.

"You shouldn't be spoken to—"

The German cut off a person who hated not having the last word, and I felt a spike of pleasure fill my chest at the flash of annoyance in Cordero's eyes. "Her judgment was sound. Nothing was said that didn't need to be said. I don't require an apology from either of you."

"But—"

"I was out of place with my behavior and we have come to terms with it, haven't we, Miss Casillas?" the *sauerkraut* asked, turning his attention to me.

Why, yes, yes, we had, hadn't we? I nodded. "Yes, we have."

Cordero's eyes moved from one player to the retired one. I didn't miss the pink blossoming on his neck. That sure as hell told me I needed to get out of the room as soon as possible before I said something I would regret. "Coach Kulti, excuse me, but Miss Casillas's actions are unacceptable. I can't allow—"

The man sitting next to me raised a hand to cut off the team's general manager. "It's acceptable and we've dealt with it. I'm going to be upset if she's punished for being honest and upfront with me, two traits that should be celebrated instead of persecuted. Nothing else needs to be said. Is that all this meeting was for?" the German asked, already rising to his feet.

What the hell had just come out of his mouth? He'd saved me. Hadn't he?

"Yes, that's all. I just thought you deserved an apology for—"

"I don't. If I wanted one, I would have gotten one." Those brown-green eyes slid over to me. "I have somewhere to be now."

Cordero was too busy looking at Kulti to notice me getting to my feet and grabbing my bag. I felt like a coward, but at least I'd be a coward that still got to play. I think. "I need to get to work, too. I think we're going to have a great season!"

Yeah, I hauled ass out of there. I didn't even bother telling Mr. Cordero's rude minion goodbye as I left. I could hear another set of footsteps as I made my way toward the elevators. A moment after hitting the down button, Kulti stopped next to me, watching the numbers go up on the small screen above the doors.

Well, in less than two hours he'd made my dad's day, shaken my hand and saved me from saying words I either would have regretted or hated myself for. I knew damn well when to be gracious. Eyeing him, his muscular silhouette, the reddish-brown stubble that had grown in on his face over the course of the day, and his overall proud face, I scratched my cheek and made myself turn to face him completely. There was no half-assing this.

"Thank you for that," I said, "in there." Like he didn't know what I was thanking him for. Idiot.

His gaze slid over to mine and he tipped his chin down.

That was it. No groups of unnecessary words, no smiles, nothing extra. All right.

At least it wasn't one person threatening the other or calling each other offensive names, right?

# 10

It sounds pretty stupid to say that I felt like a small weight had been lifted off my chest, but it was the truth.

While this new and ever-so-slightly improved version of Kulti—at least the coach edition—wasn't nice or even polite, he was present and in the moment during each practice. I was pretty sure he didn't actually know any of our names because all he did was call us by our numbers, but the point was, he was actually calling out our numbers. Like they were curse words, sure, but he was speaking. He was participating, and every player on the field soaked in his suggestions and demands.

We won the first three games of the preseason by more than four goals and managed to keep the opposing team to no more than one goal a game.

Was it because he suddenly gave a shit and was giving us pointers? I wouldn't give him that much credit. We usually won period, but whatever, winning was winning.

I could live with that.

We practiced, we played and continued the repetitive cycle.

Kulti stayed on his side of the field and I stayed on mine, and if by chance our eyes happened to meet, we looked at each other and, as amicably and indifferently as possible, we looked away.

That totally worked for me.

* * *

"Do you want to go watch a movie later?" Jenny asked right before lunging to the right to block one of the penalty kicks I'd just taken at her. She blocked it in time. Bah.

"Maybe." From off the side of the field, Gardner kicked another ball for me to attempt another shot. "I was thinking of having a boxed wine type of night."

She snickered. "What happened?"

Of course she'd understand that something had driven me to drink. "I talked to my sister on the phone last night and she called me a know-it-all, nosey bitch after I told her she needed to chill out and quit giving our dad a hard time. Every time I talk to him on the phone, she's always yelling at him for something or another. I don't know what the hell is wrong with her."

She grinned at me. Boxed wine was our cheat meal-slash-comfort food. Nothing said how truly crappy you were feeling like boxed wine. But hopefully it wouldn't come down to that. It wouldn't... I hoped. But apart from waking up aggravated because of my conversation with Ceci the night before, I'd just felt a little on edge all morning. Pissed off maybe, though I wasn't sure what the hell I had to be mad about. It was just one of those days, I guess.

"I'm sure she'll grow out of it eventually." Jenny offered what I'd already considered years ago when Ceci's hormones kicked in and she began going through these phases. Sometimes we were best friends, and then suddenly I was her worst enemy in the universe.

"I hope so. I've told her a hundred times that there's no comparison between any of us. She knows Mom would have rather I'd chosen something else to do with my life, but she still acts like she's the black sheep of the family. She thinks she's the letdown, because according to her she's not good at anything." I rolled my eyes. "Such a drama queen. I wasn't like that when I was younger. Were you?"

Jenny shook her head. "No, but my older sister was the devil. She used to hide my cleats, draw penises on them with a Sharpie, and stab my practice balls because she thought it was funny."

We made eye contact with each other and then burst out laughing together. "You win, Jen. Holy shit."

She made a little curtsy in acknowledgment.

I backed up four steps and eyed the top right of the goal, making my way like I was aiming in that direction, but at the last minute, kicked the ball left. Nailed it.

"Good one, Sal!" Gardner cheered from his spot. I gave him a thumbs up.

Jenny frowned but waved me on. "Another one."

I backed up five steps and aimed for the right of the goal, chest level. Jenny's outstretched hands managed to block the shot and made the ball go flying out. Out of the corner of my eye, I spotted someone blocking the ball's rogue trajectory with his chest.

It was Kulti.

Holy crap, it was like a high-definition flashback of him from a few years ago.

He let the ball roll down his sternum and onto his knee, where he bounced it a few times. Somehow I just knew to take a step away, just like Jenny knew to squat a little to get into position to block the shot that was coming. In the blink of an eye, Kulti let the ball fall to the top of his foot, one bounce and then another, and then it was whizzing through air, lightning-fast in his signature way, on a one-way ticket into the goal.

Then it got detoured by Jenny's freakishly large hands.

"Holy shit!" yelled Gardner.

I clasped my hand over my mouth in shock.

How I didn't make a big deal out of the block, much less manage not to say anything, amazed me. I was an adult most of the time.

"Hey, pass me the ball," I called out to her, giving her this 'dang, girl' look that showed how impressed I was. I mean, Jenny was the best goalkeeper on the team. She was probably one of the best goalkeepers in the last decade but... whoa. Kulti had been one of the best players in the world, ever.

She started to do a little bow before eyeing Kulti on the side of the field, and she stopped, thinking better of it. She'd just blocked his shot; maybe it wouldn't be the best idea to rub it in his face. *Maybe*. But seeing her do it motivated me. I let the ball stop where it finished rolling, took two steps back and went for it. The shot just barely cleared the top of the frame, swallowed by the net. Score.

"Once more," Kulti called out from his previous spot off to the side of the field.

Gardner passed him a ball. The King took two long steps back, eyed the round white object and then eyed the goal, and he went for it. The ball sailed through the air, a quick sharp arc that flew—and hit the side bar of the goal.

What the hell was happening?

"Again."

Jenny passed him the ball the third time. He backed up again and went for it. That time, it did manage to escape Jenny's reach and once more, it was just short of making it in the net. I don't think I'd ever seen this man miss a penalty kick—ever. *Ever*. Not once in any tournament or season game. Never. There were videos on the internet of him nailing ridiculous shots that defied gravity, nature and pure good luck.

I made sure to school my features so that I wouldn't have an expression on my face that gave away how surprised I was. If I were him… oh man. I'd want to crawl under a rock and die. And if he still had a fraction of the ego he did before… Jenny met my eyes in silence for a moment before she tipped her face back to make it seem like she was wiping her eyes. I was well aware of the fact that I should have looked around or pretended like I hadn't just seen Kulti miss three shots. It was a sign of the apocalypse.

Unfortunately instead of looking anywhere else, I looked right at him, trying to figure out what the hell had just happened. It'd been two years since he'd retired, so obviously he probably wasn't playing anywhere near as much as he used to. But, regardless.

*Poop. Poop.*

Okay, right. He was human. Humans made mistakes.

I felt myself nibbling at my bottom lip and looked from side to side. Scratching the tip of my nose, I waved Jenny forward. "Another ball, please."

She nodded way too sharply and threw a ball overhead. I stopped it with my chest and let it fall to the ground. I backed up even further and intended to let the ball arc up high to make it into the net. Jenny really went for it, the ball tipping off her fingertips, but it still managed to get past her and make it in. I almost cheered, *almost*, but then I remembered Kulti was there, and I reined it in.

"Let's do some upper body work today," the fitness coach called out from the edge of the field.

We went about grabbing things lying around and put them up. I couldn't help but think about what had just happened. Once we were done, Jenny and I sort of wandered together toward the section of the field where they'd set up some suspension equipment for body weight exercises. The moment we met up, bumping our shoulders against each other, I held a hand out to her, palm facing up.

Jenny slapped her big Hulk-smash hand down to mine in a

low-five, each of us giving the other a discreet, sly smile. Sure my palm felt like it got hit with a sledgehammer, but I managed not to wince.

I squeezed her fingers. “Freaking ninja skills.”

She chuckled and thankfully refrained from squeezing my fingers back. “I know, right?”

We both laughed.

I’m not positive why I turned around. Whether it was to check and make sure no one was too close behind to overhear what we were saying, or whether it was because my subconscious had picked up on something being different, but I did. I looked over my shoulder and met that distinctively familiar stare.

Maybe for all of ten seconds, I felt bad for celebrating that Jenny had not only blocked Reiner Kulti’s shots, but that I’d managed to score where he hadn’t. Ten seconds of guilt, possibly.

Then I really thought about it and decided I had no reason to feel bad or ashamed. Whatever the hell was going on with him was his business. Wasn’t it? I practiced and practiced some more to keep my skills on track.

But still… how in the hell had he missed so many shots? What a sucker. What a human, mistake-making sucker.

THE NEXT DAY, toward the end of practice, I was working on my PKs again—penalty kicks—this time with one of the other goalkeepers on the team. The woman was about my age and it was her first year on the Pipers after playing in New York for the past two seasons. She was good, but she wasn’t on Jenny’s level yet.

That was the point of practice though, wasn’t it?

The goalkeeping coach was standing off to the side, monitoring us as we practiced against each other for the second time since this season had begun.

I reared back a couple of steps and went in with my right foot, only at the very last minute, switching it up to kick forward with my left. The ball went in with a satisfactory journey as the coach stepped forward to talk to PJ, the goalkeeper, about what she could have done differently.

"You're anticipating it," she said. "It's because you know Sal that you think she's going to keep going to that right foot when she strikes, but if you didn't know her, you would have noticed..."

When they kept talking for a couple more minutes, I walked over a few feet and started volleying one of the balls lying around on my knee. I used to do it for hours, to see how long I could keep the ball in the air with whatever body part was closest, my knees, chest, head or foot, every and any combination that included those body parts or my feet. For practice, for fun, both were so tightly wound together they were one and the same. Rain or shine, I could do it in the garage or outside.

"Sal, can you go for it again?" PJ asked.

I dropped the ball and nodded at her. "Same thing?" I checked with the coach, who gave me a nod in response. All right. Six steps back to spice it up; I decided to try the same fake-out again, thinking that she'd assume I'd try to get her with my other foot next time to catch her off-guard. That time, she was watching like a hawk and only just barely missed blocking the ball. Another ball came at me from the goalkeeping coach's direction and I went for another shot. It went in again.

When the coach approached PJ again, I took in the other girls on the team to see what they were doing. That was when I saw Kulti standing about fifteen feet away, watching me.

Not knowing what else to do I gave him a smile that was probably a lot more grim than it needed to be. Awkward all right, it was downright awkward. Jenny yelled in the background as one of the defenders nailed a shot on her.

He didn't look away and neither did I. So...

PJ was standing off to the side of the goal with her coach. When I looked back, Kulti was still there. I'm not sure what the hell I was thinking or doing, but I thought back on his missed shots the day before and the next thing I knew, I kicked the ball I'd been using over to him.

If he was surprised that I kicked it over, his face didn't register it. When those murky eyes met mine again, I tipped my head in the direction of the goal just barely. A silent 'go for it.'

I wasn't a very good goalie; I didn't have the fearlessness in me that was required when people kicked super-fast balls at my face. So was I going to try and block? Hell no. I didn't want my face coming between a man that had been the leading scorer and a net.

As I turned and began walking back toward the goal, a white object shot past me. It went in effortlessly. I didn't miss the look PJ or the goalkeeping coach shot each other as they realized who had just kicked the ball, but I wasn't surprised when neither one of them said a word or made a move to retrieve the ball. I went in, grabbed it and threw it overhead in Kulti's direction, getting out of the way a second later so that I could watch him go for it again.

For the first time in a long time, at least long enough in recent history, he didn't let me down. Another shot soared through the hot spring-summer air and caught the back of the net. I didn't smile or make a big deal out of it as we did it twice more. Me getting the ball and throwing it back at him, Kulti kicking it in.

Four times total, that was it.

It was... I wasn't sure how to describe it. Beautiful was lame. Nostalgic was weird. It was something to witness in person.

This man I'd seen on television a hundred times playing in person just feet away—it was definitely something.

But I'd done this thousands of times with other people, and I reminded myself that it wasn't any more special because this was Reiner Kulti. It sort of reminded me of when I worked with kids during the youth camps and how excited they were when they improved. Sure he didn't smile or thank me for kicking a ball back to him, but I let the moment sink in. Just for a second, I let myself accept that this was Reiner 'The King' Kulti whom I was kicking a freaking ball to.

And then I looked at PJ and asked if she wanted to keep practicing.

* * *

"You know, I was thinking we'd have a better turnout by now," Jenny noted from her place right next to me.

With a sad look around the bleachers surrounding the field we usually practiced on, I felt inclined to agree with her. While the college team's stands were decently filled considering it was a weekday, our side had exactly thirty people. Thirty people total.

Needless to say, it wasn't anything out of the normal for a preseason game. But with the way everyone had been hyping up having the German on staff, and how it would help out the team, we'd all been expecting more.

"Yeah, I know what you mean," I told her. Every game so far had low numbers, and that was even more sad considering that at least a third of the people in the audience had Kulti jerseys on. My money was on the fact that they weren't even really paying attention to the game and were instead focusing on the brown-haired man who sat in the sun the entire game, actually paying attention but managing not to say any of his reassuring words of 'is that what you all call a pass?' He gave us commentary during practices, but he'd yet to make any suggestions during a preseason game. Whatever.

"Actually, I heard that they were only posting the regular season games on the website, and that they weren't putting playing times for any of our preseason games. The only people with times are season ticket-holders or friends and family," Genevieve, the player sitting on my other side explained, though we hadn't been speaking to her.

That was interesting. "Really?" Jenny and I both asked at the same time.

Genevieve nodded. "Yeah. For security or something like that, I think. It was an agreement his management and the owners had to come to before he took the job. At least that's what my friend in the office said." She didn't have to be specific about who *he* was. "Too many psychos would lose their crap and try to come watch him for free."

That made way too much sense.

I eyed the German sitting at the far end of the bench from a side-view. What would that be like? To have psycho fans that would stalk you, or possibly be such a danger to you, that an entire association had to agree to not post times you'd be present without putting you at risk? I couldn't imagine that. I didn't want to. The simple idea of it made me feel claustrophobic.

He was just minding his own business, living his life, and...

Poop.

I faced forward again to watch what was left of the game.

We won. Again.

After the two teams high-fived each other in good sportsmanship and we congratulated each other for kicking ass, we were all ready to leave. There was still some equipment around the field we'd finished using and I wasn't one of those people who just pretended not to see it and left. It made me feel bad, so I went ahead and started grabbing things, helping the rest of the staff along with a couple other players that hadn't immediately taken off.

"Thanks for helping out," Gardner called out as we walked right past each other, me heading toward the bag as he walked away from it.

I nodded at him. "Sure, G." My parents hadn't raised me to be a lazy ass.

There was a sudden loud yell—a scream really. High and just barely distinctively male, it made my ears hurt at the same time it embarrassed me because it was almost deranged-sounding. Sure enough, the noise had originated from way too close. A man was halfway on the field, his gaze locked on the six-foot-two retiree about ten feet away from me, shoving dirty towels into a bag.

I watched as the man let out another shriek—it was a happy one, I guess—and took two baby-bird steps forward before stopping again.

"Kulti?" he wavered the name, and then he went charging.

I'm sure I stood there with my mouth open in awe as Kulti took it all in stride, smiling gently for what had to be the first time I'd ever seen—possibly ever?— and made it seem like it wasn't a big deal at all that this guy was flipping out. I didn't stare, but I kept an eye on them, watching as Kulti talked to his fan in a low voice, signed something the man presented him, and gave him a handshake while the remaining players finished putting equipment up. Out of the corner of my eyes, I watched as he looked around the field. There were only four other people; one coach, two other players and me.

He still kept on looking around like someone would magically appear. Over the course of the next five minutes, he glanced up five more times. It was finally on the last look-around that I sighed and realized what he was doing.

He was searching for help.

By the looks of it, no one else in the general vicinity seemed to be catching on, or they just were unwilling to help. That little voice in my head that seemed to be my conscience reminded me that if I didn't help him I'd feel guilty later.

Not that it made it any easier.

One more sigh and I started walking toward the German, bag over my shoulder, hands knotted behind my back; I thought about what I was going to say to get him out of his encounter. Kulti looked up as soon as I got about halfway to him, his features calm and even as he listened to the fan talking.

I raised my eyebrows and made my eyes go wide in a 'just go along with it' gesture.

He blinked in response.

While I was a shitty liar, I could bend the truth so I wasn't really lying... mostly. I plastered on a smile as soon as the fan saw me coming. "Hi," I greeted him before turning my attention to Kulti. "I'm sorry to interrupt, but would you mind helping me change my tire, please?"

Yeah, I almost winced at myself for inventing such a girly make-believe situation. I could damn well change my own tire. When I moved away from my parents for the first time, I made sure to look up an instructional video and watch it enough times that the steps were ingrained in my memory. But it wasn't like anyone else knew that. Plus, it'd been the first thing that had popped into my head when trying to think of an excuse to save Kulti.

There was no hesitation on his behalf when he nodded and said way too sincerely, "Of course." The German Chocolate Cake—which I was not a fan of, for the record—turned his attention back to the other man and quickly thanked him for his support and something about it being a pleasure meeting him. Before I knew it, The King was walking alongside me across the field in the direction of the parking lot.

I repeat, Kulti was walking alongside me.

Poop. Poop. Poop.

I took a mental breather and swallowed, glancing at the man next to me.

"Don't turn around," he ordered in a low voice.

All right. The 'how about you don't tell me what to do' lived and died in a split second right on my lips.

Instead, I shot him an annoyed glance.

He happened to be looking right at me as I did it. Fantastic.

Almost as if he could read my mind, he explained, "He's watching. I'm sure of it."

"All right." I scratched at the place behind my ear as we kept walking, stepping over the curb that led to the parking lot. "Do we need to pretend like you're actually helping me?"

"Let me take a look when we get to your car." He said the longest sentence I'd ever heard from him.

I nodded and steered him toward the little brown Civic parked on the second row. "This is me."

Kulti made a noise of acknowledgment as we came to my car. Popping the trunk open, I threw my stuff inside and watched him angle his body so he could look back at the field nonchalantly. I wasn't exactly known for being inconspicuous —Eric liked to refer to me as an elephant—so I didn't bother trying to look.

Instead I looked at the tattoo that barely peeked out from beneath his shirtsleeve, and the small scars that had to have been edited out of all the pictures he'd had taken over the years because I'd never seen them before. I noticed the way so much red mixed with the brown of his facial hair that had started growing in. Tall and still in fantastic shape, my poor, stupid, stupid heart gave a little thump in recognition of an attractive man.

Then I stomped it to death and reminded myself he was just a guy. I'd grown up around guys. They weren't anything special. They were fun, funny and complete pains in the asses just like women, who were also fun and funny.

I was fine. Totally fine.

So maybe he had a slight accent, okay. And he'd won a few championships. Right.

But he wasn't a god. He hadn't found a cure for cancer. And he'd upset my dad, even if he'd made up for it.

I was one hundred and eighty percent fine.

Apparently from the looks of it, his face was a little flushed. I didn't need to glance at the field to know we were still being watched.

"He's looking?" I asked quietly, like his fan could hear me.

Kulti nodded, the sunlight hitting his face just right so he looked just as young as he had fifteen years ago.

"Okay, then let's pretend to change my tire real quick. I have to get to work." It wasn't like I'd get in trouble with Marc or anything if I was late, but I still didn't like taking advantage of him or screwing him over. The sooner we got started, the sooner we finished.

The German made a face when I told him I needed to get to work but didn't say another word. I got the wheel lock key out of my glove compartment, jack out of my trunk and pulled the spare out, just to be safe. Was I actually going to change it? No. But I'd go through all the steps and make it seem like we did.

We gave each other side glances as I crouched down on the concrete, as he did the same. I handed him the tire iron and let him loosen a bolt.

"I know how to change my own tire," I felt the need to tell him for some reason, as if not knowing made me less of a person.

Those green-brown orbs slid back over in my direction as he loosened the rest of the bolts.

I slid the jack to him and watched as he put it under the axel.

"Don't turn around," he said once he'd gone through the long act of raising the car and pretending like he was taking the bolts completely off. What a freaking actor.

No argument or question came out of my mouth. I just crouched there with him as we pretended to change my tire for a few more minutes. Eventually he finished and we stood up. It wasn't until then that Kulti turned around to look back at the field.

"The coast is clear?" I asked.

"Yes," he responded in that low voice that caught my interest a little more than it should have.

I nodded and lifted up my shoulders. "All right." What was I supposed to say after that? I wasn't sure and from the looks of it, he wasn't either. Okay. "I guess I'll see you tomorrow then," I offered up, unsure.

Kulti gave me a sharp nod. No thanks, *nada*.

One awkward smile and two retreating footsteps, I deposited the jack and the spare into the trunk. I got into the car and let myself grip the steering wheel for a second. Just as I was pulling out of the parking lot, I looked in my rearview mirror and watched Kulti make his way toward a black car parked off the curb in the lot.

He got into the back seat, not the driver's.

# 11

"Casillas!" Gardner yelled.

I stopped, just like that, in the middle of the game I was in. The ball was right by my feet after I'd taken it away from one of the defenders I was playing against. Said defender was now on the ground.

Things had gotten a little intense.

I held my hand out to the girl and helped pull her to her feet. She knew there were no hard feelings. She'd gone for the ball at the same time I had, and obviously only one of us was going to get it. Needless to say, we both really wanted it. With only a few days left before the start of the season, we all thought we were Highlanders. At one point, I had been the one knocked to the ground, I mouthed to Jenny 'There can be only one.' She didn't even bother trying to be discreet when she burst out laughing.

But it was true, mostly.

When Gardner didn't get to the point, I yelled, "What is it?"

He held up a hand before turning around, discussing something with the German. He was standing a few feet to the side and behind the head coach, facing the field I was on. Gardner's posture changed, he leaned forward a little bit as they spoke, his hand occasionally jabbing backward for emphasis.

I rolled the ball onto the top of my toes and tapped it into the air, bouncing it up and down.

Out of the corner of my eye, I spotted the special edition RK running shoes coming toward me. I looked up so quickly I lost control of the ball and let it drop. Those light-colored eyes were focused in on my face, making me so incredibly self-conscious.

How the hell had I gone from someone who didn't really pay a lot of attention to my looks, to suddenly asking myself if I should start slapping some make-up on?

Wait. *Poop*. Poop. Poop.

We'd been squatting right next to each other when he 'changed' my tire, and that was close enough to see pores.

If I could go without make-up ninety percent of the time in front of practically everyone, I could do it in front of him. Easy. I might not be the one on the team with a cosmetics deal, but I wasn't a troll either. And if I was, so what?

Okay, so maybe I wasn't that above petty things, but beauty was way down the list of characteristics in life that really mattered to me. I was a good soccer player and a pretty good person. I repeated that to myself a few times before holding my head up a little higher. That mattered more to me than whether or not I had a line of men who wanted to date me.

At least that's what I kept telling myself.

I took a deep breath in through my nose and took in those hazel-green orbs straight on. "Yes?"

He tipped his head down at the ball, still looking me dead on. It wasn't the first time I'd talked to someone who looked at others so intensely, I'd been around high-strung self-confident people who didn't know how to communicate in any other way. "It's better if you do this..."

Kulti toed the ball to himself and started to move around me, making his way toward the goal as he spoke in a low voice that conveyed how tedious he found talking to be. It made sense, even if it sounded like the words were getting ripped from his throat. What he was saying and explaining made total sense. When he was finished, he kicked the ball back toward me and walked off like nothing happened.

Reiner Kulti had just dribbled the ball around me effortlessly, despite not being able to land a few PKs recently. I'd be a liar if I said that the hairs on my arms hadn't responded to what I'd just witnessed. Having him yell your shortcomings was one thing, but actually getting on the field and participating... Jesus Louise-us.

I rubbed my tongue over my teeth and took it all in for a second.

"Thanks!" I called to his retreating back.

Was there a response? Of course not.

"What's that look on your face for, Sally?" Harlow asked as she walked by.

"He just helped me."

She gave me an impressed look. "Your bratwurst?"

I nodded.

"How about that? Maybe he's finally getting his head out of his big ass and really pitching in around here."

The fact that Harlow both noticed and commented on Kulti's big sculpted butt amazed and amused me. I snorted and then I snorted again as we both took a quick peek at his retreating buns. They were pretty perfect. Time and gravity hadn't affected them at all.

When we both looked back at each other a good fifteen seconds later, we shook our heads and said at the same time, "Nah."

Some things were too good to be true.

* * *

One week and two preseason games later, the man formerly known as Silence of the Lambs had branched out to make exactly three other demonstrations. The second time had been again with me during another three-on-three mini-game, and the other two times had been with two of the younger forwards on the Pipers. The girls had stood there and just nodded as he moved around them. It wasn't like I'd done much better, I shouted out a "thanks!" awkwardly both times.

But the point no one was missing was: he was helping. It was only a little, but something was something.

Were things still weird? Yes. No one really spoke to him except the staff—Grace hadn't said anything to him since that argument they'd gotten into after Kulti had been ugly with the two Pipers. Mostly everyone gave him his distance and went about their way.

But it worked. We won all of our preseason games and life kept going for each of us.

* * *

"See you later!"

Jenny winked at me just as her phone rang and she took off toward her car. I rubbed a hand over the back of my neck with a sigh. Marc was already waiting for me at our next job, and I was incredibly tired. Insomnia had kicked me in the ass hard the night before, and I'd stayed up way too late watching half a season of *Supernatural.*

Grabbing my bag off the grass, I swung it over my shoulder, ignoring the pain that shot through me at the movement. Most of the girls had left already after practice finished, but I'd stayed and talked to Jenny about having dinner and a movie on Saturday. We hadn't spent too much time together off the field since practices had begun, and I couldn't remember the last time I'd hung out with another girl outside of practice. Maybe when I'd gone to the mall with Ceci almost two months ago?

I was busy trying to remember the last time I'd spent time with someone who wasn't Marc or Simon, my brother's other childhood friend, when I came up to the tall man standing at the curb in the parking lot. It didn't take more than a single brain cell to recognize who it was, but for the life of me I couldn't figure out what the hell he was doing.

He ignored me as I walked past him. To be fair, I didn't make an effort to say anything to him either, on the way to my car. But I dropped my stuff off in the trunk and got inside, still watching the German at the curb as he looked at his phone and then held it up to his face, over and over again. In between he looked around the lot and went right back to the phone again.

I pulled out of the spot and thought about whether I'd feel bad if I kept going or not when he could have needed help. How many times had someone helped me when I needed it, damn it? Nerves squeezed my stomach as I pulled up alongside the curb and rolled the passenger window down, leaning over the center.

"Do you need help?" I asked, hesitantly.

Kulti looked up from his phone, the skin between his eyebrows already wrinkled in either annoyance or confusion that someone had stopped to do something so preposterous as to ask if he needed help. Once he saw that it was me, he just blinked. His eyebrows didn't smooth out or anything like that, but with one last glance at his phone, he looked at me again.

I widened my eyes but kept my gaze on him. "Yes? Or no?"

He gave me a look I couldn't interpret. "Could you give me a ride?"

Could I…?

An extra-nice person wouldn't have asked where, but I had to get to work. "Where to?" I asked slowly.

"I believe it's called Garden Oaks," was his answer. "Do you know where that is?"

Of course I did. Marc and I worked there every other week usually. Garden Oaks was a nice neighborhood not exactly too far or too close by; and it was just that: a neighborhood. A quiet sort of expensive neighborhood—at least for my taste, *and the exact area where I'd picked him up from the bar*. It wasn't where the super-wealthy resided. On my income there was no way I could ever afford to live there unless I had five other roommates.

I smiled in response and nodded, pushing away my curiosity at what exactly he was doing in Garden Oaks. "Okay. Come on."

He gave me a curious look but didn't ask anything. Instead he got into the passenger seat, wordless and stiff. As soon as he was in, I was pulling out of the parking lot.

Was I taking him home?

The only answer to my mental question was silence, obviously. I hadn't used the radio in forever and hadn't plugged in my phone to the car's stereo system in the distraction of having Reiner Kulti in my car. My dad was probably going to shit his pants when I told him.

Damn it. Poop. Poop. Poop.

I cleared my throat and made sure to keep my eyes on the road. "Do you need to call a towing company or something? I have a service on my phone in case of car trouble you could use."

His attention was focused on the view outside the window. "No."

All right. "Are you sure? I don't mind."

"I said no," he replied forcefully enough that I felt it in my chest.

Jesus freaking Christ. All I was trying to do was help. What a prick.

Suddenly angry with myself for making an effort to be nice to someone who obviously didn't want it, I clenched my mouth and kept my eyes forward.

This was exactly what I got for trying. Why did I even bother anymore? Sure, he'd been nice to my dad by making up for being a freaking bag of nasty dildos, and he'd gotten me out of my crap with Cordero and given me a couple of tips on how to improve some playing skills, but it wasn't enough. Not everyone was like this. I'd been nice to thousands of people in my life, and most didn't act like pricks.

Especially not ones that I'd idolized.

Embarrassment at being snapped at made a knot form in my throat as I got on the freeway. For a second, I thought about turning on the radio to avoid the awkwardness that had settled in the car, but I didn't. I hadn't done anything wrong, and it wasn't me who deserved to feel awkward. He did.

"What exit should I take?" I asked in a controlled voice when we were close enough.

He answered.

I exited and then asked whether to turn right or left.

Step by step, I asked him to tell me when to turn again and he did. What lane to get in, he told me. Two more turns and I was driving my car down a street I had a client on. Go figure.

Right before an immaculately landscaped two-floor modern monstrosity that seemed to take up two lots, Kulti gestured. "Here."

I pulled the car closer to the curb and stopped, keeping my eyes forward; it was immature. I didn't have to do that. I didn't have to let him know that what he'd said bothered me, but I couldn't help it. In hindsight later on, I'd curse myself for letting him see that he'd upset me, but right then I couldn't stop myself. I just kept staring out the windshield.

I waited patiently, hands gripping the steering wheel gently.

He didn't move. He didn't get out. He didn't say anything.

I didn't look at him or ask him to get out of my car. I just waited. I could wait. I wasn't impatient. Chin up and face relaxed, I out-waited him for what seemed like five minutes but was probably only thirty seconds.

Finally he reached for the handle and got out. There wasn't a sigh or an apology out of his mouth, or even a freaking thank you for the ride.

The minute the door was closed, I pulled away. I didn't peel out or act like a jackass as I tried to get away; I got back on the street and on the way to work like he hadn't just hurt my feelings.

But he had, a little.

It was enough that I didn't give a single shit about whether the big house in the family neighborhood was his or not. I didn't even bother telling my dad about it.

* * *

"...LIKE THIS," he said in that deep voice with a hint of a watered-down accent in it.

I blinked at the ball on the ground and nodded. "Okay."

"Yes?"

Scratching at my neck, I nodded again. "Got it."

Maybe he expected me to jump for joy or kiss his feet for working with me for the third time, but I couldn't find it in me to drag enough of a shit together to care that he had singled me out again. After having the weekend to cool off, I'd come back to practice with my head straight yesterday. Needless to say, that included me deciding to avoid Kulti as much as possible. I had better things to waste my time and energy on, and jackasses with short tempers and no manners weren't at the top of my list.

I managed to make it through one whole practice without expending any calories on him.

Then today he decided to jump into the middle of a five-on-five game I was playing.

To be an adult, I really watched what he did and listened. I sure as hell wasn't going to do more than that. I lifted my head and gave him an affirming nod, my face neutral. Moving around him, I went back to where I'd been and gestured to the defender I was playing against that we should restart. We did.

Fifteen seconds later Kulti interrupted us again. His long legs ate up the turf as he stopped right between us. "You're doing it wrong," he said, showing me what he wanted me to do differently.

I nodded and went back at it.

Another fifteen seconds of uninterrupted playing time went on before he stopped us again. "*Watch*. You're not watching," the German insisted.

I was watching. I was watching him very carefully.

"All right, I got it," I said as soon as he'd finished his demonstration.

The other player shot me a look that I returned.

Not even ten seconds later, "Twenty-three! What the hell was that?" exploded out of Kulti's mouth.

My hands clenched at my sides, and I asked myself, *why*? Why it'd been decided that this ass-wipe would make an appearance in my life ten years too late?

Taking a deep breath to steady my frustration, I put my hands on my hips and slowly faced him. "Please tell me what I did wrong because I have no idea what you're talking about," I said before I could even comprehend the fact that words had come out of my mouth.

Catching him so off-guard must have been a testament to how much he was not accustomed to people talking back to him, or at least not accepting his word as something holy to be treasured.

Those light-colored eyes narrowed on me, and his eyelids

dropped just enough to shield the interesting shade. "You would have a clearer shot if you—" He broke off his words as he quickly changed the foot he was leading with and turned around with the ball.

I looked at him and asked someone, somewhere for patience. "Wouldn't it be better if I passed the ball?" Of course it'd be better, I was asking a hypothetical question.

A question that he obviously didn't understand by the way he shook his head in response. "No."

No?

"If you have the shot, take it."

I glanced at Genevieve, my teammate who was standing off to the side watching us, and then looked back at Kulti. "I'm not sure I'll have it."

"Unless you're not paying attention or you suddenly can't move your feet, you'll have it," he ground out in an irritated tone.

Fighting the urge to pinch my nostrils, I squeezed my fist tighter. "All right. Whatever you say." *Whatever you say* for me usually meant *yeah, sure*, and then I'd end up doing whatever the hell I wanted anyway. He was wrong. What he was telling me to do was too risky, and it was selfish. But, whatever. I knew how to pick my arguments.

For some reason he didn't look appeased by what I said at all. It was almost as if he knew I was just saying the words to get him off my back, which I was, but he didn't know that. At least he shouldn't.

He didn't say anything else, and a minute later time for our game ran out. Another ten players headed out onto the field for their practice game. I watched and shouted out encouragements, Harlow receiving some of them. As much as I tried not to pay attention to Kulti, I couldn't help but notice that he didn't stop that game to make any suggestions.

Of course not, I thought almost bitterly.

Sometime later practice ended and I found myself walking to my car. I was debating whether to try and catch a yoga class that night, or just do some serious stretching at home, when I happened to look up and find someone standing by the driver side door of my car.

Only it wasn't just someone. It was the German.

My muscles immediately tensed up at the sight of him leaning so casually against my beloved car.

I took a calm casual breath and tried to push my emotions down as I kept walking. Kulti had his duffel bag thrown over his shoulder, his hands tucked into the pockets of his white polyester workout shorts. He looked exactly like he had a dozen other times on a magazine cover. Show-off.

Oddly enough, I wasn't affected in the least bit.

I felt smug and disinterested. Mostly I didn't find myself giving a single crap that Reiner Kulti was standing by my car. Not anyone else's, mine. He wasn't the first guy I'd seen doing it, and he wouldn't be the last.

My face didn't betray me as I closed the distance between us. I didn't think about the fact that I'd ripped my headband off as soon as I finished cooling down, that I hadn't tweezed my eyebrows in a week or taken care of my upper lip.

My muscles were tight from exercise, I felt strong mentally, and that was more than enough for me.

Kulti's lake-colored eyes stayed locked on my face as I walked right in front of him to pop my trunk and drop my things inside. I hadn't finished slamming it shut when I said, "I have to get to work. Do you need something?"

"My driver isn't here."

So that's why he'd gotten into the backseat the one day I saw him getting into his car, and why he'd hitched a ride with me the day before.

I left my hand on the trunk and looked at him over my

shoulder, at his short hair, his stern face, his full mouth. Yeah, I still didn't care. "Okay. Do you need to borrow my cell?"

"I need a ride," he said in his low voice.

What was I? Driving Miss Daisy?

"Could you give me one?" he asked.

Was this real life? Was this really happening? "You want *me* to give you a ride again?"

To give him credit, he didn't break eye contact once. "It would be appreciated."

*It would be appreciated.* My eyes almost crossed in response. "I have to get to work," I told him in a calm voice because it was the truth. Sure I was meeting Marc at a house about a mile away from Kulti's, but he didn't know that. Also it wasn't like spending one-on-one time with an ungrateful jerk was at the top of my list of things I wanted to do.

The look he gave me in response said that he didn't exactly believe me. At all. For one second, I felt guilty for lying. Then I remembered how I'd tried being friendly with him time and time again and for what? To get snapped at? I didn't owe him a thing.

The corners of his mouth tightened and a noticeable deep breath made its way out of lungs that used to carry him across the length of a full-sized soccer field effortlessly. The "please" caught me totally off-guard.

I faltered. For one split second I faltered, and then I found myself again and reached for the door handle. My attention stayed forward. I almost said I was sorry, but that would be a lie. "I'm sure just about anyone would give you a ride if you asked nicely."

A hand that wasn't my own pressed down on my window, long fingers with short fingernails extended wide, his palm as big as I remembered from our handshake. "I'm asking you."

"And I'm not the only person that can give you one. I need

to get to work." I jerked the handle, but the door didn't budge. At all.

"Casillas."

Holy shit. My name came out of his—

Poop.

I glanced at him over my shoulder; this wasn't a big deal. So he'd said my name when I didn't think another player's name had crossed his lips... hell. Ever?

"I would appreciate it," his deep voice insisted.

I didn't say a word, I just jerked on the handle again.

His forearm flexed as he held my door down. "I can pay you," he offered, casually.

The hell?

No one in my life had ever offered to give me money for doing them a favor, because it wasn't necessary. Here was a person who made more money retired than I would in a decade. He had a freaking driver yet, he wanted to pay me to give him a ride.

*Ugh.*

What was I doing? I might feel like a badass right now telling him that I wouldn't take him home, or wherever he was going, but later on there was no doubt I'd feel like an asshole for not doing a favor that was easily within my reach. I didn't want to be that person who was an asshole just to be an asshole; it wouldn't make me any better than this jerk-off.

I fought the urge to tip my head back and groan; instead I let out a resigned sigh and waved him on. "I'll take you."

Kulti blinked and then quickly nodded, getting in. Wordlessly, I pulled out of the lot and made my way in same direction we'd gone on Friday.

"Same place?" I asked with only the slightest hint of an attitude in my tone as I pulled onto the freeway.

"Yes" was his solitary answer.

All right. This time I did turn on the radio, and I drove

quietly to the same house in the same family neighborhood I'd just been in.

Just as I was pulling over he started shifting in his seat, and I glanced over to see him pulling a slim black wallet out.

Jesus. I pulled over to the curb in front of the square white stone home. "Don't."

His silence was deafening as he sat there, duffel on his lap, one hand on the car door, and the other holding a slim coffee-colored leather wallet.

"I'm giving you a ride as a favor. I don't want your money," I explained to him carefully.

He started to pull out a bill from his wallet regardless.

"Hey, I'm not joking. I don't want your money."

Kulti started to shove a fifty at me. "Here."

I reached up and cupped his hand, crushing the bill between us. "I don't want it."

"Take it." He pushed against me.

I pushed back. "No."

"Stop being stubborn and take the money," Kulti argued, his face exasperated.

Well if he thought he was the only one getting aggravated, he was dead wrong. "I said no. I don't want it. Just get out."

It was his turn to start with the one-word replies. "No."

Screw this. I put some muscle behind it and slowly started pushing our hands back toward him. Well I made it two inches before he realized what I was doing and then began pushing back, only he was stronger and he advanced more than two inches.

"Quit it. I'm not joking. Take your money." I grunted a little, putting more weight into my push, almost futilely.

Those green-brown eyes flicked up to with an even look that had annoyance written all over it. "I said I would pay you—"

"I don't want your money, you hardheaded ass—"

Oh dear God.

I stopped pushing the second I realized what I said. It must have been so unexpected that he wasn't paying attention because the next thing that I knew, he was punching me in the shoulder.

It didn't hurt at all.

But for some reason, instinct had me saying "oww" anyway.

We both looked like we'd violated the other. Like I'd back-stabbed him for saying 'oww' and I'm sure I looked at him like I couldn't believe he had the nerve to hit me. Sure it was an accident, and an accident that didn't hurt on top of that, but...

"I'm sorry," he said quickly, looking down at his hand like he couldn't believe what he'd done.

I opened my mouth and then I closed it.

Reiner Kulti had just punched me in the shoulder.

I had driven him home, argued with him over how I didn't want his money, and then he punched me in the shoulder.

I closed my eyes, pinched my nose and burst out laughing.

"Get outta here," I said when I started laughing harder.

"I didn't mean to—"

I threw my head back against the headrest and felt myself shake with how stupid this was. "I know. I know you didn't. But just get out, it's fine. I need to get to work before you punch me in the other shoulder."

"This isn't funny," he snapped. "It was an accident."

Suddenly I stopped laughing and snapped right back at him, "I know it was, jeez. I was just messing with you." I gave him a wide-eyed look. "A joke, do you know what that is?"

I mean, I'd already gone for calling him a hardheaded ass, and he hadn't thought twice about it, but that might have been because he'd punched me immediately afterward.

"Yes, I know what a joke is," he grumbled back.

Whether it was because I was tired of this shit, his shit or whatever, I found myself caring less and less who he was and how I should probably treat him differently. Maybe not totally, but at least a little bit. "I'm happy to hear that." I scooped the fifty bucks that had fallen on my lap after the meeting of his fist and my shoulder and tossed it at him. "I really do need to get to work though, so…" I tipped my head in the direction of the door at his side, indifferent to how rude I was being.

Did he look confused that I was kicking him out? I think so but he didn't argue, and he took the wadded-up money and held onto it as he got out of the car. Straightening up, he held the door in one hand and looked inside. "Thank you."

Finally.

I blinked at him and nodded. "You're welcome."

Just like that, he shut the door.

* * *

"CAN you confirm that his license is suspended?" the eager man asked.

I rubbed at my eyebrow with the back of my hand and stared at the reporter awkwardly.

What I could confirm was that he had an unreliable driver and I had yet to see him behind the wheel. Then again, didn't rich people have drivers? I'd met a few who did. It wasn't an uncommon thing. Hell, if I could afford it, I'd have someone drive me around too. Driving in traffic, in Houston traffic, sucked.

But his question nagged at me, right alongside the incident at the bar. Marc had given me the impression he hadn't carried around any car keys with him, and I'd just never gotten around to investigating or finding out if Kulti had left a car at the bar or not. It wasn't like I'd really cared anyway.

"I can't confirm anything; I don't know. I'm sorry, but I really do need to meet up with the team, I'm running late." I was. I'd overslept big time.

"Have you seen him drive?" The man was relentless.

I hadn't but I still wasn't a dick enough to admit it. He might have been an asshole, but obviously he liked his privacy, and I wasn't about throw him under the bus. Then there was the whole issue with Pipers' management being really uptight about all things Reiner Kulti-related, so I sure as hell wasn't about to dig myself into that hole. What did that mean? I needed to abort this mission, pronto. That's exactly what I did.

"I haven't paid attention. I'm sorry, but I really do need to get going. Sorry!" I hated being rude but in the long run, I'd rather come off as a jerk than turn out to be an unemployed person with a big mouth.

His license was being suspended? Wow. Really. Wow.

Whether it was true or not, and regardless of how much it wasn't my business, I couldn't help but think about it and how something like that could backfire on the team if the rumor got loose. Shouldn't his agent or publicist or someone deal with it?

The longer I thought about it during practice, the more convinced I became that maybe I shouldn't keep quiet about it. Most of the other questions I'd been asked had been harmless, but this wasn't.

Damn it.

Finally about an hour into practice, I caught Kulti off to the side, going over our playbook. As casually as possible, I made my way over and in a voice just loud enough for only him to hear, I said, "Someone from the *Houston Times* this morning asked me if I knew about you having your license suspended. I don't know anything, and that's what I said, but I thought you should know so you can tell your PR person to take care of it, or whatever it is they do."

It didn't escape me that the moment the nine-letter word made its way out of my mouth, he stopped. His entire body strung itself into a tight immovable bow.

His body language wasn't mine to analyze, I reminded myself, as I walked away to let him absorb what he'd learned.

But seriously, wouldn't he have needed to get a DUI or a DWI to have a suspended license?

I wasn't disappointed by the possibility that there was a chance he had one, I'd learned from a friend when I was younger that things like that were more luck-based than anything. How many people didn't drive home after having a few drinks? Sometimes you got caught and most times you didn't. Whatever.

Then again I'd grown up reading about Reiner Kulti's strict regimen. How anal he was about his food and his workouts and his life in general. So...

*It's not your business.* It really wasn't, my business was on the field. I had to remind myself of that.

# 12

I shouldn't have been surprised to find the German waiting on the curb. Mostly, I wasn't. Mostly.

"Need another ride?" I asked, stopping right next to him so that we were side by side.

He cut straight to it. "Please."

Please. Well, how about that. I was almost tempted to look around and make sure pigs hadn't started flying. "Come on, then."

Kulti threw his bag into the trunk alongside mine. Neither one of us said anything as we got inside, and I couldn't help but feel a little awkward that I'd said something to him about the license rumor. About halfway to his maybe-house, I finally broke the silence. The radio wasn't on, and the quiet was stifling.

"Can I ask you something?" I asked, slowly.

"Yes." There was a pause. "I might not answer."

I hated it when people said that. "All right." I psyched myself up to ask the question I couldn't stop thinking about. The possibility of getting reamed was very real, but screw it, you only live once. "Why are your PKs sucking so much?" I went for it. I just blurted it out. Good God, I should have been proud of myself. "I don't get it."

In an ideal world, he would have yelled at me and said that I was a lowly peasant in his universe who had no right to speak to him, much less ask questions like that.

In the real world, he made a choking sound.

I gave him a side look to make sure he was still alive. He was.

Was his face red?

"No one can say you aren't honest, can they?" he asked. Another choking sound—or maybe it was a snicker?—came out of him before he continued. "You can say I'm out of practice."

All right, that was something. Not enough, obviously. "How long out of practice?" I was hesitant asking. I felt like I was trying to pet the mean dog on the other side of the fence.

He raised a hand and ran it over the short hair on his head. That hard jaw might have jutted out to the side, but I couldn't be sure. The one thing I *was* sure of: he did glance over in my direction like he couldn't believe I had the nerve to ask.

Honestly, I couldn't believe I'd actually gone through with it. What I really couldn't believe was that he replied.

"Do you know when I retired?" he asked in that strict voice with only the slightest hint of an accent. I remember hearing somewhere that he spoke four different languages fluently, or was it three?

Poop. Who cared how many languages he spoke?

Of course I knew when he retired, but I didn't say it like that. I could be cool about it. "Yes."

"That's your answer."

Wait.

*Wait.*

"You haven't done what since you retired?" The question was careful.

It couldn't be. It just couldn't.

Kulti's mouth twisted to the side at the same time his nostrils flared. "I haven't played since I retired. If you tell anyone—"

I almost slammed on my brakes.

Okay, I didn't, but I wanted to. I couldn't believe him. I eased the car to a stop at a red light as he finished his stupid threat that I chose to ignore. Slowly, incredulously I said, "You're joking." Who was I kidding? He didn't have humor in his DNA.

Sure enough, he confirmed it. "I am not."

"No."

He arched a dark eyebrow. "I don't lie."

I let my head fall back against the headrest as I took in what he'd admitted. Two years. Two years! He hadn't played in two years! "At all?" My voice was all low and whisper-like.

"Correct."

Holy fuck. It felt like the world had been ripped out from under my feet. Two freaking years for a player like him? What in the hell was that?

I wanted to tell him something, to apologize or something, but I could only open my mouth and close it, good intentions present.

But I knew that my pity wasn't what he'd want. If I had to bet money, I would have said that the longest length of time he'd ever taken off from playing was when he tore some ligaments in his foot but, I wasn't about to bust out my Kulti-psycho-stalker-knowledge.

Keeping my eyes forward, I cleared my throat and then followed up by doing it again.

Because—two years! Two years!

Holy shit. How was that even possible?

I dwelled on the number one more time, and then locked it away to process it later in the privacy of my own home. Two years was a lifetime and yet it was more than long enough to explain why he had such a huge stick up his ass. The poor guy was like a eunuch. No soccer was pretty much the equivalent of losing your balls, at least that's what I figured.

Compassion and understanding rolled through me.

Easing off the brake, I told him my own story. Although later on I'd wonder why I bothered. It wasn't like he'd care. "When I was seventeen, I tore my ACL during a game, and I was out for almost six months. My parents and coaches wouldn't even let me look at a soccer ball or watch a game because it drove me nuts to know there was nothing I could really do to speed up the healing process."

Those were some of the worst months of my life. I'd never been really bitchy but toward the end of my recovery, I'd gotten so short-tempered I wasn't sure how my parents didn't slap me for being such a pain in the ass. "It was the longest six months of my life and probably the most miserable," I added, shooting him a sidelong glance.

His attention was focused forward, but I did see him nod. "I've been there."

I knew he had, but once again, it was Kulti-psycho-stalker-knowledge that I'd take to the grave with me.

We stayed quiet the rest of the way to the house, his house, whatever. Only this time as soon as he opened the door, I told him, "I won't say anything about your dry spell."

Kulti nodded, and I could have sworn he had something that could have been considered the smallest smile in the history of smiles pull at the corners of his mouth. Then he was at my trunk getting his bag and actually raising a hand in a half-assed goodbye as he walked up the stone path to the front door of the big house.

I'd be lying if I said I didn't think about Kulti, and how he hadn't played in two years, the rest of the day.

* * *

THE NEXT DAY, during practice, I couldn't help but keep staring at Kulti and wondering how the hell he hadn't murdered anyone since he'd quit playing.

I mean... he hadn't played at all? Or just... I don't know, hadn't played a regulation game? By the look of his movements and his body language, it didn't seem like he'd completely stopped playing, but what did I know? Two years couldn't completely erase a lifetime spent with a white and black ball.

Harlow elbowed me in the ribs as she stopped right by me. "Did he just call you a slow-ass?"

The team was running drills, and I'd been in the first group of players.

I hunched my shoulders up, saying nothing. What was there to say? Kulti had called me slow during a drill, and then asked another player if she had two left feet. She was the same girl I'd run with in the morning a few times by then, the one that always wanted to beat me at sprints.

Was she slow? No. Hell no. Sandy was really good.

"I would like to finish drills in this lifetime, can we move on?" a voice bellowed from the other side of the field.

Absently, I reached over to the shoulder that had been punched. At that moment, Kulti glanced over. The space between his eyebrows crinkled, and for a split second, I debated hunching over and pretending I had a shooting pain going through my shoulder so I could mess with him. He hadn't brought it up the day before and neither had I.

I didn't do it though. Harlow was a little too attentive. She'd notice. Plus, I had no idea how he'd handle it.

Really I had no idea how to handle any of this. Was I supposed to not be saying anything about giving Kulti rides home? Because I hadn't. Not even my dad knew, and I usually told him everything. He wasn't treating me any differently than he had before I gave him rides, so it didn't mean anything.

There wasn't anything to tell. Was there?

"Is your shoulder bothering you?" Harlow's voice tore me away from looking at the German.

"No." My face flushed as I turned back to her. "Ready?"

She shoved me to the side and took off. "Catch up, slow-poke."

Little did I know that the 'slow-ass' and 'slow-poke' nicknames were only the beginning. Before practice was over Kulti had called my passes sloppy, and then followed up by saying I needed to learn how to play with both legs.

This was coming from the man who played with his right foot ninety percent of the time? Ha.

I didn't let his comments get me down or bother me. I also didn't worry too much about whether he was being overbearing because I'd recently learned his secret, or if it was because I just took his shit. Regardless, I listened to what he said and took it all in stride. I wasn't going to let myself take it too personally.

When the end of practice rolled around an hour later, I was already expecting him in our usual spot, and he didn't disappoint.

Skipping the obvious, I asked as I approached, "Ready?"

"Yes," he answered.

That familiar silence followed us as we got inside and continued as I drove for a little bit.

Two minutes was as long as I could contain my curiosity before I broke down. "Do you miss it?"

Not a total idiot, he asked, "Playing?"

"Yeah." As much as I tried to reason how he'd made it so long, I still couldn't really comprehend the idea of not playing. I couldn't.

He slid his gaze over to me as he nodded, so honest and straightforward it caught me off-guard. "I miss football every day." Just as quickly as his gaze had moved to mine, it moved back as he swallowed.

So… "Why haven't you, then?" I asked before I could talk myself out of it. What was the worst he would do? Not answer? Tell me to mind my own business?

Curiosity killed the Sal. Let it be said I went down in a blaze of glory asking Reiner Kulti about a secret I wasn't sure he would share willingly.

Why he'd decided to share it with me, I still wasn't positive, but I'd take what I could get.

A slow steady exhale made its way out of him. "Do you know why I retired?"

He'd torn his ACL for the third time. There'd been rumors from the prior tear that he wouldn't come back one hundred percent, or even ninety or eighty or seventy percent. He was too old, people had said. When it finally happened, stacked on top of arthritis in his toe, and other small injuries that managed to add up over the years, everyone thought it was inevitable.

Reiner 'The King' Kulti had announced his retirement shortly afterward, ending his legacy.

Was I going to say that? Definitely not.

I settled for a nod and a "yeah."

"It took a long time for me to heal," he said. Then he didn't say anything afterward.

I found myself slowly turning my head to give him an incredulous look I realized I had no right to give him. "Okay. Then what?"

He shrugged.

Reiner Kulti shrugged like 'oh, my ACL took a long time to heal' was reason enough to explain why he hadn't played his beloved sport in two years. He wasn't fooling me. He still loved it. You didn't give up a great love so easily. I could tell by the look in his arrogant eyes when he watched the team. He looked at some players like they were complete pieces of crap he wished he could shake until they got things right. You didn't look like that unless you still cared.

He wasn't fooling me.

"That took what? Six months? Eight months?" I asked, blinking at him slowly.

When he said, "It hasn't completely healed," it was proof enough for me he was full of shit. He didn't strike me as the type to want to make a big deal about his injuries.

So I said something I would have said to any other player I had a decent relationship with—he didn't exactly count —"Bullshit."

"Excuse me?"

I laughed. "That's bullshit. Your knee still hurts? Come on. Do I look like I was born yesterday? I've been in some sort of pain since I was sixteen, and I'm sure you have been too." I shook my head and laughed again before focusing back on the road. "Jeez. Next time tell me to mind my own business instead of telling me something so ridiculous."

What the hell else had I been expecting? He'd said more than I would have bet my life on to begin with.

"You don't know anything," he snapped back.

Once again, another thing I shouldn't have been surprised at. "I know enough." Because I did, his bullshit was evident from a mile away.

"What the fuck is that supposed to mean?" Kulti's voice was laced with just a bit of anger.

He'd finally dropped a 'fuck.' How about that.

I was almost in awe—almost, and I definitely couldn't find it in me to get all bent out of shape at his ugly tone and words. "You know what I mean. Look, you don't need to get an attitude. All I was asking was why you haven't played in so long. It's none of my business, fine. Sorry I asked."

There was a pause. "Explain what you meant."

He wanted to understand, but I knew in my heart he didn't really want me to tell him. I kept my attention forward and shook my head, the laughter and amusement dying off my face. "It doesn't matter."

"It matters," he insisted.

I kept my mouth shut.

"Say it."

Yeah, I wasn't saying anything. Nobody was handing me the shovel to dig my own grave.

"You think I'm lying?" Kulti asked in a cold voice.

I swallowed. Well he asked, right? I picked my words carefully and answered. "I'm not saying you're lying. I'm sure your knee hurts, but there is no way that's why you haven't played. Even if you're only back at sixty percent, fifty percent, it doesn't matter; you still would have played with friends at least, or something. Kicked the ball on your own. You have the money to build your own field, I'm sure, if you don't want everyone in your business. It seems like you're selling yourself out. You already told me you miss playing. I just don't believe something like a little pain would stop you from at least... you know what? It doesn't matter. I'm glad you finally started kicking some balls around. Good for you."

Hours later, I'd realize how differently I could have handled the situation. How horribly I'd actually gone about it. I knew better. *I knew better*. I understood people who held their pride and arrogance like a shield and how they handled someone attacking them. Or worse, someone feeling sorry for them.

I knew because I was well aware how much I hated anyone feeling sorry for me.

Pitying a man with the ability to make my life a living hell on the field, a man who had once upon a time held a passion for soccer that seemed to light him up from the inside out, it was like I turned a force of nature against me.

Forget that I'd tried to be nice to him, that I'd driven him home and never insisted on knowing why he had me take him instead of his driver or a taxi or Gardner or Grace, or just about anyone else that had more of a relationship with him than I did.

In the words of my brother, I did it to myself. I brought the attention of a perfectionist down on me, and there was no one else to blame for it.

* * *

THE NEXT TWO weeks of my life could be summed up in three keywords: physical and emotional hell.

Any kind of bond I'd formed with Kulti had been shattered the day I pressed him for answers in my car. Proceeding to give him shit for using his injury as an excuse was just the icing on the cake.

Since then I hadn't given him a single ride home. I wasn't surprised after that initial first practice, following what I would call Interrogation Day, when he took ripping me a new one to a totally different level.

Seriously.

"*What the hell are you doing*?"

"*Listen to me!*"

Blah, blah, blah, fuck, blah, blah, blah, something-something-shit, blah, blah, blah.

But my favorite thing that came out of his mouth was "Is that how girls play soccer?"

*Oh man.*

I'd heard that one before. It still got me every time.

But if what he wanted, was for me and the team to show him just how girls played, he got his wish. We were all out for blood. Most of us had grown up playing with boys and from experience, we all knew their asses got kicked just as easily as other ladies did.

I couldn't remember the last time any coach had been on top of me with such a vengeance. There wasn't anything friendly about the things that came out of Kulti's mouth. It was all business. All tough-love, I'm-going-to-break-you-down-to-get-what-I-want love.

Each day was worse than the one before. Gardner didn't say anything. He patted me on the back and told me to hang in there.

It got hard to keep my head up and brush off the ugly words. I tried my best to focus on the things that came out of his mouth that had knowledge beneath them, but it wasn't easy. Toward the end of the first week Jenny, the world-class athlete, was the one who panted out, "What did you do to him?" after Kulti yelled at me for passing the ball to another player when he felt like I should have taken a difficult shot instead.

What could I tell her? Nothing. I couldn't tell her anything without bringing up that I'd driven him home a few times. "I have no idea," I told her.

"Did something else come up with Eric?"

"No." I'd been getting fewer and fewer messages about Eric and Kulti over the course of the last few weeks. I seriously doubted that the team photos with us standing by each other had anything to do with it, and Sheena hadn't brought up anything else about releasing clips from the press conference I'd done with Gardner at the beginning of the season.

Jenny scrunched up her face, wiping at her neck with her shirt collar. "Bring him a cupcake or something then Sal, because this is getting out of control. I don't know how you haven't started crying yet."

That's how bad it was. My whole body was tight before practice began and it stayed that way afterward. Marc went out of his way to tease me more often to get me out of my exhausted funk.

It barely helped.

And then, I finally had enough.

* * *

"If you would have—"

If I would have. If I would have done something differently, we could have won by five goals instead of one.

He was being unfair and everyone knew it. Did anyone say anything though?

Of course not. No one wanted to be the one getting their ass chewed out, and I couldn't exactly blame them.

Most importantly, did I say anything? Nope. I stood there as Gardner and Kulti went back and forth over what we could have improved upon in our last preseason game. I stayed quiet as Kulti hung the weight of an almost-loss on my shoulders and nodded when I was supposed to.

He was right. I did miss a few opportunities. I wouldn't deny it.

But so did half the members on our team. Yet did anyone bring that up? Gardner made some generalizations, but he didn't name anyone directly even when it was obvious someone had messed up big time. He didn't get a kick out of embarrassing players, and instead would pull a person aside and talk with them.

And this fucking *frankfurter*...

I swallowed the fucking bratwurst bitch, *sauerkraut* shit, German pieceofshit Chocolate Cake insults, which were all throwing a party in my mouth. They each begged me to let them come out and play.

Inside, oh my God, inside I was raging and trying to talk myself out of doing something that would land me in jail. I wouldn't cut it. I enjoyed being outside too much.

"Sorry guys," I said in a deceptively calm voice once Kulti had finished his rant.

Harlow and Jenny's faces stood out at me from the semicircle we were standing in. Harlow looked like she was on the verge of laughing, and Jenny looked like she was contemplating how quickly she could grab me in case I decided two to fifteen years behind bars wasn't that long.

None of the girls said a word.

Our post-game meeting finished soon after that, leaving a clammy awkward feeling in the air that I'm sure I was responsible for.

Like a sane rational person, I grabbed my things and casually went about preparing to leave. Harlow gave my arm a squeeze as she walked by me, not saying anything, but I felt like she was giving me her blessing—her inner fearlessness. Jenny crept over to me and wrapped her arm around my shoulders and in a low voice said, "Salamander, please don't make me visit you in jail. Orange isn't your color, and I don't think you're cut out to be some lady's... you know... *bitch.*"

Leave it to Jenny to make me lose focus. I laughed and wrapped an arm around her waist. How did she know me so well? "I swear I'm not going to do anything violent."

"You promise?"

"I promise."

She didn't exactly look like she really believed me, but eventually she dropped her arm. "Please." Jenny looked me right in the eye as she pleaded.

I couldn't help but smile at her and nod. "Promise."

Her eyes dropped low but she eventually nodded. "See you tomorrow?"

I assured her I would, and she bid me goodbye. The area had mostly cleared out by then, but the person I was looking for was still there. Taking a deep breath, I calmed my nerves and told myself I was doing the right thing. I couldn't keep doing this crap with him.

I wouldn't. I knew exactly what I needed to do to resolve it.

There he was standing, just as I finished sending Marc a text letting him know I'd be late. Standing at the curb where I'd picked him up time and time again. He wasn't expecting me to come up behind him. Or maybe he was, except possibly with a knife in one hand.

"I can't do this with you anymore," I warned him. I wasn't having any of this being-discreet crap. I stood there and I faced him. There wasn't a doubt in my mind that my face was flushed, I was sweaty everywhere. There was a slight chance that I might smell too, but I had to get this out. Now. I pointed at the field behind us. "Come on."

Kulti reared back, his face scrunching up. "What are you talking about?"

I waved him onward more insistently. "Come on. I'm not going to be your punching bag the rest of the season. You and me, whoever makes it to seven first, wins."

His bottom lip dropped and he blinked. Then he blinked again, confused.

"Come on."

"Absolutely not."

"Come on," I repeated.

"Twenty-three, no."

"Kulti." I waved him forward, giving him one more chance to do this the easy way.

"You're being ridiculous."

All right. I sniffled and took a deep breath. "And you're being a coward."

That might have not been the smartest thing to say because the next thing I knew his shoulders stiffened, and his mouth had slammed closed. Well I couldn't say I hadn't gotten the job done. "What did you say?"

"I said you're being a chicken." I did it. Holy shit, I called Reiner Kulti a chicken and a coward, and there was no coming back from it. In for a penny, in for a pound, I told myself. "Come on. What are you scared of? You know you're better than me. I know you're better than me, so let's get this over with. Play me so you can get over this crap."

"I'm not doing this with you, little girl," he stated evenly, his jaw gritting.

Little girl.

Could I have let it go? Sure. Of course I could. But I hadn't been lying when I said I couldn't do this with him any longer. All that repressed anger he had, and the frustrations he took out on me because I unfortunately had so much knowledge of him, the tension was out of this world. It wasn't like I'd forced him to tell me the truth, but regardless we couldn't keep this hateful dance up.

"Yeah, we are."

"No, we are not."

Clenching my hands together, I was about two seconds away from going Super Saiyan on his ass. "I know I'm going to lose, Kulti. I fucking hate losing, but we're doing this anyway, so let's get it over with."

He raised both hands into the air and scrubbed his palms over the back of his head. Jesus Christ, he was tall. "No."

"Why?"

"You're a pain in my ass," he snapped.

It was my turn to blink at him. "You think I'm going to beat you, don't you?"

He rolled his eyes upward as he huffed. "Hell hasn't frozen over."

Based on his tone, I wasn't sure if he really thought so or not. Or maybe I was just being egotistical. Maybe. But I knew that I needed to set my ego aside and make him do this. Some part of my gut recognized that it was necessary, so I needed to do everything possible to make this happen.

Even if it meant pissing him off.

I tipped my chin up at him and looked right into those light-colored eyes. "Then quit being a pussy and play me."

Yeah, that did it.

"I am not a pussy." He took a step forward. "I can and will kick your ass."

Whoa. I held my hands up and guffawed. "I said you were going to win, *sauerkraut*, I didn't say you were going to kick my ass."

That look I recognized all too well crossed over his features, and I was honestly torn between shivering in fear and... well I wasn't going to say it, or even really admit the other emotion. He had the look of the old Kulti—the borderline psychotic competitor.

Oh my gosh, he was going to wipe the floor with me.

And then I almost laughed because, *really*? I wasn't about to bend over and let him win. Please.

Something flared within my chest, and I let the fire of competition burn in my heart. "Let's do this."

And we did.

John the Baptist, Mary Magdalene and Peter Parker all spewed out of my mouth at some point.

It was one thing to have watched him play from the safety of my television or from the stands. To a certain extent, it was an advantage because I knew how he played almost as well as I knew my own game; the kind of moves he tended to stick to, his tells. My body was instinctively aware without me really thinking about it, that he faked leading with his right foot before switching to his left. I knew his tricks.

And yet...

Two years of not playing barely slowed him down. Barely. I was fast and he was just as fast, if not faster. His legs were a lot longer than mine, and he ate up the turf like no one's business. There was a reason this man was an icon, why he'd been the best for so long.

But *fuck that*. I wasn't going to let him win without a fight. I kept what I knew about him in the front of my brain, and I moved my legs as fast as I could. I tried to out-think him and play smarter more efficiently. The ball stayed as close to me as possible. Later on I would wonder if it really looked like we were playing 'keep away' from each other or not.

He cornered me at one point and managed to get the ball. While he did it, he shouldered me a little more than was necessary. I mean he was a foot taller and at least fifty pounds heavier, yet he was playing as rough as my brother and his friends did. I'd been playing with the boys since I was a kid, and they'd missed the memo that said I was a girl seven years younger than them. Apparently, Kulti had too.

"Playing a little rough, aren't you?" I asked as I ran up behind him, trying to block him from getting a clear shot of the goal.

He looked up at me from under his eyelashes. "Are you whining?"

I huffed. Asshole. "No, but if that's how you want to play, then that's how we'll play." Between the people I played with for fun and Harlow, I could take it.

We ran after each other for what felt like forever. I'd steal the ball from him; he'd steal the ball from me, over and over again. Sweat poured down my face, arms and lower back. He was breathing hard—had he ever breathed hard before?

It was a miracle that he was playing pretty sloppy, and I think that's the reason why he didn't manage to score. I wasn't egotistical, I knew I was good, but I wasn't as good as he was. But I watched and I learned. That was all I ever wanted.

"You've had like... eight opportunities... to score...on me..." I huffed.

His back was to mine, butt pressed to my hip. "And... you've.... had three...if...you'd known what you were—doing!" He kicked the ball up high and tried to do a header to get it in. My miracle was obviously still in effect because he didn't score.

We both hauled ass for the ball, and I might have slammed

my body up against his pretty rough, but whatever, he could take it.

"I know what... I'm doing..." I pushed my shoulder into his chest and took the ball away from him.

Back and forth, we went chasing and stealing, chasing and stealing, until I was breathing hard from the spike of adrenaline. We played aggressively, battling it out. In a real game, you knew how to keep your energy perfectly balanced. You had ninety minutes to get through, and you couldn't wear yourself out within the first fifteen.

You also had ten other people on the field to move the ball back and forth.

My morning run and practice had already taken their toll. Playing with Kulti made every muscle feel that much more intense, even the backs of my knees were wet with sweat.

But when his breath was in my ear and his body was right behind me, I could hear and feel the exhaustion radiating from his own body. I smiled.

"Getting winded?"

He grunted but didn't respond; a second later, I realized why. In a move that was Reiner Kulti at the height of his career, he stole the ball from me and powered toward the goal using the advantage of his long legs. I saw it coming but I still didn't slow down as I ran to catch up.

With a swift kick I didn't have a chance of blocking, the soccer ball flew through the air in a sharp powerful line. Perfect. It was a perfect shot.

I smiled and shook my head despite the fact that under normal circumstances, I would have been pissed off I was down one.

But that had been beautiful.

And when Kulti turned around with the most smug triumphant smile I would probably ever see, and that was saying something considering I'd played against some pretty egotistical people, it pleased me. It went straight into my sternum because it was so... *him.* It wasn't the blank indifferent man I'd seen so many times over the course of the last month.

"One-zero, Taco," he said like I was an idiot and had no idea what the score was.

Just like that, that pleased feeling in my chest that had appreciated the joy of his brief triumph disappeared.

Had he...?

"Taco? Really?" I wanted to laugh, as demeaning as the nickname was, but I'd kind of asked for it, hadn't I?

He shrugged in acknowledgment.

I waved him on. "All right, pumpernickel. Come on, six more to go."

* * *

YEAH, we only made it to four-three, and even then it was a miracle we hadn't keeled over.

"You look like you could use a break." How the hell I managed to get that out in one sentence, I had no idea. I was wheezing. He was wheezing. When the hell was the last time I'd breathed like that? Never?

Kulti was soaked in sweat, and on top of that, his face was a little pale. "I'm fine."

Fine? He looked like he wanted to puke. I'd also noticed that his right quad was pulsing. Why I noticed that, why I'd even looked down there, I had no idea. But I wasn't going to think about it either.

"Positive?" I stuck my tongue as far out of my mouth as I could and took a deep breath to calm down. Ugly, but it worked, and my lungs thanked me for it.

He rolled his eyes but kept struggling to catch his breath. Jeez. Were we really playing that roughly? "Unless... you want to."

I did. I did want to. I had no idea how I was going to push a lawnmower even if it was self-propelled. This was too much, and I'd been stupid for putting myself through it. But fuck if I was going to admit it. "I do if you do."

His cheeks were puffing full and empty, reminding me of a frog. "You're... losing. I don't care."

I was losing and that sucked, but later on, I could pat myself on the back for hanging in there as long as I had. So I shrugged at him.

He lifted his eyebrows in return but didn't agree to anything.

"You choose." *Please say yes. Please say yes.*

Kulti took a deep inhale through his nose. "You look like you're about to pass out," he noted.

Asshole.

I was losing and, apparently, I looked like I was going to pass out. Please, compliment me more.

I hoped his knee was sore later.

"I don't think you should overdo it either." I smiled, biting back my words. "Since you haven't played forever and all."

His started chewing on the inside of his cheek from the way his facial muscles moved.

It's the little victories in life that really mattered. Sticking my tongue out once again and sucking in another ragged breath, I calmed down a little more. My head was gently throbbing from how exerted I was, and I reached up to rub at my temples.

The German slowly hunched over until his palms rested just above his knees and took deep breaths. His eyes were on the grass before slowly moving them up. His shirt was plastered to his shoulders and his biceps, his hair matted down to his scalp.

Neither one of us said anything for a while.

Squeezing my eyes closed, I bent over to do a quick stretch

of my hamstrings, then my quads and finally my calves. When I straightened, I shook out my shoulders and watched as my coach straightened up and began to stretch. All those long, lean muscles...

I cleared my throat and looked at the sky. No need to make this awkward or give him a reason to rub his stupid win in my face. Would he do it? Yeah, he would. It was time for me to get the hell out of there and feed the goblin in my stomach.

"Well I'm leaving now. I'll see you tomorrow."

I had just turned around and started to make my way off the field when he piped up. "You're a good loser, Casillas!"

I started to shake my head as I walked off...

I kept shaking my head, even as I realized that he'd used my last name again.

* * *

"SOMEONE FINALLY GOT LAID."

I scrunched my face up and looked around. "Who? Phyllis?"

"Sal, that's disgusting." Harlow shuddered. "No. You know who I'm talking about," she said with that look that said 'you know who I'm talking about.'

"Heh." I crossed my eyes at her and zeroed in on the overly aggressive bratwurst walking around the field, helping set up equipment with the rest of the staff. This was normal, except for the fact that he *was* freaking sort of smiling. It was as much of one as a man who had more in common with a robot was capable of, I guess.

Still, the smile went straight to my gut.

"Look at him. He looks happy. It's weird and wrong, isn't it?" she muttered under her breath.

It was weird and slightly wrong.

Tipping my head to the side, I kept rolling my socks up my shins and watched him for a second longer. The smile didn't last long, and there was something else different about his face, his entire demeanor. He looked like a smug son of a bitch, the same smug son of a bitch that used to dominate the field.

Oh God. He was back. My gut said that he might have gotten laid, though he didn't strike me as the type that sex would have made that big of a difference in him, but it was beyond that.

Those greenish-hazel eyes looked around the field as he shoved a big yellow obstacle into place, and he caught me looking at him. His eyelids lowered and one corner of his mouth pulled up into a smile that was one fourth the size of a normal one. It morphed into a smirk a second later.

I knew what he was thinking: loser.

That smirk said it all, though. I was right. Maybe he'd gotten laid, and I didn't really like the way that thought made my ears feel strange, but I knew why he'd been smiling.

Because maybe he'd kicked my ass the day before.

But the truth was, at least the version of the truth I wanted to accept, he'd finally played soccer for the first time in years.

And you know what? As much as I hated the fact that he'd won, I had to snicker to myself. *You're welcome, pumpernickel.*

Damn that was annoying. *He* was annoying.

"Pssh. He probably stayed up doing inventory on his trophies last night." I laughed.

Harlow snickered and laughed.

Waggling my eyebrows, I elbowed her in the side and gestured toward where the mini-bands were located for stretching. Jeez Louise, I was sore. I probably looked like a lumbering bear getting to my feet. Busy adjusting my bun and headband so my bangs wouldn't get into my face, I barely happened to look up just as I was passing by Gardner, Kulti and Phyllis, the fitness coach.

"Morning," I greeted them.

"Good morning," Gardner replied.

Phyllis said something that was probably "good morning."

The German grunted, "morning." This stupid expression crossed his eyes, and I pretended to ignore him as I kept on walking. Well it was more of a limp than a walk.

My limp only got more pronounced after the first half an hour of practice. It got so bad that I started daydreaming about actually taking an ice bath. I mean, who dreams about an ice bath?

The cherry topping on my sundae of pain happened when I jogged by Kulti. He shouted after me, "Are you planning on running any faster today, Casillas?"

It took everything inside of me not to flip him off with both my middle fingers.

Practice wasn't the best. I was sore all over; my hamstrings were too tight, my shoulders were a little sore, and I was tired. Yesterday had been too much. So yeah, I dragged ass. It didn't help that everyone pointed it out. Two hours felt like ten and by the time the equipment was put away, I was beyond struggling. But I'd accomplished what I had set out to do, hadn't I? I'd gotten Scrooge to sort of smile and he hadn't talked a whole bunch of shit to me.

I might have lost our one-on-one, but I'd won the real battle.

I shouldn't have been surprised when I heard a snicker. "You seemed to be struggling today."

Slowly pushing up to my feet from the crouching position I was in, I instantly rolled my eyes at Kulti's question. He stood a few feet away, having pushed one of the heavy metal obstacles off to the side of the field.

"Oh, I'm perfect. How are you feeling?"

His mouth went into a straight line that said exactly how full of shit he thought I was. "Wonderful."

So full of shit. "Oh yeah? I thought I saw you favoring your left leg a little bit, but I guess not."

As if bringing it up made it hurt more, his leg jerked at the same time his eyes narrowed. Voice flat and dry, he said, "My leg is fine," but he still had that funny look in his eye. As if he was only barely frustrated with his knee hurting—or in his case 'not hurting.'

I purposely glanced at his knee and said, "huh" before looking right back at his face.

Tipping my chin up, I stared him right in the eye. He seriously had the most intense face I had ever, and probably would ever, see. His gaze was unflinching and solid. If someone could have light sabers in their eyes, it would be him. He had the demanding stare that boxers and fighters seemed to perfect when they were face to face with their opponent during weigh-ins.

Wait a second. Why was he looking at me like I was his enemy?

For one brief second, the idea bothered me. Later on, I'd wonder if I was just so subconsciously bored that having Kulti look at me like I was a real opponent was exciting. But then... I'd take it.

I smiled at him, *no*, smirked at him. I was pleased with myself.

His nostrils flared in response, and he just kept right on staring, head held high, neck elongated. He was such a proud asshole.

And as much as I would have enjoyed standing there, staring at him, I knew how important it was for me to do something about my body pain. I let my smile grow bigger and then took a few steps backward. "I'll see you later, Coach." Two more steps backward, I eyed his leg. "Keep off your leg."

It wasn't like he needed me to tell him what to do. Ha. I bet that was irritating.

Sure enough, he was a master at being just as equally irritating. "Make sure you ice down. I don't need you being useless again next practice."

I ran my tongue over my teeth and nodded. "You got it."

* * *

THE NEXT DAY his limp was worse. Despite the ice bath I'd taken, which should be said even if you've taken one a hundred times before, it never stops sucking a massive amount of donkey nuts; I was still in pain everywhere.

And when Kulti spotted my bowlegged walking, just as I noticed how he kept taking weight off his left leg, we each just gave each other dirty looks.

# 13

"Are we going to win or are we going to *win?*" Grace, the Pipers' captain, belted out at the top of her lungs.

The energy in our circle was tangible—more than tangible. It went straight into my bones, into the very center of me. In each of us there was anticipation, joy, eagerness and even a little violence that made up the wattage coming out of our group.

On the evening of our first game of the regular season, there was blood in the air.

Months of practice and years of experience, had led each member of the Pipers to this point. We wanted to win and needed to win. The first game was always so instrumental to how each team would treat the rest of the season.

I loved this. It was the endless possibilities, the opportunities and the ability to start all over again, regardless of how our last season went. It was my favorite. Knowing that my parents were there, Marc, Simon and a few other friends that had been along the long path with me, only pumped me up that much more. This wasn't just about me, this was about all of them. My parents who had worked so hard to put me through youth leagues, teams, clubs, camp after camp, youth national teams, college, the WPL. Marc and Simon had been with me since I was a little kid tagging along with Eric, who they loved to bully and teach horrible habits to—like elbowing and tripping. They'd played with me almost as much as Eric had.

I was hungry for a win, for all them.

This moment in time was for all of my teammates. It was love. It was perfect.

From the sound of everyone belting out a "*We're gonna win!!!*" I wasn't the only one who felt so deeply about it.

Our arms linked over and around each other, every single female who had made it to this moment, yelled "PIPERS" at the top of their lungs.

We were off.

* * *

"IT WAS A CLOSE GAME—"

That was an understatement. We barely managed to squeak by with a win.

"—but we did it, ladies. Don't take this for granted—"

Standing together, sweaty and worn out, I bumped arms with Genevieve, a younger player standing next to me, who'd scored the winning goal in the last five minutes of the game. She shot me a huge excited smile that I returned wholeheartedly.

A heavy damp arm wrapped around my neck, in what would have been considered a chokehold, if it had been anyone other than Harlow. It was just the way she hugged me. Her mouth pressed up against my temple, as she spoke low and excited. "We fucking did it, Sally."

I wrapped my own arm around the middle of her back and squeezed tight, nodding up at her with a grin on my face. "Of course we did," I whispered back, excitement still thrumming through my veins.

Gardner continued his spiel about setting a standard for the rest of the season and bringing up a few things we needed to work on. Finally after a few minutes, he held up his hand for all of us to try and reach for, and he said, "I'm going out tonight. Who's coming?"

I wasn't. My family was in town, and I usually celebrated with them and the rest of the gang. I'd just finished burning hundreds and hundreds of calories playing the entire game; I could fit in a reasonable Mexican meal with a gallon of water all to myself. Jenny was coming with us, like she usually did, on season openers.

A few staff members cheered and claimed that they'd go out with him.

I finished changing in the locker room and met up with Jenny outside, so that we could go find my family. Gardner and his small group were ahead of us, making their way out to the parking lot too. I couldn't help but notice that Kulti wasn't with them.

As we crossed the double doors, I spotted a black Audi idling by the curb.

Then I spotted the crowd of people wearing various versions of Reiner Kulti uniforms, close by it. I watched as long as I could, curious to see whether the German would make his way out or not. By the time I got in my car and pulled out of the spot, nothing had changed. I'd spotted Gardner's truck zipping out of the lot ahead of me.

But still, the black Audi hadn't moved and neither had the people hovering by it.

* * *

A FEW DAYS later I heard, "Twenty-three!" and wanted to bang my head on an imaginary door.

How many times had my number been yelled in the last hour and a half? My best guess was somewhere between a dozen and twenty. Anything more than two, was too many.

I wanted to punch him in the dick. Any guilt I felt for how he hadn't played in two years, or how the poor guy wasn't able to walk to his car after a game without being surrounded by people, didn't matter at all at that point. Not even a little bit.

*Patience, Sal. Patience.*

I walked quickly over to where he was and tipped my head back, ignoring the fact that three weeks ago, I hadn't been able to talk to him in a complete sentence. "Yes?"

"Don't you have some drills to do?"

"No." I hiked my thumb back. Twenty seconds had possibly passed since I'd finished them and when he'd called my number. "I'm waiting so I can start stretching."

Those lazy eyes did that lizard blink. Keeping his gaze on mine for what seemed like a minute straight, he finally lowered his voice and asked, "Do you want to play today?"

Uhh.

I felt like I had stadium spotlights and a dozen cameras on me. I had to fight the urge to look around and make sure I wasn't getting pranked. My quad gave a pulse of nervous anticipation. "I can't?" I said it like it was a question, taking in the confused look in his eyes. "You almost killed me the other day. Maybe this weekend?"

He only missed a single beat. "Fine." Was that disappointment in his eyes?

Oh hell. I think it was.

I watched his face while I suggested, "I have some friends that play recreational softball. They're all pretty good and sometimes I play with them. They're having a game tonight. We could go."

He blinked at me.

"My contract says I can't play any type of regulation soccer on a team, but it doesn't say anything about any other sport," I explained.

He seemed to mull the thought over for a minute, and I was pretty convinced that he was going to tell me to screw off, but out of the blue he nodded. "Fine. Text me the address and the time."

Was this for real? "I don't have your phone number," I kind of croaked out.

"Give me yours." He had his phone out of his pocket a split second later, and I rattled off my number. Another long moment later, he nodded. "Now you have it."

It didn't hit me until much later what exactly he said and what it implied.

I had Reiner Kulti's phone number, for one.

And I was going to text him—two.

But three seemed to be the one that really snuck into my chest cavity; he had asked me if I wanted to play with him.

He had asked me to play. With him.

Instead, he was going to play softball with me and a few of my friends. Huh.

* * *

**Seven P.M. at Hershey Park. I'll wait for you by the bathrooms near the parking lot.**

I checked my phone one more time to make sure that the message really had gone through. Then I checked it again to make sure that I hadn't missed a text in response. I hadn't.

With my bat, glove and bottle of water in one hand and armpit, I fidgeted with my headband with the other. I'd accidentally grabbed a thick one from my glove box, which fit over my ears, and those made me feel a little claustrophobic. I messed with it some more as I looked around the nearly full parking lot. It was only five minutes before seven, and Kulti still hadn't shown up.

It then hit me again with the same strength it had the first time, Kulti was coming to play softball, only after he'd asked if I wanted to play soccer with him. Why hadn't he asked anyone else to play with him?

Well I was probably the most aggressive forward on the team, so we had that in common. Harlow didn't count because... she was a defender, right? I was the fastest. Without really tooting my own horn, it was a fact. So really, who else would he play against? My style was the closest to his, and he'd enjoyed beating me the first time.

So there.

No big deal.

I was an obvious choice.

Plus, maybe he had asked someone else? I doubted it, but you never knew.

Possibly another minute ticked by, and I looked around the lot again, anxiously. I was nervous. Why was I nervous?

For Kulti's sake I'd already decided not to tell anyone who he was. I wasn't positive how they would all react, especially Marc and Simon, or even if they'd let him play, and I didn't want him feeling under a microscope from the start. I was going to tell them he was my friend who had recently moved to Houston.

That wasn't *really* a stretch, I figured.

The headlights of a car illuminated my body for a split second, before the car pulling into the lot turned and then finally took a spot one row down. It was the same nondescript plain black sedan that wouldn't have called my attention, even with the Audi emblem on it.

Of course he'd be in an Audi.

I smirked to myself as a long body folded out of the vehicle's back passenger door, slamming it shut before heading to the back and grabbing a bag from the recently opened trunk. His tall lean body seemed even more imposing without his team T-shirt or polo. The graceful lines of muscle that lined his shoulders and arms for the first time since he quit playing soccer full-time were delineated perfectly in the shadow of the setting sun. What I really caught a good eyeful of though, was the wide earband he had on that looked similar to mine, matting down his short hair and making him look like a different person. Not like himself at all, unless you really knew who you were looking at. The length of his hair on top of his larger frame and facial hair was an excellent disguise.

Poop. Poop, poop, thisisyourcoachstupid, poop.

He gave me what could have been considered a smile, if you closed your eyes and looked sideways, the minute he spotted me standing there, which was almost immediately.

"Hi," I greeted him.

That sort of smile grew maybe a millimeter. He grunted his greeting, looking around at the three fields that seemed to form a U-shape. Two of them were already full, but the one that my friends usually played on was mostly empty, with only a few people gathered.

"Come on, before we get stuck on a shitty—" I winced at myself. Was I allowed to cuss in front of him even though we weren't on Pipers hours? "—crappy team."

He tipped his head down in a lazy nod and followed after me as I led him around the outskirts of the field. "They're all really nice," I told him, not that he'd care, "but I think we should keep your identity a secret."

Kulti shrugged but didn't say a word as we approached what I quickly counted to be seventeen people. Damn it. Recognizing more than half of the people hanging around, I waved at the ones I knew and headed toward Marc and Simon, who had their backs turned to me. As soon as I was close enough, I kicked each one in the ass with the side of my foot. "Hey guys."

Marc turned around first, frowning at getting kicked until he realized I'd been the one to do it. "You shit, you could have told me you were coming."

I rolled my eyes and shrugged. "Last-minute decision. Live with it."

Roughly, the man I worked with every day shoved me toward Simon, who gave me a big grin before pulling me into a full frontal hug that made it seem like it'd been weeks instead of days since we'd seen each other. "Glad you came, Salmonella. We need you."

"I told her weeks ago that she should come out, but someone's too good for us regular folks," Marc added just to be a pain.

"You, shut up. I'm here and I brought reinforcements." I finally waved at Kulti, who had stopped a few feet behind me and to the right. "My friend and I wanted to play, so I figured I'd come down and see if you had spots for us."

Marc and Simon looked over and around me to view a reconstructed version of Kulti. Neither one of them said anything for so long, that I started to think they recognized him.

It was Marc who raised an eyebrow, mouthing 'friend?' And Simon, who didn't have a filter in his big trap, asked, "You finally got a new boyfriend?"

"*Friend*," I insisted. I looked at Kulti for some clue as to what I was supposed to call him, but he didn't catch on to the question in my voice. "...Rey? This is Marc and Simon. Marc and Simon, this is... Rey." Saying his name out loud, like we were actually friends, was strange. It was like writing with my left hand. I almost felt like I'd get in trouble for saying it out loud, but I didn't let myself think about it too much.

The two men I'd grown up playing with, didn't miss a beat.

They were obnoxious, but they weren't impolite. Each one made sure to shake Kulti's hand before settling back into place. Simon didn't look twice at him, but I noticed Marc staring at him a little too intently.

Shit.

I'd tell him the truth later, once I was sure he wouldn't lose his shit and start crying. Would he be pissed? Of course but it was either him being mad at me or the possibility he'd fall to the ground and start kissing Kulti's feet.

"So, you have room? I think I counted seventeen people, right?" I asked, rocking back on my heels and swinging my stuff with my other hand, keeping a steady eye on Marc.

Simon made a noise as he looked behind at the people who had gathered. "I'll see if somebody wants to sit this game out and play the next one instead."

"All right, if not then I'll sit it out and see if someone will swap with me next game," I offered, still watching the dark-haired man I'd grown up with.

Simon, a tallish blond, rolled his eyes and scowled. "Right. You know you can ask half of these assholes if they'll let you play and they'll fight over who will do it."

I snorted and let him head toward the group, leaving me with Kulti and Marc. Marc was looking at Kulti like he was trying to undress him. Lines furrowed his forehead and a second later, he slanted his gaze over in my direction and the confusion deepened.

"Hey, Sal?" he asked slowly, cocking his head to the side.

Kulti was busy looking around, aloof. Thankfully.

I shot Marc a look that clearly said *shut up*. "Later."

"Come here," he insisted in a low voice, eyes narrowed just a bit more.

Fortunately, Simon chose that instant to call everyone together to choose teams so I turned away. With my boss-slash-friend on one side, and one ex-professional soccer player on the other, we made our way toward Simon.

But Marc wouldn't leave me alone. Knocking his fist against mine as we walked, he leaned toward me. "Sal, is that—"

"No."

"Holy—"

"Be quiet about it at least, big mouth," I hissed under my breath so that Kulti wouldn't hear me.

Marc stopped walking. His normally tan face went white. "Are you shitting me?"

"No."

I kept on going. If I didn't pay attention to him, then I couldn't confirm anything.

They figured out who were going to be the team captains by a process of guessing numbers. The winners were one man I'd played with a few times before, whose name I thought was Carlos, and the other I didn't know. After an intense game of paper-rock-scissors, Carlos got to pick first. He immediately looked over and waved me forward. "I'll take Sal first."

"What a suck-up," Simon said, as I walked by him, an affectionate smile on his face. "I'm Sal and I play professional soccer. Look at me," he added in a high-pitched girly voice right before kicking me in the butt.

The other captain called Simon's name, and I swatted his leg away with a laugh.

Each person was chosen until the only people left were Kulti, a girl I'd played with before and another guy. Marc had been picked for Carlos' team too, and I could see him making faces, tipping his head over in Kulti's direction not very subtly. Finally understanding what was going on, Carlos pointed at the ex-star. I would forever hold onto the fact that he'd gotten chosen almost last for what had to be the first time in his life, and said "I'll take him."

I couldn't help but snicker to myself. When I caught Marc's

eye, he slid me a sneaky evil grin that had lost its surprised pallor. For all I knew, Kulti could suck just as much at softball as my brother did, so I really wasn't sure what Marc was excited about. This could go horribly.

As we circled together once the other girl had been chosen, gear was grabbed and we got ready to play. I looked at Kulti and said in a low voice, "I should have asked you before, but do you know how to play?"

From the expression on his face, you'd think I asked him if he knew what a yellow card was. Sheesh.

I held up my hands in a peace offering. "Just asking." There was one more thing, in case he happened to be really good with a bat and a glove. "Look, this is for fun, all right? I don't think they can handle your superhuman skills, so tone it down a little. Yes?"

His pleased little baby grin said everything, and he finally nodded once in acceptance. "Fine. We're going to win anyway."

"Duh." Like anything else was even a possibility. I put my hand up and shoved his shoulder before I even realized what I was doing, and I froze. Then I snatched it back and frowned. "Ahh, sorry."

Anddd this was awkward.

I don't know what I was expecting him to do, but flashing a grin at me so wide I swear my heart stopped, wasn't it. I'd seen him win championships on television before, of course he'd been smiling then but... what just came across his face so abruptly was beyond unexpected.

All I did was stare dumbly back at him for a moment, long enough to look like a complete idiot, before I forced myself to remember *poop,* and I grinned back at him.

"Sal! We don't have all day, get your ass over here!" Simon called from somewhere behind me.

I met Kulti's eyes once more, flashed him a smile like the one that had since melted from his face and made my way over to the rest of the group. Marc was looking back and forth between my coach's headband and mine, the expression on his face smooth and curious. It wasn't until he swallowed what looked like a grapefruit that I could tell he was dying on the inside, and when his eyes shot over to me, it was confirmed.

"I like to play shortstop," Carlos, the team captain for the game, announced.

A couple other men spoke up and announced the positions they thought they were good at. This had me rolling my eyes because everyone thought they were good at the popular positions. It happened every single time. All you had to do was nod and smile and eventually things worked out fine. I wasn't impatient, and I didn't mind playing the positions no one else liked.

Carlos looked at the four of us: Marc, Kulti, another man I didn't know and me. "You guys fine with playing outfield and second?"

I was only a little surprised when Kulti didn't pipe up and voice his opinion, but when it was silently and unanimously agreed that we'd play whatever, those green-brown eyes met mine, and a smirk covered the lower half of his face.

Two seconds later, we were positioned across the field. I was in the outfield and so was he.

Approximately ten minutes later, Simon was screaming off the sidelines, "This is horse shit!" after I'd caught the third out, following Kulti's first catch, and a second one that he'd sent flying to third base with time to spare. Who would have known he'd have an arm on him?

We switched to batting and not much changed. Kulti knocked the ball close to the fence to make it to third base on one run. I hit the ball far enough, allowing the player on first base to cross home. I ran fast enough and made it to second.

Thirty-five minutes after that, the other team captain was practically foaming at the mouth, yelling at our team captain about how they needed to pick different players for the next game. "They," and he pointed at Kulti and me, who had surprisingly, or maybe not so surprisingly, played like we'd been teammates for years, "can't be on the same team together!"

So maybe it was a little unfair.

A little.

I mean, this was softball and we were soccer players. I'd been a tomboy most of my life, and I happened to be good at most sports. I'd never been a great student, I always chose practicing over studying, but you couldn't have it all unless you were Jenny.

It just so happened that Kulti was good at catching and throwing a ball. Whatever.

I never played all-out during 'fun' games of any type; first, I couldn't afford to get hurt and second, I didn't like to dominate the games when I was fully aware that the people who played did it to unwind. They didn't need my competitive butt ruining it. Even Kulti hadn't run as fast as we both knew he was capable of, but at fifty percent, he was still leaps and bounds better than the average man. He ran slower, held back and I noticed that he really did try to give other people a chance.

But the point was he didn't like to lose. I didn't like to lose. So if people weren't taking advantage of the opportunities opened up to them, well, one of us was going to do something about it. And for some reason, I was fully aware of where he was on the field constantly. He was catching balls and throwing them the entire game.

In the end, we won nine to zero.

Finally deciding to move *Rey* to the other team, I met those crazy eyes from our positions on opposite sides of the field. He didn't have to say it and neither did I. This was going to be our rematch. Round two. This might have been a completely different game, but in reality this was going to be me versus him.

That fiery burn I got in my chest during games flared inside of me as we each locked gazes, and I shot him my own *bring it* smirk.

Was he going to make me eat dirt? Hopefully not.

* * *

"Son of a bitch," I muttered to myself when Simon's wristwatch beeped with the time.

Marc trotted up next to me, his face flushed and shocked. "Did we lose?"

I nodded slowly, halfway in a stupor. "Yes."

"How?" he asked. We never lost, especially not when he and I were on a team together.

"It was him," I answered. There was no need to point. We both knew who I was referring to.

We both just looked at each other and silently went off to cower in our disappointment. I grabbed my bat, tucked my glove under my arm and stretched. Halfway through a body settled onto the ground next to me, and I knew it was Kulti.

Asshole.

When he didn't say anything, I felt my frustration race up. When I didn't find it in me to say anything either, my anger just ticked up a little higher. Eventually he looked over and kept his expression blank. "A coach of mine used to say that no one likes a sore loser."

My eyebrows went into a straight line. "I find it hard to believe that you listened to him."

His brown eyebrows went up and a hint of an angelic, serene look took over his features. "I didn't. I'm only telling you what I have been told, Taquito."

What a smart-ass.

* * *

We were at the airport in Seattle on the way back to Houston, following our second game a few days later, when I spotted the crowd surrounding our sensation of a coach.

Not again.

I hadn't said anything about the crowd around the Audi after the first game, and I hadn't heard anyone else say anything about it either. To be honest, I hadn't given it much thought. Since then, I'd played softball with the German and even joked around with him for a little bit, at least as much as his dry humor was capable of.

On the other hand, nothing had changed while we were on Pipers time. He still ripped me a new one each chance he had. I hadn't given him another ride home, either. The black Audi was always there after practice, its tint so dark I'd bet a dollar it was illegal.

Everything seemed to run normally, not bringing any unwanted attention to this new buddy I had. No one had a clue, with the exception of Marc, who wasn't speaking to me unless he had to because I'd brought Kulti to softball and hadn't warned him. He'd get over it eventually.

Besides that, everything was fine. The Pipers played another game and won, and now we were heading home. I'd gotten a ride in the last van to the leave the hotel along with Jenny, my hotel-room buddy.

The chunk of the team that had arrived before or with the German, was scattered throughout the gate. Several airport security stood close by, while the people who recognized Kulti stood in front of him, staring. Oblivious to his audience or simply settling for pretending they weren't there, Kulti was looking down at his iPad like he didn't have people treating him as if he was in a fishbowl.

Why wasn't he in the colonel's lounge, or whatever it was called, like he'd been on the flight over?

Kulti looked up and around. His face was expressionless,

but he caught me watching and something passed between us, something that only my gut understood. He was doing the same thing he had back during the preseason game when that fan had stopped him. So he knew that he was surrounded. He was looking for help.

I could have ignored him. I was well aware of how easy it would be to pretend I hadn't seen him. Damn it.

"Jen, do you have your Uno cards with you?" I really hoped this didn't backfire on me. I wasn't sure my pride could handle it.

Standing right next to me, as she sipped on the Americano she'd purchased on the walk over, she nodded. "Always."

"Are you ready to do your good deed of the day?" I asked her, knowing damn well what her answer would be.

"Sure. What are we doing?"

"We're going to see if Kulti wants to play."

Her almond-shaped eyes didn't even blink once. "We are?"

"Yes."

It took her a second to catch up when I made my way over to the lonely German, but she followed, without an argument. He looked up as I took the open seat on his left, his backpack was on the other seat, and Jenny took the open one on my other side. His eyebrows made a funny line, like he wasn't sure what exactly was going on and was undecided about whether or not it was a good thing.

Jenny passed the deck of cards over to me—sneaky, sneaky, sneaky.

I raised my eyebrows as I moved the cards onto my lap for him to see. It didn't escape me that his crowd of onlookers was watching us curiously, but knew better than to say anything. I kept my attention on Kulti the entire time, watching as his eyes went from the cards to my face and then back to the deck again.

Part of me expected him to say no.

He didn't. He took his iPad and slid it into his backpack,

raising his own thick eyebrows. "I haven't played in a very long time."

Jenny popped her head in from around, smiling wide. "We'll teach you."

I snorted and pushed her face back with my hand on her forehead.

Not fifteen seconds later, the three of us sat on the floor at Sea-Tac, playing Uno with a small group of Kulti fans standing around. It made me feel awkward. I couldn't help but glance up every so often and smile at the people watching us because I didn't know what else to do. But it didn't stop the three of us from trying to beat each other.

And exactly six hours later, when our plane landed in Houston, I had an email from my dad that said: **You're famous.**

There were pictures of Jenny and I sitting with Kulti, laughing our asses off during one of our games. Someone had posted the picture on a fan website. Below the image was an italicized caption: *If one of these lesbos is his girlfriend, I'm gonna kill myself.*

# 14

Exactly one week after the softball game, days after pictures had gone on the internet of Jenny, the bratwurst and I playing Uno at the airport, I had Kulti pull me aside after our cool-down following practice.

We rarely spoke during practice unless it was him calling me a different synonym for slow, or asking me if I was going to finish my passing drills in the next decade. I didn't take it personally and tried not to think about it too much. We'd just played softball. We hadn't gotten married.

*Awkward thought.*

So... whatever. I was learning and growing, and I was busy enough that this weird friendship didn't live at the front of my brain.

"Are you playing again tonight?" Kulti whispered the question when I was close.

I kept my eyes forward, no matter how badly I wanted to look at him. "I was thinking about it." I paused. "Do you want to go?"

"Yes," he answered quickly. "Same time, same place?"

"Yep." I waved at Harlow as she walked by; totally not

missing the raised eyebrow she was giving me. "I'll wait for you in the same spot."

Kulti grunted his agreement.

We both went our own ways, wordlessly.

I couldn't help but think about the fact that he wanted to go play again. He wanted to play softball of all things.

Then it hit me just like it had the first time; Reiner Kulti wanted to play with me. He'd asked. Again.

I was on such a one track mind that I wasn't paying attention as I prepared to leave. My mind was on the fact that I had his phone number—poop—and that I really hoped Marc wouldn't say anything this week either, when a reporter snagged me on the way to my car.

"Casillas! Sal!"

I slowed down and turned. A man not much older than me was sitting off the side under the shade, a tape recorder clearly visible in one hand and a messenger bag over his shoulder. Whatever media showed up was always before practice, no one ever stayed after.

"Hey," I told him.

"I have a few questions for you," he said quickly, rattling off his name before skipping the whole 'if you have time part.' I didn't have time, but I didn't want to be rude.

Instead I said, "Sure. Shoot."

The first two questions were easy, normal. What I thought about analysts saying we had a tough road ahead for the championship, with the inception of two new teams in the WPL? Why would it be a tough road? I enjoyed a struggle. What we were doing to assure we would continue to move up past the regular season? He must have thought I was dumb enough to give away the imaginary tricks we had planned. No one ever wanted to hear that it was hard work, practice and discipline that were the key to winning at anything. Then finally, it happened: "What do you think about the rumors circulating that Reiner Kulti has a drinking problem that's been kept confidential?"

*Again?*

I tried to think about all of my PR training in the past. There could never be any hesitation when journalists asked questions like that. You absolutely couldn't let them see that they'd rattled you. I especially wouldn't since I'd grown *almost* fond of the German bratwurst lately. Well at least I think there was more beyond his crispy exterior. "I think that he's a fantastic coach and that rumors are none of my business."

Fantastic coach? All right. That was stretching the truth a bit, but it was a white lie. At best I'd say he was trying.

"Has he given the impression that he might be drinking excessively?" He snapped out the question quickly.

I allowed myself to blink at him in disbelief. "I'm sorry but you're making me feel really uncomfortable. The only thing he does excessively is push us to better ourselves in any way he can." What I didn't say was that he did it by yelling at us like we were the scum of the earth, but did the method work? It most definitely did. "Look, I like him. I like him a lot as a player and as a coach. He's one of the most decorated athletes in history, and he's a good man." Lie? Not so much. He'd sent my dad a present. How? I wasn't sure, but it didn't matter. A complete prick wouldn't have thought twice about my little dad. "If there's something in his past or if there isn't, I could care less. I know him and respect him now more than ever. To me, that's all that matters."

"So, you're neither confirming nor denying that there might be a chance—"

"Look, you can't be that caliber of player without extreme self-discipline in some form. I've tried to drink a Coke before a game once, and it nearly killed me. I will gladly answer any questions you have about our upcoming games or practices, or just about anything else related to Pipers, but I'm not going to bad-mouth or spread gossip about someone that I value and respect when I don't have a reason to."

Value and respect? Meh... Another stretch of the truth.

He didn't exactly look sure whether to believe me or not, but fortunately, I guess I'd frustrated him enough that he looked back behind me to see another player coming. Hallelujah.

"Thanks for answering my questions," he said, not exactly grateful. But what did he expect? Me to trash talk Kulti?

I'd had people I played with in the past do that to me, and I had sworn to myself a long time ago that I would never be that person. If you don't have anything nice to say, don't say anything at all, right?

* * *

THE GERMAN WAS WAITING for me in the parking lot when I pulled in that night.

Impressive.

Until I realized I hadn't decided whether or not to tell him about Sherlock Junior asking dumb questions after practice. His response could go one way or the other, and I really didn't know him well enough to predict which one.

By the time I grabbed all of my crap, I hadn't made a conscious decision.

A minute later after we'd greeted each other with a, "Hi," and a, "Hello," on the sidewalk, I was still undecided.

But apparently, my brain had chosen for me. We had barely taken three steps forward when I blurted out, "There was another journalist asking about a supposed drinking problem." Well it wasn't so *supposed*. I wasn't going to base his drinking off one experience, but I couldn't forget about it either.

Kulti didn't jerk or react in any outward way. "Who?"

I rattled off the man's name.

"What was his question exactly?" he asked.

Word for word, I repeated what the man had asked. Slowly, making sure to watch Kulti's face, I told him verbatim how I responded. Well, mostly. "I wouldn't violate your trust or your image in any way."

Those green-brown eyes looked into my own, making me think of a rusted lime. "I know you wouldn't."

What? That easy? He knew I wouldn't? Nothing was ever that simple, and his easy acceptance made me feel uncertain. "Okay." I paused. "Good."

He did that European short nod of agreement that consisted of a chin jerk. "Thank you, Sal."

There were two parts of that statement that had me stumbling, mentally at least.

The t-word again. Thank you.

But the most shocking in my book was... the Sal. *Sal.*

Honest to god, I think I said something remarkably close to, "Ermghard." What the hell did that even mean? I had no idea, but it seemed fitting.

In a split second, I got it together and offered him a tremulous smile. "Thank... you." Wait. What was I thanking him for? Stupid, stupid, stupid. "For that," I explained quickly, even though it sounded more like a question than a comment. My face went all warm suddenly at the compliment he'd just paid me.

He'd given me his trust, or at least something close to it.

What do you say after that? I couldn't think of anything intelligent that didn't end up with me smiling like a goofball afterward, so I kept my gaze elsewhere as we approached the field.

"You came back!" Marc greeted us, his eyes immediately flashing toward Kulti, with that deer-caught-in the-headlights look. Or maybe he was constipated, both expressions were strangely similar. He'd finally started willingly speaking to me today, when he asked if I was planning on going to softball that night.

"You know I don't like to lose." With a smile, I eyed Kulti and tipped my head over to Marc. "Marc, Rey. Rey, Marc, again. Just in case you didn't remember."

Extending out his free hand, my brother's friend shook my coach's hand and I swear—I *swear*—I saw Marc eye his palm like he was never going to wash that bad boy again. We were going to need to have a talk, seriously. He was just as bad as my dad.

"Is there room for us?" I asked.

"Yeah, except I'm positive no one is going to agree to let you both be on the same team together." A familiar arm was thrown over my shoulders. "I want to be on his team this time."

I groaned and tried to elbow him in the ribs. "Traitor."

"You ladies ready to play?" Simon called out from where he'd quickly gotten surrounded by multiple people.

To no one's surprise, Kulti and I were chosen for two separate teams, in a way that told me the captains for the week had planned it, before we arrived. A look passed between the two of us that was a mix of a smirk and a grin. Splitting up into our respective teams—my team was playing defense and I'd been assigned second base—I suddenly felt like we were two boxers circling each other, or two rams about to go head to head.

This was going to be fun.

* * *

"TAG HIM! TAG HIM!" someone yelled.

It was the last inning, with only one out to go. I was playing second base, and a ball had been hit straight at first base. The player on first was barreling toward me as the first baseman ran up behind him.

One of my legs was braced behind me, the other one out in

front so I could tag the runner out, if the first baseman didn't get him first. I should have recognized the look on the guy's face —pure determination. I was just a girl in front of someone insistent on not getting out. Muscles contracted, my hand was out to catch the ball in case first baseman decided at the last minute to throw it.

But he didn't.

A second later the runner was on me, one foot stomping down on mine, in an attempt to make it to second. What did I do? I got the hell out of the way, even though it was too late to avoid the heavy-ass shoe on my instep.

Holy freaking *shitttt*.

A giant puff of air escaped my mouth, and pain flared up through my foot and shin. It was one thing to get stepped on and another to have an elephant-sized foot try and trample me.

"Out! He's out!"

"Are you blind? He made it!"

Hands gripping my foot over my shoe, I looked up at the sky and breathed through the pain while I tried to convince myself that I was fine. Some of the players were arguing about the call, but I stood off to the side cradling my freaking foot.

"Are you going to live?"

Breathing out through my nose, I looked just slightly down to see Kulti standing in front of me, his thinner bottom lip pulled into a straight line. "I'll be fine." Yeah, that didn't sound convincing at all.

From the shape his eyebrows took, he didn't believe it either. "Put your foot down."

"In a minute."

"Put it down."

I should and I knew it, but I didn't want to.

"Now, Sal."

I gave him a look that said just how much I disliked it when he got bossy and set my foot down anyway, gingerly, gingerly, gingerly—

I groaned, grunted and whimpered just a little at the same time.

"You're done," he ordered.

Yeah, we were. I needed to ice myself because there was no way in hell it wasn't going to bruise spectacularly. Marc and Simon were two of the people arguing about the outcome of the game, those assholes not giving a crap that I'd gotten practically crushed.

"Losers," I called out. Sure enough, they both looked up. Ha. "I'm leaving now. I'll call you later."

They nodded, with only Marc adding, "Are you all right?"

I gave him a thumbs-up.

With a quick wave at the people I did know, the ones who hadn't tried to hurt me, I walk-slash-limped around the outskirts of the field, following two steps behind a slow-paced Kulti. He didn't stop or turn around to make sure I was following after him; he just kept heading in the direction of the lot. As we got closer, he jogged toward his car. In the time it took me to walk the rest of the way toward the bathrooms where I'd found him, he had already opened the trunk of the Audi and set a small blue cooler on the lip of the bumper. He pulled two small white things out and closed it again.

With a large hand, he pointed at the bench right off the curb. "Sit there."

I squinted to see what he was holding, as I sat dutifully.

"Shoe off." He continued to order me around and I didn't fight him on it, realizing he had two ice packs stacked together in one hand.

Toeing my tennis shoe off, I pulled my foot up to rest the heel on the edge of the bench. Kulti handed me one of the packs before sitting down next to me. He didn't have to tell me what to do; I rolled my sock down until it just covered my toes and placed the still very cold cloth material on what was already inflamed pink skin.

Kulti folded his body so that his leg was partially propped up on the corner of the seat and placed the other pack on top of his knee.

We were sitting on a bench nearly side by side, with icepacks.

I burst out laughing.

I laughed so hard my stomach started cramping and my eyes got all watery and overwhelmed, and I couldn't stop.

The German raised an eyebrow. "What is it?"

"Look at us," I laughed even harder, unable to catch my breath. "We're sitting here icing ourselves. Jesus Christ."

A small smile cracked his normally stern face as he looked at my foot and then at himself.

"And why do you have icepacks in your car anyway?"

His small smile eroded into an even larger one, which eventually cracked into a low chuckle that lightened his face in a way that had me admiring just how handsome something so insignificant could make him. "If I want to walk tomorrow, I need to ice immediately." There was a brief pause before he added, "If you tell anyone—"

"You'll ruin me, I know. I got it." I grinned. "If you tell anyone about this, I'll kill you, so I guess we're even, right?"

His expression fell into a flat one. "I won't say a word."

I lifted up a shoulder.

He must have thought I didn't believe him because he kept going. "If you get kicked off the team, I wouldn't have anyone else to play with."

My little heart wrapped up that comment in cling wrap to preserve it forever. "What about Gardner?" I offered.

He shot me a look. "Once was enough."

What? "You played with him?"

"Two days after you."

"It couldn't have been that bad." Gardner had played college soccer.

Kulti sat back against the old wooden bench. "Have you ever played with people that were significantly worse than you?"

That was an incredibly rude way of putting it, but I nodded.

"Picture it, and then imagine that they thought they were a much better player," he explained.

Ooh. I grimaced and he nodded.

I fought the question that had been living in my brain since that first time he asked me to play and then decided, why not? What if I never got this chance again? "I wondered why you asked me and not anyone else."

He sat back against the bench and adjusted the ice-pack on his knee, his attention steady, and his words careful. "You play how I like. You don't hold back."

"Didn't you tell me yesterday that I think too much when I have the ball?"

His biceps flexed against the back of the seat. "Yes. You play better when you follow your instincts and not your head."

Was that a compliment? I thought it might be.

"What about Grace, though? I thought you two were friends."

Reiner Kulti gave me a look. Yes, I was nosey and no, I wouldn't apologize for it. "Her husband and I have known each other for a long time. He was a trainer in Chicago when I played there. She and I aren't on speaking terms anymore. Even if we were, I would not have asked."

Because of what he'd said to the girls that day? Maybe that question was pushing it, so I dropped it and just nodded in understanding.

The part-time model, who once upon a time appeared half-naked in underwear ads, blinked his long eyelashes at me. "I owe you my gratitude. I never thanked you for what you did that night at the hotel. Most people would have handled the situation differently. I—" his eyes moved from one of mine to the other, gauging me, "—appreciate it. Greatly."

"You're welcome," I said, though now that we were on the topic I wanted to ask why he'd gotten drunk in such a public place. It was probably a little too soon, so I kept my mouth shut. Wiggling my toes, I sat back against the bench, his hand brushing my shoulder and sighed. "And thank you for the ice pack. Hopefully tomorrow I can walk."

His index finger nudged me. "You will."

What he wasn't saying was that I had to. How the hell else would I explain that I'd taken a hoof to the instep? Accidentally? That definitely wasn't believable.

That didn't mean I wanted to have him telling me what to do all the time. "Are you going to boss me around even when we're not on the field?"

He didn't even blink before he answered. "Yes."

# 15

The next day almost immediately after warming up, the German who had shared his ice pack the day before, sidled up next to me discreetly. With his arms crossed over his chest as he prepared himself to rip us new assholes, he asked in a voice so low only I could hear, "Your foot?"

I crouched down and retied my shoes. "It's bruised."

Kulti looked unimpressed when I glanced up, like I was a total baby for succumbing to something like bruising. "I have oil that will make it go away faster," he mumbled his reply. "Find me after practice."

I almost choked on my saliva. No joke. Somehow by the grace of God, I managed to get out, "Okay."

But of course nothing with him was easy. If playing softball outside of practice hours was our dirty little secret, then we were going to keep it that way. "Deal with it until then."

Ding, ding, ding. There was the man I knew and... respected?

Meh. Something like that.

"I will."

He nodded. "I know."

I'd been playing for myself for so long because I loved it, that it took a moment to recognize the flare of pleasure I got from someone else believing in me. Like a flash flood, his words from yesterday filled my veins and had me forgetting about the pain in my foot. He might not ever say it to my face, but the fact was Reiner Kulti had sort of worried about me.

How about that.

* * *

LIKE MOST INJURIES, the worst didn't come until two days later.

Within eighteen hours, what had started as a pinkish mark had reddened to a rusty color. After forty-eight hours, the pain had peaked. At least I hoped it had peaked. I could put pressure on my heel and the outside of my foot, but if I tried to walk flat-footed... fuck me. I wasn't a complete sucker. I handled pain and played around it all right most of the time. While I definitely wasn't a masochist, I'd adapted that 'mind over matter' mentality years ago. If you didn't think you were sick, you weren't sick.

So I had iced the crap out of my foot every chance I had after practice and even during work. I applied the arnica oil that Kulti had handed me like it was steroids after practice, all sneaky-like, and kept off it as much as possible.

And every single time that flash of pain shot up my shin, I cursed the day that little fucker at our rec game was born. I hoped he fell face first into a pile of fire ants. There, I said it, and I had no regrets.

When our next match came, before heading to the stadium I drank some turmeric tea and popped two painkillers in the car. I hoped to make it through the next few hours without getting caught. It bothered me so much that I didn't even care that we were playing New York, when usually I'd be restless beforehand, almost dreading it.

Unfortunately, my sneakiness only lasted until I was in the dressing room. I was wrapping my injury in some athletic tape before putting on socks that went with our team uniform. Harlow leaned over and 'oooohed.' "What in the hell happened to your foot?" She made another noise. "You break something?"

I rubbed some more oil on top of it before beginning to wrap the arch and instep as comfortably tight as possible. "It feels like it, Har."

"I got some extra strength Tylenol in my bag if you want," she offered.

"I took some right before I left home, but I might take you up on it during halftime."

"You got it, Sally. Grab 'em if you need them." The defender smacked me on the back of the shoulder. "Those girls give you a hard time today, you let me know and I'll take care of them for you," she winked before walking away.

The New York players. Ugh. I wasn't even going to worry about them.

I finished wrapping my foot while muttering curses under my breath, and rolled up my sock before anyone else noticed what I'd done and why. Usually we all complained about the small amount of healthcare professionals we had access to, unless you were on the national team, but in this case, it worked out for the best. A trainer would probably make the coaches sit me out if they saw the disco-like colors going on under my shoe.

Unfortunately there weren't any secrets on our team, at least not between me, Har and Jen. Within ten minutes, I had Jenny hanging over my back. "What happened to your foot?"

"Nothing." I tipped my head back and blinked at her. "Just a little bruise."

"Harlow said it was more than a little bruise," she noted.

I noted that Harlow had a big freaking mouth. Then again, what was new? "It's fine."

Jenny made a 'hmph' noise in her throat. "Take something for it."

"I already did, Mama Jenny," I assured her.

"Well, be careful with it. Don't leave yourself open on that side and ignore those idiots if they say anything to you."

"Yes, dear." Of course I already knew that. But her intentions were in the right place, and I wasn't going to act like an ungrateful douche for no reason.

Knowing I was being a bit of a turd, Jenny yanked on my ear and then slid away before I had a chance to retaliate. A few minutes later, Kulti, Gardner and the rest of the coaching staff came into the locker room and reviewed the plan we'd gone over during practice the day before. They revisited our opponent's weaknesses, our own weaknesses, things to focus on. Win, win, win.

Our semi-circle of hands together had us all yelling and cheering. Shortly afterward the game started in a one-third packed stadium.

Within the first five minutes, someone shouldered me hard with a nicely added "slut" thrown in. I made sure to shoulder her back, just as hard, the first chance I could without getting caught. A few minutes later, the big broad that had been eyeing me from the moment I got on the field, slipped her leg out to trip me when I ran by her. She got a yellow card, only a warning, and I let it go.

I made it through about half the game before my shoe started to feel too tight over the bruised area of my foot. Our halftime break was a blessing because I had the chance to take off my shoe for a bit. Another fifteen minutes in the second half passed before I made myself retie it a little looser. Eighteen minutes after that, I was praising the lord the game was over, and that we'd scraped by a two-to-one win—one goal I helped score when I managed to pull several opponents away from the goal and kicked the ball to the closest open player.

The little snickers I'd heard from a few of the New York players the rest of the game had just gone in one ear and out the other.

Was I going to be able to walk the next day? That was debatable, but I'd worry about it when I woke up in bed with a foot that thought it would never be the same again.

That freaking jackass at the park. I really, really hoped he fell into an ant pile. Fucker.

While Coach talked in the locker room, I snagged an ice pack from a nearby fridge and let it sit. I showered, changed and waved goodbye to everyone, counting down the steps until I was at my car. There was a small strip between where the locker rooms ended and the parking lot began, so I knew to expect a few fans hanging around who wanted autographs. My parents hadn't made it to this game since it was on a Thursday and they had to work the next day, but Dad had texted me good luck before the start. Sure enough, a group of about twenty fans were waiting, and I started signing a few of the posters that had been given away at the entrance, as well as taking pictures with a few little girls that had me smiling big time.

"Goodnight, thanks for coming!" I gave the last kid a side hug, before she waved at me once more and followed along with her mom.

It was kids like that and moments like those that made playing in pain totally worth it.

And then I heard the chorus of several loud voices talking at once, moving closer and closer. I sighed, knowing there was no way to escape and feeling a little cowardly for wanting to avoid hearing crap come out of people's mouths who shouldn't matter. Nothing they said should have bothered me; mostly, it didn't.

By the time I managed to turn around and start making my

way slowly toward my car, several of the players for the New York Arrows walked by me. I exchanged greetings and handshakes with a few of them, the ones that hadn't called me a variation of a slut on the field earlier.

"Hey, Sal," I recognized the person speaking behind me.

I stopped and slowly turned around, plastering a smile on my face. "Hey, Amber."

But in my head I was really thinking, hey, you freaking bitch. Was it justified? Yeah.

She'd cost me the national team. Her and her stupid-ass estranged husband.

The tall brunette had a sweet smile on her face, but her eyes said it all. They said how much she disliked me and blamed me for something that had been a complete accident. The hate in her gaze called me a whore, in the same way she'd verbally whispered the name, when I'd stolen the ball away from her during the first half.

"Nice seeing you again," she said in her deceivingly sugar-stained voice. She waited a moment until two other players on her team kept walking, leaving the two of us standing there. I was surprised her two buddies left; they'd called me a bitch and a tramp during the game, too. I just pretended like I hadn't heard them by that point.

"Messed around with anyone else's husband lately?" Amber asked the minute we were relatively alone in the parking lot.

Bitterness crept into my throat. Maybe even a little embarrassment too. I hated what had happened but as much as I'd explained the situation to her, it hadn't mattered. Amber, being a fantastic forward several years older than me, and a star player for the national team, had taken my chance and my position away.

I would never forgive her for it, despite how horrible I felt about her husband, ex-husband, estranged husband, whatever the hell that ass-wipe was now.

I steadied my heart and shook my head. "Grow up."

Her blue eyes flared with indignation. "Fuck you."

Oh brother. "Really? Fuck me? That's the best you can come up with? I'm a whore, a bitch and a slut, and I can also fuck myself. Real nice. I wish everyone could hear how pleasant you are in person."

"You are a slut, you home wrecker."

Guilt flashed through my belly, but I beat it back like I had every other time. I wasn't a home wrecker. *I wasn't.* I felt terrible, fucking *terrible*, but it wasn't like anything had been intentional. I would never in a million years be interested in a married man, but when you don't know he's married... "I'm sorry, all right? I've told you I was sorry about a hundred times and you know it. If I could go back in time and mind my own business, I would. So, stop. You got what you wanted and you should be happy and let it go. It's been three years; it's about time you quit with your shit."

Beautiful Amber, with her great legs and competitive spirit, bristled. "Don't tell me what to do. I hate your fucking guts, Sal."

Acid stirred my chest. "I know you do, and trust me, I'm not your fan club president either. I just don't feel the need to remind you of it every time I see you."

She wanted to fight. I could tell. She had the same look on her face that she'd had three years ago when she approached me during practice one day, three days after I'd gone on a second date with her husband. "That's why I hate you. You always think you're so much better than everyone, but you're not. You're even more of a bitch because you fool everybody with that angel act. I know the truth—I know you're a fucking whore."

Getting called that? Yeah, it wasn't exactly fun and games. I would definitely never admit that out loud or show it to someone like her, but it was the truth. Sticks and stones and all that crap.

"You," the voice from behind me said. "Run along before I call Mike Walton and repeat what you said to him."

Who Mike Walton was, I had no idea.

But the person behind me? I definitely knew him.

The bratwurst.

From the look on Amber's face, as the steps behind me got louder with Kulti's approach, she knew exactly who both Kulti and Mike Walton were. Her face might have paled, but it was too dark to know for sure. What I did know was that she was pissed. Real pissed.

"Today," Kulti snapped.

The rate at which she moved said exactly what words didn't. Amber was one of the stars of the national team and had been for years. A few months ago, I'd seen a lotion commercial with her in it. She wasn't used to having someone tell her what to do.

He didn't even wait until she was out of earshot before he asked, "What's her name?"

"Amber Kramer," I replied, looking over my shoulder.

His face didn't register the name. "Never heard of her." He turned his head to look at me. "Do you want to tell me what that was about?"

I said exactly what I meant. "Not really." I'd gone this long with keeping what happened between me and a select group of people, mainly members of the national team back when I'd been on it. It was how Jenny and Harlow knew. Having more people know about one of the dumbest things I'd ever done, wasn't exactly on my list of things to accomplish. And though I'd been assured I wasn't to blame, I thought I was smarter than to fall for someone's lies. He hadn't been wearing a wedding band or even had the tan line for one, damn it.

"I heard what she called you."

Shame filled my belly, and I felt my face get all warm, indignation flaring up in my throat. "I'm not like that."

"You don't have to tell me you're not." The expression on my face must have been unsure enough that he stared me right in the eye as he said, "I've met a lot of women in my life. The only women I don't like are the ones who are interested in a person's money and fame."

His second sentence was the one I got hung up on. The thought of him and a lot of women was probably an understatement. For some reason I found the idea disgusting. "I'm sure you have."

I knew how bad some girls were with college soccer players, and I'd seen firsthand how women reacted around my brother. Some of the guys weren't even attractive, or had particularly nice personalities, but regardless after a game, they were swatting groupies off left and right. And Kulti, well Kulti was on a level of his own. I couldn't imagine.

And for one brief second, something flared in the pit of my stomach. It was jealousy or something equally stupid, that I could blame on the thirteen-year-old Sal who still lived inside me someplace.

I stomped her back down to her little room under the stairs.

I smiled weakly. Still feeling a little weird that I'd run into Amber and that he'd overheard her calling me something ugly; I really wanted to get home. Gesturing toward the parking lot, I asked, "Do you need a ride?"

"My driver is here." He pointed to a corner of the lot furthest away, in the same direction as my car.

I nodded at him and we started walking, looking back to make sure there weren't any other Kulti fans standing around like there had been at our last home game. Parked a lot closer than he was, I pointed at my car. "If you're free tomorrow, I can squeeze in a quick game if you promise not to play too rough or long." I needed the rest.

"Where?"

It took a second for me to think of a field; the one that came to mind was a small one but it worked. I rattled off the name. "Need an address?"

He shook his head. "What time?"

We agreed that the earlier the better.

"Your foot will be fine?" he asked.

"As long as you don't step on it," I said, dropping my bag into my trunk. "Goodnight, Coach."

"*Gute nacht,*" he responded, tipping his head as an indication for me to get in my car.

I got in and waved at him through the rearview mirror.

* * *

**9:30?**

It was 9:29 the next morning when I was pulling alongside the curb to Kulti's home.

I was picking him up.

Poop.

I looked at house through my passenger window and took in the big new two-story construction. He'd sent me a message at eight in the morning, asking if I could come by to get him after all. I didn't ask why he couldn't have his fancy driver take him to the field, but did I wonder? Of course I did.

I was picking up The King from his house to go play soccer.

At no point in my life had I had any signs that this would ever happen. This was friendship or something like it. Even if it felt like driving to his house was more of a date than hanging out.

I got out and marched up to the door he'd walked up to on all those occasions I dropped him off. The house was big, but not obnoxiously large, despite the fact it was at least twice the size of the home I'd grown up in. But who cared? I'd been in bigger houses before.

Ringing the doorbell, I took two steps back and found myself clasping my hands behind me while I waited. Less than a minute later the door swung open and Kulti stood there, dressed in black athletic shorts and a blue T-shirt, holding a big glass of something green.

"Come in," he ordered, standing to the side to let me in.

I did, trying to be discreet as I looked around at the bare cream walls. "Good morning."

"Morning." He closed the door. "I need ten minutes."

"Okay." I eyed both him and his drink as he walked around me and headed down the main hallway of his house.

It was impossible not to notice how empty the walls were, or when we walked by the doorway leading into his living room, how there was only a three-seater couch with a massive television in front of it. No framed jerseys or mounted trophies, no signs of who the owner of the house was. The next doorway led into a stainless steel and granite countertop kitchen, big, open and airy, it looked like a more expensive version of something out of an IKEA catalogue.

"There's water, milk and juice," he said going in, already tipping his green glass back to chug down whatever concoction he was drinking without a single flinch.

"I'm fine, thanks," I answered absently, admiring the view of the backyard from the big window above the sink. There wasn't much to it besides newly laid grass that could use a good watering. Most of the lots in the neighborhood had been old homes that had been torn down to build these new ones, and the house took up so much space it only left a small rectangular yard that didn't have much room for anything besides a patio set, if he'd wanted one.

Kulti brushed up against me as he leaned into the sink to rinse out his glass.

I leaned away from the view and him. "Your house is really nice."

He seemed to absently look around the kitchen, nodding.

"Did you just move in?"

"Two months now, I think," Kulti answered.

What a freaking talker. I watched as he placed his glass inside the dishwasher. "This is a really nice neighborhood." I cleared my throat.

He shrugged. "It's quiet."

Something about what he said nipped me. "No one knows you live here, huh?"

The German shot me an incredulous look I couldn't comprehend before answering. "No one." He kept on giving me that strange look. "I'm ready to go now."

So he didn't want anyone to know where he lived. That wasn't surprising, but I let it drop. "Let's go."

Kulti had a bag waiting in his nearly empty living room and followed out after me, setting the alarm and locking the door. The Audi he'd been riding around in was parked in the driveway when I peeked through the wrought-iron fence that sectioned off the back part of his house.

"So none of your neighbors know you live here?" I asked again once we'd gotten inside the car.

"No. I leave the house before they do and get back before."

"What do you do for groceries?" I was really curious about that. "Order them online?"

"I walk. It's three blocks away."

All this walking and riding around in cars he didn't drive, and all these mentions of a suspended license from people that got paid to investigate things... I gave Kulti a curious look but didn't dig in too deeply. So what? Maybe the signs were all there, but it wasn't my business to ask, the same way I didn't want to talk about Amber and her dumbass husband.

"I guess I don't understand how no one has recognized you.

I mean, your face is on a billboard off the freeway by my house," I told him, shaking my head. Then again, I'd seen his face hundreds of times on my walls. I could probably do an ink blot test and find him.

"People don't pay attention. I wear a hat, and the only people that speak to me are the elderly in the motorized scooters who need assistance reaching something."

Glancing over my shoulder, I shot him a smile. "I don't know how you do it, honestly. We have fans but it's different. The only people that wear my jersey are my parents and brother. I don't like being the center of attention, so it works for me."

His head moved so that he could look out the window. His voice was so serious, so distant; it made me look at him longer than necessary. "I've had enough attention in my life, I don't miss it."

That was why he lived in this neighborhood and wore a hat to the grocery store.

I guess you figure that some people have it all. Why wouldn't they? Looks, money, fame. What else would they need? A friend? Companionship? Something to take the boredom away?

Personally I knew hundreds of people, yet I was only really close to seven. They were all people that I'd known for a long time, but out of those seven I was confident that five would still be in my life even after soccer.

I eyed Kulti again and repressed a sigh. Feeling bad for him hadn't been part of the plan.

* * *

"Close enough?" I grunted.

Kulti pressed into me even more. "No."

He was backing me into a corner, defender and striker at the same time, to keep me from stealing the ball from him. Somewhat rough and playing like I was just a smaller man, by not avoiding the full body contact that came so naturally in soccer, he crowded me, he held me back. And I fought for every inch I made it forward, having to tap into my short bursts of speed to try and out-trick him.

It didn't really work.

With him on me, I only managed to get my feet on the ball about four times during our game, and each time he made me lose it out of bounds or stole it away. It was aggravating and exhilarating at the same time, especially when I ran after him and tried guarding against his big-ass body.

Playing with someone bigger, faster and more talented than you are, isn't exactly an ideal situation, but I tried and in the end, Kulti won, one to zero, nailing a clean shot right between the two goals we'd made out of sticks and empty water bottles we'd found in my backseat.

Freaking pumpernickel.

"Again?"

Hands on my hips, I took a few deep breaths in through my nose and nodded at the man standing in front of me, breathing just as hard. There weren't very many people at the park we'd gone to about twenty minutes from Kulti's house, but there were more than there'd been when we first arrived.

Against my better judgment, I said, "One more."

We went for it.

We both might have been more tired than we'd been when we started, but it didn't matter. Kulti was on me from the second I got the ball, constantly less than a foot away. He was definitely slowing down, and I used it to my advantage. I was just as tired as he was, our game the day before had drained me, but he was thirteen years older than me and didn't train as hard. And I was almost as fast as he was.

"Slowing down?" I panted as I tried to fake him out and make a run to the left.

He grunted, raw and rough. "Quit talking and play."

Yeah, he was definitely pooped.

Out of the corner of my eye, I noticed a few people sitting along the edge of the small field we were on, watching. But it was right then that Kulti snuck his foot into my path to try and trip me.

"You ass," I hissed, just barely missing him.

He used me being distracted and pissed, to steal the ball.

In the end I took it back when I summoned the last bit of energy I was willing to spend, and really put in the effort to power toward the goal, scoring. I threw my hands up in the air and stuck my tongue out at The King. "I win." Yeah, I totally wasn't being professional or mature about it.

Just to rub it in even more, our audience on the edge of the field began clapping.

Someone wasn't amused. I'd actually say he looked a little pissed.

I liked it.

"*Oye! Muchacha! Es el Aleman?*" someone from the field yelled.

"*Callate tonto!*" someone else replied, telling the guy asking to shut up.

I eyed the sore loser in front of me, not knowing what to do. Now that I got a better look at the people on the sidelines, they were all Latinos, in their late twenties and older. The German didn't say anything with his eyes or his body language.

"*Amiga! Es Kulti?*"

There were only about six of them...

I looked at Kulti again but the only thing he did was shrug, damn it.

"*Si es,*" I admitted. "*Pero no le digan a nadie.*"

The group erupted. "*No chinges!*" No shit was right.

The next thing I knew they were on their feet, hands on their heads, losing their minds. The guys went up to the German, speaking quick Spanish and watching him like they had never seen anything like him before.

It wasn't until I heard the first one who had spoken, say, "*No me digas!*" that I heard Kulti reply in perfect Spanish, explaining that he was real and not a ghost, "*No soy fantasma.*"

The guys lost it again. "You speak Spanish!" one of them exclaimed in the same language.

The German shrugged and gave them an easy smile.

For the next couple of minutes, I watched as the strange men blasted off several questions, and they were answered in an accent that rivaled mine.

I'm not going to lie, not even a little bit. Besides a big butt, I had a thing for guys that spoke different languages. While Reiner Kulti was every bit as impressive of a male specimen as you could get physically, the way he spoke Spanish multiplied his attractiveness by about thirty percent.

Okay, thirty percent minimum.

But it wasn't like I could or would think about that too much. He was my coach.

And I was his friend. Or something like that.

# 16

The first sign that something was off was when I spotted the three people on the edge of the field halfway through Pipers practice two days later. Two of them I recognized from the team's office staff, and the other person, carrying a kit, was a stranger. It was only on rare occasions that management showed up during training, if there were photographers on the field or if there was an exhibition game going on, but never without a reason.

The second sign that something was up was when they approached Gardner. It was the way he reacted to whatever they were telling him that had me a little worried. He looked annoyed and possibly outraged. Easygoing and calm ninety-nine-percent-of-the-time-Gardner, angered?

Yeah. No.

Then the clapping started. The meeting of palm on palm that paused our warm-up. "Ladies, we're taking it easy today."

Easy?

Apprehension rippled down my spine.

"Apparently, we're doing a round of drug testing today. It's nothing to worry about. As most of you know, you are subject to random drug testing throughout the season. If we can have your cooperation we can get through this quickly, and after your sample is received you're free for the rest of the morning," Gardner explained, frustration tracing his words.

Random drug testing? The last time I'd been randomly drug tested had been back in college. The stipulation included in everyone's contract was more of a blue moon-type occurrence. If they wanted to they could test you, but apart from the health exams and blood tests we took at the beginning of every season, I'd never heard of it happening.

So, yeah, that was freaking weird.

I had nothing to hide. The hardest drug I took was an over-the-counter painkiller and that was only in a dire situation like with my foot.

There was no reason for me to think the testing had anything to do with me.

Then Gardner called me into his office that afternoon.

* * *

"SAL, TAKE A SEAT," Gardner said from his spot behind his desk.

I gave him an uncomfortable smile and sat down.

Coaches just didn't call you after practice was over, the day a random drug testing went on, and ask you to come in for a chat. They didn't. I'd been in the middle of a nursery with Marc choosing some annuals for a project, when the call came through. I'd been shitting bricks since.

There were only a few reasons why Gardner wouldn't just tell me over the phone what he wanted: they were trading me, dropping me or some super-fast test had come back and found something in my urine that said I was doping.

Me, doping. Jesus Christ.

I wasn't so badass or indestructible that I wasn't on the verge of losing it. First, I didn't want to get traded. Second, I sure as shit didn't want to get dropped from the team; even though my contract was good for another year, you still never knew. Third, I sure as hell wasn't ingesting anything that was remotely illegal.

But still.

I managed to tell Marc what was going on, and the 'oh shit' look he'd given me was enough.

Taking a deep breath, I gripped my thighs and steeled myself. I might as well bite the bullet. "So, what's going on, G?"

He sat back, crossing his arms over his chest and smiled. "Always to the point, that's why I like you, Sal."

Gardner might like me, but he wasn't telling me what was going on. "Are you letting me go?" To my credit, I sounded calm, not at all like I was on the verge of taking a bat to his office furniture.

A bat to his office? Dear God. I needed to tone it down.

"No." He reeled back. "Where the hell would you get that from?"

"You asked me to come to your office to talk to me privately, and we had a drug test this afternoon." I just barely kept the *hello* to myself.

His eyes rolled up to the ceiling, a hand going to the back of his neck. "Damn. I didn't think about that. I'm sorry. That's not why I want to talk to you."

Yeah, that wasn't entirely convincing.

"I'm not worried about the results. I'm sure they're fine, but I did ask you to come in because of the drug test. I had an interesting conversation with Sheena earlier."

"Okay."

"She told me that an email came in this weekend with your name and some pretty wild accusations on it."

That bitch. That fucking bitch. It didn't take a genius to know where the email had come from. I squeezed my thighs a little tighter, controlling the rage bubbling up inside of me.

First it was someone on the team tattling on me to Cordero, and now Amber was making crap up? I didn't think I was a bad person. I did community service work from time to time, I mowed my elderly neighbors' lawn for free, and I smiled at strangers. Sure sometimes I had bad thoughts about people, but it was never for any reason, though that didn't make it any better. There were better people in the world than me, and there were sure as hell people a lot worse too. So I couldn't help but take it a little personally that these miserable hags were taking their crap out on me.

"Any idea where something like that would come from?"

"Amber." I gritted my teeth. "It was Amber. No one else would do something like this."

Gardner wasn't surprised. I'd told him what happened years ago, when I'd gotten back from the last national team tournament and burst into tears in front of him. "Christ. She's still not over that mess?"

I couldn't say that if I were in her shoes, I would have gotten over it either, but I liked to think that I wouldn't go as far as she had. Actually, I knew that I wouldn't. Only a total ass-wipe would call and make bogus allegations that could jeopardize someone's lifetime of hard work.

I swallowed the bitterness back, reminding myself of all the good things in my life. "Nope."

With a sigh, he shook his head and scratched at his neck. "In that case, I'm sorry for asking you over. I kept my eye on her during the game, but it didn't seem like she was doing anything unusual."

Of course he hadn't heard all the names she'd been calling me during the game, but whatever.

"I'm going to give her coach a call and tell him he needs to get her under control."

"Don't worry about it. It's fine. If she does something like this again we'll figure it out, but really, don't worry about it."

She was a crappy person who had to live with the effects of her awful personality for the rest of her life. That was bad enough.

Gardner's eyebrows went up in disbelief, but he didn't argue. "You let me know if you change your mind."

I nodded and stood up, ready to get out of there so that I could think of as many bad names for Amber as I could in private. "I will. Thanks for letting me know though, G. I appreciate it."

"Anytime." He watched me for a second before saying, "Sal, you know you can come to me with anything, right?"

"I know." It was the truth. "You're a good guy, Coach."

Gardner smiled as I made my way out of his office with a wave. "Rest up tonight. I need your head in the game tomorrow."

"You got it," I said, closing the door behind me.

I made it about ten feet down the hallway before an amount of anger I didn't think I was capable of, filled my entire soul. Amber had taken away the national team from me, fine. But now she was stooping low enough to try and jeopardize my career in the WPL?

That bitch.

I went home and took my anger out on the bathtub with a sponge and cleaner.

* * *

A LITTLE MORE THAN halfway through the game the next day, I accepted the fact that I was playing like complete and total crap.

All right, that was a bit of an exaggeration, but the point was I was playing pretty terrible. I was distracted and angry. For once in my life, I couldn't push everything else down to focus. The maliciousness in Amber's actions made my head want to explode. It wasn't like she hadn't done enough in the past to begin with either. Talking to her after the last game ended up stirring up some real resentment from me that not even my dirty bathroom could make go away. My head and my heart weren't in it, and I was too pissed off to give a shit.

So when my number went up on the board in red, and another girl's number went up in green, I wasn't totally surprised they were taking me out. I couldn't get angry about it either. Embarrassed and resigned, yes. I'd only gotten substituted a handful of times, and it had always been for a good reason: unavoidable cramps and torn muscles. There was also that one time I got too aggressive after a player elbowed me in the kidney and hadn't gotten caught, but Gardner took me out before I did something I might regret. But this time there was no valid excuse for how sloppy I was playing, or how absent-minded I was today.

It was pathetic. I knew better. I did better. I could handle more than this without blinking an eye, and I failed spectacularly.

I slowly jogged off the field, avoiding everyone and anyone's eyes, as I stared straight forward. Just as I was heading to the bench, the only route available was a sliver between Kulti and Gardner, a hand grabbed my wrist. Gardner wasn't the grabbing type, so I knew before even looking over my shoulder who it was.

Those crazy-colored eyes stared down at me from their position eight inches above mine. A furrow creased the space in the middle of his auburn eyebrows. "What the hell is going on with you?" he snapped.

I took a sharp inhale and met his gaze directly with a single shrug. "I'm sorry." I wasn't going to make any excuses. There weren't any.

That must have pissed him off because his nostrils flared. "That's it? That's all you're going to say?"

"There's nothing else *to* say. I'm playing like shit, and you're taking me out. I get it."

Honest to God, if Kulti was the type of person that smacked himself in the forehead, he had the expression on his face that said he'd be doing it right then. "Get out of my face right now; I'll deal with you later."

Even though I was sort of expecting his response to be similar, I still recoiled. But even as I did I bit my words back, swallowed my pride, accepted my fault and marched over to the bench. Elbows to my knees, I sat forward and watched the rest of the game, mentally kicking myself in the ass for being such an idiot.

An hour later, our team had barely squeaked by with a 1-0 win in thanks to a ball that hit the tip of Grace's foot just perfectly. We headed to the locker rooms and listened to the coaching staff drone on about what we did wrong, and what we *really* did wrong. Kulti didn't even bother looking at me when he decided to speak, but it was obvious to me that he was referring to all my screw-ups. Normally that would have put me on edge, but I had already accepted reality. As a wrap, Gardner gave his bit of motivational advice for the next week, and we were released to get out of the locker room.

Showering, getting dressed and heading toward the bus for a ten-hour drive back to Houston, I managed to avoid talking to anyone. I was too angry with myself for slacking off to be good company, and everyone gave me space. Sternum burning with embarrassment for playing like such an asshole, I managed to make it halfway to the bus before I caught Kulti standing off to the side as he spoke to... a woman. Was that a woman? I squinted.

"Casillas!"

I hesitated. Did I want to listen to him rip me apart in front of a stranger that might have been a woman or a slim man wearing skinny jeans? No. Definitely not. But it'd be obvious if I ignored him and kept on walking toward the bus.

"Casillas!"

Fuck. Fuck, fuck, fuck.

I guess I'd been warned. 'I'll deal with you later' wasn't exactly a vague threat. If I were a really religious person, I would have done the sign of the cross as I walked over to where the German was standing. Yeah, it was definitely a woman next to him, so I put on my Big Girl Socks during the short trip.

It took me until I was about five feet away to recognize the person he was talking to. An ex. Blah. She was an ex-girlfriend that I was certain was an actress or had been one at some point.

In the blink of an eye I was pissed off, and every step I took closer made me more and more angry. He wanted to do this now, in front of an old girlfriend?

"Are you sure you don't want to meet up tonight?" the attractive redhead asked, ignoring my approach.

Kulti wasn't even looking at her; instead he was staring at my face. My-aggravated-as-shit face. His one-word answer sounded as brutal as usual. "No." So at least he was an asshole with everyone. There was that.

The woman bent a long leg and moved her head over to get into his field of vision. "Positive?"

It was too dark to tell whether his eyes glanced over in her direction or not. "Yes," he confirmed

"Kulti—" A hand went to rest on his shoulder, and I didn't miss the way he shrugged her off.

"It took you long enough," he grumbled, when I stopped close but not too close to them.

I was looking at him, instead of the woman who was obviously still trying to get his attention.

I just stared back at him, not exactly wiping off the irritated look on my face. Was he planning on chewing me out? Did he really think this was the right time to do it?

Pulling together an amount of bravery that I really didn't have in me, I forced a calm look on my face, relaxed my shoulders to not give away how tense I was, and I blinked at my coach, Reiner Kulti.

"Yes, Coach?"

His luminous eyes bore down on me with the power of a strobe light, the biggest strobe light in history. By the shape of his mouth and the tic of his jaw, I was about to get reamed.

He didn't even bother looking at the woman next to him, hopeful and still attentive to a man who wasn't giving her the time of day, before he lowered his voice. Unfortunately I recognized that he wasn't lowering it to be inaudible, he was just that pissed, before laying it down for me. "What the hell was going on with you tonight?"

He was just as to the point as I expected. All righty. I licked my lips and gave him a solid shrug. "My mind wasn't in it and I'm sorry about that." It was implied that I wouldn't let that happen again.

"That's it?" he spat.

"There's no excuse," I told him, watching the woman look back and forth between us. "I know better, and I'm sorry."

His lids got heavy. If I didn't know him any better, I would have assumed he was sleepy. He wasn't anywhere close. "You played like an imbecile."

Seriously? Did he have to call me that in front of another person?

"Kulti?" The woman waved her hand around in his face.

The German turned his head and stared at her long enough that she scrunched up her face and stepped back.

"God, I forgot how much of an asshole you can be. I don't even know why I bother," she hissed at him.

The man who guarded his words like they were gold didn't let me down. He didn't say a word. Kulti looked at her for maybe five more seconds and then turned his attention back to me as if she hadn't spoken.

What an asshole.

"Your team deserves your attention, and I deserve better from you. Do that shit again and I'll have you coming in as a sub for Thirty-Eight," he threatened, oblivious to the woman who shook her head as he spoke, before finally turning around to walk off.

That time, I flinched and winced. I probably sucked air in through my nose. Thirty-Eight was one of the younger forwards, Sandy, a rookie on the team who would be a force to be reckoned with in the near future.

"Learn to compartmentalize your life, do you understand me?" he asked in that somber crisp voice I had a feeling he had learned to wield perfectly in the last few weeks.

As much as I hated to admit it, my face went hot, and I knew I was blushing with humiliation. He would try to take starting a game away from me? For playing crappy during one single game? More embarrassment flooded my system, lined carefully with anger.

The idea that I thought we were friends floated right up and center.

But Pipers time wasn't friend-time. It never had been. The man who called me Taco, and played soccer and softball with me, was a completely different person from the one standing before me in that moment.

Learn to compartmentalize your life, he'd said. Do what he did.

The only thing I could do was nod jerkily and accept the ultimatum he'd given me. I wasn't going to remind him this was one bad game out of so many. I wasn't going to promise anything or apologize. It hurt my pride, but I balled it up and tucked it neatly into my sternum. In a voice that I was extremely proud of for how solid it sounded, I said, "Okay. Fine.

But maybe next time call me an imbecile when I'm not in front of your girlfriend, would that work for you? "

When he closed his eyes and began grinding his teeth together, I wondered if I said the wrong thing. It wasn't until he started scratching at his cheek and then erupted a second later, I figured the answer was: *yeah*. I had.

"Are you fucking kidding me?" he burst out.

I took a step back and gave him a crazy look because seriously, what else did he want from me? "No."

"I'm threatening to bench you, and you're complaining about who overheard?"

I'd bet a dollar that my hair kind of blew back a little bit at his question, but I wasn't going to puss out. No fear. "Yeah, I am. If I'm playing bad consistently, then I don't deserve to start. That sucks, but I understand. I'm not going to argue with you over an obvious fact. What I do have a problem with, is you being rude to me in front of other people, and you were a dick to her. Jesus F. Christ. Manners, Germany, ever heard of them?"

Kulti didn't hesitate to throw his hands up behind his head. The short brown strands crept through his fingers. "I want to shake you right now."

"Why? I'm only telling you the truth."

"Because—" he snapped something in German I thought was the equivalent of 'fuck', "—you're going to sit there and let me take this away from you? Just like that?" he growled.

"Yeah, I am. What do you want me to tell you? Do you want me to beg you? Get mad? Throw a fit and stomp off? I understand. I get it. I played one bad game; I'm not going to play two. That's fine. It's your tone and choice of where we're having this conversation that I have a problem with."

He might have started pulling on the shortest of short ends of his hair in what was a mix of annoyance and frustration. "Yes, goddamnit, get mad! If my coach had ever even hinted at taking me out of a game, I would have lost it. You're the best player on the team—"

I'd swear on my life that my heart stopped beating. Had he just said what I think he said?

"You're one of the best I've ever seen, period, man or woman. What kills me is that you are a complete fucking pushover who's hung up on worthless words in front of a person that doesn't matter." His cheeks were flushed. "Grow some balls, Casillas. Fight me for this. Fight anyone that tries to take this away from you," he urged.

His words went through my brain like molasses, clinging and slow. Yet I still didn't understand. Then again, maybe I did. This was the same man that owned the field each time he went on. Most of the time, each of his plays had begun with him and ended with him. He was a greedy asshole with the ball.

And we were arguing over two completely different things. Dear God.

I took a deep breath and gave him a steady look. "Of course I freaking care about getting benched, but I also care about who you call me an imbecile in front of. Do you think I want a complete stranger thinking I'm some kind of doormat that lets you talk to me like that? I might be when we're on the field, but I'm sure as hell not going to let you treat me half as bad as you just treated her, buddy."

Kulti looked like I was speaking a completely different language, so I took advantage of it.

"This is a team sport. If I'm not playing my best, isn't it better for someone who is playing better to take my spot?" Not that I wouldn't fight for it, tooth and nail. I was going to get my shit together and get back into the game, so that no one would take me out. On the other hand, I didn't feel the need to promise him that. I'd show him. Yet everything that he was telling me went against my natural instinct. This was a team sport, there definitely wasn't an 'I' in soccer.

Obviously my response went completely against his natural instinct, because his eyes bugged nearly out of their sockets.

I held out my arms and shrugged.

It wasn't until he started shaking his head that he finally spoke again. "*You* have to watch out for you. Not for anyone else, do you understand me?"

I blinked. Apparently he was going to ignore me complaining about the girlfriend thing. Okay.

"No one else is going to watch out for your best interests but you. Just for agreeing with me that you played like you've never seen a soccer ball before, I should make sure you sit out the next game."

What? I never agreed that I played *that* bad.

"But—"

"No buts. You play like shit and I'm going to give you hell for it, but you should never let anyone take this away from you."

Amber's actions seared through my belly, a painful reminder of what I'd already had taken away from me.

Then again I guess I had let her take it away from me. I didn't fight when she'd said, "It's her or me." I'd felt so consumed with guilt for going on two dates with a man who was separated from my teammate, I'd willingly stepped aside and given up my position. I was a serial monogamist and possessive as hell. If I'd been her, who knows how I would have felt.

Maybe I could have fought for it. I could have told Amber she was being an idiot because it wasn't like I had known that jackass was married, much less married to her. Even then, I hadn't slept with him. I had kissed someone who I thought was single and seemed like a nice guy. That was absolutely it. The second man I'd kissed since breaking up with my college boyfriend had been a cheating, lying piece of donkey shit and been married to my teammate. I hadn't just backed up the toilet; I'd made the septic tank flood the house.

Two stupid dates had taken away my lifelong aspiration.

I felt my eyes get watery with disappointment in the team and the coaches who hadn't fought to keep me on. More than anything, I was disappointed with myself. I sniffled, then sniffled again, trying to control the water works creeping up in my eyes. It had been years since I cried over leaving the national team. One month was all I'd given myself to be upset over it. Since then I'd locked it up, accepted reality and moved on with the rest of my life. When something is broken into too many pieces, you can't stare at them and try to glue them back together; sometimes you just have to sweep up the pieces and buy something else.

"Are you crying?"

Clearing my throat, I blinked hard twice, lowering my gaze to the small cleft in the German's chin. "No."

His fingers went up to push at my shoulder lightly. "Stop it."

I lifted my chin and pushed his shoulder right back, sniffling while doing it. "You stop it. I'm not crying."

"I have two eyes," he replied, looking down at me with a troubled expression on his face.

Just as I was about to sniffle again, I stopped. Those green-brown eyes were way too close and too observant. The last person in the world I would want to show any signs of weakness in front of would be him. Instead, I let my nose get all watery and avoided wiping it as I stared right back at him. "Obviously, I do too, Berlin."

The 'Berlin' did it.

To give him credit, he settled for giving me a scowl instead of an ugly word for how much of a jackass I was for calling him that. "I'm not from Berlin."

A fact I was well aware of. He didn't know how much I knew about him, and I wasn't about to tell him. Something about that little secret made me relax.

When I looked right back at him with a clear expression

and relaxed shoulders, as innocent as I could possibly make myself out to be, Kulti tilted his head back to look up at the dark sky. "Get on the bus, Sal."

So we were back to 'Sal.'

Knowing damn well when it was time to either retreat or answer some question I wouldn't want to, I took two steps back. "Whatever you say, sir."

* * *

GAME?

I flexed my foot inside my boot and typed back: **Sure.**

**Same time?** Kulti texted back.

**Ja.** I smiled at the screen before setting my phone on my lap.

"What the hell are you smiling at?" Marc asked from his spot behind the driver's seat.

The smile eased itself off my face. "Nothing."

"Liar."

I rolled my eyes as the phone vibrated from between my legs. Bringing it back out, I made sure Marc's attention was back on the road.

**Go make a quesadilla.**

I started laughing hysterically.

"Goddamnit, Sal!" Marc shouted. "You want me to get into a wreck?"

Despite Marc yelling at me for bursting out so suddenly, it didn't stop me from cracking up.

* * *

HE WAS WAITING on the bench by the time I pulled my car into the park's lot, headband on, bat leaning against his thigh and a glove on his lap.

I kept my face even, like he hadn't sent me the most ridiculous text message earlier in the day. "Hi."

"Sal," Kulti said my name like he'd been using it forever, standing up with his things in hand. He had on the same variation of an outfit he usually did: white athletic shorts, a plain black T-shirt and black and green RK signature running shoes.

"Ready?" I asked, eyeing his muscular calves for a split second.

"*Ja*," he answered.

I looked up at his face and snickered, but he wasn't smiling at me, he was just watching like always. We walked toward the field together silently. The awkward conversation we'd had during the Pipers game a few days ago seemed forgotten. I understood what he meant and where he was coming from, so I didn't take it personally.

Not surprisingly, we were split up into two different teams. Most of the players at the park were people we'd played with the last couple of times. One of them was the douche-bag that played whack-a-mole with my foot, who was standing off with a couple of other guys, all of them staring at me.

Weird.

An open palm smacked me in the shoulder. "Watch it." Kulti leaned over to meet me eye to eye, his index finger pointing low in the direction of my shoe.

Definitely. I stared up into his murky green eyes and nodded. "I will. Good luck."

Instead of saying anything, he walked past me, bumping the side of his upper arm against my shoulder, lightly... playfully.

"Come on, you punk. I wanna start the game before I turn forty," Marc shouted, waving me onto the side of the field. Our team was batting first.

"That's like next week."

He shot me the middle finger.

We lined up to bat and only made it through four batters before we got three outs and had to switch positions. Six outs later, I managed to get three of six opposing players out, and my team was back playing defense. It was a fast-moving game with a lot of quick inning changes. It seemed like I was going to be able to go to practice the next day without a limp.

At least that's what I thought until I realized how competitive and petty some guys could be.

Not even two batters in I had one of the opposing players clothesline me, as he ran to the base while I caught the ball to tag him out.

I landed on my ass and back pretty hard because I hadn't been expecting it at all—because seriously, who the hell plays like that?? Last week should have been an anomaly. I took a deep breath to control how pissed off I instantly became and how out of breath I was from practically being tackled. Once I was calm, I shoved him off and gave the jerk a dirty look. It was one of the guys the idiot from last week had been standing with, also one of the three people I'd tagged out earlier.

I took another deep breath, fighting back a groan as I watched him get up to standing position from his hands and knees. *Patience Sal. Patience.*

But it wasn't working.

Rolling up to sit, I bit back the curse words that were molding to my gums.

*Patience. Patience.*

I swallowed and clung to the tiny bit of patience I found inside myself. "I don't play like that," I told him in a careful controlled voice, getting to my feet slowly. I straightened to my full height, still a good five inches shorter than the man who shoved me to the ground. I tipped my head up and looked him right in the eye. He was somewhere around my age and good-looking enough to be an egotistical dick with his gelled hair and trimmed beard. I'd learned early on playing with my brother, Simon, Marc and their friends that as a girl—as a person—you couldn't back down. Plus, I wasn't scared of these idiots. Not even a little bit. "Don't do it again."

"Whoa, whoa, whoa." Marc's voice came from somewhere in my peripheral vision before he appeared. Close enough, he shoved a hand between our bodies and moved the stranger back a foot. "Dude, we don't do that shit. You especially don't do that shit to her, so watch it or your ass is out of here. That goes for all of you."

The tension was like a thick mist over the field, as the guy finally took another two steps back and nodded. Anger buzzed through my ears as I watched his stupid head retreat.

A hand whacked me in the stomach hard, and I didn't have to look down to see that it was Marc, leaning over to get in my face. "I thought we talked about you taking risks," he hissed.

I blinked and felt my nostrils flare. "His friend stomped on me last week and now this ass-wipe went WWE on me. What did you want me to do? Sit here and take it?"

We both knew he was part of the trio who had taught me as a child that it was acceptable to shove my elbow into the soft spot beneath people's ribcages and sometimes in their kidneys, if it was needed. It wasn't until I was a little older playing in a league that my coach had finally explained that it wasn't right... even if it got the job done.

With a sigh, Marc's dark eyes stared into mine. "Of course not, but you know the last thing I want is for you to get hurt because these pussies get their panties in a wad."

"I know, but that was bullshit."

A strained smile stretched wide across his mouth. "It is bullshit, but sometimes I want to push you to the ground, Sal, and I love you. Chill out. We'll let the air out of his tires in a couple of weeks, when he isn't expecting it."

Bah.

I snorted, and then I snorted again. He was such a great

person in my life, more like an illegitimate bastard brother than a friend, really. I kissed the tips of my fingers and followed up by smacking his cheek with them in a light slap. "I love you too, but I don't know if I can wait a few weeks."

With a roll of his eyes, he straightened up and scowled. "Try. Keep the anger in check, mini-Hulk."

I rolled my eyes right back at him, took another breath for control, collected what remained of my patience and held it close to my heart. Out of the corner of my eye, I saw Kulti at the sideline, one foot forward, his hands down at his sides, those muscular forearms flexed. I noticed even his calves were taut. His jaw was locked as he stood there, ready for who knows what. But he didn't move. He didn't say a word, and I was still too pissed to put together his body language.

Was it an accident? I highly doubted it, but I'd played with rough people in the past, and I'd let them get away with maybe an elbow or a shoulder if it let them sleep better.

But still, he was a fucking asshole.

Then it happened again.

A few minutes later, once the teams had switched positions, I was running—not full speed—toward third base after stealing second. Just as I was coming up to the base, someone from behind me sped up, and completely unnecessarily, shoved me forward as he attempted to tag me out.

I went flying, straight on a mission to eat a whole bunch of dirt.

Under normal circumstances, I would have been able to stop myself, but with the added push, I had too much momentum going. The image of falling awkwardly on my knee or ankle, and the possibility of tearing something flashed through my brain. There was no graceful way to stop without really hurting myself. So I went forward, hands up in the sloppiest slide that wouldn't break a wrist, and I belly-flopped. I mean, *belly-flopped* and still skidded a bit. The fall was hard and painful. It reminded me of that time I dove off the platform when I was a kid and knocked the wind out of myself, almost feeling like I might have cracked a rib.

But the point was, I fell, I slid. I'd been shoved. And I was not okay with it, especially not when the silly, stupid man decided to stand over me, six feet of douche-bag supreme.

My stomach burned, and my lower ribs ached as I tried to push up to my hands and knees.

Holy shit.

I sucked in a breath and hissed it right back out, one hand going under my shirt to palm the skin that I knew was scraped to hell.

Before I could even successfully sit up on my knees, the culprit had been shoved to ground. I mean he was *shoved* hard. It wasn't Marc, and it wasn't Simon. It was Kulti standing with his back to me. Kulti had pushed the full-grown man to the ground.

Reiner 'The King' Kulti stood over the fucking weasel, straddling his body in a squat. "You coward," he spat.

Literally, I saw saliva coming out of the German's mouth as he said words in his native language, which I didn't understand but got the gist of. They weren't friendly, not at all.

"You're pathetic." Honestly, I thought he was going to slap him and was only slightly disappointed when he didn't. His face kept moving lower and lower until I was sure the blood rushed to his head.

What followed was an explosion of German that made the hairs on the back of my neck stand up. Vicious and sharp-edged, I only understood a few words here and there. Something about dying and *his investment*?

What the hell that meant, I had no idea. What I did know was that it sounded incredibly ugly. It sounded so ugly; I felt a little shiver roll down the length of my spine even as I froze in place on my knees, mere feet away from the action.

"It really is him," Marc whispered in a reverent voice, scaring the crap out of me because I had no idea he was so close.

"Shh," I hissed so I could hear if anything else was said to the idiot on the ground.

Sure enough, I wasn't left hanging. Kulti straightened until he was standing up, legs on both sides of the guy's body. "Next time, I'll break your hand." With that, he turned around. I'd swear on my life he cocked his leg back as if planning to kick the man, but at the last minute changed his mind and kept going... toward me.

What did I do? I just stayed there. I just *stayed right there.*

Had he, the man who hadn't even batted an eyelash when a teammate of his had gotten two broken vertebrae after a cheap shot, defended me? *Me?*

That imposing six-foot-two frame stopped four steps later, eyes down at the hand I had under my shirt; why, I wasn't sure. I was so wrapped up in Kulti's actions that I couldn't have been sure about anything.

His nostrils flared, and I swear his entire upper body seemed to expand as he reached forward, his finger barely grazing my chin. Kulti muttered something that sounded suspiciously like, "so lucky," under his breath, his chin turning to pause just above his collarbone, like he couldn't bear to look at me. Adam's apple bobbing, he seemed to struggle for another breath before getting himself under control.

His intense gaze ignored the gaping mouths surrounding us. He said in a crisp tone, hands wrapping around my elbows, "We're done here. I'll get your keys."

All I could do was nod. I might have even forgotten to breathe from the shock and excitement as he continued holding me, helping me up to my feet. My ribs sang a sorrowful song as I stood up with a groan. The skin over my stomach hurt, but I managed to make eye contact with Simon and Marc.

"I'm fine," I said, for once in my life not caring that all these people I didn't know well, were staring at the sideshow known as Kulti Kicking Ass.

"You sure?" Marc asked, his face creased with worry. I nodded. "Call me later, okay?"

I swallowed and waved at my two longtime friends, breathing through the pain as I turned to walk off the field. Kulti was ahead of me. He'd already reached down and grabbed my glove, his own tucked under his armpit, one arm extended out in my direction in a gesture for me to come toward him.

I did.

My abs and sides ached with every step, but I managed to keep it together as we walked nearly side by side, the German ending up just slightly behind me. He veered off for a second to grab both of our bags, snatching them up off the floor. The anger coming off of him was suffocating, but I took it all in, okay with it. He'd been about to beat the crap out of that guy in my honor.

I'd seen Kulti lose his shit for much less, but for someone else? Never. Marc was going to scream over the phone later, I just knew it.

I eyed him as we walked toward the parking lot, going through a million different ideas of how to thank him for what he'd done. From the way his body was strung, tight at the shoulders and down through his chest, I figured it'd be best to give him a minute. So I kept my mouth shut and kept walking.

My car was so close I could almost touch it. All I wanted was to get home, maybe throw some Epsom salt into the bathtub and soak for a while as I drowned my pain in over-the-counter painkillers.

"Jesus Christ," I groaned when my ribs gave a strong throb, as we stopped right by the hood of my car.

The big man dropped both of our bags on the ground, and I

couldn't help but notice the big vein in his neck pulsing. His fingers were curled at his sides. "Let me see."

"I'm all right," I insisted, debating whether or not to bend over and grab my bag.

"You are the worst liar I have ever met," he said. "Pull up your shirt or I'll do it for you."

"Uh..."

He wasn't exaggerating.

When I didn't immediately pull up my T-shirt, he did it for me. One hand fisted the worn cotton material at the hem, and the next thing I knew, he was jerking it up. Way up. My shirt went high over my breasts, my black sports bra and all.

I tried to smack his hand away. "What the hell are you doing?"

It was useless. He had a death grip on the material, and his eyes were laser-focused on the middle section of my body.

Maybe I should have been self-conscious, but I wasn't. Not really at least. I ate well, I exercised a lot, and frankly, I just didn't give a crap if he found me lacking or thought I was too much. Because I was in pain. The skin covering my abs was inflamed and red; right down the middle, tiny beads of blood dotted my poor stomach. Luckily, my ribs weren't swollen or blue.

But tomorrow... I cringed.

As I shuddered at the thought of how much I'd be hurting tomorrow, Kulti yanked down on the elastic hem of my royal blue running shorts two inches. It was low enough for the elastic band of my pastel blue cotton panties to make an appearance.

"All right," I muttered and pulled them back up, out of his grip.

Kulti flicked his gaze up, chin still down, my shirt still bunched in his other hand. "I didn't take you to be shy."

"I'm not." Unless it was in front of a camera, that was more along the lines of a complete and total meltdown.

"You're acting like it."

A small part of me was well aware that he was just egging me on, challenging me so I'd do what he wanted. I wasn't shy. I was used to people—okay, physical therapists, chiropractors and masseuses—putting their hands all over me when I was half-dressed. Practicing in sports bras when it got too hot, or when I wanted to work on my tan wasn't out of the usual either. I didn't have any real issues with my body except for a few stretch marks in key places along my glutes and quadriceps. At some point, I'd gotten over the idea that beautiful faces and traditional feminine bodies whether they were slender or curvy, were the only standard of beauty in the world. The fact that I wasn't built slim or voluptuous and would never be anything close to any kind of bombshell, was fine with me now. My body and build were a hard fact.

My arms, stomach and legs were a sign of the craft I'd been working on my entire life. It was my machine: short torso, wide-ish shoulders and muscular thighs. They were mine, and I wasn't embarrassed of it. I was happy with myself. Sure I'd had people tell me my quads were too big, or that I needed to stop lifting weights before I looked too manly, whatever the fuck that meant. My arms couldn't be scrawny, I needed my legs to take me to the end of the universe and back, and they did. On the other hand, I'd also had teammates and coaches tell me I should put more muscle on. I could have been more and I could have been less, but I was just me. At some point, you just have to decide to be the best version of yourself, the one you can live with and look at in the mirror day after day.

Eventually, I'd found that person. Not a model and not a physique competitor in a bodybuilding competition. Just me.

Plus, I'd seen Kulti's ex-wife and his ex-girlfriends. He liked them tall-ish, long-haired with small breasts, just between the line of slim and fit.

Which was not my small C-cups that didn't shrink no matter how much bench pressing I did, or my hamstrings and butt that only fit into the most stretchy of jeans after ten minutes of wiggling, jumping and tucking. I didn't even think about my face because that was a whole different matter. It had scars and freckles that I couldn't and wouldn't do anything about.

"Fine." Dropping my hands, I held them up before pulling my shirt over my head. Screw it. What were boobs and some freckles, when he'd seen me without make-up nearly every day for the past two months?

His lids dropped low over his hazel-ish eyes, but he didn't say a word. Instead he watched me with that heavy gaze as his hands wrapped over my sides just below the smallest part of my ribs. They were cool and firm. I couldn't help but notice his hands were big. I only just barely managed not to make a sound at his touch. I mean, Marc touched me all the time. It was no big deal.

His hands slid up, his palms so wide and fingers so long, he could almost reach all the way around.

Then he squeezed, and I let out a really unfeminine grunt.

The German didn't break eye contact with me once, even as his thumbs pressed into the hollow between my ribs, the pads resting on the scraped-up skin above the flat muscle of my abs. My nostrils flared as he squeezed a second time, my heart racing, racing, racing under cover. The hair on my arms prickled in response to him.

Did he need to look at me while he did this? "I'm fine. If anything, they're just a little bruised," I said in a controlled voice that didn't even hint at the fact the big organ right in the center of my chest thought it was heading into Nascar.

One thumb absently stroked a line upward to the elastic

band of my bra, which I couldn't help but remember was literally just a centimeter from the bottom swell of my breast. "You'll be fine," he stated confidently like he had x-ray powers that told him everything was all right.

His hands dropped from my stomach.

I swallowed, trying to get myself together. "My, uh, keys are in the side zipper of my bag. Can you grab them for me or pass me the bag so I can get them?"

He shot me a look, reaching for my bag off the ground before unzipping the pocket and fishing my keys out, holding them clasped in his palm. "I would drive you home but..." His lips curled over his teeth, almost as if he were going to smack them.

*But.*

"Don't worry about it." I didn't ask him if he couldn't. He couldn't. It was that simple. I didn't know why exactly, but the clues were there.

He didn't even blink or look mildly uncomfortable, I understood that much. He nodded once, his lips still tight. "I'll follow you."

Follow me home? "That's all right. I promise. I can make it home in one piece."

"I'll follow you."

Dear God. "I'm sure you have better things to do. Trust me, it's fine."

"I don't. I'll follow you home," he insisted. I opened my mouth to argue, but he cut me off. "Get in."

That was exactly how I found myself leading an international soccer icon to my garage apartment.

## 17

It was the knocking.

It was the freaking knocking that finally made me roll out of bed.

I was going to kill whoever was on the other side of the door. Okay, maybe not kill but seriously maim.

The fact that my feet were dragging behind me at ten o'clock in the morning was the first example of how horrible I felt. Though I knew better, I wasn't actively stretching any of my muscles, which explained why I felt even worse than the day before.

"Coming!" I barked out when the knocking became even more obnoxious.

Murder. Screw it. Maybe I could get away with a crime of passion.

When I looked through the peephole that my dad had installed the minute after he'd finished helping me move in, I thought about slapping myself in the face to make sure I wasn't dreaming.

"Coach?" I asked as I unlocked the top lock and then the bottom, pulling the door open just a crack.

His big German face stared at me through the slit. "Rey is fine. Let me in."

He would like being called Rey—king in Spanish.

I let him in.

Only after I opened the door, did I think about the fact that I'd just rolled out of bed a second earlier. My hair must have resembled something out of John Frieda's worst nightmare and my face... puffy. It was definitely puffy and drool-stained, definitely. "I just got up," I explained weakly, watching him lock the door once he was inside.

"I can tell." Those brown-green eyes gazed at my face for a second, straying a little lower briefly, before finally taking a look around my small living room. "I called you," he said absently.

"I put my phone on silent after I called Gardner to tell him I wasn't coming in," I explained. First, I'd slept like complete crap. A comfortable position to sleep in had eluded me the entire night, I'd been miserable. When my alarm went off at six and I'd rolled over to turn it off, my ribs had told me very calmly that there was no way I was going for a run, much less making it through practice.

Fortunately in the last four seasons I'd been with the team, I'd missed practice on only one occasion that wasn't injury related. My grandfather had died, and I'd flown to Argentina for the over-the-top funeral thousands had attended. *A country in mourning,* a telecaster had called it that night when I'd sat in my hotel room watching the news recap the day. Gardner didn't even hesitate to tell me to feel better and come back once my mysterious 'virus' went away.

I hated lying, but at least I had promised to visit the doctor and stay in bed.

"I see." He took a couple more steps in, his eyes looking to the small kitchen and the counter island where I had two barstools in lieu of a table.

I stifled a yawn. "Are you okay?"

Kulti inspected me from head to toe, frowning. "I'm fine. I came to make sure you were alive."

I had a brief flashback to the night before, when he'd rolled down the window as his car sat idling in the driveway, ordering me to take something for the pain. "I'm fine. I feel like roadkill, but I'm all right."

"You missed practice. You're not fine."

He had an excellent point. "I have a doctor's appointment at noon, just to make sure nothing is broken."

His expression darkened as he walked around me to head into the kitchen. He stopped after taking two steps and looked over his shoulder, his gaze going to my legs. "Do you ever wear pants?"

"No." I had shorts on, damn it. Plus, this was Houston. No female wore pants in the summer unless they had to.

He looked for a second longer, glanced up at my face, and then continued his journey into the kitchen. "Do you have tea or coffee?"

I pointed. "Both."

He made an indiscriminate noise as he searched my kitchen cabinets.

All right. "Well make yourself at home. I'm gonna go shower and put on some pants, I guess." I might have given him a dirty look at the mention of putting on bottoms, but he wasn't paying attention. His back was turned.

Thirty minutes later, I was freshly showered, my teeth brushed, my hair… well, up in something that could be considered a bun, deodorant applied, jeans that could have passed for leggings and wearing a real bra on, I made an appearance back in the living area of my garage apartment. Kulti was sitting on the couch, drinking from a black coffee mug with an owl picture on it and watching television.

The fact that the man I'd had on my wall for nearly a

decade was sitting on my couch, drinking coffee because he'd come by to check on me, didn't really hit me much. I wouldn't say it was normal, but I wasn't choking up to talk to him or freaking out that I hadn't dusted in a couple of weeks. It was just... okay. No big deal.

No big deal that Reiner Kulti was sitting here, hanging out.

"Are you hungry?" I was starving. By this point in the day, I'd normally already be on my second meal.

"No," he replied, still not turning around from his focus the television.

I eyed him and started looking through my freezer for something easy to cook. There were some frozen turkey breakfast patties, fruit and a whole grain baguette. The frozen fruit I set aside to blend into a smoothie as I got the rest of it ready. Kulti didn't say anything as I made my meal, but I knew he was fully aware of what I was doing.

When I was done, I had a blender filled with a weird smoothie of almond milk and leftover frozen fruit. I poured two drinks and put my makeshift breakfast sandwich on a plate.

"Here," I said, holding a glass over his head from behind.

He took it from me without a word, setting the glass on the coffee table. Stiffly, I took a seat on the opposite end of the couch, plate on my lap, smoothie on the coffee table and sat there watching the survival show on the screen. Kulti manned the side table as I ate my food, making a mess all over myself, because it hurt too much to try and have manners.

"Why do you have so many recordings of this show?" he asked, browsing through my DVR.

"Because I like it," I told him. Though, okay, it was only the partial truth. I did like it. I also thought the two guys who tried to survive in different conditions and environments were really attractive.

Kulti made a humming noise but clicked on the oldest episode at the top. I definitely wasn't going to complain.

Not even fifteen minutes into the show, the German completely turned his entire body in my direction, his face suspicious.

I set the plate on my lap and blinked. "What?"

"You like them or the show?"

Oh brother. Marc had laughed hysterically when I admitted how hot I found the two men—they were in their early forties, both graying, one at an early stage of hair loss, but I didn't care. They were really attractive and the whole survival thing only helped. What did I have to be ashamed about? "Them, mostly."

Kulti's facial expression didn't change, but his tone said it all. "You're joking." He couldn't believe it. What was the problem? They were both good looking.

"No."

He blinked those green-brown eyes at me. "Why?" he asked, like I'd just told him I drank my own pee.

I picked the plate up and held it directly under my mouth before taking a bite of my sandwich. "Why not?"

"You are young enough to be their daughter," he ground out. "One of them doesn't have hair on half his head."

I took another bite of my food and watched him carefully, not even *thinking* it was weird that he seemed so outraged at who I found attractive. "First off I doubt they're old enough to be my dad, and secondly I could care less about a bald spot."

Kulti shook his head slowly.

*Okay*. "They're both in good shape, have nice smiles and nice faces." I glanced at the screen. "And I like their beards. What's wrong with that?"

His mouth gaped a millimeter.

"What?"

"Do you have father issues?"

"What? No. My dad's great, jeez."

His mouth still hadn't closed that tiny gap. "You like old men."

I bit both my lips, eyes wide. I'm sure my nose flared a little bit. How close to the truth he was, and it almost made me laugh. Instead, I shrugged. "I wouldn't say *old,* merely... mature?"

Kulti stared at me for so long I started laughing.

"Stop looking at me like that. I don't think I've ever been attracted to guys my own age. When I was younger..." *I'd been in love with you*, I thought but didn't say out loud. "I thought they were dumb and then it just stuck," I explained.

He still didn't say a word.

"Quit it. Everyone has a type. I'm sure you do."

Kulti blinked. "I'm not attracted to senior citizens."

I rolled my eyes. "Okay, fine. You don't like older men or women."

He ignored my jab at him being attracted to men. "I don't have a type," he said slowly.

Yes, he did, and I knew exactly what it was. "Everyone is attracted to certain things, even you."

Those hazel-green eyes blinked at the speed of a moving glacier. "You want to know what I'm attracted to?"

I was thirty seconds too late to realize that I didn't want to know after all. Did I want to hear him spout off prerequisites I didn't fit? No. Hell no. While I completely understood his place in my life, that didn't mean I wanted to be the antithesis of Reiner Kulti's dreams. My pride could only handle so much.

But it wasn't like I could back-down by that point. Gritting my teeth, I nodded. "Go for it since you think I'm such a weirdo."

"I like legs."

Legs? "And?"

His eyes narrowed just barely. "Confidence."

"Okay."

"Nice teeth."

Hmm.

"A beautiful face."

My eyelid may have started twitching.

"Someone who makes me laugh."

The twitching went into overdrive. "Are you making stuff up?" Because, really? Kulti laughing? Ha.

"Is there something wrong with my list?" he asked with a stony even glare.

"There wouldn't be anything wrong with it if you weren't randomly blurting stuff out. Someone who makes you laugh? I feel like you're going to start describing a unicorn after that."

He prodded at the inside of his cheek with his tongue. "Just because I'm not attracted to women old enough to remember the last Great War, doesn't mean my list is made up," Kulti said.

Oh my God. That made me burst out laughing. "You make it sound like I hit up retirement homes for dates. Those men are probably only a couple years older than you are, so think about that, creaky knees."

And that got his mouth to close. "You are the most insolent person I have ever met in my life."

Smiling, I took a bite out of my sandwich.

What felt like five minutes later, Kulti finally turned his attention back to the television, one cheek pulled back like he was biting down on.

When the episode was over, I got up slowly and took my dishes into the kitchen, grabbing Kulti's right along the way. "I have to leave in thirty. If you promise not to steal anything that you could easily afford on your own, you can stay here and watch more TV."

There was a pause as he scrolled through the DVR recordings. "My driver is downstairs. He can take us."

Us? My plate clattered into the sink. "You want to come?"

"I have nothing else to do."

That wasn't the first time he'd said something along those lines. I walked back around the couch and carefully sat down, eyeing him. I knew what I was about to ask was completely out of my league, but whatever. "What exactly do you do all day?"

It was an honest question. He didn't have to have a normal job, but I figured he had other things to keep him busy. He had a few projects, some businesses I'd heard about throughout the years, but apparently he also had a lot of time to spare. So what did he do when he wasn't at practice?

He kept his attention forward, but I could see the way the shoulder closest to me tightened. His answer was simple. "Nothing."

"You have nothing to do?"

"No." He amended his answer, "A few emails and phone calls, nothing significant."

"Don't you have businesses and other stuff?"

"Yes and I have managers that handle everything so that I don't have to. I've minimized my obligations recently."

That sounded... awful.

"You could do things if you wanted to," I offered lamely. "Community service, get a hobby..."

Kulti shrugged his shoulders.

That didn't help me feel any less weird about how bored he must be. Not having things to do drove me nuts. How could it not drive him crazy too? To stay in his house all day...

I suddenly remembered the night I picked him up from the bar. All right, so maybe he didn't stay in his house all day. Regardless, a lot of things suddenly made sense. Why he played softball, asked me to play soccer with him, why he was in my apartment.

This sense of obligation stirred in my chest. But I didn't say anything or do anything. Mainly because I wasn't planning on forgetting what he'd admitted.

There was such a thing as too much too soon, wasn't there?

Leaning back against the couch for a few more minutes, I

kept the thought in my head. "In that case, you're going to have to grab one of my hats before we leave."

"Why?"

"Because my doctor is a fan of yours." He had a framed jersey in his office.

He cocked an eyebrow.

"Your picture will be all over the internet before you leave," I explained. "Then everyone will ask what you were doing at a doctor's appointment with me, and the next thing I know everyone will say I'm pregnant with your baby."

Kulti huffed. "It wouldn't be the first time."

He was right. I could remember at least a few times over the years that some tabloid or magazine reported that he'd impregnated someone he'd been seen with. They speculated on a new relationship every time he stood next to a woman.

Then there had been his divorce.

It'd been bad. *Bad.* People had put a timeline on his marriage from the moment pictures had been released, which at the time, I thought had been one of the worst days of my life. My first love—this asshole who now called me Taco now—had married some tall, skinny, beautiful bitch.

All right maybe she wasn't a bitch, but back then you couldn't have paid me money to think otherwise.

Exactly one year after his huge spectacle of a wedding, his divorce papers to the Swedish horror-flick actress were filed. Rumors of them cheating on each other, of him starting and ending relationships before things were finalized, talk of an insane pre-nuptial agreement, flooded tabloids and entertainment channels alike. The real kicker had been that the team he'd been playing for that year hadn't even qualified for the finals. People had ripped Kulti apart. I mean, *ripped his ass open.*

While I'd initially forced myself not to follow his career, not to look him up on websites, or even pay attention when his name was brought up, it'd been impossible to ignore all the drama, despite how much I wanted to.

Then he'd come back the next season and won a championship.

I hadn't watched or paid attention to the European League that year, or the two following. By that point, I was too focused on myself and my career. Reiner Kulti had become someone who had nothing to do with me.

"That's the price of fame, huh?" I asked, feeling a stab of pain right through my chest. It really shouldn't have hurt as much as it did. It was weird how even now, when I was fully aware there would never be anything between us, my body still had a severe possessive streak in it. He'd gotten married to someone, and pledged his life to another person.

Bah. I didn't have time for this crap.

Kulti's cheek ticked like he was remembering everything he'd been through too. It wasn't like he was a talkative forthcoming person to begin with, but when he answered with one word, I figured it was still a touchy subject for him. "Yes," was the only thing he said.

All right. I cleared my throat and sang under my breath, "Tough shit, frankfurter."

There was a pause before he let out a snicker. "Sal, I don't know how you haven't gotten elbowed in the face yet."

I opened my mouth and pressed the tip of my tongue behind my upper teeth for a second. "One, at least I tell you things to your face and not behind your back. And two, I have gotten elbowed in the face. Multiple times." I pointed at a scar right smack on my cheekbone, then the underside of my chin and lastly right above my eyebrow. "So, suck on that, pretzel face."

To be fair, he was fast, but I also wasn't expecting it.

The couch cushion hit me right in the face.

* * *

"SAL, I haven't seen you here in forever," the receptionist on the other side of the window said as I handed her a clipboard with my paperwork, driver's license and medical card.

"You make it sound like that's not a good thing," I told her with a smile.

She winked. "We'll call you in for your x-rays in a few."

I nodded at the older woman and smiled at the couple waiting patiently behind me. I walked back to my seat in the corner of the room where the German was sitting with the television remote in his hand, flicking through channels on the mounted flat-screen. I muffled a groan as I sat, my hands gripping the armrests on the journey down.

He was eyeing me, only slightly shaking his head.

"What?"

He looked down, whether at my hands or the v-neck T-shirt I had pulled on I wasn't sure, and then returned his gaze to my face. "You."

"Be quiet. The last time I took time off from training was when my grandfather died. I don't play hooky without a good reason." I blew a long breath out of my mouth and stayed upright, back straight, hands braced to help me up when they called my name.

He reached over and smacked the side of my knee with the back of his hand. "I'll be back."

I opened my mouth and let a huge grin take over my face, the action halting him halfway up. The only reason I didn't laugh was because it would hurt, but I still snorted. "Okay, Arnold."

Kulti didn't look particularly impressed. "He's Austrian, not German, you little shit," he deadpanned, his face saying I was annoying him, but his eyes said he thought I was a little funny.

Besides, I hadn't meant that I thought Arnold was German, but if it annoyed him, it was all the same.

Stretching up to his full height, he hit my knee with his and made his way out of the small reception area in the direction of the restroom. I pulled my phone out of the black leather purse my parents had bought me for Christmas and started typing a message to Marc. I let him know I made it to my appointment, and I'd be going in for an x-ray pretty soon. I hadn't screwed him over too bad today by taking the day off, there wasn't anything terrible on the schedule, but still. I felt bad, even if he was the one who told me I better not tag along until I knew for sure I wouldn't be doing more damage to myself by working.

"Do you mind turning the volume up?"

I glanced up from my phone to see the man who had been behind me checking in with his wife, looking expectantly from his seat across the room. He was referring to the television. "Sure," I said, taking the remote from Kulti's empty seat and absently raising the volume on the television.

It took me a second to realize what the topic on television was for today.

"...it isn't the first time money's bought one of these guys out of trouble. How many times do their handlers hide things that they don't want the public to find out about? There are employees for every big sport you can think of, who follow these superstar athletes around, dragging them back to their hotels after an entire night spent at a strip club or partying. Some fans don't want to hear about their favorite athletes doing normal, human things. Honestly, I'm not surprised if there is a DUI on Kulti's record that no one can find solid proof of it. The guy is a German national hero, even if half the country hates his guts. After the two seasons he spent with the Men's American League, he's practically an American hero—"

I changed the channel, my heart beating up in my throat.

Jesus Christ. They were discussing him having a DUI on

freaking *Sports Room*? Didn't they have anything better to talk about?

"Excuse me. You mind putting it back?" the man across the room asked.

I was suddenly unbelievably thankful that I'd told Kulti he needed to put on one of my hats before we left my apartment. Feeling like a little bit of a dick, I shook my head. "In a minute. I'm sorry."

The stranger couldn't believe I said no, and honestly I was surprised I'd said it too. But when it came down to it, I would rather this stranger think I was rude than Kulti walk over and see that crap playing. He hadn't been acting weird so I didn't think he knew he was being talked about on cable television, but what did I know?

"Are you the TV police or something?" the stranger asked with a frown.

I tried to reason with myself that he was just being a dick because I started it. "No," I said calmly, looking him right in the eye because being shy when you're being rude just makes things worse. "I'll put it back on in a sec."

Hopefully if I waited a minute, the anchors would be talking about something else.

The guy just stared at me. Sometimes you didn't need to actually say the word 'bitch' to get the message across. This guy had obviously mastered that talent.

I sensed Kulti before he actually made it back. He purposely walked right in front of me, the side of his leg bumping into my knees, before taking his spot on the chair next to mine. It took him all of a second to catch onto the ugly vibes the other man was sending.

The German leaned forward, one elbow on his knee and half his body facing me, but his head was cocked at the stranger. Fortunately my hat was pulled down low on his forehead. "I'm sure there's something else you can look at, friend."

"I'd be looking at the TV, *friend*, if your lady hadn't turned it off," the man explained.

Kulti didn't ask me why I turned it off or why I didn't turn it back on. He stayed in the same position he was in, his free hand resting on his other knee. "Instead of worrying about the television, maybe you should be worrying about your cholesterol, no?"

Oh God.

"Miss Casillas, will you follow me?" A voice spoke from the door.

I stood up and lightly punched Kulti in the shoulder as he stared across the room at the other man. He stood up after me, not giving the man another thought. Lowering my voice so only he could hear, I whispered, "You might want to call your publicist. They were talking about Kulti on *Sports Room,* and it wasn't about him playing soccer." I tipped my chin down. "Do you know what I mean?"

His eyes moved from one of mine to the other before he nodded his understanding.

I'm not sure why I did it, but I reached over and gave his wrist a squeeze. "You didn't steal anything or kill anyone. Whatever anyone else who doesn't know you thinks, isn't a big deal."

"Miss Casillas?" the medical personnel called my name once more.

"I'm coming." Making my eyes go wide at the German, I took a step back. "Let me go get this over with."

The last thing I did before heading to the back for my appointment was drop the remote on the seat next to the man's wife. The x-ray went by quickly, mostly because I was thinking about the situation with Kulti. He hadn't confirmed or denied anything. So what did that mean?

Thirty minutes later, I was sitting in a room with my doctor as he showed me a great set of films. "Nothing is broken. See? Not even a hairline fracture," he confirmed.

"That's what I wanted to hear." I smiled at the doctor I'd been going to since I moved to Houston. His medical assistant stood in the corner of the room.

"You should look into doing some milk commercials. You've got some strong bones on you, Sal," he joked around, scribbling something into my file. "I recommend you take a week off to be on the safe side—"

I choked.

"—but at least four days if you choose to be stubborn and get back." He looked up with a smile.

Yeah, that wasn't much better.

"I'll get you a note if you need one, or else just have someone shoot me a call or an email if they want to speak to me," the doctor said. "You don't want to make it any worse. Your body needs the rest."

Four days off would really be five because I'd miss the game and have Sunday off by default.

Handing my file to his assistant, the older man smiled. "My wife and I went to your season opener," he noted. "You've got a real talent, kiddo. I haven't seen anyone move like you since *La Culebra*. You've heard of him, haven't you?"

I only barely caught my smile before it fell off my face. "Yes, I have. That's very nice of you to say." I cleared my throat and ignored the weirdness I felt at the mention of the Latin American star. "Thanks for going to the game, by the way. I can probably get you a set of comp tickets for another one if you'd like to go again."

"That'd be great. Any game would be fine."

I made a mental note to see who I could con some tickets out of.

"So, ah, what's it like working with Kulti?" The doctor's cheeks were pink at the apples.

I was suddenly thankful the German hadn't followed me into the exam room. I could only imagine how much the doctor would flip out if he knew Reiner 'The King' Kulti had been sitting in his waiting room. "It's... great. He's tough, but he knows what he's talking about."

The doctor got this dreamy look in his eyes. "I bet. I've always wanted to meet him. "

So. Not. Obvious.

"I was pretty nervous around him at first." That was the truth. "But he's just like everyone else," I said as I slid off the exam table as gently as possible, not exactly believing the words coming out of my mouth. Kulti wasn't really like everyone else. Not totally. Edging toward the door, I told him, "I'll email you the tickets once I get them."

If he was disappointed that I didn't make an offer to introduce him to the German, he didn't show it. The medical assistant passed me my file and instructed me on how to take care of my co-pay. Thanking the doctor and his assistant once more, I opened the door and found Kulti leaning on the wall next to it.

"You scared me," I said, glancing back to make sure the doctor was still in the room. I gestured toward the exit where the receptionist sat. "Come on."

I made my payment as quickly as possible, trying to get the heck out of there before the doctor saw my friend. My friend who didn't say a single word as we took the elevator down to the lobby, and the same friend that stayed quiet as we got into the car his driver had brought us to the doctor in. His jaw was hard, his shoulders even harder, and I didn't miss the way his hands were fisted as he stared out the window the entire ride back to my place.

I swallowed and looked out the opposite window, not sure what to say to make the situation better. Honestly, I didn't even want to ask what he'd found out. While I was pretty sure he considered me a friend, I didn't fool myself into thinking that he was going to spill his troubles to me. Considering there were things I still would rather he not know either, I figured I wasn't in a position to be a hypocrite and ask.

When the car pulled into the driveway that led to my garage apartment, I hesitated. The German was still looking out the window; apparently he wasn't getting out, I guessed. "Hey."

He didn't turn to look at me completely, but his jaw flexed. He was like a little freaking kid that was pissed off. Avoiding eye contact and not speaking.

All right. "You know your reputation is just what everyone else thinks of you, your character is what you really are."

I knew from the moment he licked his bottom lip that he wasn't yearning for my support. But knowing I was about to get it wasn't enough warning. "If I needed your inspirational bullshit, I would ask for it."

Well, all right.

Bottling up my aggravation, I tried to put myself into his shoes. I would *hate* it if my personal life went public and everyone started talking about it. He was right to be frustrated, but I really was just trying to help. So, okay. *Patience.* Sure he had experience with being under a worldwide microscope, but that didn't mean it would get easier to deal with over time, right?

I sucked in a breath through my nose, my hand squeezing the door handle. "I'm only trying to tell you this isn't the end of the world. You'll get through this like you always have. At the end of the day, this isn't a big deal, all right? "

Kulti kept his attention forward; his index finger went up to scratch at the side of his nose. I could feel the arrogance coming off of him. Good gracious. "How many endorsements do you have?" he asked in a cold voice.

"What does it matter how many endorsements I have?" I replied evenly. I wasn't going to let him make me feel insignificant just because I didn't have the backing or the fan base he did.

"You're a kid with one endorsement who makes in one year what I used to make playing ten minutes of a single game. I don't think you're in any position to tell me what's important and what's not important."

Indignation burned my throat. I straightened up my spine and shot him a really miserable look, which would have been a lot more effective if he was actually facing me. Because *what a fucking douche-bag*. I had this horrible urge to kick him right in the balls. "I'm okay with you being upset that your private life is getting joked about on national television, but I didn't think you'd be a snob when all I'm trying to do is put this in perspective for you."

"You don't know a damn thing," he muttered.

Jesus Christ. "I know enough. You're not the only person in the world that's done something they've regretted. So what if you have your license suspended? Whoopty freaking do, Rey. But it's done and over with, and all that matters is what you do with yourself from now on. Being a prick isn't the way to go about it. But what do I know? I'm poor and I'm young, right?"

Knowing there was nothing left to do or say, I opened the door and turned my whole body to exit the easiest way possible for my ribs. "Thanks for the ride and for coming with me," I said right before hoisting myself out.

Nothing. He didn't say a word as I shut the door.

Well.

# 18

To be fair, I had been warned.

Jenny had sent me a text message letting me know that practice on Friday had been bombarded by reporters wanting the scoop on Reiner Kulti's supposed DUI.

I had just begun wondering why people would care when I reminded myself that I didn't—I shouldn't. Especially not after someone had been a massive asshole to me. For four days I stayed at home, and for three of those days I let myself fume over how he'd spoken to me.

*I made more money in a day than you do in a year for doing the exact same thing*. Of course it pissed me off. The salary scale was a hard fact, as much as it sucked, but he didn't need to be a pretentious dick about it.

Then to top it off, although I hadn't exactly expected an apology, I had definitely not gotten one. Not a text, not a phone call, nothing. So maybe I wouldn't have been so bothered by the overabundance of media sectioned off from the soccer field if Kulti wouldn't have been rude when I was only trying to be a good friend.

"Sal! What do you have to say about your coach's public record?" one yelled.

"How do you feel about—"

I waved them off and kept walking toward the field. "Sorry! I have to get to practice!" It was the truth; I wasn't lying. I did have to get to practice. After four days off with my ribs still the slightest bit sore and my stomach still brushed over with scabs, I had to get back into the swing of things.

My bout with an imaginary virus needed to be over.

"You're back!" Genevieve, one of my teammates, greeted me as I walked passed her. "Are you feeling any better?"

As long as no one punched me in the rib, I would be. Unfortunately that wasn't what I could say to her. "Way better. Good job on Friday, by the way."

She smiled at me and went back to putting on her cleats.

Most of the other girls greeted me as I walked by them, saying that they were happy to see me back or that they'd missed me. It was an exaggeration more than likely but I'd give them the benefit of the doubt. I sure as hell had missed them—at least the field—and Jenny and Harlow for sure. Getting stuck indoors for four days had been torture.

Arms came up from behind to wrap around my neck. "I'm so happy you're back," Jenny said into my ear, giving me a squeeze that had me freezing in place.

"I missed you too," I gripped her forearms before reaching back to smack her in the hip.

She only hugged me harder before pulling away. Standing back, Jenny tipped her head over in the direction of the media, waggling her eyebrows at the same time. "Nuts, huh?"

The fact I had been the one to tell Kulti about the coverage was nuts. The other fact, that Marc was the only one who had any idea that I spent time with the German, was nuts. I wasn't the type to have secrets—and this one made me feel bad. I was lying to my friends and family, and it wasn't like I could stop this deep into it.

All I could do was nod, turning around to face her. "Yeah. I don't see what the big deal is."

"Me neither." Jenny shrugged but quickly reached up to tap my elbow. She lowered her voice to a whisper. "He's been in a horrible mood since then." She paused like she was really thinking about what came out of her mouth. "In a *worse* mood. I overheard him tell Grace she should look into retiring."

My eyes bugged out.

Jenny just nodded.

Jeez. I thought about it for possibly five more seconds and then shook off my Kulti-related thoughts. I had better things to do.

"Come help me stretch. Everything is tight," I told her.

She reached up and squeezed my shoulder. It took everything inside of me not to buckle my knees in order to get further away from her. As casually as possible, I stepped out of her reach. Seriously, I wondered if her boyfriend let her get anywhere near his privates.

I was in the middle of wondering if she'd ever given a hand job when I spotted Gardner and Kulti walking toward the field together. Whether they were talking or not, I couldn't tell, but my teeth responded to the sight of the German.

If he'd apologized the next day or the one after that, I would have forgiven him with only giving him a minimal amount of shit. It wasn't like he was the first person to make an asshole-ish comment to me in my life, and there was no way he'd be the last. My own mom had said some pretty rude things to me at one point or another, but I always forgave her. I wasn't even going to get started with the stuff Ceci, my little sister, had said to me over the years, which only reminded me of my upcoming trip back to San Antonio for my dad's birthday; I still needed to get him something.

"I'll grab you a mini-band," Jenny said, tearing me out of my thoughts, thankfully.

I needed to focus.

* * *

SQUEEZING MY EYES SHUT, I fell back against the turf to try and catch my breath after running sprints. My back hurt, my lungs felt like they were wrapped in an iron band that was shrinking by the minute, and as much as I wanted to pull up my shirt to fan off, I couldn't without showing everyone my belly.

Good grief.

A shadow came over my chest, followed shortly by, "You have more in you, *schnecke*. Get up."

I kept my eyes closed. The temptation to ignore him was overwhelming, but I couldn't do that. Pretending like he wasn't there would just give him more power. On top of that, *schnecke?* What the hell did that mean? It didn't matter. Whatever. "I'll be up in a second," I told him on a long exhale.

My own personal eclipse didn't move despite the fact I had at least responded to him.

I didn't bother opening my eyes either as I finished catching my breath.

The shadow shifted to the right as something hit the side of my foot. "Are you well enough to play today?" Kulti's voice was low as he spoke.

His nudge got me to open my eyes and stare straight up at the blue-gray sky. "No."

Kulti was standing by my feet, his hands behind his back as he looked down at me.

I glanced at him for a second then rolled to sit up gently and get to my feet. Sparing him another look, I gave the German a tight smile I wasn't feeling at all. "I need to get back."

That's exactly what I did.

* * *

AT EIGHT O'CLOCK THAT NIGHT, my cell phone dinged with a text.

From my spot on the couch with my socked feet up on the coffee table, I glanced at the screen and saw 'German Chocolate Cake' pop up.

I went right back to watching my show. If it was life or death he'd call, and he didn't.

* * *

AT FIVE O'CLOCK the following afternoon, my phone beeped with an incoming text message again.

'German Chocolate Cake' appeared on the screen.

For a second I thought about picking it up and possibly reading the message, but I'd ignored the one the day before; during practice today, he'd given me a massive amount of hell during my one-on-one game. Basically, he was acting like nothing was wrong, and like he hadn't been an ass days before.

Now he was texting me again.

"Did they get your phone number?" Marc asked from behind the wheel.

I set my phone back between my legs and shook my head. Marc already knew about the insanity at practice with the reporters and the mystery behind Kulti's driving record. He'd been warning me that it was only a matter of time before someone got desperate enough to call, especially since Jenny and I were the only players that had pictures with him floating around the internet.

"No." I smiled at my friend and before I realized what the hell was coming out of my mouth, I made something up. "Wrong number."

* * *

"ARE YOU DONE?"

I pulled my bag up and over my opposite shoulder and straightened, wiping at my forehead with the back of my hand. "I have to get to work."

The German had his own bag over his shoulder. His handsome, handsome face was tight as he ran a hand over his head.

I raised my eyebrows, forced a smile on my face and turned to start walking.

Kulti's hand whipped out to grab my wrist, stopping me in place. "Sal," he hissed, turning me to face him.

I took a breath through my nose and tipped my head back to look him in the eye. "Kulti, I need to get to work. "

His head jerked back, the corner of his cheek rounding like he was sticking his tongue there. "Kulti, really?"

"That's your name, isn't it?" I slid my arm up and out of his grip, keeping my gaze locked on those green-brown eyes that seemed lighter today than usual. "Look, I really need to get to work. I need my job to help me pay bills." So maybe my smile turned a little condescending, a little smug and just the tiniest bit bitchy.

"You shouldn't give me the power to make you angry." He lowered his face to mine and I had to fight the urge to roll my eyes.

"What I shouldn't do is waste my time on someone with an attitude problem."

Kulti's Adam's apple bobbed, his gaze intense on me as he took his time replying. The words were even and steady out of his mouth. "I used to make more money in a day than most people do, you aren't the only one—"

This wasn't helping at all. My eye twitched. "Yeah you made more money in a day than most people in third world countries make in a lifetime. Trust me, I understand, and I could care less about how much money you make or don't make. Don't be an idiot."

He wasn't used to being called an idiot if the look on his face said anything, but by that point I couldn't have cared less. "I've worked as hard as you did to get to where I'm at. Just because I don't make as much money as you doesn't make me any less worthy."

Kulti shook his head. "I never said it did."

"Well, you sure made it seem like it did. Just like you made me feel this small for having another job," I told him, holding my thumb and index finger about an inch apart.

"Sal," he grumbled my name.

I raised an eyebrow at him. "I do landscaping. Did you know that? Because you've never asked, but I think you should know if you didn't. Sorry I'm not sorry that I can't live up to your standards."

"What standards?"

"Your standards. I can't give you advice because I'm too young? Or is it that I'm poor? Wait, it's because I'm a girl. Is that it?"

"Why are you being so stubborn about this? That isn't what I meant."

That had me letting out a sharp laugh. "If our roles were switched, you really think you wouldn't say something similar if not worse? Seriously?" He'd tell me to eat shit and kiss his ass for sure, and that was the PG-13 version of it.

He knew it was the truth from the way his tongue poked at the side of his cheek.

I gently tugged my arm away from him, and he let me that time. "Look, I'm not in the mood to talk to you right now. You don't get to take your anger out on me and expect me to get over it like nothing happened. The fact is, I would never say what you said to me to anyone. I thought we were friends and that's my mistake. I don't want to be friends with someone that looks down on me. I really do need to get to work." I took a couple steps back and offered him a smile that I wasn't feeling. "I'll talk to you later."

I have no idea if or how he responded because I took off. I hadn't been lying. Marc and I had a lot of work to do.

* * *

I STARED at the images on the tablet.

"Is it?"

*Was it me in the pictures?* Yes, it was. Clasping my hands and settling them between my thighs, I looked away from the photographs that had been taken right outside of my doctor's building.

The first picture I'd been shown was of me walking alongside Kulti with my head down. The second was of me standing by his car right before getting in, and the third showed me getting in while the German stood a little too close behind.

It was definitely me. There was no denying it; anyone with decent vision could recognize who it was.

So the fact that Gardner, Sheena and Cordero, the Pipers' general manager, had invited me to a meeting to talk about this had me on edge.

*Is it you*? Cordero had asked shortly before Sheena slid the tablet over.

It was a trick freaking question and I didn't like it. Maybe it was a good thing that I wasn't a liar and that I didn't have anything to hide. Regardless, I was still on edge.

I looked at the man behind this crap right in the eye and nodded. "It's me."

None of them looked remotely surprised. Of course they wouldn't. Mr. Cordero knew damn who was on the photographs; he just wanted me to slit my own throat with a lie.

Digging my hands a little deeper into the crack between my

thighs, I shrugged at them. "He went with me to my doctor's appointment when I wasn't doing well." *Doing well* was vague enough so that it wasn't a total lie. Keeping my face neutral, I kept my gaze steady on the team's general manager. "I haven't done anything wrong."

The Argentinian man settled onto his hip, his chair the closest to mine. "'Wrong' is a bit subjective, don't you think?"

"Sure." I shrugged. "But in this case, I haven't violated any terms of my contract or done anything I wouldn't be upfront with my dad about."

Well... I had told my dad hardly anything about my friendship with the German. Or anyone else really, but that was mainly because everyone would make a big deal over it and there wasn't a deal to make, big or small.

A knock on the door prevented anyone from saying another word. Gardner instructed the person to come in, and I couldn't say I was shocked to see Kulti. His eyes caught mine as he took the seat nearest the door. His face was expressionless, his broad shoulders loose. Still in his clothing from practice, track pants and a Pipers T-shirt, he leaned back against his chair and stared straight at Mr. Cordero. "What's going on?"

The general manager reached for the tablet on Gardner's desk and passed it to the German. "These images were released a couple of days ago."

Kulti glanced at the screen for a second, and only a second before handing the device back with an impatient look. "What's wrong with them?"

"These are pictures of you and one of the team's star players on one of the most popular tabloid websites in the world," Mr. Cordero explained in a cool voice that sounded just shy of crossing the edge into smart-ass town.

In what would begin two of the most unreal moments of my life, Kulti crossed his muscular arms—so lean, I could see veins crisscrossing his forearms and one or two running up his biceps—and shrugged. "What I see is a picture of me taking my friend to the doctor."

"Your friend?" Cordero asked in disbelief.

"That's what I said," Kulti snapped back. His volume was low but there wasn't any mistaking his irritation with the conversation.

Mr. Cordero turned to me, like I could possibly be handling Reiner Kulti calling me his friend in front of three Pipers staff, well. "You're friends?" It wasn't my imagination that he sounded like a bit more of an ass when he'd been speaking to me than he had when speaking to the German. Then again, I wasn't some country's national icon.

I nodded at the Pipers' general manager, my emotions twisted into knots at Kulti's admission. "Yes." We were friends when he wasn't getting on my nerves at least.

"Friends," he said absently. "What kind of friends?"

Yeah, I wanted to smack him. I mean I knew what it looked like, but *seriously?* I'd given up so much for the Pipers, and he would think that I'd do something to jeopardize the only part of soccer I really had left? My face flushed red as I tried to talk myself out of saying something that could only hurt my career more than it already had been.

I knew what he was trying to do, and I sure as hell wasn't going to let this man who worked in an office make me out to seem like I didn't take this job seriously. "We are the kinds of friends that have a lot of things in common." Jesus Christ.

Before I could say anything else logical, the German cut in with his response. "The greatest kind. I don't understand why that's a problem."

If I was one to swoon, I would have, but instead I let my brain react to his comment instead of my heart. Had I been expecting him to denounce me? Yeah, I guess I had.

All right. Okay.

He'd still been a dick a few days before. What he said didn't change anything.

"There isn't a problem or a reason for us to be here," the German stated in a way that left little room to argue. "You were well aware of the media coverage my coming here would bring, and you wanted me here either way. You can't pick and choose what people publish."

Sheena let out a tight laugh. "Mr. Kulti, it doesn't look good—"

"You can't tell me who I can or can't be friends with," he cut her off. "It doesn't really matter what something looks like if it isn't what it truly is, no?"

Wait a second, that sounded sort of familiar...

Sheena turned her attention to me, her face slightly flushed. "Sal, with your history—"

This bitch started to go there. I needed to cut it short. "I haven't done anything wrong in this case. If I had I wouldn't have a problem taking responsibility for my actions. He's my friend and there isn't anything inappropriate about our friendship. I have nothing to be embarrassed about."

The sting of guilt that I *hadn't* told anyone about him was there, but I would swear I had only kept it to myself because I didn't want this type of attention. There were some things people couldn't understand, and obviously this was one of them.

Kulti uncrossed his arms and leaned forward, elbows on his knees, his face even further away from the back of the chair. "This wouldn't be a problem if it wasn't for the PR issues going on with me at this moment. There's nothing here that is worth us having a conversation. She's my best friend—"

I shot him a look out of the corner of my eye, reminding him of the shit that had come out of his mouth outside my apartment. It said *is that how best friends treat each other? Really?*

Apparently he saw my facial expression and didn't care that

I wasn't feeling particularly friendly at that point. "Nothing any of you say is going to change that. That's the end of the story. If there's something else you want, call my manager."

"Sal—"

I was torn between panicking at why they were making a big deal out of this and debating whether or not it was worth standing up for myself. "They're just pictures of us getting into his car," I argued halfheartedly, unsure what route I needed to take.

I was a good player, one of the most consistent on the team, but the truth was everyone was replaceable. I couldn't afford to act like a diva, but at the same time the little voice inside of my head wanted me to tell these people—and by people I really meant Cordero—to fuck off.

"Miss Casillas, I think you've made it clear your decision-making skills are nothing to—" Cordero began ranting.

Kulti lurched forward in his seat, and I felt my eyes go wide at his defensive posture. "I'm going to tell you right now that you don't want to finish that sentence."

Gardner coughed. "There's no reason for anyone to get bent out of shape. I believe you, Sal, if you say that you're friends, you're friends. You've never given me a reason to not trust you. I think we can all agree that we want this season to go smoothly or at least smoother than it has been going."

"This is my fault. I will take responsibility for the negative attention, but I won't let you put the blame on her for befriending me," Kulti said. "Sal has done nothing wrong."

"I don't think you all understand. This doesn't look good," Sheena said quickly, before anyone cut her off. "Do you think you could... I don't know, Mr. Kulti, I'm just throwing out ideas for you to talk to your publicist about, but... do something publicly to pull rumors away from... this... friendship?"

"Go on a date?"

Kulti didn't even hesitate. "No."

"But—"

"No," he repeated.

Sheena's desperate eyes met mine. "Sal, what about you? Could you go on a date? Post some pictures—"

"No."

That was definitely not me that answered her. It was Kulti who answered almost angrily. I let him.

"Sal—"

"No." That was Kulti again. "Absolutely not."

"But—"

"Stop asking," the German snapped. "I'm not doing it and neither is she."

"I've done just about everything that's ever been asked of me. I don't want to do this," I explained gingerly, trying to ease over the hostility radiating off the man next to me.

Cordero guffawed.

Ten minutes later, I found Kulti waiting outside of Gardner's office. Mr. Cordero had left first, with the German following immediately afterward. Sheena stayed in the office to discuss something. What else could it be besides me or the German?

"There's nothing for you to worry about," Kulti's deep, heavy voice assured me.

I scratched my forehead, trying to urge away the frustration I felt at the conversation that had just finished up. A nasty nagging feeling had taken up residence in my belly. This wasn't sitting well with me, and honestly I was really worried they were going to try and find something to use against me. I wasn't sure why I felt so pessimistic, but I did.

An elbow nudged at mine. "Stop worrying," he ordered.

I blinked at him and didn't even think about pulling my elbow away. He'd called me his best friend; I'd give him half-credit for that... though he was still a douche. "I can't," I whispered to him as we approached the elevator in the office building. "Cordero doesn't play around. He isn't a fan of mine."

Kulti made this face that told me I needed to chill out. "He's like every general manager on every team. He thinks he's a god and he's not." He nudged my elbow once more. "You don't have anything to worry about."

My stomach and my head said otherwise. Nerves had started eating up my organs. "I don't want to get traded, and I don't want them to bench me."

I wasn't going to have a panic attack. I wasn't going to have a panic attack.

This wasn't going to be like the national team all over again. I hadn't done anything wrong.

I pressed my hands against my hips and squeezed, willing myself to calm down.

"Sal." Kulti stood right in front of me. "Nothing is going to happen. I won't let them do anything, understand?"

My knees started to shake the same way they did when I was in front of a camera. Oh God, I was going to throw up. Sometime in the last two minutes I had started sweating.

"Sal," the German's voice got even louder, more determined. His big hands landed on my shoulders. "No one is going to make you do anything that you don't want to do. " He kneaded the muscle there, his voice a gentle reassuring cadence. "I promise."

It was the 'I promise' that had me glance up at him; I felt this huge ugly knot of dread creep up to the center of my chest. "I like it here."

His green-brown eyes seemed so close to mine. "Remember all that money I made?"

The urge to punch him in the gut was still there, but instead I nodded. "What about it?"

"I can afford the best lawyers."

"You want me to sue them?" I coughed out.

"If it's necessary."

Holy shit. "I don't want to. I just want to play, here."

"I know." He gave my shoulders a squeeze. "If it comes to it," the German continued, "we'll worry about it. You're the best player on the team. They won't get rid of you."

Another shot to the heart. Jesus Christ. The best player on the team? I felt greedy, like I needed to gobble up all these nice things and store them for a rainy day when he called me a slow-ass, or even one day when I was older and couldn't play anymore. I could think back and remember the day the five-time World Player of the Year, The King, told me I was the best player on my team.

He shook my arm. "Yes?"

I nodded, still the slightest bit unsure. "Yes."

Kulti nodded and blew out a breath. There were dark circles under his clear eyes, and he looked conflicted. "When I get angry I have a hard time controlling what I say," he said, his chin tipping down.

"Oh, I know. Trust me." I blinked. "Or don't."

The German gave an exaggerated sigh. "You are my best friend."

I started to make a face like 'yeah, right.' Me? His best friend? I'd take 'friend'. I took the title in the office because it seemed like such a monumental thing to say in order to get me out of trouble.

But... as soon as I started to make a face, I stopped. Kulti wasn't a man that wasted his words, so... "You have a horrible way of showing it."

"I know." But he didn't apologize. "I've done a great deal of things I regret now, and it's difficult for me at times to cope with them."

My eyes narrowed, curiosity prickling at me. I might never get a chance to encounter an apologetic Reiner Kulti again. Taking a quick look around, I made sure there wasn't another person within listening distance and I whispered, "Did you really get a DUI?"

Answering the question wasn't as easy as I'd hoped it would be, but with a great gulp, Kulti tipped his chin down.

Well. That wasn't exactly shocking. He'd been blitzed out of his mind when I'd picked him up from that bar months ago. People made mistakes all the time. He had a right to make them as much as the next person. "Okay," I told him simply. "Thank you for telling me."

His gaze flickered from one of my eyes to the other before he took a shallow breath and swallowed, his Adam's apple bobbing with the force. "I was in a bad place after I retired," he explained in that low voice that I liked, unexpectedly. "I was very angry and I picked up a bad habit I'm not proud of."

I nodded slowly, still keeping an eye out to make sure no one was around. "Do you need help?" I whispered.

Kulti's eye started to twitch, but he shook his head. "I've been sober for over a year."

I closed one eye and made a face. His timeframe was debatable.

"With the exception of that one day, I have no problem not drinking, but once I start..." Kulti knuckled his brow bone. This *was* hard for him to admit. Who wanted to admit their failures? Not me. Definitely not him. "I let myself down, and I know there are people that this news could disappoint even more. There won't be any bars in my future anymore either way. I would rather stay home." He nudged me. "Or at your home."

Yeah, I was a total sucker, forgiving people way too easily.

My facial expression must have said that because he nudged me again. "You and I fight, yes? It's in our nature. I think you should get used to the idea." The corners of his mouth tipped up just a bit. "Are we fine now?" he asked earnestly, expectantly.

Were we? I knew what the polite thing to say would be, but

I wasn't a liar. At least I wasn't usually. I told Kulti the truth. "Mostly. You're still a jackass for what you said, but I'll forgive you because I know you were upset and some people say things they don't mean in the heat of the moment. So as long as you don't say something so stupid again, I can live with it this once, Reindeer."

The look he gave me was blank for so long, I wasn't expecting him to react the way he did. I thought for sure he'd argue with me some more about how I needed to get over being pissed at him, however small the amount.

He didn't.

Instead almost a minute after I finished talking, the doors were opening to the main level of the office building; Kulti burst out laughing. I swear he said something like "Reindeer" under his monster laughs.

# 19

"Hey, Gen. Good morning," I said to Genevieve as she walked by me the afternoon of our next game, two days after the meeting in Gardner's office.

The younger girl, who had always been friendly with me, kept on going. Her eyebrows went up as she walked by and that was that.

Now, I didn't think too much about it. I was used to being around girls. Girls with all kinds of reactions to their periods: the ones who got unnaturally angry, the ones that cried, girls who retreated within themselves, the ones who wanted to stuff their face all day—all those and more. It wasn't a big deal. Mood swings, been there done that.

I figured maybe she was having a crappy day or something. There was also the possibility she was on her period. Who knows.

Not even fifteen minutes later, right at the beginning of the team's warm-up, I overheard someone behind me. "Did you see the pictures?"

I couldn't exactly pinpoint the person speaking, and I didn't want to turn around until I heard a little more. It wasn't like there were any other pictures besides mine and Kulti's, but whatever.

"What pictures?" the other voice asked in a regular volume.

A second later, the original speaker said "Shut up," and was then followed up by "Ouch."

Now speaking in a lower voice, the second person asked, "What pictures?" in a whisper.

"The ones of—" there was a pause, "and Kulti."

"What? No. What of?" the second voice asked.

There was another pause followed by "—was coming out of some building with him, and it shows them getting into his car."

"Really?"

"Yeah. It's—" pause "—for sure. I heard they had a meeting with Cordero and Gardner about it and that they didn't deny it—"

I felt awkward, so, so awkward. Even after I made myself stop listening to what they were saying, I still felt aggravated. It had already begun, the rumors and the stretched truths. The urge to turn around and tell them that wasn't exactly how it'd gone was overwhelming, but I had to practice what I preached.

I hadn't done anything.

The only problem was that the longer practice went on, the more I felt the weight of multiple stares on me. I overheard a few of the whispers. It wasn't every girl, but it was enough of my teammates to make me feel dirty,

I knew that I hadn't done anything to be embarrassed about and Kulti knew that we hadn't, so it shouldn't matter what everyone else thought.

If I reminded myself of it enough, it was easier to ignore the girls that gave me funny looks.

Besides the looks and the whispers, practice went okay. The last game before our week off, on the other hand, didn't go so well. We lost in overtime. The locker room was filled with disappointment afterward. It wasn't until the coaching staff had left and I'd started changing, intent on showering once I got back to my place, that Jenny saddled up next to me on our way out.

The expression on her face prepared me for what was going to come out of her mouth. "Sal, I didn't want to say anything but some of the girls are talking about you."

I gave her a smile over my shoulder that I wasn't totally feeling. "I know."

That didn't make her look any less concerned.

"It's fine, Jen. I promise. I haven't done anything I shouldn't have, and I'm not going to run around defending myself."

"I know." Her dark almond-shaped eyes were long. "I don't like hearing them say things about you."

My neck got all hot. "Me neither. It doesn't matter though." I looked my friend in the face, understanding that she really did believe me when I said I hadn't done anything with the German. At least someone knew better. "You know I didn't and I know, and I'm okay with that."

Jenny pressed her lips together and nodded stiffly. "If there's anything I can do—"

"Don't worry about it, really. There's nothing to get mixed up in. They'll get over it." Or they wouldn't. Blah. But I wasn't about to let people who would so easily talk about me behind my back get me down.

And wasn't that kind of shitty? I would have done just about anything for the girls on the team, even if it was someone I wasn't close to. Yet here they were, gossiping like I hadn't worked with most of them, trying to help them improve, or trying to motivate everyone when we needed it. On top of that, someone within that group was the person that had thrown me under the bus with Cordero weeks ago.

Whatever. *Whatever*. I'd been through this before, but this time I wasn't going to let guilt get the best of me. I had nothing to feel guilty about.

My friend made a face before slipping an arm over my shoulder as we walked. "I know who's gotten a nose job," she offered. "I also know who has a yeast infection. What you do with that is up to you."

I started laughing and hugged her back. "That's all right, but thanks anyway."

Jenny eventually dropped her arm as we got out to the parking lot. Her face still held worried lines at her mouth but she changed the subject. "Are you still going home for the break?"

"Yeah, it's my dad's birthday and I haven't been back in a while. You?"

She undid her high ponytail and let her long, black hair fall down her shoulders. "I'm leaving tomorrow morning. We have a couple of exhibition games coming up in a few days. I won't be back for almost two weeks." The 'we' she was referring to was the national team.

I was a supporter of Jenny and Harlow, and I always rooted for them. But for once in a long time, I felt a twinge of something like grief.

"Fun," I told her, only half-meaning it. I mustered up some enthusiasm for the person that was always supportive of me. "I'll make sure Harlow tells Amber I said hi," I said with an evil smile that made Jenny snort.

"You're bad."

I smacked her butt. "Only when I need to be."

* * *

THE FAMILIAR KNOCK that I'd come to associate with Kulti started up at seven-fifteen the next morning. I'd already been awake for almost an hour and a half, finishing up my morning run and making it home to pack my bag before showering so that I could head out on my drive to San Antonio. The last thing I expected was for the German to show up on my doorstep, especially not at seven in the morning.

I grabbed a sweatshirt off the pile of clothes on my bed with every intention of putting it on when the knocking became even more persistent. *Impatient ass.* I carried it to the door with a sigh, not even bothering to check the peephole.

"Bratwurst?" I asked as I undid the deadbolt again.

"*Ja.*"

I swung the door wide and started to wave him in, only slowing down my movement when I noticed what he was wearing—a shirt, jeans and scuffed brown leather boots. It was the first time I'd seen him in something that wasn't workout pants or shorts. Huh. A second later, I noticed something else.

There was a backpack over his shoulder.

And he was staring at me.

I didn't miss the tic in his jaw as he looked from the seven-year-old tank top I had on over my sports bra to the stretchy shorts that looked more like underwear than anything else.

I also didn't miss the way his eyelid started twitching right before his gaze finally slipped upward and the twitching got worse.

"What?" I asked him when he hadn't moved his body or his gaze.

Those murky green eyes flicked down to what I was wearing again. His voice was too steady and slow. "You open the door half naked all the time?"

Oh dear God. "Yeah, Dad." I blinked at him and stood off to the side to give him room to come in. "You coming in—" I eyed his bag again "—or are you leaving?"

"I'm leaving," he said even as he walked into my place, still giving my workout clothes this disapproving scowl.

"Where are you going?" I closed the door behind him.

Kulti dropped his bag right by my work boots. "To Austin."

"Really? Why?" I mean, I liked Austin as much as anyone. I'd been there a hundred times in my life, but it wasn't my favorite city in the world. I wouldn't expect this guy to want to spend his days off in Austin when he could afford to go just about anywhere.

The German made his way toward my kitchen and straight to the cupboards, pulling out a mug. "I have an appointment this afternoon."

Why the first thing I thought he was referring to was plastic surgery, I had no idea. I planted my hands on the counter between us and leaned forward, giving him a disbelieving look. "*No.*"

He glanced over his shoulder as he found a small pot and began filling it up with water from my fridge. "Yes?"

"Rey, buddy, don't do it. You're still really handsome, and honestly you can always tell when someone's had surgery done to them. I don't care what the plastic surgeon says, it's noticeable," I told him totally seriously.

He set the pot down on the stovetop but he didn't turn the burner on. His broad shoulders slumped forward as he lifted a hand and pinched the tip of his nose. When he turned around to face me, his eyes were closed and the tip of his tongue was at the corner of his mouth. "Burrito." He opened one eye. "I'm getting my tattoo worked on."

"Ohh." Well, I felt like an idiot.

He nodded, the movement all smart-ass.

"The one on your arm?" It was the only one I knew of.

He nodded again.

Why he was going all the way to Austin when there were about a million tattoo shops in Houston was beyond me, but whatever. "That's neat. I'm going back home." I then realized he didn't know what 'home' was to me. "San Antonio. It's close to Austin."

Kulti shocked the shit out of me when he said "I know. I'll pay you a thousand dollars to take me to Austin."

"What?"

"I will pay you a thousand dollars to take me to Austin." He gestured with his head toward the bag that had been left by the door. "Gas as well."

I scratched my nose, trying to make sure he wasn't joking. My gut said he wasn't. He definitely wasn't. "You want me to drive you to Austin for your appointment?" I couldn't help but ask.

The German nodded.

"All right." I narrowed my eyes at him, debating how to go about this and deciding there was no pretty way. "I don't know how to say this without sounding like a bad friend who doesn't appreciate your generous offer, but… why don't you have your driver take you?"

"His daughter's birthday is today," he explained.

"And you want me to drive you, even though you could just pay someone else less money to take you?" I asked slowly.

"Yes."

Oh brother. The lazy part of me that was dead set on spending four days with my parents, didn't want to drive Kulti around. Then the other half of me felt bad telling him no. "I was planning on spending the weekend at my parents', I can't drive you back here right after your appointment."

He lifted up a single bulky shoulder. "I don't have anything else to do."

Score one for Sal being a fucking douche bag.

He didn't have anything else to do.

Why did that make me feel so shitty?

But I couldn't let him make me feel bad. I couldn't back out on my parents. "Rey, I'm spending the weekend there. I can't drive you back. I already promised them I would go."

"I heard you the first time," he replied in a tone I was not a fan of. "I said I don't have anything else to do. I'll stay with you."

He'd stay—

He'd stay with me?

An image of my dad fainting flashed through my mind.

"Stay with me at my parents'?"

He lifted another lazy shoulder. "Yes."

"For the weekend?"

The smart-ass rolled his eyes. "*Ja*."

Snarky bastard.

"Is that a problem?" he asked after a moment of me not saying anything.

I cleared my throat and thought of my dad again. "Remember my dad was a big fan of yours?" He nodded. "He's a huge fan, you have to understand that if you want to go and—" I gulped, "stay with them. He might faint and act like he doesn't speak English the entire weekend." Then I thought about it. "And stare, he might stare at you and not say a word."

The German seemed to think about it for all of five seconds before he shrugged, like none of what I said would bother him at all. Not even a little bit. "Yes. Fine."

I took a deep breath because I suddenly couldn't comprehend what I had just signed myself up for. "Are you sure?" I asked him slowly.

He gave me a look right before turning back to grab the pot again. "Yes. Now go shower and put on something that covers you up more."

I had no idea what I was getting myself into. Not a single freaking clue.

* * *

"So, why did you decide to come here instead of some place in Houston?" I asked nearly nine hours later as I pulled my car into a parking spot in front of the nice building Kulti's phone had directed us to.

We hadn't left my place until a little after ten, since there was no point in us rushing around because his appointment wasn't until four. The drive was a little less than three hours. To kill time we stopped for lunch at one of my favorite barbecue places along the way, stopped and walked around the Capitol and visited a dollar store. Kulti had asked in the office supply section, "Everything costs one dollar?" Then he proceeded to inspect every item we came across.

Unbuckling his seatbelt, he gave me another look still clearly insulted that I had assumed he was getting cosmetic surgery earlier. "I saw their work in a magazine."

That was all the information he gave me. All right.

We got out of the car and made our way toward the door inscribed with 'Pins and Needles' in classy simple font. Kulti reached forward and opened it. In the back of my head, I'd figured the German wouldn't have chosen some seedy place where you'd probably get crabs if you sat on the toilet, so I wasn't surprised by how clean and modern-looking the tattoo parlor was. Heavy metal played softly in the background.

A redheaded man was sitting behind the black desk at the front, working on something with a pencil. He looked up when we went in and gave us a friendly smile. "Hey, how's it going?"

When I realized Mr. Non-Congeniality wasn't saying anything, I smiled back at the man while elbowing Kulti in the arm for being rude. "Good, and you?"

"Great." He glanced at the German and something like recognition flickered in his gaze, before he set his pencil on the desk. He swiped the computer mouse next to his hand and glanced at the screen before slowly sliding his gaze back to Kulti. "Dex will be out in a minute, if you want to take a seat."

"Thanks." I smiled at him again and turned back to sit on

one of the black leather couches. Kulti stayed standing, walking toward the wall where multiple magazine articles were framed.

Not even thirty seconds later, the sound of boots on the tiled floor didn't prepare me for the black-haired man who made his way from the back of the business. Tall, broad shouldered and with tattoos that went all the way down to his wrists, I couldn't help but stare at him.

I'd never been a fan of guys that looked like they'd gone to jail, but you'd have to be blind to not appreciate how good-looking the man was, even if he wasn't my type.

Because, Jesus Christ.

"He's wearing a wedding ring," Kulti's low voice murmured from right next to me.

"That doesn't mean I can't look," I muttered right back, noticing that yeah, he was wearing a shiny yellow-gold wedding band right above a tattoo of what looked like a letter.

Something came down over my eyes and I realized that the German had pulled his beanie down over my head. "Hold this," he said, continuing to tug the material down over my nose.

"Hey, man." A voice that I knew had to belong to the tattooed black-haired guy, sounded closer. The sound of two palms slapping together was right by my head as I rolled the dark green beanie up over my forehead.

Sure enough Kulti and the other guy were right in front of me, shaking hands. The German was only slightly shorter than the man, who was probably just a little younger, but as I took in their differences, Kulti looked down at me and gave me a look that had me smirking. His face was one I was nearly as familiar with as my own, so good-looking and stubborn and proud.

I'd still stare at Kulti over the tattooed guy any day, every day.

"You wanna look at the sketch one more time before we do the transfer?" the tattoo artist asked, taking a step back and not looking down at me once.

"Yes. How long will everything take?"

The dark-haired man shrugged. "Couple hours."

The German nodded before speaking to me, his hand resting on my shoulder. "*Schnecke,* I'll pay you to—"

"Shut up and get your tattoo fixed. I'm not taking your money anyway, loser."

He looked at me for a second and then pulled the flap of his beanie back down over my eyes.

By the time I managed to roll it back up, the wet-dream-worthy men were walking toward one of the work areas behind the front desk. I settled back into my seat, prepared to watch some Netflix on my phone while I waited, when the tattoo artist made his way back to the desk.

"If Ritz isn't back in ten minutes, give her a call," he said to the redheaded guy.

"You got it, Dex. She sent me a text twenty minutes ago saying she was on her way, so I'm sure she'll be back in no time."

The dark-haired guy grunted and before he got a chance to reply, the door opened and a girl around my age came in carrying a car seat in one hand and a diaper bag in the other. The guy named Dex immediately came around the desk, scowling.

"What the hell are you doin', babe? I told you to give me a fuckin' call when you parked so I could help you out," he snapped in a harsh voice, taking the car seat from her with a heavily tattooed arm. He held the seat up to face level and peered inside, what looked like dark blue eyes narrowing before a smile broke across his harsh face. "How's my little man?" he whispered, dipping his head even closer into the cocoon of the seat and making an audible kissing sound.

Dear God. A man like that making kissing sounds at what I could only guess was his baby. My vagina, my vagina didn't know what to do with itself.

The girl smiled, not even remotely fazed at the way the guy had been talking to her or by the way I sat there in awe looking at them. "I'm not going to call when I know you have an appointment, and I scored a spot on the street so it's no big deal." She was still looking at the man with the baby before adding "hey, Slim" with a glance at the redhead behind the desk.

The ginger blew her a kiss. "I've missed you."

"I've missed you too," she said.

Dex lowered the baby carrier back down and frowned at the girl. "Give me a fuckin' kiss, will ya?"

She rolled her eyes and cut the distance between them, coming up to her toes to plant her lips against the dark-haired man's. He wrapped his free arm around her waist and pulled her right into the broad frame of his body, deepening the kiss even though he was holding a baby carrier in his free hand.

I had to look away.

Maybe it was time I started looking for someone to let into my life. It'd been five years since the last time I'd had an honest real boyfriend, and I wasn't traveling as much anymore.

I could make it work. Couldn't I?

My stupid eyes moved over to Kulti's direction for one split second before I forced them down to my lap. I slipped my headphones on, peeked up again to see Dex holding the baby carrier in a hand as he and the girl walked to the back, and then started up a movie on my phone to keep me busy until the German was done. Sometime later, a hand waving at me from the front desk caught my attention. It was the redheaded guy.

"Hey," I said, taking my headphones off and pausing the movie.

The girl from earlier was sitting next to the desk with him, no baby seat in sight, but there was a baby monitor on the desk. "I don't usually act like a fan-boy," the man said, his voice a whisper. "But... is that Kulti?" His face was really hopeful.

I set my phone on my lap and watched as he leaned forward for my reply. "Yes."

The guy pumped his fist in the air and turned back to the girl. "I told you so!" he whisper-hissed at her, which only made me smile.

"His hair is different," she responded to him in a low voice, looking back to make sure she wasn't being overheard.

"He does look different with his hair short," I agreed, stretching my neck up but only able to catch a glimpse of the guy they'd called Dex hunched over.

"Do you think he'd give me an autograph?" the redhead asked.

I nodded.

The guy grinned all teeth at the girl, who smiled at me. "He's the most famous person we've had in here, at least since I started. There was that boxer guy that was a friggin' jerk but no one was impressed," she explained shyly. She turned back around before adding, looking at the ginger, "I used to have a big crush on him. He was so cute."

"Don't let the boss hear you," the redhead laughed.

Or he'd get jealous? How adorable was that?

So sweet it made me feel a little weird. With how busy I was, I didn't spend much time around couples. Even when my friends had significant others, I still didn't do a whole bunch of stuff with them.

Oh hell. I had almost exactly what I'd always wanted. I had nothing to complain about.

"Are you dating?" the guy blurted out a second later. The girl hit him in the arm.

I felt my neck get hot, and though I realized I didn't have to answer, I did anyway. "No."

"Oh."

"We're just best friends."

* * *

"LOOK, I need to warn you: I think my dad's going to lose his shit," I said as we pulled into my parents' neighborhood. "I already warned him that I had a big surprise while I was waiting for you at the tattoo place, but I really think he's going to lose it."

I could feel the weight of his gaze from the other side of the car even though it was almost eight o'clock at night. "I'm not worried."

Of course he wasn't worried.

But I was.

My dad was going to crap his pants. I hadn't found the balls to even warn my mom because I wasn't sure how she'd handle it either. There was a chance she'd freak out and say she needed a warning beforehand.

"Rey, you don't understand how big of a fan of yours he is."

"*Schnecke*, I'm not worried. I've seen it all."

Not that I didn't doubt it, but it still didn't help my nerves as we got closer and closer to the house my parents had lived in for as long as I could remember. The fear that one of them would spill the beans on my childhood crush had been nagging at me for hours.

What was I going to say, though? That he wasn't welcome? That wasn't very nice and that wasn't the way my parents had raised me. Plus, I'd brought Jenny home with me a few times during breaks. That wasn't counting the other teammates and friends that had been in and out of my life over the years who had come by for holidays.

The small three-bedroom house was right at the end of the cul-de-sac. My mom's new-ish car and my dad's work truck were in the driveway, as I parked on the street. The house wasn't new in any way, but my dad took care of it.

I shot him a smile as Kulti grabbed our bags from the trunk, holding my hand out. "I can take that."

He gave me a single look before he kept walking right up the stones my dad had laid as a path to the doorway. The German didn't even bother waiting for me to catch up before he was knocking on the door, a little more subdued than the way he banged on mine every time he came over.

I shoved him to the side as the locks began turning.

"*Quién es?*" Of course it would be my dad.

"Sal!" I called back, putting my index finger up to my mouth when Kulti looked at me.

"Sal? You lost your key?" The bottom lock turned and a moment later, my dad's face appeared in the crack of the door.

"No." I grinned, happy to see him. "Happy early birthday. Don't freak out—"

His forehead scrunched up as he swung the door wide. "Don't freak—?" He stopped. His gaze swung from me to Kulti, then back to me and finally back to Kulti. The weirdest breath escaped his mouth.

Then, he shut the door in our faces.

Kulti and I looked at each other, and a second later I started laughing as a big grin that caught me totally off guard cracked across his lightly bearded face.

"Dad," I cried his name out.

There was no reply, which only made me laugh even harder.

"*Papi*, come on." I pressed my forehead against the door, my shoulders shaking as I replayed the look on his face when he spotted the German next to me. "Oh God."

Twisting my head to look at Kulti again, he was still smiling.

"Salomé? *Que paso?*" My mom's voice came from inside the house a second before she opened the door, her forehead scrunched up in confusion already. "*Porque—ay carajo!*" she said, immediately spotting the much taller man standing next to me. Her face went a little pale. Her mouth gaped in surprise for all of three seconds before she cleared her throat, looked back at me and cleared her throat again. "Okay. Okay." Her eyes swung back over to the German before she smiled warily. "Come in, come in." She spoke in Spanish, ushering us inside.

"Hey, Mom," I said, giving her a hug before stepping aside as she closed the door behind us. "I brought my friend with me." I gave her a look with wide eyes that said *please don't bring anything up*. "Mom, Rey...Reiner...? Kulti...?" I looked at him for a clue as to what I should have my family call him. He just shrugged in response casually, extending a proper hand out to my mom. "Rey, this is my mom."

My mom was too busy looking him up and down like she couldn't believe he was real, and honestly a small part of me couldn't believe it either. Reiner Kulti was standing in my house. I'd watched hundreds of his games in the living room. I'd sworn to my dad I was going to be as good as The King in this exact place more times than I could count. He was here. *Here*. As my friend, spending the next few days because he had nothing else to do.

Jesus Christ.

"*Hola, Señora Casillas,*" Kulti said in his perfect Spanish, continuing on in it, "It's a pleasure to meet you. Thank you for having me."

Who was this man with manners? I watched him, not really surprised at how polite he was but... a little bit caught off guard.

A small slow smile crossed my mom's face, pleased with his introduction. "It's nice to meet you too," she said, thankfully avoiding anything like *I've heard so much about you* or something really incriminating. Mom finally looked over at me, not switching back to English. "I was wondering why your dad shut the door and walked into the bedroom. He's in there now. Go find him while I get Reiner a drink."

So she decided to go with Reiner. How about that.

I gave him a small smile as he stood there with our bags in hand. "I'll be right back. You can leave the bags there, I'll move them later."

He gave me what I was starting to call his 'shut up Sal' look.

I smiled at my mom and gave her another hug despite the fact she was more focused on the man next to me. "I'll get him out of there."

Sure enough, the bedroom door was closed when I came up to my parents' room. I knocked on it twice before saying, "Dad? I'm coming in. Don't scar me for life."

Sitting on the edge of his bed, with his head between his knees, was the man who had raised me. His rough dark hands were gripping the back of his head and it took everything inside of me not to start laughing at his mini-panic attack. Choking it all back, I took a seat beside him and put my hand on his back.

"Surprise," I whispered with only the slightest hint of laughter in my voice.

Slowly, his head turned and I caught one light-green eye staring back at me. "I don't know whether I want to hug you or beat you," he said in Spanish.

"You've never even spanked me," I reminded him with a big smile.

Dad managed to scowl with only the small part of his face visible. "*No la chingues, hija de tu madre.* Are you trying to give me a heart attack?"

It should be said that my dad was the second most dramatic person in the family, only outranked by my little sister. Eric, our mom and I were the sane, stable ones.

So yeah, I shook my head at him knowing he was full of crap. "With the way you drive, it's going to be another car that —"I dragged my thumb across my neck "—gets you not a heart attack, all right?"

Dad tilted his head so that both of his green eyes were visible. I'd always wished I'd inherited his mom's gene but I hadn't. None of his kids had. With his super-tan skin, the color always seemed to pop. Lucky dog. Mom had told me once it was the first thing she noticed about him. "With the way you're treating me, I'm going to end up on blood pressure medicine soon." He sat up and continued to give me an impertinent look. "You brought *him* to our house and you didn't warn me? You didn't even tell me you were on speaking terms the last time we talked." He shook his head. "I thought you were my best friend."

The kicker was that my dad genuinely did sound hurt. Not much, but enough that I felt guilty I hadn't said anything to him about my friendship with the Bratwurst King of the World. Dad *was* my best friend. I usually told him everything. While I would never say I loved one parent more than the other, my dad and I had always had a special relationship. He'd been my buddy, my champion, my co-conspirator and my backup for as long as I could remember. When my mom had tried to force me to play every other sport besides soccer, Dad had been the one who argued that I should do whatever I wanted.

So his words were enough to wipe the smile off my face as I leaned into him. "I'm sorry. I didn't know how to tell you. I wasn't even sure we really were friends. At first he was just kind of an asshole, and then we became friends."

"Hmph."

"I'm serious, Dad. It's just weird. I had to think about him pooping for the first two months so that I wouldn't stutter every time I was around him."

That made him to crack a small smile.

"We played soccer together a few times, I took him with me to play softball with Marc and Simon, and he took me to the doctor a week ago," I explained, surprised he hadn't seen the pictures of us that had been posted on Kulti's fan websites.

And even when my dad's favorite athlete in the universe

was within walking distance, the number one man in my life put me first. "What the hell did you go to the doctor for?" he snapped.

Ten minutes later, I'd told him everything—mostly. From the softball game that had gone wrong, to Kulti taking me to the doctor, to the conversation with Mr. Cordero, and finally to the German showing up to my place that morning.

Dad was shaking his head by the end, anger apparent in his eyes. "*Cabrones*. We'll sue them if they do anything," he said, still hung up on Mr. Cordero.

What was it with these men and suing people? "We'll worry about it later. I didn't violate any terms of my contract, so I don't think they can do anything." I really hoped. "You-know-who told me not to worry about it."

His eyes narrowed, but grudgingly he nodded.

"Ready to see your true love?" I asked with a smile on my face.

Dad smacked me on the back of the head lightly. "I don't know why we didn't put you up for adoption," he said, getting to his feet.

I shrugged and followed him out of the room, noticing how slowly he was walking and the way he looked around the corner like he expected someone to pop out of nowhere and scare the crap out of him. In the kitchen, we found Kulti sitting at the small round table crammed into the corner of the room, a plate of watermelon, jicama, celery and broccoli, with a glass of water in front of him. My mom was digging in the fridge for something.

The German stood up and extended a hand out to my dad, not saying a word.

And my poor star-struck dad glanced at him, and in a way that wasn't at all like his usual self, timidly stuck his hand out—only slightly trembling—and clasped Kulti's.

"Nice to see you again, Mr. Casillas," Kulti said in flowing Spanish, keeping eye contact with my dad.

I had to pinch my nose when my dad nodded rapidly in return, sucking in a loud breath when their hands broke apart. Coming up from behind, I squeezed my dad's shoulders and whispered in his ear about how he needed to imagine him pooping, before taking a seat next to the German and sneaking a piece of watermelon off his plate.

Dad grabbed a seat next to me and across from Kulti, looking everywhere but at The King. This was the same man who didn't know how to behave in a movie theater, much less church. Loud, outgoing, opinionated and stubborn with a temper that was well known... he sat quietly in his chair.

This was exactly what I'd been worried about with bringing Kulti to San Antonio. I wanted to spend time with my parents, not to have my dad so freaked out he refused to talk. I wasn't going to embarrass him by pointing out how weird he was acting in front of the German, and I decided to try and show a little patience. We, or at least I, were going to be here for the next three days; Kulti and I hadn't talked about whether he'd figure out another way to get back to Houston, but the fact he hadn't mentioned leaving hadn't escaped me either.

So, we'd see how it'd go.

Kulti nudged the plate in my direction and I smiled as I took a piece of jicama. Then it hit me.

"Where's Ceci?" I asked my parents.

Dad raised his eyebrows, but it was my mom who answered. "In her room."

Of course she was. There was no way in hell she didn't know I'd gotten home. The little pain in the ass.

"Who is Ceci?" Kulti asked, holding a piece of broccoli in his hand.

"My little sister."

He blinked.

I shrugged. What else was I going to say? That my sister hated my guts during different moon cycles?

Fortunately he didn't ask anything else. I know Dad took it personally when Ceci acted like a turd, and then my mom would get mad that we weren't more understanding and patient with her. I was patient with her. I hadn't punched her yet despite the dozens of times she'd deserved it.

My mom took a seat at the table and started asking if we had any plans for tomorrow, and then saying how my aunts and cousins wanted to see me. Pretty soon it was close to ten and I was yawning up a storm, wondering how the hell my dad hadn't cracked a single sigh when I knew damn well he was used to going to bed early, too.

The silence was just weird, with me trading looks with Kulti and my mom while Dad avoided everyone's eyes.

All right, I'd had enough.

"You want me to show you where you can sleep?" I asked the German.

He nodded.

There was only one guest bedroom and since my little sister wasn't even going to bother coming out to tell me hi, I guess sleeping in her room was out of the question. As Kulti followed me out of the kitchen and we passed the small living room with its hard couch that had been bought for durability rather than for comfort, I felt my eye twitch a little. That thing was unforgivable, but there was no way I was going to banish my friend to that cloth-covered rock.

What had once been my brother's room long, long ago, had been painted and converted into a guest room for whoever was in town. My parents weren't fans of buying new things if the old things still worked, so I knew exactly what I'd be walking into. Ceci and my old furniture back when I'd lived with them before college.

Bunk beds.

It was a full-sized frame at the bottom and a twin at the top. I almost smiled when Kulti didn't even blink an eye at the accommodations. "Welcome to Hotel Casillas," I held my hand out in presentation mode, letting him take in the black metal bunk beds, the thirty-something-inch flat screen mounted on a dresser and the various posters and articles of Eric and me on display that my parents had moved in there after Ceci had ranted her mouth off. She couldn't live with our achievements constantly in her face, or something like that. She acted like we'd been given what we had. Ha.

'Natural talent' and genetics only went so far.

"Where are you sleeping?" he asked, dropping our bags on the floor.

"Umm—"

"In there," my dad piped up as he walked past the bedroom; his was at the end of the hall. Like he'd been talking all night, he said over his shoulder, "*Buenas noches!*"

Sleep in the same room with him? The two times I'd brought my ex with me, Dad had made him sleep in the living room, but with Kulti over? I seriously doubted my age had anything to do with why he was throwing us together in the small bedroom. If he would have known I was bringing him, I'm sure he would have taken the twin mattress out.

Typical.

I could have argued, but did I really want to sleep on the floor in my parent's bedroom or squeeze onto the couch? No thanks.

"You mind if I sleep on the top one?" I asked.

Those hazel-green eyes took in the bed and I could see either amusement or something similar in the way he looked at it. He shook his head, still eyeing it. "No. You can have the bottom one."

"You're too tall for the top one," I explained to him. "Take the bottom. The mattress is newer too."

He gave me a side-glance and nodded before scooting our bags deeper into the room and then crouching down to dig through his.

"There's a bathroom right next door. Get whatever you want from the kitchen, my house is your house. Everyone sleeps solid so you won't bother anybody." I drummed my fingers on my leg, trying to figure out if there was anything else I needed to tell him. There wasn't. "I want to see if my sister is up before I get ready for bed."

The German just nodded and mumbled something I didn't completely understand.

My little sister's bedroom was on the other side of the bathroom door. The slit beneath the door was lit up and the television was loud enough for me to hear it, so I knocked pretty loud. "Ceci?" I rapped my knuckles. "You up?"

No answer.

"Cecilia?" I knocked again.

Still nothing.

"Ces, seriously?"

There was no response. I wasn't delusional enough to think she'd fallen asleep with the television on. I knew my sister. She couldn't sleep with any light. She was just being a little shit. Again.

I'd never done anything to her. I'd never given her a hard time, discouraged her or said anything mean. Maybe I'd been wrapped in my career for all of her life, but I'd been there as much as I could. From the moment she was old enough, maybe around six or seven, she'd turned into the fucking 'woe as me' devil.

I had to take a deep breath and let out a deeper sigh to not let her bring my mood down. She wasn't going to open the door, and I wasn't going to beg her either.

More disappointed than aggravated, I went back to the bedroom I was apparently sharing with Kulti just as he was coming out, a toiletry bag in his hand. It was easy to forget how much taller than me he was, how much bigger in general too, but I didn't notice it much then either, especially with my little sister acting like a jackass pulling away my focus.

He went into the bathroom while I grabbed clean underwear, a regular bra I could slip out of once I was under the sheets, my nightshirt and my own toiletry bag out of my duffel. I could shower once the German was done. While I was at it, I pulled out some clothes for my run the next morning. On a piece of paper by the television, I jotted down the Wi-Fi password. Just a few minutes later, he came back into the room and his face a little damp, but everything else the same.

"I'm going to shower. The TV remote is on the dresser, and the Wi-Fi password is by the TV, all right?" I asked, already edging around him to go to the bathroom so I could take a shower. It'd be a miracle if I didn't fall asleep inside, but I was so used to showering at night I wouldn't feel comfortable going to bed without one.

"I'm fine," he said putting his things back into his bag.

"Okay, I'll be back, then."

Less than fifteen minutes later, I'd blown through one of the fastest showers in history, brushed my teeth and put on my pajamas. Back in the room, Kulti was sitting on the edge of the full-sized bed in a thin white undershirt, the lower part of his bicep visibly wrapped in some kind of plastic, and his jeans were still on. He looked up as I entered the room and gave me an expression that was mostly a smile as he peeled off a sock.

"Are you fine?" he asked after I dropped my pile of dirty clothes by the door and crouched to grab a pair of knee-high socks from my bag.

"Yeah, why?" I straightened, making sure that my double extra-large T-shirt, basically a muumuu, wasn't tucked into the waistband of my underwear.

He peeled off another sock. "You're mad over your sister,"

he said casually, tossing the two surprisingly long pieces of cloth onto my pile of clothes.

I started to argue with him, telling him I was fine, when I realized that I'd be lying and he'd know it. I threw my own pair of clean, striped socks up to the top mattress, my bare toes wiggling in the carpet. I didn't have the cutest feet in the freaking universe, I mean they weren't ugly, but they'd been through hell and back with me. I wasn't often barefoot.

"Ah, yeah. I'm a little mad she decided to hide out in her room," I sighed, scratching my cheek with a sad smile. He had leaned forward, his elbows on his knees, his forehead furrowed. Reiner Kulti on my bunk bed. What a vision. "It's rude and I'm sorry. I'm sure you'll get to meet her tomorrow."

The German shrugged like he was completely indifferent about whether or not he got to meet Ceci, and I couldn't blame him. Why would he care? "If she's going to upset you, I would rather not. She sounds like a brat."

"She's not a brat," I defended her. "She's just... a pain. It's been hard for her to grow up with me and Eric. We're close— my brother and I, but there's almost seventeen years between the two of them. There are ten years between me and her, and she almost killed my mom during the delivery, but we don't ever talk about that," I added, imagining Kulti bringing up the subject to get a rise out of her.

"She's the only one that's never shown an interest in soccer so she thinks everyone is disappointed in her for being 'normal.'" I snickered. "She says it like it's a bad thing. You know how it is, how much you have to give up. It isn't like what we do is easy or anything."

His eyes drilled into me, straight into my chest. In understanding? In kinship? I wasn't positive until he nodded slowly, solemnly, like he was remembering every single thing he'd sacrificed in his life for the dream he no longer had. "No, it's not an easy life, Sal. Most don't understand that."

"Right? I get enough crap from other people; I don't want it from my sister too. I just want her to be happy. I could care less if she's good at soccer or not. Anyway, my mom likes to say that you always fight with the people you love the most, so oh well. My dad and I are always bickering about something. I guess she's right." I walked over to the ladder on the side of the bunk beds, hands gripping the sides of it. "You have a brother, right?" I asked, knowing damn well he definitely had a brother, an older one.

"Yes," he answered, scooting back further onto the bed. Something weird stirred in my chest watching him sitting on my bed in his pants, thin shirt and big bare feet. It was so *homey*, so natural. For so long I'd had to remind myself that he was just a regular man, but seeing him there like that really nailed it home.

It was so cute. He was so cute.

"I haven't seen him in three years," he added unexpectedly.

I looked at him through the rungs of the stairs. "Jeez. Why?"

"We've never been close. He has his own life and I have mine."

How lonely did that sound? Sure I wanted to strangle my sister sometimes, but she was usually in a good mood at least a handful of times a year. "Not even when you were little?"

Kulti hunched his shoulders up casually, settling back against the two pillows propped on the wall. "I left my parents' home when I was eleven, Sal. I haven't seen them for longer than a month at a time since then."

The 'holy shit' was apparent on my face, it had to be. I'd known he'd gone to some soccer academy before his career took off, but he'd been eleven when he left home? That was one of the neediest times in a kid's life. He'd been so *little*. Jesus.

"You were there all the time?"

He nodded.

"Didn't you ever... get lonely?"

Kulti studied my face. "At first, but you get over it."

Get over it? At eleven? Good gracious. Where was the nurturing?

"Do... you still see your parents?" I asked, not sure whether I was going into territory he didn't want to get into or not.

A small sharp snicker came out of his mouth. "My mother called me a few days ago saying she's ready for a new house."

I had to fight back a wince. Him buying it for her was implied, wasn't it? "It's nice that you take care of her." I trailed off, not really sure if it was nice or not, or whether he genuinely wanted to provide for them. Because I mean, who demands a new house? Where the hell do you get the balls to do that?

He blinked and confirmed my suspicion that he might have been getting forced into buying his mom a house. Feeling uncomfortable that I had brought up something a little sensitive, I reached forward and ran my index finger up the sole of his foot, surprised when he jerked it away violently.

I stood there and watched him with a big dumb smile on my face. "You're ticklish?"

With both knees now to his chest he scowled over. "No."

"Ha." I laughed. "That's cute."

He didn't look like he was amused.

I gripped the bars and smiled over at him before climbing up to the bunk bed, conscious to keep my long T-shirt tucked between my thighs on the way up. "Will you get the light or should I turn it off? I'm ready to go to bed but you can leave it on, it won't bother me. The remote is by the dresser."

"I'll get it," he said, the mattress making some creaking noises as I heard him settle in.

Getting comfortable, I pulled the sheets up to my chin and rolled onto my good shoulder, facing the wall. "All right. Night, Rey. Wake me up if you need something," I yawned.

From below, the German said, "Goodnight, *schnecke*."

"You're not calling me a shithead or anything, are you?" I yawned again, drawing the sheet up higher to cover my eyes.

"No," he replied simply.

"Okay. If you want to go home tomorrow or if you'd rather stay in a hotel if you aren't comfortable, let me know, all right?"

"Yes."

One last lion-like yawn made my chest expand wide. "Okay. Night, night."

He might have said "Goodnight" again, but I was pretty much out the second I finished talking.

* * *

I CREPT down the bunk-bed ladder when the room was still dark. It didn't matter if I set an alarm; more often than not, my body just knew it was time to get up. As quietly as I could I fumbled around for my clothes, barely able to see. I pulled my nightshirt up over my head...

Then the fan light came on.

I froze. I froze there in my underwear, wearing nothing else.

"What are you doing?" Kulti's sleep-thick voice asked.

Well then. I could freak out and make a big deal out of standing there mostly naked, or I could take it like a champ and make it seem like it wasn't a big deal that I was topless and in one of my oldest pairs of value-pack panties.

"I'm going for a run," I said slowly in a whisper, still not moving an inch. "Go back to sleep."

There was a pause and then the mattress started creaking. I knew beforehand what he was going to say. "I'll come."

Oh dear God.

I went to my knees as fast as possible and now that I was able to see, pulled my sports bra on as fast as lightning just as the shrill squeak of what had to be Kulti getting off the bed warned me my time was up. I didn't even let myself think that he'd probably caught a glimpse of side boob. It wasn't like he hadn't seen hundreds of boobs before but these were mine. Wearing a sports bra was one thing, boobs flopping freely was another.

I yanked a racer-back tank on before standing up, already holding my running shorts in one hand, ready to pull them on as soon as possible. But I sure as shit wasn't going to bend over and put them on with my butt facing him.

Except just as I turned around, I stopped. Because the German was facing me, watching me as he stood there in boxer briefs. Only boxer briefs. Was his face all sleepy? Maybe, but I sure as hell wasn't looking at his face when I turned around. All I saw were his flat six-pack abs and square pecs, the low rise of his heather-gray boxer briefs and wood.

The morning wood tucked against his thigh.

I coughed and eyed his thigh one more time before quickly stepping into my shorts and pulling them up my legs, just as he pulled up his own pair of running shorts.

I couldn't breathe, and I really couldn't look him in the face as I grabbed my socks off the floor. "Umm, I'll, uh, wait for you in the kitchen."

He grunted his agreement and I hauled ass out of there, walking out before I remembered I left my shoes in the room. I went back in, grabbed them without looking at the boner—I mean, Kulti—and going back out. My dad was already gone, the coffeepot was on for my mom who was already getting ready for work. I filled up two water bottles from the collection I had here and drank a glass while I waited for the German. It didn't occur to me until he arrived in the kitchen that I should have brushed my teeth.

"Ready?" I asked.

Sleepy and his eyes and cheeks puffy, he nodded.

*Don't glance at his crotch, don't glance at his crotch.*

I glanced. Just real quick.

"Eyes up here, Taco."

I wanted to die. "What?" I slowly looked up to see a smug look on his swollen mouth.

By some miracle, he decided not to embarrass me and say he knew I was full of shit playing dumb. Was I going to take advantage of the pass he was giving me? Hell yeah.

I waved Kulti forward, noticing he'd taken the wrap off his freshly inked tattoo. A hint of dark lines peeked out from his shirtsleeve. "Come on. I'm not going to take it easy on your old knees, so you better keep up."

* * *

"IF YOU WANT to go somewhere, you can borrow my car," I told the German over breakfast a couple hours later.

He leaned back in his seat, polishing off a hardboiled egg. "I don't."

"Think about it if you want. I'm going to trim the yard first, and then I want to head to the mall to buy my dad his birthday present. It'll take me a couple hours until I'm ready to go. "

"You're mowing the yard?" he asked.

I nodded.

Those green-brown eyes focused in right on my face and a moment later he said, "I'll help you."

"You don't have to—"

"I want to."

"Rey, you don't—"

"I'm not lazy," he cut me off. "I can help."

I eyed him for a second, the brief image of what I was sure was a good fat eight inches under his boxer briefs filling my head, and then pushed the image back, remembering what the hell we were talking about. "All right, if you really want to."

Because, seriously? I doubted he cut his own lawn, but he

wanted to help me do my dad's? All right. I was stubborn, but I wasn't dumb enough to not take help when it was offered.

A few minutes later we were outside, and he was helping me take my dad's ancient mower out of the garage—he took his good one with him to work—and his back-up edger and weed-eater. "Which would you rather do?" I asked him once all our equipment was on the driveway.

He shrugged, looking at the mower with interest.

I would have bet my life he hadn't mowed a lawn in a couple of decades, if ever. Hadn't he just told me the night before how little time he'd spent with his family once he started at the soccer academy? Even then had he ever spent time doing housework when he was so busy being a childhood prodigy?

I was tempted to tell him I could do it all myself, but I couldn't. I couldn't.

He'd come to San Antonio with me because 'he had nothing else to do.' He'd offered to help me probably for the same reason. The poor guy was alone and bored. I had a feeling he didn't have many friends, he'd admitted to not being close to his family, and all that together made me just sort of sad. It made me want to help him, to include him in things. I wanted him to get his feet wet with life.

What was the best thing to do?

"You mow, and I'll take care of the edging and weeds," I told him, making sure I wasn't giving him a look of pity. "All right?"

His long fingers wrapped around the upper bar of the mower and he nodded.

I handed him a pair of disposable earplugs, safety glasses and a smile that was encouraging but not too encouraging. I said a prayer that we'd make it through this intact.

Reiner Kulti took almost an hour to cut my dad's front and back lawn. He had to take two passes in the front to get the lines even, and he almost ruined the engine once when he didn't empty out the bag. It was my fault, I hadn't told him how. He did it without asking a single question, and I didn't offer any advice either.

He looked so damn proud of himself, I almost cried. Honestly. I felt like a mom dropping off her baby boy at preschool.

I slapped him on the back and kept the 'good job, buddy' to myself before putting up the equipment.

* * *

HE HAD that look in his eye again. The same one he'd had when he'd been looking at the lawn mower.

"Have you ever been to a mall before?" I asked him once we were through the glass doors.

Kulti had his attention on everything around us. His hair was concealed by the baggy beanie he had pulled low on his head, and he'd been thoughtful enough to wear a long-sleeved button-down chambray shirt that I had a feeling cost more than my entire outfit put together. With his hair and tattoo covered, we were pretty confident that he wouldn't be recognized.

I hoped. I really, really hoped. The idea of a mob lusting after him was something out of my worst nightmares.

"Yes I have been to a mall before," he muttered.

"The Galleria doesn't count," I told him, referring to the huge shopping center in Houston with all the designer stores.

He blinked those beautiful light eyes down at me. "I've been to several malls," he insisted. "A long time ago."

I groaned and shoved at the elbow he hadn't gotten work done on, earning a small smile. "Well don't steal anything because I won't bail you out, okay?"

"Yes, *schnecke*."

"Good." I grabbed his wrist and gave him a tug in the direction of one of the stores I needed to visit.

The German looked at every store and booth we walked by until I found one of the businesses I was looking for. Right in the center of the aisle were the massage chairs and masseuses my dad loved coming to every time he went to the mall. "Let me get a gift certificate real quick," I told him after I'd stopped right by the booth. He nodded and watched as one of the male masseuses rubbed down a woman's shoulders.

"You want one?" I asked after paying for a gift certificate.

He shook his head.

"Sure?"

He nodded. "What's next?"

"A new pair of tennis shoes." I pointed at the store close by. "He never buys himself new shoes, so we all have to buy him some, otherwise he'll wear the same pair until they're taped together."

I could have sworn he smiled as he walked alongside me into the shoe store. I knew exactly what I was getting, even though I wished Kulti wasn't around to watch. He was busy looking at the rows on the walls when the store employee came over.

"Can I help you?" the young guy asked, eyeing me with a little too much interest considering I was probably almost ten years older than him.

I pointed at the pair I wanted, careful to keep my back to the German a few feet behind me and said, "Size nine and a half, please."

The employee nodded in approval. "The RK 10s in black?"

I bristled at the fact he was talking about them out loud. "Yes, please."

"We have the Kulti 10s on sale for women," he offered, pointing at the shoes on the opposite side of the store.

"Just the men's," I smiled at him.

"The 9s are buy one, get one half off," he kept going.

"I'm all right. Thanks, though."

He shrugged. "I'll be back, then."

Thank God. I turned around to see the German holding a running shoe up to his face with interest.

"Those are nice," I chipped in.

Those green-brown eyes flicked up to mine and he nodded in agreement. "Did you find what you wanted?" he asked, setting the shoe back on the rack.

"Yes." I scratched my cheek and his eyes immediately narrowed. "The employee is getting them for me right now." Knowing I needed to change the subject, I asked, "Are you getting anything?"

"Here you go," the unfamiliar voice said from behind me a second before the employee walked around and held out the box.

The big swoosh mark on the top of the box wasn't a big deal, but the guy pulled the lid and tissue paper back and there they were. The Reiner Kulti 10$^{th}$ edition in black.

"Perfect," I sort of choked out, avoiding the gaze that had locked on my face. "I'll take them."

"Absolutely not," the German snapped from right next to me.

"I'm taking them," I insisted, ignoring him.

"Sal, you are not buying those," he insisted.

The employee looked back and forth between us, his expression confused.

"I buy my dad shoes every birthday and I'm getting these for him. This is what he'd want," I gritted out, still avoiding his gaze.

"Sal."

"Rey."

His hand touched my elbow. "I can get these for you for free," he said in that exasperated tone he used when his accent really began to bleed through. "In every color. Next year's edition." His fingers pressed into the soft indent of the inside of my elbow. "Don't buy them."

"Do you work for Ni—" the employee started to say, his eyes wide and way too interested. Thankfully he wasn't paying enough attention to the man standing in front of him, otherwise he would have known.

"You mind giving us a second?" I cut him off with an apologetic smile.

What was he going to say? No? Grudgingly, he nodded and turned away.

I finally cradled my guts to me and faced Kulti, who had put his hands on his hips looking just shy of exasperated. *Patience, Sal.* "Tell me why you don't want me to buy them."

"I don't want you to spend the money."

Oh dear God. "Rey, I'm going to buy my dad shoes regardless of whether they're yours or not." Later on I could dwell on the fact I was hanging out with a man that had his own signature shoe line, but now wasn't the time. "I'd rather you make... what? How much do you make, five dollars a pair? Anyway, I'd rather get yours and you make my five dollars than someone else, all right?"

That didn't seem to help matters at all.

If anything, Kulti's jaw went tight and the corners of his mouth pulled down flat. And his shoulders and biceps might have tightened, but I wasn't positive. "I can get every shoe in this store for free. I haven't bought a pair of shoes in over twenty years. You shouldn't have to pay for shoes either. You're the best player in the country—"

Every cell in my body froze.

"—you shouldn't have to, and I'm not going to let you buy some of my *fucking* shoes that you had to work all day to pay for. While we are at it, I'm not going to let you buy any shoes in this store. Not for you and not for your father," he snapped. "I can get you whatever you want, just tell me."

I would have opened my mouth to argue with him, but I couldn't. I just stood there, looking up at him at a complete freaking loss.

Kulti's fingertips touched the outside of my wrist, his expression hard and serious. "If you were me, wouldn't you do the same thing?"

Damn it. "Well, yeah." I don't know why I hadn't noticed before how golden his eyelashes were. "I don't want to take advantage of you. I swear I didn't bring you along to guilt-trip you into getting them. I promise. I would have bought them in Houston but—"

I stopped talking when I noticed something in his body language change, when I felt his deep breath wash across my cheek. He looked deflated but not necessarily in a bad way.

He put his hand on top of my head, the bottom of his palm resting just barely on my forehead as he let out another chest-filled breath. "You are..." The German shook his head and sighed. "No one could ever make me do something I don't want to."

I could believe that.

"Understand?" He dipped his head. His face, so deeply tanned from years of being in the sun, looked younger for some reason in that instant.

"Yes."

Kulti nodded. "You would do it for me if you were in my position, *schnecke*."

"Did you guys decide if you're getting the shoes?" an unexpected voice asked from behind me.

It took me a second to tear my eyes away from the almost-hazel ones so close to mine. "I'm sorry for wasting your time, but I'm going to have to pass."

The frown on the employee's face wasn't unexpected. He

moved his gaze over the German with even more interest. "Say, you look familiar—"

I hated being rude, but I grabbed the German's wrist and led him out of the store before the kid could think about it too much more. Once we were out, I let go of his wrist and smiled up at him as we walked through the spacious corridor, but he was already pulling his cell out of his other pocket and pecking at the screen with his thumb.

"*I need you to send me RK 10s, size nine and a half*—" The fact he'd paid attention to the shoe size on the box didn't escape me, "—*in men's*... What's your address?" He turned his attention down to me, and I rattled off my parent's home address. Kulti repeated it to the person on the other end of the line. "*I want them there tomorrow... and a sample of the pair you sent me last week... yes, those.*" He hung up, just like that. He just called, said what he wanted and hung up. No thanks, no goodbye, nada.

After he finished putting his phone back into his pocket, he looked down at me and frowned. "What?"

"People don't get aggravated with you when you're rude to them?"

Kulti blinked. "No."

"Never?"

He lifted up a shoulder in the most perfect gesture of how much of a shit he didn't give.

Good God. "If I hung up on someone like that, which I wouldn't because it's not nice, they would tell me to go screw myself." I blinked at him and thought about what he said. "If you hung up on me like that, I would tell you to go screw yourself. Not that I don't appreciate you getting the shoes for my dad, but it wouldn't kill you to be polite, you know."

He shrugged. He freaking shrugged, and I knew me telling him how he could handle the situation differently wasn't going to change a single thing.

* * *

"THIS IS the worst game of Uno I have ever played in my entire life."

Kulti looked up at me from across the table and smiled his little smug baby smile. The freaking bratwurst. "You're being a sore loser."

My mom and dad both nodded from their spots on either side of me. I looked at both of them and shook my head. Traitors. "I'm not being a sore loser." Much. "They kept giving me all their crappy cards so they wouldn't make you draw!"

"It sounds to me like you don't know how to lose," he said calmly, taking the cards from the middle of the table to shuffle.

I made a choking noise and turned my attention to the mute sitting next to me. Dad had said maybe six words in the last three hours. He got home and found the German and I in the driveway washing my car. Dad said exactly two words, "Oh, ah, hi," gave me a kiss on the cheek and hightailed it inside. We'd eaten dinner my mom made with him saying another two words, "salt" and "*si*." And the last two words he'd said were, "yellow" and "blue" when he made us change colors playing cards.

My mom on the other hand, had decided not to be fazed, and it wasn't like I could blame her. She wasn't particularly impressed by famous soccer players for longer than a second. Been there, done that.

"You've never liked to lose," Mom noted as Kulti slid a card in her direction, which she took with a smile. "When you were little, you would make us play games over and over again until you won."

She was right. I remembered being a competitive little kid. Whoops. "You guys are ganging up on me. I'm just saying it'd be a fair game if you two quit making me take more cards every turn."

She smiled again when the German passed her another card. "It's just a game."

It was just a game.

I made sure Kulti met my eyes when I got my next round of cards. Nothing was just a game.

* * *

"DAD?" I knocked on the door an hour or two later. "*Papa*?"

He said something from inside that was along the lines of 'come in,' so I did. Standing in the doorway between his bedroom and en suite, Dad had a toothbrush in his mouth, already dressed for bed.

"I just wanted to tell you goodnight." I smiled at him.

He held up a finger and went back into the restroom where I could hear him turn the water on and rinse out his mouth before coming back. "*Buenas noches.* I had fun tonight."

"You did?"

My dad nodded seriously, sitting on the bed next to me. "Do you know how hard it's been for me to not tell anyone that he's staying at my house? *My house*, Salsa!" Dad erupted, seriously. This was more like him. "The King is sleeping in my house, he mowed *my* lawn, and he's friends with *my* daughter." He put a hand to his chest and took a big, walloping breath. "This is the best present anyone has ever given me." He paused. "Don't tell your mom."

And he was completely, one hundred and ninety-nine percent serious.

I didn't bring up how he hardly talked, but I did grin at him. I was happy that at least he was acting normal in front of me and eating up just having Kulti in the house. "Are you sure? I don't want you to feel weird."

"Am I sure? *Pues si.*" He wrapped an arm over my shoulders

and pulled me into his side. "I'm going to remember this for the rest of my life."

I laughed and leaned into him. Only he would be happy just having Kulti in the house even though he didn't talk to him. "Thank you for not telling everyone." My parents had decided not to have my extended family come over with the German staying and honestly, I was a little relieved.

"You think he'll take a picture with me before he leaves so I can send it to your *tios?*"

"Yes."

Dad nodded in pleasure. "I can rub it in their faces later, with their *pinches fotos* of their grandkids. Why do I want grandkids when you bring The King home with you?"

I rolled my eyes and patted his leg. "I want you to tell Mom those exact words the next time she asks me when I'm finally going to get married and give her a couple of babies."

He gave me another side hug. "You know I'll love you if you play or not."

I did. "I know."

"I just want you to be happy."

"I know."

"I mean it," he insisted.

And I smiled. "I know, Dad. I promise I know."

With one more side hug, he let me go. "Tell your friend I said thank you for doing the yard."

"You could just tell him yourself," I said, getting up.

He shook his head. "No. You tell him for me."

Stubborn mule. "Okay. Goodnight."

"*Buenas noches, amor.*"

I backed out of his room with another smile and closed the door behind me. My little sister's door was closed and that time I didn't hold back my sigh of annoyance with her. She'd gotten home with my dad after school, said 'hi' and then walked into her room and stayed in there for most of the day, only coming out to grab a plate of food and go back in with it. For a second, I debated whether to knock on her door and tell her goodnight just to be a troll but decided against it. We were going out to dinner for our dad's birthday the next day, and I needed her to chill out as much as possible so it wouldn't turn into a nightmare.

She was still a turd though.

By the time I made it back to the guest room, Kulti was already lying in bed with the sheets pulled up halfway to his stomach, his legs propped up and his tablet reclining against them. I grabbed my nightclothes and stuff from my bag and went back into the bathroom to shower, put on another long T-shirt and socks that went up almost to my knees.

"Are we going for a run in the morning?" Kulti asked from his spot on the bed once I was back in the room, pulling out a new set of running clothes for the next day.

"As long as you can keep up again," I teased him, setting the clothing on top of my bag and turning around to see him scowling at me. Not saying a word, I winked and climbed up to the top bunk, settling in before I remembered what my dad had said. I got up to my knees and leaned over the edge so I could see him, sitting there on the too-small-for-him bed. "Thanks for helping me today with the yard. My dad asked me to say thank you too."

Squeaky clean and so relaxed-looking on the bed I'd grown up in, Kulti looked refreshed. He tipped his chin down. "It was my pleasure."

I flashed him a smile and sat back up, crawling under the covers one more time. I'd barely pulled them up to my chest when Kulti spoke again.

"That was my first time using a lawn mower."

I fucking knew it! I didn't say that of course, instead, I stuck with a very grown-up, "Oh really?"

There was a pause before he kept going. "I enjoyed it. I can see why you went to school for it. It's fitting."

Wait a second, wait a second. I knew for a fact that I'd never once told Kulti that I got my degree in landscaping. He'd never asked, not once. Sure, I had told him out of anger that I did landscaping work, if he hadn't already known, but that was the extent of it. There wasn't a single doubt in my mind that I had never mentioned what university I went to school at, much less what I majored in.

"How do you know what I went to school for?" I asked him casually. I'm sure I was making some kind of stupid face.

"I looked you up. You have it on your profile," he said without skipping a beat.

What? I sat up again and looked over the edge of the bunk bed. "You did?"

Even upside down, I recognized that he nodded. "Yes."

"You... have an account?"

He might have frowned, but I wasn't positive with all the blood rushing to my head. "Get down before you fall over the side of the bed and give yourself more brain damage than you already have."

Rolling my eyes, I did as he said but only because it wouldn't be the first time I'd fallen off a bunk bed. I climbed down way too quickly and went and sat on the edge of his mattress, way too interested. "You use social media?"

Kulti stared at me. "Yes." Then he added, "I have a fake account."

"No!" I laughed.

"Yes," he confirmed.

"Can I see it?"

The German looked like he wanted to deny my request but he finally nodded, and a minute later, handed me his tablet. The blue and white page had "Michel Reiner" at the top and some bogus, generic picture of a sunset as the profile picture. His number of friends? 25.

Twenty-freaking-five.

I looked at him over the top of the tablet and felt my little heart break just a bit. "Do you know how many people like your fan page?"

He shrugged.

I looked it up.

The Reiner Kulti Official Fan Page had one hundred and twenty-five million likes.

And 'Michel Reiner' had twenty-five.

Something watery pooled in my throat as I handed him back his tablet. "I don't get on there much but you could add me as a friend if you wanted to," I offered in a wobbly voice.

"What an honor," the bratwurst said, but he said it with a small smile so I knew he didn't mean it like an asshole.

I still reached under the cover and pulled his leg hair. At least I hoped it was his leg hair.

Whatever it was, he let out a grunt-squeak noise of surprise as he jerked away, a big smile on his face that seemed to fit into skin that wasn't accustomed to forming those types of facial expressions. "Do it again Sal, and you'll get it right back."

I made sure he was watching when I crossed my eyes at his threat. "I don't have hair on my legs, so good luck with that." I eyed the small screen again. "Who else are you friends with on there?"

"Some old teammates, my mother, my manager and publicist." He tapped my name into the search and hit the 'add' button once my page came up. "You."

My phone beeped a second later, and I saw the alert of a pending friend request. I accepted it and set my phone back down on the dresser before taking the seat I'd left next to the German.

The German who was already busy browsing my profile.

"Nosey much?" I asked.

He grunted, clicking on my main album and scrolling down. They were mainly all pictures that friends or family members had posted and linked me to. Birthdays, games, get-togethers, more games... it was a timeline of the last eight years of my life through other people's eyes. Kulti didn't say anything as he looked through them, until he suddenly stopped scrolling.

"Who is this?" he asked.

He didn't need to point at the picture for me to know who he was referring to, and honestly, I was a little surprised Adam still had pictures of us up. We hadn't been together in five years, and he'd dated more than a few girls since then.

But there we were on the screen.

I was in my early twenties, him in his late twenties and me on his lap, with his arm around my waist. My ex-boyfriend of four years was blond, built like an Abercrombie model, really cute and just as nice as he'd been attractive.

"That's really old. It's my ex-boyfriend," I explained to the German.

The man who rarely used words didn't change his tactic, but he slowly started looking through more pictures with dozens more of Adam and I popping up along the timeline. It made me feel a little sad that I hadn't tried harder to work things out with him. We'd always gotten along really well, and he'd been the exact person I needed and wanted back then.

"How long were you together?" he asked once we'd scrolled three years further back.

"Four years. We met my second year in college."

"He looks like an idiot."

It took me a moment to comprehend what came out of his mouth, but it made me laugh once it finally took hold. I nudged him with my elbow. "You're rude. He wasn't an idiot. He was really nice."

Those green-brown eyes slid over to me. He didn't look amused. In fact his jaw was tight, and he looked a little pissed off. "You're defending him?" He sounded like he couldn't believe it.

"Yeah. He was really nice. He's the only man I've ever really dated, Rey. We'd probably still be together if I would have wanted to have kids right after college."

Kulti's head jerked to look at me directly.

"What?" I asked, surprised by his expression.

"Have you kept in contact with him?"

I shrugged. "He calls me between girlfriends, but that's it."

"To get back together?" Why his voice was so low I couldn't understand, and I gave him a weird look.

"Yeah, but it wouldn't happen. He's slept around a lot since we split. I'm not one of these girls that think men who have slept with hundreds of women are sexy. That's gross. I don't loan my body out to just anyone, and I don't like the idea of a bunch of girls knowing what someone I love's penis looks like, you know?"

A muscle in Kulti's jaw ticked and I swear his eye twitched. Then I realized what had just come out of my mouth.

"No offense to you. It's your business whatever you decide to do with yourself. I'm not going to judge. I'm just old-fashioned and picky. That's probably why I haven't been in a relationship since him, huh?"

His eye definitely twitched that time, and I felt bad for pretty much calling him an unattractive man-whore.

"Look, I'm sorry. Just because I can't imagine being intimate with someone I don't love doesn't mean there's anything wrong with it. It's not for me. Different strokes for different folks."

Kulti's eye twitched again. I didn't miss the way he was biting down hard and making his cheek flex either.

"What?" I asked when he didn't say anything.

Nothing.

The German tipped his head back and closed his eyes, his fingers going for the bridge of his nose. One inhale, one exhale. Another inhale, one more exhale. What the hell was wrong with him?

"Rey, are you okay?"

One eye opened as his chest puffed. "Stop talking about sex."

Jeez. "Okay. Sorry. I didn't take you to be a prude."

He choked, his other eye opening. But did he say a word? No, he didn't.

I sat there waiting for him to make another comment, but nothing came out of his mouth. I really hadn't taken him as a person who would get offended so easily. The 's' word hadn't even come out of my mouth, much less anything raunchier. So I didn't completely understand why he was getting so bent out of shape.

When he continued to say nothing and he kept looking at the support for the bottom of the top bunk bed, I fidgeted. "Can I see your tattoo now?" He'd been a little too secretive about it, and I'd been wondering what the hell he was hiding all day.

Mr. Secret's chin moved just a tiny bit to the side before he nodded almost belligerently. Setting his tablet flat on the bed, he arranged his body to the side and carefully pulled the sleeve of his undershirt up. Where less than forty-eight hours ago there had been a tattoo nearly as old as me, a cross, it had been covered as if by magic with the outline of a bird. It was a beautiful, regal-looking bird.

"A Phoenix," Kulti explained like he could read my mind.

"I can't even see your old one at all," I told him, still inspecting the great, beautiful wings and the eccentric-looking crest on its head. "This is amazing, Rey." I wanted to touch it but the skin was still a little irritated, and I didn't want to be the one to accidentally scratch it and mess it up before it was healed. "Seriously, way better than that cross you had before. What made you decide to get that?"

The German eyed me as he scooted back into place and tugged his shirtsleeve back down. "Someone told me I can't take back what I've done, but what I do from now on is what matters. It seemed fitting."

Damn it. I hated when he actually listened to me, but I smiled anyway and dropped the subject when he didn't meet my eyes. All right. "Are you ready to go to bed?"

"I'm going to stay up and watch a movie on here," he explained, gesturing to his tablet. With the bed above shadowing half of everything below, I couldn't see his face well. "Would you want to watch it?"

Was I sleepy? Yes. But...

"Sure, at least until I start to fall asleep," I agreed.

He slid over all of half an inch and angled his upper body toward me. Well. Scooting in next to him close enough so that our elbows were touching, Kulti propped the tablet back onto his bent knees as I tucked the hem of my shirt between my thighs. It had ridden up but it wasn't like he could see my underwear, and it wasn't like he hadn't seen just as much of my legs practically every other day we'd hung out. I fixed the pillow behind my back and eased onto the bed so that my shoulder touched his bicep.

"What are we watching?" I asked.

Apparently the man wasn't a cheapskate because we didn't go with a Netflix movie; instead he bought a digital copy of some newly released suspense thriller.

I'd guess that I probably made it twenty minutes into the movie before I fell asleep. With his body heat on one side, even through the barrier of the sheet he had pulled over himself and the comfortable bed beneath me, I was out.

I woke up to find that my bent knees had fallen over and were resting on Kulti's hip, my shirt had somehow ridden up past my hips leaving my underwear out for anyone to see. My hands were crossed over my chest and tucked into my armpits, and the entire right side of my body was huddled into the left side of the German.

I sat up and gave him a sleepy yawn. "I'm going to bed." I squeezed his bent knee before throwing my legs over the side. "Goodnight, Rey."

"Sweet dreams."

Sweet dreams? Had that really just come out of his mouth? I think I might have fallen asleep with a smile on my face thinking of him using those words.

* * *

"YOU'RE WEARING A DRESS."

I turned around and frowned, my hands smoothing down the front of the blue sundress I'd put on five minutes before. "*Yes.*" It was going to be bad enough when my parents saw my outfit. They acted like they'd never seen me in anything besides sweat pants or shorts.

Now I had to hear it from the German too.

He stood in the doorway in the same jeans he'd had on when we left for Austin. He'd added a black checkered and blue shirt and his tennis shoes.

I smiled.

He didn't say anything. He only kept looking at me as if he hadn't seen me in less clothing plenty of times, even thought that made me sound like a nudist. I twitched. "What? I dress up sometimes. Birthdays, Thanksgiving, Christmas, New Year's." I pulled on the hem of the light dress that almost reached my knees… if I hunched over and yanked.

His gaze slid back up to my face after watching me fiddle with the skirt and he blinked, slow, slow, slow. "You have make-up on."

"I wear make-up." Not much but enough.

"No heels?" He glanced at my feet, which were in a pair of black suede ankle boots my parents had bought me for my birthday a couple years ago.

"Trust me, you'd end up spending the night peeling me off the floor or laughing when I walk around like a newborn baby giraffe." I smiled at him.

His eyes flicked up to mine and a small smile cracked the corners of his mouth. "You're good at everything."

I snorted. "I wish. I'll make you a list later at all the things I'm horrible at." I grabbed my purse off the corner of the bed and pulled it over my head. "Are you ready to go?"

"Yes," he answered, dropping his gaze to the scooped neckline of my dress for a split second.

I had freckles on my chest, but it wasn't like he hadn't seen those before.

I pushed the acknowledgment of him staring out of my head and drew in a breath to relax. That morning, he'd woken up when I'd been half-naked again, only wearing a sports bra and underwear, and he hadn't said a word as I pulled the rest of my clothes on. Sure I could have gone into the bathroom to change, but I kept the same thought in my head that I had from the beginning. I had nothing to be embarrassed about. I accepted my body as it was and if I started acting all goofy about it now, well, that just looked stupid.

I wasn't out to impress anyone.

Plus, it wasn't like he hadn't seen better—and hopefully worse—before.

Whatever.

I felt good, and I didn't care how much crap I was about to get from everyone that enjoyed teasing me just because they could.

Sure enough we found my parents, Ceci and her friend in

the living room waiting for us. It was my dad that made the first crack when he saw me.

In a dress shirt, slacks and dress shoes, he must have forgotten he'd been acting like a timid little bear around the German because he immediately nudged my mom with his elbow. "Look, it's a Christmas miracle. Sal put on real clothes."

I exaggerated a laugh, making a face at him at the same time. "Funny."

My mom came forward and squeezed my shoulder. "Look at how pretty you look when you wear a dress. If you dress like this more often, maybe you'd find a boyfriend again. *No?*"

Once upon a time, her comment would have really hurt my feelings. Actually, she'd said the same thing to me in the past at least a dozen times. If I dressed differently, if I put some effort into my appearance, if I didn't play soccer, maybe I'd find someone...

Someone who didn't know me at all could only love me if I was half myself.

I forced a smile onto my face and patted my mom's arm, ignoring the intense gaze coming from Kulti. "Maybe one day, Ma."

"I'm just telling you because I love you," she said in Spanish, picking up on how her comment irritated me. "You're just as pretty as any other girl, Sal."

"You're all ugly. I'm hungry, let's go," Dad said with a clap of his hands, his face too cheerful.

He knew. He knew how much Mom's comments bothered me. Maybe they didn't piss me off or make me cry, but they bothered me. The fact she was saying it in front of my friend didn't help.

Staying in place, I smiled at my sister and her friend as they followed my parents out the door. Ceci hadn't said a word to me, and I didn't want to start crap with her tonight. I gritted my teeth and tamped down my emotions. Today was about my dad, not about my mom or Ceci.

Since we wouldn't all fit into my mom's sedan, Kulti and I drove separately. It was the same restaurant we'd gone to for the last three years so I knew exactly where we were heading.

I had barely turned the ignition and driven to the corner of the block when the German spoke up. "I don't like the way your mother speaks to you."

My head snapped over to look at his face.

He on the other hand, was busy facing forward. "Why do you let her belittle you in that way?"

"I..." I turned back to face out the windshield and tried to tell myself that this moment was real. "She's my mom. I don't know. I don't want to hurt her feelings and tell her that her opinion doesn't matter —"

"It shouldn't," he cut me off.

Well... "She just has a different view on how I should live my life, Rey. She always has. I'm not ever going to do what she wants me to do, or be the person that she wants me to be. I don't know. I just let her say whatever she wants to say and I suck it up. At the end of the day, I'm going to keep living the way I want, regardless of what she says or thinks."

Out of my peripheral vision, I could see his head turn. "She doesn't support you playing?"

"She does, but she'd rather see me do something else with my life."

"Does she understand how good you are?" he asked completely freaking seriously.

I had to smile, his belief in me almost made up for my mom trying to guilt me into having a boyfriend and dressing up to feel like a woman. Blah. "You really think I'm good?"

"You could be faster—"

I knew he was only trying to piss me off by calling me slow. I turned to look at him, outraged. "Are you serious?"

He ignored me. "But yes, you are. Don't get a big head about it. You still have quite a bit of room for improvement." He paused. "She should be proud of you."

I was torn between wanting to defend my mom and wanting to give him a hug for the nice things he was saying. Instead I went with "She is proud of me. It's just... it's hard for her with me, I guess. I know she loves me, Rey. She goes to my games, wears my jerseys. She's proud of me and my brother but..." I scratched at my face, debating whether or not to tell him for a second. It'd been years since the last time I told anyone. Not even Jenny or Harlow knew. Marc and Simon did but that was only because they'd been in our lives forever. It hadn't helped that Cordero had been the last person to talk to me about it, and he'd left a bad taste in my mouth. *Everyone should know*, he'd said. He hadn't liked when I told him *no. No way*.

My brother Eric had started early in his career putting a stipulation in his contract about the type of personal information that could be released about him. I'd followed in his footsteps with my Pipers contract and fortunately it had paid off to be so secretive. But if there was one person that I could tell, it would be Kulti.

Swallowing, I asked, "Have you ever heard of Jose Barragan?"

"Of course I have," he said with an insulted snicker.

Jose Barragan was a legendary Argentinian soccer player who had lived as big off the field as he had in real life.

I would know. "He was my mom's dad."

The silence in the car was no great shock to me.

"*La Culebra* was your grandfather?" he asked me gently. The Snake. My grandfather had been called The Snake for a dozen different reasons by millions of people.

"Yup." I didn't say anything else because I knew he was going to need a second to process it.

*La Culebra* had been a star. He'd been the king of a generation way before mine. He'd led his country to two Altus Cups; he'd been a superstar in a time before technology and social media. My mom's dad had been a sport's shining star, their flesh and bone trophy.

"Does anyone know?" he finally asked, that creepy calm silence still ringing in my ears.

"Yeah, a few people do."

Another pause. "No one has ever said anything to me about it." I could see him out of the corner of my eye shift in his seat. "Sal, why is it a secret? Do you understand how much money you could make off endorsements?"

Cordero had asked the exact same question. The only difference was, Cordero was an asshole only trying to make himself look better. *La Culebra*'s granddaughter on his team? Especially when he came from the same country? He immediately saw dollar signs, but I wasn't about to let him exploit me or my family. I'd never figured out how he'd found out, but it hadn't mattered. No meant no.

"I wouldn't want to put my mom through that," I explained. I squeezed the steering wheel a little tighter. "Did you ever meet him?"

"Yes."

"So you know he wasn't the nicest man in the world."

His lack of a response was more than enough.

"Rey, I met him maybe ten times in my life. I saw him on TV more than in person. He told me once when I was eleven that I was wasting my time with soccer. He said people didn't like to watch athletes that were women. He told me I should be a swimmer or a ballet dancer. Fucking *ballet*. Could you imagine me in pointe shoes? When I was seventeen, he showed up to the U-17 game I was playing with the national team and tore apart my game afterward. When I was twenty-one, he came to the Altus Cup match and asked me why I didn't play for Argentina instead. Nothing was ever right or enough for him.

"That was just him. From what I've heard my mom say, he was a really shitty father and a worse husband. Supposedly, he'd hit my grandma when he wasn't cheating on her. My mom wasn't a fan of his, and I know she blamed soccer for his behavior. I don't blame her. She met my dad on vacation in Mexico; they got married and moved here. The last time I saw him, he called my dad a stupid Mexican and told my mom she wasted her life marrying someone so beneath her.

"I love my dad and I owe my parents everything. They're the hardest working people I've ever met, and I don't appreciate anyone talking badly about them. When my mom says something unsupportive, I try to be understanding that my mom hates that my brother and I play soccer. She can't stand that we took after him.

"Once my agent did try to sell me to a company by telling them *La Culebra* was my grandfather. You know what they told her? If I was his illegitimate daughter's daughter, they'd want me. Or if I were anything but Hispanic, it'd be a story. They made it seem like I cheated to get to where I was, like his genes and my Hispanic heritage immediately gave me an advantage. As if I didn't bust my ass day after day, working harder than my teammates to improve."

I took a calm breath and blinked back the tears of frustration. It had been so long since I had made myself feel so small. "I've had to work twice as hard as everyone else to prove to myself that I didn't get here because he's my mom's dad.

"I'm sorry I didn't tell you sooner but," I shrugged, "I just... I want to be me. I want people to like me for me, not because of who my brother or my grandfather is, or what I freaking wear... I would have told you eventually. Someday."

In the five minutes it took from that point until we were pulling into the parking lot of the family-owned restaurant,

Germany didn't say a word. I was familiar enough with him to recognize when he was pissed off or annoyed, and I couldn't sense either of those emotions from him. He was simply silent.

I didn't feel like talking about it much anymore either, so I didn't force the conversation. Talking about that old man always gave me indigestion and a heavy heart. It really nailed home how lucky I was to have the people I had in my life.

We didn't speak to each other as we met up with my family; they were waiting by the entrance. We didn't say anything as we walked into the establishment and took two seats next to each other. My dad was seated at the head of the table, my mom on one side with Ceci beside her and her friend at the opposite end.

"What would you like to drink?" The waiter had started with my mom and made his way around, getting to Kulti before me.

I'm not positive what I was expecting, but it wasn't "Water."

"And you, *señorita*?" the waiter asked me.

I'd been planning on getting a margarita because that was usually my treat, but I had a possible drinking problem sitting right next to me and I was driving. "Water too, please."

My mom started talking about one of her brothers calling earlier to wish Dad a happy birthday and how he was planning on coming to visit within the next month, when the waiter came back with our drinks and to take our orders.

"For you?" he asked Kulti.

The jerk-off did it.

"Tacos," he paused dramatically and I had to be the only one that really caught it, especially when he knocked his knee into mine beneath the table and shot me a side look, "*al Carbon*."

I snorted and tapped my knee back against his, curling my lips over my teeth to keep from smiling. I barely remembered rattling off my meal because I'd asked, knowing damn well they didn't, "Do you have any German Chocolate Cake?"

Why would they have German Chocolate Cake at a Mexican restaurant? They wouldn't, but I was going to be a pest and look like a moron at the same time.

"Umm, *no.* We have *sopapillas* and *flan*?" the man offered.

Before I got a chance to answer, someone pretended to drop his napkin on the floor and in the process of bending over to retrieve the imaginary item, decided to dig his sharp elbow right into the meaty part of my thigh.

It lasted all of a second, but the squawk that came out of my mouth was so ugly even my dad, the king of ugly noises, made a face at me.

"We don't know her," Dad said to the waiter in Spanish.

I laughed and turned to Kulti, way more amused than I was embarrassed, "You're going to get it later, bratwurst," I muttered under my breath.

He knocked his knee against mine again, his actions saying so much more than any words right after getting out of the car could have. Where the hell had this playful man come from, I had no idea, but I loved it.

I reached beneath the table and squeezed his denim-covered knee.

"Who wants to give me my present first?" my dad asked once the waiter had walked away.

Mom and I met each other's eyes from across the table and we both barely shook our heads. Who asks that? My dad. My dad asks for his presents.

Mom turned her attention back to the brand-new fifty-seven-year-old and winked. "I'll give you your present at home."

I cringed.

From down the table, Ceci said, "Mom!"

Then I added, "Gross."

Our dad laughed but it was Mom that gave us both a frown. “Nasty girls,” she said in Spanish. “That’s not what I meant!”

I balled up my hand and put it against my mouth, pretending to hold back a good retch.

“*Cochinas,*” Mom repeated, still shaking her head.

“Okay. Ceci? Sal? Who wants to go?”

My little sister sighed from across the table. Sometimes it was weird looking at her. She looked so much like our mom, brown hair, fair skin, brown eyes, fine boned and slim. She was the pretty kid. The really pretty one that had had boyfriends back when she was in fourth grade, while I’d been… not having boyfriends in fourth grade. Back then my only boyfriend had been my imaginary love, Kulti, the guy who happened to be sitting next to me in that exact moment.

“I’ll go first.” She pulled a small box from under the table and had our mom give it to Dad. “Happy birthday. I hope you like it, Daddy.”

Dad tore open the paper and then the box with the excitement of a little kid. He pulled out a beautiful frame with a really old picture of him and Ceci on a swing set. He grinned and blew her a kiss, thanking his youngest daughter for her gift. Then, expectantly he turned his attention in my direction and made ‘gimme’ hands.

Kulti held his hand out. “I’ll get it.”

I grabbed my keys from my purse and handed them over. “Thanks.”

He’d barely left the table when my dad leaned over, a glassy look in his eyes. “I’m not dreaming, am I?”

Mom groaned.

“You think I can take a picture of him here?” the birthday boy asked.

I thought about what would happen if a picture of my dad and the German got on the internet. On the inside, I winced. A lot. But what was I going to tell my dad? No? Because I didn’t want the world to know that Kulti had spent time with my family? Because I didn't want rumors floating around? I didn't. I definitely didn't want any of that.

On the other hand, he was so excited and happy about everything, despite the fact that he still hadn't said a direct word to my friend.

How could I tell him that was a bad idea? I couldn't. Dad would go on to send a picture to every person he'd ever known.

There were worse things in life, weren't there?

"Sure, Dad."

The man grinned.

Yeah, there was no way I could tell him no. I handed over his gift card for the mall masseuse and earned a big wink from my dad.

Kulti was back in no time, sliding into his seat while holding two perfectly wrapped boxes in his hands. The packages had shown up early that afternoon, already wrapped and ready to go inside of a larger cardboard box. We'd stashed them in the trunk of my car before anyone caught us. The German handed them both over so I could pass them to my dad, who had a look on his face like he'd just crapped his pants and realized it.

"Happy birthday from the both of us," I said, without even thinking about how it sounded.

Dad didn't care because he wasn't paying attention. He was eyeing Kulti and then the boxes, and then Kulti and then the boxes all over again. Very gently, he tore off the paper of the first one and pulled out the same RK 10s I'd been trying to buy at the shoe store the day before.

He opened his mouth to say something, but then closed it again and reached for the next box. Inside was a plain white shoebox with no brand or logo on the cover. My dad pulled the lid back and stared before pulling out a shoe I hadn't seen before. The familiar stitched 'RK' was on the back and so was the familiar swoosh on the side.

"Next year's edition," Kulti explained.

Carefully, Dad set the shoe back into the box and took a deep breath before meeting my eyes and in a very low voice said, "Tell him I said thank you."

I put a fist over my mouth but I wasn't sure whether it was to keep from laughing or sighing in exasperation. "Dad, tell him yourself."

He shook his head, and I knew that was as good as I was getting.

Biting my lip I turned back to Kulti, who I was sure had heard what my dad had said and repeated what I'd been told.

Very seriously, the German nodded. "Tell him he's welcome."

Jesus Christ.

"And tell him there's something else in the box."

Something else? "Pa, there's something else in the box." Also, like they hadn't heard each other from four feet away.

Dad blinked, and then rifled through the nameless white box and pulled out a greeting card sized envelope. He removed something that looked like an index card. He read it and then read it a second and then a third time. He put the card back inside the envelope and then the box. His dark face was somber as he took a few breaths. He finally raised his green eyes to meet Kulti's hazel ones.

"Sal," he said, looking at the German, "ask him if he wants his hug now or later."

* * *

"What's wrong?"

I gave Kulti a look as I sat on the edge of the bigger bunk bed, ready to take my shoes off. "Nothing. Why?"

The German blinked at me. "You haven't said a single word."

I hadn't. He was right.

How could I talk when something huge had lodged itself into my chest? Something monstrous and uncomfortable had picked up and moved in, stealing the space where my breath and words usually lived.

Kulti had stolen that piece of me when he hugged my dad back...

He'd given him two front row seats to a FC Berlin game, along with a voucher for flights and a hotel.

What do you freaking say after that?

"Are you upset?" he asked.

I made a face. "About what?"

"Berlin."

Oh my God, he looked so earnest... "Rey." I shook my head. "How could I ever be upset over that? That was the greatest thing anyone has ever done for my dad. I can't even..." I stared up at him as he stepped right in front of me, looking down. "I can never pay you back. Okay, maybe I can if I pay you installments over the next five years, but I don't know what to say."

He shrugged those brawny shoulders. "Nothing."

I rolled my eyes. "It's a big deal."

"It isn't."

I stood up and held my arms open. "It is, so quit arguing and give me a hug."

He quit talking but he didn't hug me. I should have taken it as a compliment that he didn't shrink away from me or simply say 'no.' Kulti just looked at the arms I held a little away from my body, like it was some foreign thing he'd never seen before.

When he stood there for another ten seconds, I decided I had enough. This guy had given out thousands of hugs over the course of his life. Then I looked at his face and how serious he always was, and decided maybe he hadn't. But he had given my dad one at the restaurant, so screw it. He had to have another one in him.

I took a step forward and wrapped my arms around his waist, over his own arms like they were hostage. He rested his chin on the top of my head. "Thank you," I told him.

I held him for another ten seconds, feeling him stay stiff as a board the entire time, and then decided I could put him out of his misery. I dropped my arms and took a step back, the backs of my knees bumping into the frame of the bed.

Maybe it would have been awkward if I really cared about him hugging me back, or in this case, not hugging me back, but I didn't. Not at all. He'd given my dad something wonderful; I could live with it.

What *was* awkward was the way he was looking at the freckles on my chest and bare shoulders beneath the thin straps of my sundress.

"I should probably go change now," I muttered, taking a step to the side. "But I want you to know how grateful I am for what you did for my dad, all right?"

He nodded absently, still looking at the skin right above my boobs. Not directly at my boobs, just above them. Weird.

Well I guess this was payback time for looking at his boner the day before, and I was going to take it. "Hey, eyes up here, pretzel face."

# 20

"How was your break?"

I looked up from my spot on the ground pulling my socks up high to see Gardner standing over me. "Good. I got to spend some time with my family, and you?"

He shrugged, crouching down. "I slept a lot."

"Nice."

Gardner made a pleasant face but didn't reply. He stayed next to me as I pulled my cleat on and tied it. "Sal." His voice was so low my gut immediately knew something was wrong. "More pictures popped up this weekend. I want you to be smart, okay?"

I didn't even tilt my head to take a look at him, only slanting my eyes over in his direction as my guts crawled up into my throat. "We're friends, G. That's all."

The grave expression on his face wasn't exactly reassuring. "Look, I believe you. I'd believe you if you told me pigs flew, but I know Cordero's going to be pissed, and there's only so much Sheena and I can do."

Time seemed to slow down. "What are you trying to say?"

"I want you to think about what you're doing and what you

want from the future." Gardner put his hand on my shoulder. "I want the best for you, Sal. That's the only reason why I'm saying anything. I don't want you to get blindsided."

Blindsided by what?

Before I could even start to get my thoughts together and ask him for clarification on whether I was over-exaggerating what he was implying, Gardner straightened up and walked off.

*There's only so much Sheena and I can do for you.*

*Think about what you're doing and what you want to do in the future.*

*I don't want you to get blindsided.*

All I did was take my friend home with me. That was it. *It.*

I hadn't done drugs, flashed a crowd, stolen anything or killed anyone.

If my guesses were on track, Gardner had just warned me that my career was in jeopardy.

Maybe I should have panicked. Cried. I would have sworn that I would stop being friends with someone who so obviously needed a friend.

But I didn't do any of those things. Not even close.

While Gardner had just been trying to be a good friend and warn me, I was suddenly pissed. Really pissed.

I hadn't done anything wrong, and I knew that in my heart. Sure, there was a stipulation in my contract about fraternization, but I hadn't been freaking *fraternizing* with anybody. Not even close, and I was being punished? Or at least sort of being punished?

This was horse shit. Absolute horse shit.

And I really wanted to punch Cordero in the face. Repeatedly.

Tension screamed through my shoulders and down my arms. I had to ball up my fists to contain my frustration with this entire situation. Honestly, I liked Rey. It wasn't easy, and he got on my nerves at times, but I felt a closeness to him that I didn't feel with anyone else I played with.

The fact that only a few of the girls on the team spoke to me during practice didn't make things any better. The rest cast me side-glances that I wasn't a fan of. But they didn't say anything to egg me on, so I managed to keep my mouth closed. I knew better than to be the one to start anything. You're only young and dumb once.

When they weren't giving me snide glances, they were looking at Kulti like they were expecting to find him with my bra around his neck. The thing was, while I could keep my mouth shut, the German didn't have to.

And he didn't.

He had met my eyes early on during practice and frowned. His frown had continued to deepen the longer practice went on. Kulti didn't try to ask me what was happening, but somehow I knew that he was aware something was bugging me, and it had to do with the girls looking him up and down.

My favorite thing that came out of his mouth was, "I don't know what the hell you're looking at, but you need to be looking at the field and not braiding each other's hair!"

It was so sexist and untrue; I couldn't help but snicker and then try to hide it.

In the long run though, it didn't help me be any less pissed off.

They were still talking about me, and giving me looks. Murmuring. There was nothing I could do.

* * *

SOMEONE WAS SEATED at the bottom of the stairs leading up to my apartment by the time I got home from work that evening. It took all of a split second once I got out of the car, to recognize the brown hair and the long body that stood up, brushing off the back of his loose workout shorts.

He didn't say anything to me as I parked my car a couple feet away from him, and he didn't say a word as he took my duffel bag, even as he eyed the baggy pants and the long-sleeved shirt I had on. He hadn't seen me in my work clothes before, and I couldn't find it in me to care that I had dirt and grass stains all over my knees and that my hair had doubled in volume since that morning.

"Hey you," I said with a smile as we climbed up the steps to get to the front door.

Unlocking the door, he followed after me, locking it as soon as he was inside and dropping my bag in the same place I always left it. I sat on the floor and yanked off my work boots, too exhausted to even bother trying to do it standing up. They got tossed in the direction of the door harder than they needed to be.

The German held out his hand to me.

I took it and got to my feet, not moving an inch when we stood maybe four inches away from each other.

I'd been telling myself the second half of the day that this was technically his fault. That if I hadn't been nice to him, we wouldn't have started spending time together and become friends. If he was anyone else in the world, save for a handful of other people, no one would have given a single shit what we did together. I had spent my entire career trying to get through day by day and improve. I didn't want fame, and while a fortune would have been nice, it wasn't what got me going every morning. I'd been careful, always careful, always sacrificing whatever I needed to, to succeed.

Kulti had come in and doomed all that.

I had put time and effort into building a working relationship with the girls I played with. I helped them out, wanting them to do well, and all that hard work was now pretty much in the shitter. No one except Jenny and Harlow had bothered to—

The German squeezed the hand that I hadn't even noticed he hadn't let go of. Palm to palm, his thumb rubbed over the back of my hand, once. Just once. "If you would like me to apologize, I won't."

I closed my eyes and stood there, letting him hold my hand and not letting myself think about it too much. I was an affectionate person, and even though Kulti hadn't really been one in the entire time we'd been getting along, you couldn't be a soccer player and be weird about physical contact. So I would take everything he was willing to give me.

"What do you have to not be sorry about?" I asked him, eyes still closed.

His long fingers squeezed again. "Forcing you to be my friend."

I felt myself smile. "You didn't force me to be your friend."

"I did," he argued.

"You didn't. I was nice to you when you were still being an extra-large pain in the ass."

There was a pause. "Was this before or after you called me a bratwurst?"

I opened an eye. "Both."

The corners of his mouth tipped up just slightly, but he stayed serious. "I won't let them bench you."

I nodded, staring straight at the man who mastered the resting bitch face, and I said, "All right."

Words hung in the air between us. I felt compressed, squeezed. I was torn between knowing that I wasn't going to tell him to beat it and knowing that I probably should.

Was this worth it? Was this worth being ostracized by my teammates? Being on my general manager's hit list? Having my photo plastered on fan pages with the words 'die bitch' at the bottom?

I really had no idea.

I hoped so.

* * *

"SAL! YOU GOT A MINUTE?"

My fingers gripped the nylon strap of my bag, and I felt my insides stir. The day before I had managed to avoid the two reporters loitering off the side of the field by hauling ass while they were busy talking to other people, but now... I hadn't gotten so lucky.

I'd gotten to the field for practice early, but not early enough. Damn it.

"Come on, one minute. Please!"

With no one to hide behind or any other way to pretend like I hadn't heard the guy calling out to me, I took a deep breath and resigned myself to getting this over with.

The twenty-something guy looked friendly enough in khaki pants and a neatly tucked in, button-down blue shirt. He smiled at me, his little handheld recorder ready and waiting. "Thanks for stopping. I have a few questions for you."

I nodded. "Sure. Okay."

He introduced himself and the website he was doing the interview for, and let me know he'd be recording our conversation. "You're about halfway through the season now, how are the Pipers looking?"

All right. "Good. We've only lost one game so far, but we're trying to stay focused and get through the next few weeks so that we can move into the playoffs again."

"At what point does the pressure really start to get to you?"

"At least for me, it never lets up. Before the season even starts, I'm already worried about how things are going. Every game is important and that's what our coaching staff has really drilled into us. It's easier to stay focused when you're worried about putting one foot in front of the other rather than trying to take on a huge obstacle at once."

He smiled and nodded. "Who are you looking forward to watching this Altus Cup?"

I smiled at him, feeling a little easier. The Cup was starting in September, right after our season ended. "Argentina, Spain, Germany." Almost absently I added, "The U.S." Well that didn't sound sincere at all. "I'm pretty excited."

"Any plans for rejoining the U.S. Women's National Team?" he asked.

That now-familiar rope of anger laced my wrists, and I had to shake it off. It was easy enough to live with not being on the team before, when things had been great with the Pipers, but now not so much. I was on my last reserve of patience. "No plans," I said in a steady voice, even smiling. "I'm focusing on the Pipers for now."

"You've talked about your work with youth players in the past; are you continuing your camps this year?"

"Those camps are starting up in a few weeks. It's mainly low-income middle school kids and early high schoolers I aim for. That's usually one of the most influential ages for kids to really stick to sports, so I love doing them."

"Okay, one final question so you can get going: what do you have to say about rumors about a relationship between you and Reiner Kulti?"

Dun, dun, dun. I smiled at him and eased my little heart to slow down. "He's a great person. He's my coach and a friend." I shrugged. "That's all."

The look the guy gave me was incomprehensible, but he nodded and smiled and thanked me.

I couldn't help but feel dirty. Just a little. Like I'd done something wrong—or at least something that I wouldn't want to own up to. I could handle accepting my faults and mistakes. I didn't have a boyfriend; I wasn't married. I could be friends with whoever I wanted to. And it wasn't like he was still married or anything, either.

But...

I swallowed back the weird feeling in my chest, that strange indecisiveness that wasn't sure whether I wanted to handle all this unnecessary attention or not.

I wasn't a superstar. I was just me, a little-known soccer player. The equivalent of a bobsledder in Houston, as my sister had called me one day.

All I had ever wanted was to play and to be the best. That was it.

What was I doing?

I tried to block out all these things that didn't matter when I was at practice, but it was a lot harder than usual for some reason. I couldn't stop thinking about Gardner's warning, stupid Amber and her equally stupid husband, the national team, Kulti and all his famous-person crap. I felt like I had a noose around my neck, slowly, slowly, slowly tightening. I couldn't breathe.

Right after finishing my passing drills, I felt a hand wrap around my wrist when I wasn't expecting it.

I hadn't even realized he was nearby. To be honest, I hadn't been paying that much attention to anything besides soccer: passing the ball, blocking, sprinting. Things I had done a thousand times and would hopefully do another thousand in the future.

A deep line creased between his eyebrows as he tipped his chin down to ask, "What's wrong?"

"Nothing" started to come out of my mouth, but I decided against it at the last minute. He'd know. I wasn't sure how he'd know, but he would know I was lying. "I'm just stressed, that's all." Okay, so that was vague and understated, but it was the truth. I was.

Apparently, it wasn't enough for him. Of course it wouldn't

be. He got that über serious look on his face, the one that smoothed the angled lines of his cheekbones. Kulti met me eye to eye, not caring that we were so close or that whoever wasn't busy doing drills was more than likely looking at us. He didn't care. He simply focused on the object of his attention—me.

It tightened something in my chest that I couldn't really put together.

"Later," he stated, he didn't ask.

I shrugged my shoulders.

"Later," Kulti repeated. "Keep your head in it."

I nodded and offered him a weak smile.

He didn't smile back. Instead, he let go of my wrist and put his hand on my forehead before shoving me gently away. It wasn't exactly a hug or a pat on the back, but I'd take it.

Sure enough when I turned around, at least eight sets of eyes were on us.

Great.

* * *

A KNOCK at eight o'clock that night had me setting my latest concoction on the kitchen counter, careful not to let the spoon fall out of the bowl. I'm not sure who else I could have been expecting to show up besides the German, so I wasn't surprised to find him on the other side of the peephole.

"Come in," I said, already opening the door wide for him to enter.

Right before shutting the door, I noticed that his Audi was parked behind my Honda, the silhouette of someone in the driver's seat. All right.

"Don't mind me," I explained, walking back to the kitchen where I'd left my face mask.

"You have something on your face," Kulti stated, standing on the other side of the counter with a curious expression.

I had only managed to cover one cheek before he'd knocked so I'm sure I looked like an orange creamsicle. Picking up the spoon, I applied more of the cool mixture to my cheeks and forehead, watching the German as I did it. "It's a face mask made with Greek yogurt, turmeric, ground oatmeal and lemon." I raised my eyebrows as I dabbed some over my upper lip. "You want some?"

He eyed me dubiously. Then, he nodded.

All right, then. "Rinse off your face with hot water, and then you can put it on."

I blindly finished putting the mixture on my target skin as he went to the kitchen sink and splashed water over his face, dabbing it dry with a paper towel. It wasn't until Kulti took a seat on the edge of the kitchen counter and tipped his chin down, that I realized he wanted me to put the mask on him.

"Are you serious?"

The German nodded.

"You are really something else, you know that?" I asked, even as I stepped forward and began smoothing the gunk over his nose and across each cheekbone, gentle and slow. The facial hair that had grown in over the day prickled my fingers with each pass over his features.

"Do you do this often?" he asked after I'd covered his chin.

"A couple times a week." I smiled, noticing his eyes on mine. "Do you?"

"I've had a few scrubs before photo shoots," he admitted.

I nodded, impressed. What a metrosexual. I ran my fingers over the strip of flesh below his nose. "We spend so much time in the sun, you really have to try and take care of your skin. I don't want to look like an old lady before my time comes."

He nodded his agreement and let me finish putting the mask on him with watchful eyes. Once we were done, I told him we needed to wait at least twenty minutes before washing it off. "Don't touch anything either. The turmeric stains everything," I warned him, but I didn't really care if I got a stain on my furniture or not.

Grabbing an ice pack from the freezer, I sat on one end of the couch and watched him sit on the other. Propping my leg on the coffee table, I slapped the ice-pack down on it for a good fifteen minutes. My notebook was on the cushion between us, with a whiteboard on the table for my sticky notes, right where I'd left it before I decided to do my first beauty treatment of the week. The reporter's question earlier about the summer camps reminded me that I needed to plan the lessons for them. I hadn't finalized a single thing yet.

The German didn't even hesitate to pick up the notebook, reading over the notes I'd written about the different things that I thought would be beneficial to the kids at their ages.

"What is this?" he asked.

I fought the urge to snatch the notebook away from him. "Plans. I have a few summer camps coming up."

His eyes flicked up from over the edge of the notebook. "Training camps?"

"For kids," I explained. "They only last a few hours."

He glanced back down at the sheet. "For free?"

"Yes. I do it in low-income neighborhoods for kids whose parents don't have the funds to enroll them in clubs and leagues."

He hummed.

I scratched my cheek, feeling oddly vulnerable at him reading over the skills I planned on teaching the kids. He kept reading and it got worse. It wasn't like he was a fantastic coach, he wasn't. I had no doubt he could have been a great coach if he wanted to, but he didn't.

I scrunched my toes up in my socks and watched his face.

"Did your parents have money?" I found myself asking.

Kulti "uh-huh"ed.

I pulled my knee up to my chest and put my chin on it,

careful not to rub the yogurt all over it. "There was no scholarship for you at the academy?"

He glanced up. "FC Berlin covered the costs."

No shit. They'd recruited him at eleven? It happened, but I guess it still amazed me.

"And you, Taco?"

I smiled at him from behind my knee, surprised he was asking. "You've been to my house, Germany. We weren't poor-poor, but I didn't have a pair of name brand shoes until I was probably fifteen, and my brother bought them for me with his first advance from the MPL. I have no idea how my parents managed to swing paying for everything for so long but they did." Actually, I did know. They cut a whole bunch of things out of the budget. A lot. "I just got lucky they cared, otherwise things would have gone a lot differently."

"I'm sure you haven't made them regret anything they did."

"Eh. I'm sure I've made them wonder what the hell they were doing a time or two." Or three. Or four. "I used to have a terrible temper—"

The German snorted. Straight-up snorted, lips fluttering, too.

Ass.

I nudged at his hip with my toes. "What? I don't have a terrible temper anymore."

Those awesome almost-hazel eyes looked up again from over the notebook. "No, you don't and neither do I."

"Ha!" I nudged at him again and he grabbed my foot with his free hand. I tried to yank it back, but he didn't let go. "Oh please, my temper isn't anywhere near as bad as yours."

"It is." He pulled my foot back toward him, getting a better grip around the instep.

"Trust me. It isn't."

"You're a menace when you're mad, *schnecke*. Maybe the refs haven't caught you pinching girls, but I have," he said casually.

I sat up straight. "Unless you have any physical proof, it never happened."

Kulti stared at me for a beat before shaking his head, his thumb pressing a hard line down the arch of my foot. "You're an animal."

My shoulders shook but I managed to keep myself from laughing. "It takes one to know one."

The corners of the German's mouth tipped up. "Unlike others, I have never pretended to be nice."

"Oh, I know." I smiled at him. "There was that time you bit a guy—"

"He bit me three times before I had enough," he argued.

I raised an eyebrow but kept going. "Don't get me started on the thousand times you elbowed someone in the face." Once the words were out of my mouth, I reeled back. "How the hell didn't you get banned?"

The fact he shrugged at that claim said just how much of a crap he still didn't give about the staggering number of noses he'd broken and eyebrows he'd busted.

"All the fights you were in—"

"I usually didn't start them."

"Debatable." He blinked at me. "And don't forget about the tibias you've broken."

With that comment he just kept an even glare on me that had me smiling pretty smugly, even if it was at my brother's expense.

"You win," I stated. "All I give are bruises," and then I added, "and an occasional bloody lip or two and a concussion once."

The German leaned over, putting my notebook down and scooting closer to me, yanked my foot once more before setting it back on the couch next to him. His hand was wrapped around my ankle. "I'm positive you've thought about doing worse and in the end, that's what matters."

He had a point, but I sure as hell wasn't going to admit it.

Instead I just sat on my end of the couch and gave him a flat look of irritation, until he smiled just the slightest bit wider and finally looked back down at the notebook. I went back to the sticky notes on the poster board and reviewed what I had jotted down already.

In the middle of making a few new notes, Kulti tapped the top of the foot I still had right by him. "Tell me how I can help with this."

If anyone thought for one second that I would ever say no to help from him, they would have been insane. It wasn't just the endless endorsements he had access to. If he wanted to do any actual work with the kids, it would be like having Mozart give a kid a lesson in musical composition.

I swallowed and felt my entire body brighten. "Any way you can."

"All you have to do is ask." Then as if he thought about what he said, his eyelids hooded low. "You aren't going to ask, I don't even know why I bother. Let me see what I can do."

"All right." I smiled at him. "Thanks, Rey."

He nodded very solemnly and I found myself just studying him.

"Can I ask you something?"

"No," he said in a pain-in-the-ass tone.

I ignored him. "Why did you take the Pipers position when you hate coaching?"

The notebook he'd been holding was slowly lowered to his lap. The muscle in his jaw flexed, and his expression became very even. "You think I don't like coaching?"

"I'm ninety-nine percent sure that you freaking hate it."

Kulti relaxed a whole millimeter. He just kept looking at me for so long I thought for sure he was trying to intimidate me into changing the subject or hoping I'd forget. Maybe.

The hell I was.

I blinked at him. "So?"

The German's lips peeled back into something that was a mix between an incredulous smile and an amazed one. "Is it that obvious?"

"To me." I shrugged my shoulders at him. "You look ready to strangle someone at least five times each practice, and that's when you don't even say anything. When things actually come out of your mouth, I'm pretty sure you would light us all on fire if you could get away with it."

When he didn't agree or deny anything, I blinked.

"Am I right or am I right?"

He mumbled something that could have been "you're right" but it was said so low I couldn't be sure. The fact he was avoiding my eyes said enough. It had me grinning.

"So why are you doing it? I'm sure they're not paying you a quarter of as much as any of the European men's teams would. I'm definitely sure the MPL would have paid you a lot more, too. But you're here instead. What's up with that?"

Nothing.

It felt like a few hours had passed without him saying anything.

Honestly it was really kind of insulting. The longer he took to not answer, the more it hurt my feelings. I wasn't asking him for his bank account number or for a freaking kidney. I had taken him home with me, brought him into my house, told him about my grandfather and he couldn't even answer one single personal question? I'd understood from the beginning he had trust issues, and I couldn't say that I blamed him. My brother got all cagey around people he didn't know. At some point, you never knew who was your friend for the right reasons and who wasn't.

But... I guess I had thought we were past that.

I swallowed back my disappointment and looked away, scooting forward on the couch so I could get up. "I'm going to make some popcorn, do you want some?"

"No."

Averting my eyes, I got up and headed into the kitchen. I pulled a pot out and set it on the stove, lighting it. Collecting my extra-large tub of coconut oil and bag of kernels, I tried to suppress the feeling in my chest that I was suddenly not so fond of.

He didn't trust me. Then again, what the hell did I expect? It wasn't like anything I found out about him wasn't given out in drips. Tiny, tiny drips.

I'd barely scooped some oil into the heated pot when I felt Kulti standing behind me. I didn't turn around even when he got so close that I couldn't take a step back without touching him. His silence was incredibly typical, and I didn't feel like saying anything either. I scooped a few of tablespoons of popcorn kernels into the pot and set the lid on, giving it a shake which was angrier than it needed to be.

"Sal," he said my name in that smooth tone that hinted at a trace of an accent.

Keeping my eyes on the pot as I opened the lid to let the steam out, I asked, "Did you want some after all?"

The touch on my bare shoulder was all fingertips.

But I still didn't turn around. I gave the pot another forceful shake but his fingers didn't fall off, they just moved further up my shoulder until he was closer to my neck. "You can take the first batch if you want."

"Turn around," he requested.

I tried to shrug off his fingers. "I need to keep an eye on this so it doesn't burn, Kulti."

He dropped his hand immediately.

"Turn around, Sal," he said forcefully.

"Wait a minute, would you?" One more hard shake to the pot and I opened the lid.

The German reached around me and turned off the knob on the stove. "No. Talk to me."

Carefully, I wrapped my fingers around the long oven handle and took a breath to bottle my frustration up.

"You said a few minutes ago you didn't have a temper," he reminded me which only made the moment that much more aggravating.

"I'm not mad," I snapped back a little too quickly.

"No?"

"No."

He let out a sound that could have been a scoff if I thought German people were capable of making noises like that. "You called me Kulti."

My fingers flexed around the oven handle. "That's your name."

"Turn around," he ordered.

I tipped my chin up to face the ceiling and asked for patience. A lot of it. Hell, all of it. Unfortunately, no one seemed to answer my prayer. "I'm not mad at you, all right? I just thought..." I sighed. "Look it doesn't matter. I swear I'm not mad. You don't have to tell me anything you don't want to. I'm sorry I asked."

No response.

Of-freaking-course not.

Right. *Right.*

*Patience. Patience.*

"I took the position because I had to," that deep voice I'd heard a hundred times on television said. "I didn't do anything for almost a year except almost ruin my life, and my manager said I needed to come out of retirement. I had to do something, especially something positive after my DUI." Two warm hands that could only have belonged to him covered my shoulders. "There weren't many things to choose from—"

"Is that because you didn't want to be in the spotlight anymore?" I asked, remembering an earlier conversation we'd had.

He made a positive grunt. "Coaching was the only thing we could agree on. Short and temporary, it seemed the best fit." Kulti paused as the pads of his thumbs brushed over my trapezius muscles. That made me snicker, and it made the German dig his thumbs into my muscles. "A friend of mine suggested women's soccer. I did some research—"

I had to save that for later. I wasn't surprised he admitted he had to do research on women's soccer. Of course he wasn't familiar with it.

"—and the U.S. women kept coming up as consistently the best," he finished, but something nagged at me.

Something didn't add up.

"Why didn't you just join the national team staff?" I asked even as his thumbs really dug deep into my shoulders and holyfreakingcrap, it felt great. It'd been months since the last time I'd gotten a massage.

The German let out a sigh that reached all the way to my toes. "Is anything ever enough for you?" His voice was resigned.

He knew the answer. "No." Then I thought about it and his reluctance and I gasped. "*They didn't want you?*"

"No, you little idiot." He called me an idiot even as he gave me a massage that made my knees go weak, so I couldn't take it to heart. Actually, it was sort of his own affectionate way of talking to me. "Of course they would have wanted me if I had asked."

How the hell I fit in the same room as his ego, I had no idea.

"I won't involve myself in anything if I believe I won't win," he stated.

I rolled my eyes even though he couldn't see me. "Who likes to lose? I get it."

Those magical thumbs slid deep around my shoulder blade. "I know you do."

"Right... so...."

He stopped all movements with his long fingers; the heat

from his rough palms radiated through my skin and somehow into my bones. "You're the best striker in America, *schnecke*. Look up 'best goals in women's soccer' and four of the top ten are yours. I wasn't going to waste my time on anything or anyone but the best. With more training, better coaching, you could be the top striker in the world."

He wasn't going to...

It's like my brain stopped working.

I opened my mouth and closed it, at a complete loss for words.

"I came to the Pipers for you."

What the fuck do you even say to that?

Is there anything to say?

It seemed like the world came out from under my feet. My lungs felt punctured and bereft. Shaken up didn't even begin to explain how I felt.

*Get it together, Sal.*

Breathless and unsteady, I released the oven handle and turned around slowly to face Kulti. *Focus. Don't make a big deal out of this.* Damn it, it was so much easier said than done. This had been my lifelong dream when I was a kid. To be singled out by The King... remnants of a younger Sal were still in me, rejoicing and throwing Mardi Gras beads in the air at what he said. I couldn't think about it, not then and possibly not ever.

*I came to the Pipers for you.*

Jesus Christ. I needed to keep it together. *Focus*. "I'm not the best but that's beside the point. You didn't recognize my last name when you saw the video?"

He gave a smile that could have been sheepish if he was capable of being sheepish. He wasn't. It was more of a smirk. "I can't remember every player I've ever injured, Sal, and I wouldn't care to."

Not surprising at all, but it still made me shake my head. "You're something else, pumpernickel." My shoulders relaxed as I took in the very serious face several inches above mine. "So, you came to the Pipers even though you knew you didn't like coaching." I purposely skipped the part about how he'd chosen our team.

"*Ja.*"

"And you still hate us."

The German lifted a shoulder in the least apologetic shrug ever. "There's a few of you who should have stopped playing soccer a long time ago." He blinked. "And one of you I would love to shake on a regular basis."

I grinned at him before reaching forward to thump him on the shoulder. "Trust me; I've had the urge to punch you in the face a time or five."

"There's that temper again. A nice girl would never think about punching someone," he said with that stupid smirk. "How many people have you punched before?"

"No one," Jeez Louise, "in at least ten years. I've thought about it a hundred times but I haven't actually gone through with it. Come on."

He gave me a look that easily replaced a raised eyebrow, making a point about me *thinking* about doing things again.

Asshole. "It's too obvious and you know it. There's no way to get away with it."

The German nodded in agreement. "True. How many players have you elbowed before?"

"Enough," I answered truthfully, knowing that my number would still and forever be a fraction of his.

"You have the most fouls on the team," Kulti noted, which surprised the shit out of me. "More than Harlow."

It was my turn to shrug. "Yeah, but it's not because I elbow people left and right. I haven't done that since I was a kid and got kicked off a league for it," I explained to him with a grin.

"Such a great deal of anger for such a small body." A small smile cracked his lips. "Your parents? What did they think?"

"My mom chewed me out about it. My dad did too, but only when she was around. When she wasn't, he'd high-five me and tell me the other girl had it coming." We both laughed. "I love that man."

Kulti smiled gently, taking a step back only to grab two bowls out of the cabinet. I shot him a look as I poured half of the popcorn into each one and followed him around to the couch, where we took the same seats we'd left. Knowing that I was pushing my luck, I went for it anyway. "What about your parents? Did they go to your games?" I remembered when I was younger at the height of his career, cameras would zoom in on an older couple in the stands, pointing out that they were Reiner Kulti's parents.

"My father worked quite a bit, and once I went away to the academy, it was too far from home. They went to as many games as they could, watched more on television," he said around a mouthful of popcorn.

Well that was more than enough information to press for the day. What he didn't say was that his parents didn't go to a lot of his games when he was younger, but once he was older, they went whenever he paid. At least that's what I assumed from the way he worded it. "It worked for all of us."

I'm positive I didn't imagine the bite in his words. Obviously, I needed to steer the topic into safer territory.

"One more question and I'll quit being nosey." He might have nodded, but I was too busy eating popcorn to be sure. There was no way I could ask him with a straight face. "Did you blow that game against Portugal before you retired or were you really sick?"

His response was exactly what I expected: he threw a pillow at my face.

# 21

The next two weeks went by normally. Practices went well, Harlow and Jenny finally came back from their national team obligation, and the Pipers won the next two games in the season. I worked, exercised and Kulti came over nearly every night. We'd watch television, or get pissed off at each other playing Uno or poker, which he taught me to play. A couple of nights he showed up when I was about to start yoga. He'd help me move the couch and did it with me.

It was all fine, fun and easy.

I loved routines and knowing what to expect most of the time.

There were only two downsides, and they both revolved around females.

The girls on the Pipers gave me weird looks and said things when they thought I wasn't listening. It took everything inside of me some days to ignore them, and other days I'd just smile at them and remind myself that I could go to sleep easily at night knowing that I hadn't done anything to be ashamed of. Some days were easier than others, but as long as we kept playing well as a team, I'd suck it up and keep my big mouth closed.

Harlow on the other hand, didn't have any problem telling the younger girls to mind their own businesses and focus on soccer and not spreading gossip. She did it without once asking me anything about what was happening with Kulti.

The emails had picked up again. It had started as only a message or two from the German's female fans, but in no time picked up to three or four. By the time the picture my dad had taken of all us at dinner began being circulated, they were so frequent that I stopped reading emails from people I didn't recognize. I didn't say anything to anyone. I didn't want to. The less attention I brought to myself and Kulti, the better, I figured.

* * *

"HOLY SHIT."

I turned around to see what the sixth grade teacher was 'holy shitting' over, and I froze.

Seriously, I froze.

"Holy shit," I repeated the exact same words that had just come out of the other woman's mouth.

It was the German walking across the middle school field, which would have been a 'holy shit' moment to begin with if I wasn't already used to seeing him all the time. But there were the two men walking alongside him. One was another German who I'd seen play plenty of times growing up, and the other a Spaniard who I'd met before and happened to have a cologne commercial running on television.

They pooped. They all pooped. Every single one of them.

I took a deep breath and looked around the field at the four teachers who had volunteered to help out with the soccer camp that Saturday morning. Four small goals had been set up about half an hour ago in preparation for the twenty kids who had pre-registered.

Dear God, he'd brought these men and he hadn't said a

word about it the last time we'd seen each other. Then again, neither of us had brought up him helping since we had originally talked about it two weeks ago. I didn't want him to feel obligated to do anything.

Yet here he was with friends. Not just any friends, but *them*.

There was no way in hell I was being totally cool about this. No way Kulti couldn't tell I was thrilled. From the way his mouth tightened when he stopped just a few feet away, ignoring the two teachers standing right by me, he knew everything.

I grabbed his forearm as soon as he was close enough and squeezed hard, hoping he could understand everything I was feeling, everything I wanted to say but couldn't. At least nothing I was able to get out in that instant.

"Hello," I managed to say in a voice that sounded just like my own and not like I was on the brink of shitting a small pony. "Thanks for coming."

The German tipped his head down in acknowledgment.

Turning my attention to the other men, I thought to myself once more: *poop, poop, poop*. Fortunately, I got through it.

"Hi, Alejandro," I said, almost shyly.

It took the Spaniard a moment of looking at me before it dawned on him that we knew each other. "Salomé?" he asked hesitantly. Honestly, I was surprised he remembered my name; I had no doubt he'd met a thousand people since we'd last seen each other, and it wasn't like we'd been best friends. We both had a sponsorship with the same athletic clothing company. About two years ago, we'd had photo shoots scheduled at the same time.

"It's nice to see you again," I said, extending my hand out in a greeting.

What I didn't see were the hazel-colored eyes going back and forth between myself and the Spanish man.

Alejandro quickly took it, allowing himself to smile broadly.

"*Como estas?*" He fell into that quick, soft accented Spanish that was a little foreign to me.

"*Muy bien y usted?*" I asked.

Before he could respond, the other newcomer butted in. "*Hablo español tambien*," he said in a rougher accent, more like the Central American Spanish I was accustomed to.

I smiled at him. "Hi. It's nice to meet you," I greeted Franz Koch, one of the star players in the European League a decade ago. In his mid-forties, he'd been the captain of the German National Team years ago.

If I remembered correctly, he'd been a freaking beast.

"Franz," the man said, taking my hand. "It's a pleasure to meet you."

I cleared my throat to keep from croaking and managed to smile. "Oh, I know who you are. I'm a big fan. Thank you so much for coming." I scratched at my cheek as I took a step away from them. "Thank you all for coming. I don't know what to say."

My German was fortunately on top of what needed to be done, because he jumped right in. "Let's do what you planned, but we'll split into two groups instead."

"Okay." I nodded. "That works. The kids should be showing up pretty soon." A smile exploded over my face when the two unexpected visitors nodded in agreement. They were here for my camp. "Is that fine with you guys?"

They agreed immediately. Alejandro and Kulti went on one team—I didn't miss how quickly my German claimed the Spaniard, and Franz and I were on the other.

It turned out to be the most fun I'd ever had at any youth camp, ever.

Franz, who didn't have an ounce of an ego and understood that this was for fun, was a dream to work with. An excellent team player and leader, he passed the ball freely, teased the kids with his thick accent, even talking like Arnold for a little while. He really just took pleasure mentoring the kids. We laughed, grinned, high-fived each other and the kids throughout the game.

On the other side of the field, where we'd moved the goals over, I could hear Kulti and Alejandro arguing with each other in quick Spanish from time to time. The kids, mostly Hispanic, cracked up over whatever they said to each other.

Most importantly, the kids had been ecstatic.

Everyone knew Kulti and Alejandro. Franz had been the one with the least amount of claps when I'd introduced him, but he'd won over the boys and girls who had been frowning when they got stuck with us and not the two superstars.

It had been amazing. Was I over the moon? Absolutely. By the time the three hours were over, I felt like I'd won a million dollars. The kids left more stoked than ever, the parents were in awe from where they were relegated to standing on the side of the field, and even the coaches were all grinning.

I threw my hand up and Franz's met mine in a wild shake once all the kids and the volunteer teachers had taken pictures with the four of us. "Thank you so much for coming. It really means the world to me."

"You are very welcome. I had a great deal of fun," he said with an honest smile.

I held my hand out to Alejandro. "Thank you, too. Those kids," I couldn't help but smile, "you guys made their day. Thank you."

The Spaniard shook my hand. "You're welcome, Salomé. I had fun, though next time I would rather be paired up with you," he said, cocking his head toward the German standing next to him. "He was difficult."

"He's a pain every day." I leaned into Kulti, bumping his arm with my shoulder.

I didn't miss the mini-step he took away from me or the face he made as he did it. His forehead scrunched, and he gave me a side-look that was almost repulsed.

What the hell? Did he just take a step away from me? O-kay.

My poor heart didn't miss how crappy his actions made me feel. *All righty, then.* Apparently being playful with him only applied to times when we were alone.

I could feel the smile on my face wither for a second before I plastered a bigger one on top of it.

Well.

That was embarrassing.

I looked back over at Franz and Alejandro, unsure of what to do since Kulti was being weird. "Thank you guys for coming. I appreciate it more than you can imagine. If there's anything I can ever do for either of you, please let me know." The bright smile I gave them was genuine. I held my arms out, knowing that at least the Spaniard would give me a hug. He'd given me one before.

He didn't leave me hanging. A little damp and sweaty, Alejandro stepped forward and wrapped his arms around my shoulders in a gentle hug. "*Fue un placer ver te otra vez.*"

I looked up at him when he started to pull away and smiled. "Always," I replied in Spanish. "Thank you again."

We had barely pulled away from each other when Franz stepped forward and grabbed me for a big hug, lifting me off the ground. "Thank you for having me." He set me back down, his hands splayed wide on my shoulders as he took a step back. "I'll be at your game this evening. I'm looking forward to seeing you play."

My eyes went wide, but I nodded. "That's great and a little nerve-wracking. Thanks." Glancing down at my watch, I made a face. "Speaking of which, I should really get going so I can get ready." I took another step back and grinned at the two men before returning my attention to Kulti.

Kulti, who was standing there with his tongue in his cheek,

had his arms crossed over his chest. He was pissed. I could recognize it by the way his eyes were narrowed.

What the hell did he have to be mad at? Was he mad because I tried to play around with him in front of his friends? It was fine in front of my family, but not in front of people he knew? I brushed it off and ignored his expression, saying, "Thank you for everything, Rey." Because I was thankful, that much was true. I just wished he wasn't acting strange in front of his friends.

* * *

A HAND TOUCHED my arm as I made my way toward the locker rooms following our Pipers' game that night.

I blinked and then grinned, still on a high from our win. "Hey, Franz."

The older German stood on the other side of the railing that separated the stands from the players making their way down the ramp to the locker rooms. "Salomé," he shook his head, smiling a gentle smile that made me feel so at ease. "Your videos don't do you justice. Your footwork and your speed are fantastic."

What was it with all these compliments lately?

Before I could digest it, Franz kept right on going. "You favor your right foot too much. I do as well. I know some tricks I could show you. Are you free tomorrow?"

*Franz Koch wanted to show me some tips.* I would never say no to someone offering to give me pointers. "Yeah, definitely. I'm free all day tomorrow."

"Excellent. I'm not familiar with this city. Do you know where we can meet?"

"Yes, yes." If I sounded too enthusiastic, I didn't give a single shit. Not a single itty bitty one. I rattled off the name of the park and after repeating it twice, I typed it onto the smart phone he handed me.

The second German man to come into my life smiled as he took his phone back with a nod. "Tomorrow at nine if that's agreeable with you."

Oh. Boy.

On the inside, I was squealing with excitement; on the outside, I hoped I only resembled a little bit of an idiot. "That definitely works for me. Thank you."

When I caught Kulti's attention in the locker room, I almost opened my mouth to tell him that I was meeting up with Franz the next day, but from the look on his face, I decided to keep my mouth shut. He'd looked consistently angry since we'd said goodbye at the youth soccer camp, and I had no idea what the hell had crawled up his butt and died.

Needless to say, I decided when I was back at home that I wasn't going to bother trying to figure it out.

I had tried to be playful with him and he'd been a bratwurst, so whatever. *Whatever.*

* * *

I WAS DYING.

Oh my God, I was dying. Nearly three hours of doing various drills with and against Franz had almost killed me. Death was on the cusp, I could feel it.

"How old are you again?" I asked as we both sat cross-legged across from each other at the park closest to my house.

"Forty-four."

"Jesus Christ." I laughed and put my hands behind my back to recline. "You're amazing, seriously."

"No." He mirrored my movement. "You are. With time and better coaching..." He shook his head. "Reiner said you don't play for the American team. Why?"

I crossed my legs close to my chest and looked at the nice older man. And for some reason I didn't completely understand, I told him. "I had a problem with one of the other girls on the team, and I left."

"They let you leave because of a problem with another player?" He reeled back, his accent becoming stronger.

"Yes. She was one of the team's starting players, and I was pretty young back then. She said it was either her or me, and it was me." Yeah, it hurt a little being so frank about it.

"That is possibly the dumbest thing I have ever heard." Franz stared at me like a part of him was expecting me to say, 'just kidding!' But I wasn't, and after a minute he finally realized it. He genuinely looked astonished. The older German sat up straight, giving me his total attention. "Why are you still here then?"

"What do you mean?"

"Why are you playing in this league if you can't play for the U.S. team?"

I blinked at him. "I have a contract with the Pipers."

"When does it end?" he asked, completely serious.

"Next season."

His nose scrunched up for a split second. "Have you thought about playing elsewhere?"

"Outside of the U.S.?" I started fidgeting with my socks, his questions leaving me curious with where he was going with this.

"Yes. There are women's teams in Europe."

I leaned back and shook my head. "I know some girls who have played there, but I've never given it much thought. My brother is on loan in Europe right now, but... no. I haven't thought about it. My family is here, and I've been happy here." Until recently.

Franz gave me an even look and said eighteen words that would haunt me for weeks to come. "You should think about playing somewhere else. You're going to waste your talent and your career away here."

I would later wonder why of every person in my life, I chose to talk to Franz about my career, but in the end something in me decided he was the best option. His view was more unbiased than anyone else's. While he might have cared a tiny fraction about my future—if that—he was giving me a clinical view. He was telling me what *he* would do, what the best thing would be without taking everything else into my life into consideration. Not my parents, my job, the Pipers or anything.

Play somewhere else?

I blew out a long breath and told him very honestly, "I don't know."

"Don't give the best years of your career to a league that doesn't appreciate your talent. You should be playing on the national team—any national team, and you could do it. It isn't complicated. Players do it all the time."

He was right. Players did do it all the time. I wouldn't be the first and I definitely wouldn't be the last to play for a different country. Fans didn't think twice about it. They didn't care as long as someone played well.

"Really put some thought into it, Salomé," he said in a gentle encouraging voice.

I found myself nodding, feeling confused and the slightest bit overwhelmed by this new possibility. Play somewhere else, a different country. That sounded kind of scary. "I'll think about it. Thanks."

"Good." Franz smiled. "I'm here for three more days. Are you free tomorrow for round two?"

* * *

I WAS DRIVING home when my dad called. I let it go to voicemail and waited until I got to a red light to call him back.

"Hey, Daddy," I said into the speakerphone once he answered.

"Salomé—"

Oh dear God. He went with my full name. I braced myself.

"You met Alejandro?" He enunciated each word slowly. The fact he went with the man's first name said more than enough about how popular he was. It was like 'Kulti,' everyone knew him by one name.

"I have a picture to send you!" I immediately shot back before he could give me too much shit.

Dad ignored me. "And Franz Koch?"

I sighed. "Yes."

He didn't say anything after that and I sighed again.

"I had no idea they were coming." That sounded lame even to my ears. "Dad, I'm sorry. I should have called you right after and sent you pictures. Kulti brought them and I was so surprised, I wasn't thinking clearly. We had a game afterward and... don't be mad at me."

"I'm not mad."

He was disappointed. I knew he liked being in the 'know.' He liked knowing gossip before everyone else did, and I had let him down and made him find out that two super-star players had volunteered at my soccer camp through someone else.

"Your *tio* sent me the picture," he said, which explained everything. Dad wasn't a fan of my mom's brother.

Bah. "Franz came to our game yesterday and asked to do some one-on-one coaching with me," I offered him up. "We played for three hours. I thought I was going to die."

"Only you two?" he asked in a soft voice that was probably still the same volume a normal person spoke in.

"Yeah."

"He asked you to play with him?"

"Yes. He said my footwork was fantastic. Can you believe that?"

Dad chuffed. "Yes."

I grinned into the phone. "Well I couldn't believe it. He asked if I was free tomorrow to play again."

"You better have said yes," he grumbled, still trying to hold on to his aggravation.

"Of course I said yes. I'm not that dumb..."

Dad made a noise. "Eh."

"Yeah, yeah. Dad?"

"*Que?*"

"He asked me why I haven't considered playing in a different league." His words from earlier were wreaking havoc on my brain. "He said I was wasting my time here since I don't play on the national team."

The thing about parents, especially ones that loved their kids what some people might consider 'too much'—if that was even possible—was that sometimes they were selfish. Other times, you could hear the pain it caused them to put their kid's well-being ahead of their own wishes. So I wasn't positive how my dad would react to what I was saying. But I knew deep in my heart that my dad had always done what was best for me even if it cost him time, money and even heartache. Sure he'd been all about my brother going to Europe, but Eric wasn't me.

While I might not be his baby, I was his Sal. We were each other's best friends and confidants. Dad and I were a gang of two.

I kept going, and I told him about Cordero, Gardner and the Pipers that were talking about me because of my friendship with the German. By the time I pulled into the driveway of my garage apartment, Dad knew just about everything. I wasn't totally surprised that I felt relieved to get it off my chest.

"I don't know what to do," I admitted.

There was no hesitation on his end. "*Hijos de su madre,*" he growled. "You would never..." Dad let out an exasperated snarl of frustration. "You would never do that."

I sighed. "What should I do? I haven't done anything wrong, and a part of me doesn't want to leave..."

"*Mija*," my daughter, "Do what's best for you. Always."

* * *

"FIVE! FOUR! THREE! TWO! ONE!"

My arm was shaking as I finally let it collapse. Push-ups, freaking push-ups.

One-armed push-ups were the damned devil. I groaned and rolled onto my back, flopping my arms out at my sides to loosen them up, but it wasn't helping much. I'd spent the last three afternoons in a row playing with Franz Koch, and the guy wore me out. Add that to two days of work and practice. It would tire anyone out.

"Thirty seconds, ladies!" Phyllis, the psychopath fitness coach, yelled.

Oh God.

"Fifteen seconds!"

I rolled back onto my belly and planted both hands down flat on the ground, feeling the short crunch of turf under my palms.

"Five seconds! Get into plank position if you aren't already in it!"

She was insane.

"Up! Into a wide stance! Down! I better see your chests touching the floor!" she hollered, walking through the multiple bodies lowering themselves, myself included. My arms burned as I went down, biceps and shoulders being lit on fire. "Casillas! Do I see your arms shaking? Because I know I don't see your arms shaking!"

I gritted my teeth together and dropped even lower to the ground, arms trembling and everything, but I'd be damned if I stopped.

Especially when Phyllis started bellowing, "Roberts! Glover! You better get those scrawny arms under you and get yourselves up. This isn't high school P.E.! Get up!"

High school P.E.?

The two minutes straight of push-ups had me gasping for breath by the time we were finished. I pulled my knees under me and finally got to my feet with a tired huff.

"You had more in you," someone chipped in as they walked by.

I glanced up to find that it was the German making such a lovely observation.

He was too far away for me to return a comment, so I kept it to myself and got to my feet. The fact he hadn't spoken more than five words to me since the day of the kid's camp had grated on my nerves, big time. I hadn't done anything to piss him off besides try to play around, and he'd shut down. If he was pissed about that, then he needed to get the heck over it. We spent most days together, and all of a sudden, nothing?

I rolled my eyes and shook my head.

What was I doing? Really?

I loved playing. I didn't love the drama that went with it. I'd been doing this long enough to know that no association was perfect and no team was without its bad seeds, but...

"You all right, Sally?" Harlow asked with a slap to my back.

I nodded at my friend. "I'm good, just a little tired. You?"

"I'm always good," she claimed. "You sure you're okay, though? You've been looking a little pissed off."

"Yeah, I'm fine. Some of these girls though... they try my patience, Har. That's all."

The defender nodded, her lips puckered as she did it. "Ignore 'em, Sally. They're not worth it. You do what you gotta do and leave the rest up to other people to deal with." She slapped me on the back once more. "Now tell me about this

Alejandro that went to your camp. Is his rear end as big in person as it looks on TV?"

That had me laughing. "Oh yeah."

She let out a low whistle. "That ass, Sal. Whew. I'm not gonna even lie, I was a little jealous you didn't tell me he was going to your thing. I would have shown up with a lawn chair and popcorn."

"Thanks," I said sarcastically. "Next time I need you somewhere I'll make sure there's a big ol' butt so you have some incentive to show up."

Harlow laughed.

"What about Franz?" she asked as we walked toward our bags. "Did he have a good one?"

"Yeah, it was pretty impressive." I happened to look up in the middle of my sentence to see Kulti standing right by Gardner, and he was watching me.

What I didn't say was that Kulti had the best one.

# 22

"Did you all wake up this morning and decide you were going to play like complete assholes?"

It wasn't Kulti speaking, it was Gardner.

The game that night had gone that bad. Gardner was a firm believer in positive reinforcement. He complimented players when they did something well, and coached them through when they didn't.

We had bombed the game. It had been horrible.

He was right. It was like every player on the Pipers had woken up that morning and decided to play like we couldn't stand each other. There had been no communication between anyone, no sense of teamwork, no real effort.

To be honest, I was more than a little relieved it was an away game. At least our fans didn't have to watch the disaster unfold in person.

"I have no idea what to say to you all," Gardner continued his speech. "I don't *want* to say anything. I don't want to even look at you," he said in a lethally calm voice before looking at the other coaches standing by him. "If any of you can think of something, please feel free to jump in. I'm at a complete loss for words."

Sheesh.

"You were an embarrassment," Kulti piped up the second Gardner stopped talking. He was standing two people away from Gardner. His hands were on his hips, his face as serious as ever. "That was the worst game I have ever seen. The only person who knew she was supposed to care tonight was Thirteen, but the rest of you," his eyes met mine across the room and stayed there, "were disgraceful."

Yeah. *That* hit me right in the chest. I was fully aware that he was looking directly at me as he made the harsh comment. Sure it wasn't my best game, or anywhere close to it, but it wasn't like we'd lost because of me.

The only thing wrong I had done was snap at Genevieve in the middle of the game. After I missed my second shot of the night, she said loud enough for me to overhear, "I guess you don't get substituted if you're messing around with the coaching staff."

Could I have let it go? Sure—but during practice before the game, she'd run into me during some passing drills for no freaking reason, and then not apologized for it. Immediately afterward, she'd done it again. There's only so much you can take, really.

I'd figured that telling her to 'mind your own fucking business and focus on the game' could have been a lot worse, but apparently not. Gardner had finally taken me out of the game with fifteen minutes left in the second half.

I wasn't going to make any excuses. I sat there in the locker room and kept my mouth shut as the other assistant coach repeated everything that Gardner and Kulti had hinted at, but in a much more constructive way. His approach was more 'I'm disappointed in you all,' instead of the you-all-fucking-suck approach the other two had taken.

Jenny Milton, number thirteen, was sitting next to me; she nudged me with her elbow as she finished taking the tape off her hands. We had lost because we hadn't scored and because our defenders hadn't helped Jenny when the Cleveland team made charges toward the goal. She hadn't been able to block every attempt, and that was in no way her fault. She really had been the only one who hadn't blown it.

"That was brutal," she muttered, giving me wide eyes.

"My butt hurts from over here," I agreed, leaning over to take off my socks.

Jenny tipped her head over in Genevieve's direction discreetly. "What did she say to you during the game?" She'd been the only one who hadn't heard, I guess.

"She said some stupid crap about me not getting subbed because of Kulti." I kept my gaze down while I took off my cleats. "She was just being dumb." Not really in the mood to talk about it, I got up and quickly stripped off the rest of my uniform, wrapping a towel around myself before taking off my underwear and sports bra. "I'm going to hit the showers," I told her with a smile so she wouldn't think that I didn't want to talk to her. I just didn't want to talk about what Genevieve had said.

I was tired of it. I was tired of a bunch of stuff.

The night before when we'd arrived at the hotel, I had laid in bed and thought about everything Cordero, Gardner, Kulti, Franz and my dad had said. I'd debated calling Eric but ultimately decided against it. He would have said something stupid about how I brought everything upon myself for being friends with someone he hated.

And wasn't that the shit of it? I'd become really good friends with a moody ass who had nearly ended my brother's career. Sure, my dad had given me the blessing to move on from it without feeling guilty, but still.

The pumpernickel was still not on speaking terms with me for some reason that I couldn't comprehend.

I finished showering and getting dressed before hauling it out of the locker rooms toward the vans that were waiting to take us back to the hotel. I had just cleared the last set of doors that led outside the facility when I spotted him waiting off to the side, disguised in the shadows.

I mentally prepared myself for whatever nonsense was about to come out of his mouth. My gut said it wasn't going to be pretty, but you never knew, miracles did happen.

The instant the door snapped close, his head moved to face my direction. I didn't know what to say, so I just pulled my bag up higher on my shoulder and continued walking forward.

He didn't spare a word and neither did I, as I stopped a few feet away.

"Is there something you want to say?" I asked, a little sharper than I'd intended.

Kulti gave me that slow leisurely blink. "What the hell were you thinking tonight?"

"I was thinking that Genevieve was being a dick and not a team player." I shrugged at him. "What's the problem with that, Coach?"

"Why are you saying 'coach' like that?" he snapped, picking up on my sarcasm.

I looked at him for a second and then closed my eyes, telling myself to calm down. We'd lost and it was over with. There was no need for me to get riled up. "Look, it doesn't matter. I know I played like crap, and I'm too tired to argue with you."

"We're not arguing."

My poor eyes squeezed closed. "Whatever you say. We're not arguing. I'm going to get in the van now, I'll see you later."

"Since when do you run away from your problems?" He caught me with a hand to my wrist as I started to turn around.

I stopped and looked him dead on, aggravation simmering in my veins. "I don't run away from my problems, I just know when I'm not going to win an argument. Right now I'm not going to win against your freaking bipolar ass."

Kulti dropped his chin. "I am not bipolar."

"Okay, you're not bipolar," I lied.

"You're lying."

I almost pinched my nose. "Yes, I'm lying. I don't know if I'm talking to you, my friend, who would understand why I'd snap at Genevieve during a game, or to my coach, or to the guy I first met who doesn't give a shit about anything." I blew out a breath and shook my head. *Patience.* "I'm tired, and I'm taking everything you're saying personally. I'm sorry."

He muttered something in German that I only caught bits and pieces of, but it was enough for me to string it together. It only further pissed me off. Three years of high school German had taught me a few things.

I turned around and leveled a look at him. "The only thing I know for sure is that I don't know what the hell your problem has been lately, but I've had it!"

Kulti's nostrils flared as a vein in his neck pulsed. "My problem? *My problem?*" His accent became so much thicker when he was angry; I had to really pay attention to know what he was saying.

"Yes! *Your* problem. Whatever the hell is up your ass needs to come right back out."

"There is nothing up my ass!"

I almost made a crack about how there definitely had to be something up his ass, but at the last second decided I was too angry to try and make light of the situation.

"I beg to differ," I stuck with instead. "You're my best friend one minute, and the next minute you look disgusted when I try to play around with you in front of your friends. I'm not going to let you choose when we're friends, and when we're not."

It took me a second to realize that the words had actually

come out of my mouth. I hadn't planned on bringing it up; I really hadn't, but... well, too late now. Damn it.

I was an idiot. "I understand. It's fine. We can be friends in private, but we can't be friends in public." I swallowed. "Look, there's definitely something bothering you, but you don't want to tell me, just like you don't want to tell me anything else. That's all right."

"Who said I don't want to be friends with you in public?" He sounded surprisingly indignant.

"You did. I tried to touch you after we were done with the kids, when we were around Franz and Alejandro, and you took a step away. Remember? We're always pushing each other and messing around, and suddenly it was obviously not okay because we were in front of your friends. I know I'm not some super-celebrity or anything, but I didn't think you'd pull away like that. You embarrassed me, and I don't embarrass easily, all right?"

Kulti's hands fisted at his sides, and then he brought them up to cover his eyes. "Sal," he cursed in angry-sounding German. "You say that we're friends, but you didn't think to tell me that you've been spending time with Franz?"

Was this a joke? I made myself calm down. "I saw him three times after you started acting like I had the plague and frowning all the time. We weren't really talking and you were already walking around with a dirty diaper for some reason I don't even understand, buddy," I explained.

Those eyes, a perfect shade between green-green and hazel-brown, stared straight ahead before he laid into me.

"He's married!" Kulti shouted abruptly.

My eyes went wide, and I had to suck in a breath to rein in my anger. "What the hell do you think we were *doing*?" I asked slowly.

Kulti bared his teeth at me. "I have no idea because you didn't fucking tell me!"

*Patience*. Holy shit, I needed a whole bunch of patience.

I didn't find it.

I lost it.

"We were practicing, you jackass! What the hell is wrong with that?" I screamed at him. Holy shit.

"Then why were you both being secretive?" he growled, fury lighting up his light-colored eyes.

My eye started twitching. "We went to the field by my house. He showed me some exercises I could do to work on my left foot ball handling, you fucking, *fucking* jackass. He said I should think about playing in Europe, okay? That's the big conspiracy, the big secret, you idiot. He said I should go to Europe and join a club there so I could play for their national team..."

I couldn't let go of the volcanic-like anger seeping out of him. It became a beacon for my anger and my damn curiosity. "What the hell do you think we were doing? Sleeping together?"

He stared at me for so long, I had my answer.

Oh my God.

Me sleeping with Franz. I couldn't get over that wild assumption. What was he thinking? "*I can't believe you*. Who the hell do you think I am? Easy? You think I'm going to sleep with any guy who pays attention to me? I already told you I don't do that," I yelled at him. I didn't care if one of the Pipers could come out of the stadium and hear us, or worse, someone in the media. "Fuck!"

"Europe?" He looked about ready to blow a gasket. "You could have asked me to practice with you at any time!"

"Asked you? When? You already play favoritism with me according to eighty percent of the Pipers because we spend so much time together. If you were coaching me on the side that would come back on you, wouldn't it, Kulti?"

"I told you not to call me that," he gritted out.

"That's what you are, isn't it? Coach Kulti?" My jaw felt hard and tight. I could not get over what he'd said. "I can't believe you would think I was messing around with Franz, Jesus Christ. I really," I put my fist up to my mouth and blew a deep breath into it. "I really, *really* want to punch you in the face right now."

"I can't believe you would think about going to Europe without talking to me."

I took a step back letting his words sink in to my gut. Europe was a better opportunity, and we both knew that. There was no doubt. Before the WPL existed, Americans went overseas because it was the only place to go. But if it came down to it, most athletes would rather stay close to home. I was one of them.

More importantly, Kulti had always told me that there was only one person in the world I needed to watch out for, and that was me. Yet, here he was telling me otherwise. He was making me feel bad for even thinking about going to Europe without mentioning it to him first.

"I didn't say I would go, he just brought it up. It'd be a great opportunity if I wanted to leave my family, which I don't think I want to, but..." I felt unsure. "Why are you being like this? I don't badger you over stuff you don't want to talk about, which is just about everything. Plus, you're my friend; I figured you'd be happy someone was trying to work with me on improving my skills. You of all people should understand."

The German seemed to be trying to bore a hole straight into the center of my face. "I would have worked with you any time, any day you wanted, Sal. I could care less what management or the coaching staff think. You of all people shouldn't think twice about what your teammates say about you. They're nobody."

God, this man. "I'm sorry, Rey, am I a mind reader? Am I supposed to know you'd want to practice with me?"

"No. You're stubborn and a pain in my ass."

"I'm a pain in your ass? You're a pain in my ass. I try and I try with you, and for what? For you to be an asshole when you're frustrated or upset? Maybe other people will deal with your shit when you act like that, but I can only take so much. I like you. I like how well we get along sometimes, but I don't know anything about you really, when it comes down to it. All you do is give me these bits and pieces when you're in the mood. When you're not in the mood, you don't say anything at all. Or you go through this fucking phase where you give me dirty looks and ignore me for no apparent reason. How is that supposed to make me feel?

"I've already put enough on the line being your friend. I've shared my family with you, my home; I've told you things I haven't told other people. I've put my career at risk for this—us. You have nothing to lose, and I have everything I care about in jeopardy. I've given and I've given to everyone, and for what? To have what I valued the most in my life taken away? I've been trying, and I'm fine with that, but you need to meet me at least a quarter of the way. There's only so much I can take from you and your freaking mood swings."

I palmed the back of my head as I watched him, waiting. Waiting for something. For some assurance, some promise that he would try to keep his crap under control, or at least try harder.

Instead his face took on a hard expression, the tendon in his neck straining. "I'm too old to change, Sal. I am the way I am," he finally offered to me in a crisp voice.

"I don't want you to change. All I want is for you to trust me a little. I'm not going to screw you over, and I don't like giving up on things," I told him in an exasperated voice.

And what did he say? Nothing. Not a single thing.

I'd never been a fan of people who talked a lot. I thought it was a person's actions that really said what mattered. That was until I met Reiner Kulti, and I suddenly felt like stabbing myself in the eye.

My head gave a dull throb, a warning of a tension headache beginning. I suddenly realized this conversation was going nowhere. Exhaustion poured straight into my muscles, and for the first time in a long time, I felt defeated. I hated it.

But there comes a time when you have to listen to your gut and not your heart, and I did just that.

"Maybe we both have too much stuff going on right now. I'm overwhelmed, and I have no idea what I'm doing, and you have your own crap to work out. Maybe you need to figure out what you want to do with your life before we can keep being friends. If you even still want to be friends after this." I told him.

As soon as the words were out of my mouth he looked outraged. Absolutely outraged. "Are you joking?"

I shook my head, grief coming down on me with such a force it made me want to cry. At the end of the day though, it was like he said: no one was going to watch out for me but me. "No."

He opened his mouth and then closed it, and a second later he shook his head and was gone.

* * *

KULTI DIDN'T COME to my house the following day or the one after that.

When I started to feel a little guilty on Sunday afternoon, I sent him a text.

**Sorry for what I said. I'm under a lot of stress and I shouldn't have blamed you for my choices. You're a great friend, and I won't just give up on you.**

He didn't respond.

Then Monday came and he wasn't at practice.

He wasn't at practice Tuesday, either.

No one asked where he was. I sure as hell wasn't going to be the one to do it.

I sent him another message.

**Are you alive?**

No response.

* * *

TWO THINGS CAUGHT my attention when I pulled into the middle school's parking lot.

There was a black Audi already there with familiar license plates.

Parked right next to it, was a big white box van.

Unsure whether to feel relieved that Kulti was still alive, or aggravated that the *sauerkraut* hadn't texted me back once, I took a deep breath. I pulled into the parking spot, putting my Big Girl Socks on, though my instincts said that he more than likely hadn't gone out of his way to show up for camp if he wanted to get into an argument.

At least that's what I hoped.

I'd barely gotten out of the car and popped the trunk to grab my bag and the two cases of bottled water, when I heard steps come up behind me. I knew without turning around that it was him. Out of the corner of my eye, he stopped right beside me and pushed my hands away from the cases, hoisting them out.

"Tell me where to take them," he said simply as his greeting.

All right. "Their field is in the back. Come on," I said, shutting the trunk with my bag in hand.

We walked silently across the lot and down the paved path leading toward the field. Three teachers had volunteered and were providing the goals from the school's existing sports equipment. I spotted two of them already there and made my way toward the table they had set up for registration.

When we stopped in front of them, the man and the woman physically jolted when they realized who was standing next to me.

"Mr. Webber, Mrs. Pritchett, thank you so much for helping out. This is my friend, Mr. Kulti, he'll be volunteering with the camp today," I introduced them.

The two teachers just kind of stood there, and it was Kulti that nodded a greeting at them.

"If you can let me know where the goals are, I can start setting up," I told Mr. Webber, the physical education teacher.

He was looking at Kulti as he nodded absently. "They're heavy," he warned, eyes still on the German.

"I'm sure it'll be fine," I assured him, only just barely restraining myself from rocking back and forth on my heels.

"I'll help," Pumpernickel added, which finally got the teacher going.

Between the four of us, we pulled the soccer goals out and set them up. There were only two, but it was enough. The pre-signup sheet had fewer kids registered than the week before.

I was busy spraying lines on the grass when I spotted Kulti speaking to two female teachers who would be working the registration table. He was gesturing at something on the sheet and they were nodding enthusiastically, which didn't say much because he probably could have been telling them that he pooped golden nuggets and they would have been excited, based on the way they'd been looking at him.

Hookers.

All right, that wasn't very nice.

I finished spraying the lines just in time for the first of the kids to start showing up with their parents.

"Are you okay with doing this like we did last week? Only

working together this time?" I asked Kulti once I'd approached the registration table where he'd been standing.

He tipped his short brown-haired head at me, his eyes directly meeting mine. "We make a good team, *schnecke*, it will be fine."

So now he was back to calling me *schnecke*, whatever that meant.

I eyed him a little uncertainly.

In return, he punched me in the shoulder, which would have made me smile, but him dodging me at the last camp was still a little too fresh in my thoughts. The facial expression I made—a weak, watered-down smile you gave someone that you didn't find particularly funny but didn't want to hurt their feelings—must have said as much, because Kulti frowned. After a beat, his frowned deepened.

The German, who had reportedly gotten into a fight years ago when someone called his mother a whore, grabbed my hand, raised it and hit his own shoulder with it.

*What in the hell had just happened?*

Before I even had time to think about what he'd done, my oversized bratwurst took a step forward and he did it.

He wrapped his arms around my shoulders, bringing me in so close my nose was pressed against the cartilage right between his pectorals.

He was hugging me.

Dear God, Reiner Kulti was hugging the shit out of me.

I just stood there with my arms at my sides, frozen. Completely freaking frozen in place. I was stunned, beyond stunned. Stupefied.

"Hug me back," the accented voice demanded from up above.

His words shook off my paralysis. I found myself wrapping my arms around his waist, gingerly at first, our chests meeting in a real honest hug. My palms went flat against the twin columns of his lower back, arms overlapping.

"Am I dying and I don't know it?" I asked his chest.

He sighed. "You better not be."

I pulled back and looked up at his face, completely unsure about what the hell had just happened. "Are you dying?" I blurted out.

"No." Kulti held that same serious expression that was so innate for him; I wasn't sure what emotion he was feeling. "I'm sorry that I hurt your feelings. I only stepped away because Alejandro is... competitive. He wants what he can't have. It was my mistake inviting him." He glanced up quickly before looking back down and adding in a lowered voice, "I'm sorry for all the problems my presence has caused in your life. Soccer has given me everything, but it's also taken away just as many things."

He gave me a sad determined look. "I don't want it to take you away as well. You are the least shameful thing in my life, Sal. Understand?"

He was dead serious.

If we had not been around strangers watching our every move, I might have started tearing up. It was bad enough I had to press my lips together to keep from doing something I would regret.

I managed to suck in a tiny breath and aim a smirk at him. "Can I give you another hug or is that over your daily allowance?"

The German shook his head. "Have I told you that you remind me of a splinter I can't remove? You're incredibly annoying."

"Is that a yes?" I blinked up at him.

"That's a stupid question, Sal," he stated.

But was it a yes?

I didn't get a chance to ask for clarification because I

spotted four kids making their way across the field from the parking lot, and I knew I'd have to put off this conversation for later. I still didn't completely understand why Kulti had been such a douche the other day with the kids, but he'd apologized, and in his book that was the equivalent of giving me his kidney, so I'd take it and demand an explanation later.

More importantly, what had inspired him to give me a hug right then?

I squeezed his hand and gave him a nod. "Let's start, all right?"

"Yes." He didn't break eye contact with me once. "I brought shoes for everyone. I think it would be best to give them to the kids at the end."

"You brought..." I shut my mouth and got it together. "In that van? There's shoes for the kids?"

"Yes. I asked the volunteers to take their size information during registration. There should be more than enough for everyone. I brought nearly every size."

It's funny how things work sometimes. It really is.

I had learned and accepted my place in a stranger's life a decade ago. I'd grown up and accepted what would and could happen, and I had known that there was no future for me and a man who didn't know I existed.

And then one day, that same man for some reason decided to step into my circle, of all the circles in the world he could have chosen. Slowly, slowly, slowly, we became friends. I knew and understood that procession. I was okay with my place. Friends. Not so simple or easy, but those were the best things in life, the hard things that didn't fit perfectly, weren't they?

In one instant, in one kind deed and unexpected gesture, something inside of me woke up. There was a reason I put up with his shit and forgave him for being a dick so quickly.

I was still in love with this man.

I had no right to be. No sound reason to. I liked to think I made wise decisions, but reviving my childhood adoration for him was one of the dumbest things I could ever have let myself do. But, obviously, I couldn't take it back. My heart hadn't completely forgotten what it was like to feel this way for him, but no matter how much I tried to pretend otherwise, it had swelled and grown over the years.

Now, I understood. I had loved Reiner Kulti as a kid. I had loved my ex-boyfriend as a young adult, learning and growing. And the Sal Casillas I was today knew that I couldn't love someone who didn't deserve it.

It was the shoes for the kids whose parents couldn't afford them that tied the noose around my neck.

Him bringing his friends to my soccer camps.

Kulti buying my dad the trip of a lifetime.

Calling me his friend in front of people that he genuinely knew he didn't give a single shit about.

I was in love with this pumpernickel.

God help me, I think I wanted to cry.

I tried to find something to say—anything, and I hoped that my face didn't say, 'You are a fucking idiot, Sal.' Because I was. I really was. There was no escaping the truth when it was looking at you from two feet away, brown haired, bright eyed and six-foot-two-inches tall. I scratched my cheek and fought the urge to look away, to find my breath and sanity wherever it had gone. "I didn't think your sponsor would do something like that."

Here's the thing about the German: he wasn't one to beat around the bush or play coy or be modest. He looked me right in the eye and said it. "They didn't. I bought them."

He...

"Ms. Sal!" one of the teachers by the registration table called out.

"You," I poked Kulti in the stomach knowing I only had a

second before I needed to haul it back to the table. "I don't know how to thank you—"

"Don't."

"Ms. Sal!"

Gaze to gaze with the bratwurst, I told him in a rush, "Thank you."

He gave me a heavy-lidded glare but didn't say anything before following me over to registration.

Needless to say, the kids went wild when they saw the German. Me, they could have given less of a shit about. Kulti, they were losing it over. They listened to him and were excited out of their minds when we began different drills and exercises.

The bratwurst was right. We were a good team. I had just as much fun with him as I had with Franz if not more, because of the amount of playful shit-talking we had going on with each other.

A crowd triple the size of the one we had on the field, formed on the far end of the school's blacktop throughout the duration of camp. Camera flashes continued going off, but luckily no one approached us—and by 'us' I mean Kulti—while we were busy. I just pretended they weren't there and told myself to keep acting normal.

When the time came around for us to wrap up, I let Kulti tell his young fans that they were all getting a pair of his latest edition RK running shoes. Any passerby would have thought the kids had been told that they'd won the lottery from the way they reacted. The German hadn't been joking. There were more than enough shoes for all the kids.

"Can I get one of just the two of you?" the mom of one of the kids asked after we'd taken a picture with her son.

"Sure," I said, right before the German threw an arm around my shoulder and hauled me up to his side, roughly and deliberately.

Well.

I whacked him in the hard slab he called his stomach with a smile.

"I know this isn't my place to say anything," the lady gushed once the picture was taken. "I thought the age difference was a little strange, but seeing you together, it makes perfect sense. You two are stinking cute."

My face went hot. "Oh, it's not—" I started to say before the German reeled me up against him.

"Thank you for bringing your son," he cut me off.

*Thank you for bringing your son?*

I almost choked.

The second we were alone, I held my arms out to my sides. He had given those people the wrong impression of our relationship. "What the hell was that?"

He gave me a bored look as he began collecting the cones scattered around the field. "People will believe whatever they want to believe. There's no point in telling them otherwise."

Maybe he had a point, but still.

"Rey." The palm of my hand went to my forehead. "I don't think that's a good idea. The stuff I hear on the field is bad enough."

"Ignore them."

It was so easy for him to say that when he wasn't the one hearing it constantly. "I just don't want it to get worse. That's all."

The cone he had been in the middle of grabbing landed back on the ground. He turned his entire body in my direction. "Is the idea of a relationship with me that distasteful?"

The fuck? "What?"

He settled his hands on his slim hips. "You don't find me attractive? You like older men, you told me so. I'm only twelve —thirteen—years older than you."

I woke up that morning thinking it was going to be a day

like every other. Apparently it wasn't. What the hell was I supposed to say?

The truth. Blah.

I found myself scratching at my cheek. "You are attractive. You're very attractive and you know it, you conceited bastard. And you're not too old. It's just that..." I coughed. "You're my coach and my friend," I added absently, like that was supposed to be the big reason why I couldn't look at him any different. Unfortunately, I now knew the truth: it was a bit too late for that crap.

His response? "I haven't forgotten."

What hadn't he forgotten?

"Stop worrying about what everyone thinks. You're the one that said the only thing that matters is what you know about yourself." He kept right on looking at me until I nodded. "Let's finish up, yes?"

In less than twenty minutes we were finished putting all the equipment back and helping the teachers put away the tables they had borrowed. I thanked them profusely for their help and watched as Kulti grabbed my bag and the water bottles that had been left over, hauling it all to my car.

"I'll ride with you," he said the instant the trunk had been slammed shut.

I shot him a look as I went to the driver side. "My place or yours?"

Kulti looked at me from the other side of the car. "Yours. Mine is too quiet."

Considering we both lived alone, I didn't understand how one place could have a different noise level than the other. The only difference was that his house was at least about six times bigger than my garage apartment.

"Why don't you get a pet?" I asked.

"I have fish."

That made me laugh. He had fish? "You do not."

He tipped his shaved brown head in my direction. "I have three, a beta and two tetras. My agent gave them to me when I moved here. I have an aquarium at my flat in London."

I tried not to make it seem like his admission was a big deal. "That's neat. Who takes care of them?"

"A housekeeper."

A housekeeper. No surprise there. "How many houses do you have?"

"Only three," he answered nonchalantly.

Only three. I'd grown up the kid of paycheck-to-paycheck parents. While I knew that someone who had as much money as he did could realistically afford way more than three houses, it still amazed me. At the same time, it made me like Kulti a little more. I could respect someone who didn't blow his money on stupid crap.

Instead, he spent it on buying shoes for kids.

Damn it, I needed to quit this mooning crap, but today had been a real whirlwind.

"Where's your other house?" I found myself asking so that I wouldn't think about other things.

"Meissen. It's a small town in Germany."

I made an impressed face.

"The house is tiny, Sal, but I think you'd like it," he noted.

"I've always wanted to go to Germany," I told him. "It's on my list of places to go on my bucket list."

He slanted a look at me. "What's a bucket list?"

He didn't know what a bucket list was? I shouldn't have found that as cute as I did. "It's a list of things you want to do before you die. Have you heard the term 'kicking the bucket'?" Out of the corner of my eye, I saw the German shake his head. "Well that's what it's referring to. Stuff you want to do before you die."

Kulti made a thoughtful noise. "You have more things on your list?"

"Yeah. I'd like to see the Seven Wonders of the Ancient World, I want to bike the Continental Divide, do an Ironman, see the Northern Lights, hike a glacier, hold a baby panda and win an Altus Cup..." I sensed myself babbling and cut it off. "Things like that. I almost have enough money saved to go to Alaska after the season is over. Hopefully I can knock out some glaciers and the Northern Lights in one trip."

There was a pause. "Alone?"

"I was going to see if my brother would go with me. He's the only person I know besides you with the time and money, but we'll see. Last year we went to Peru to see Machu Picchu." I shot him a smile over my shoulder. His fortieth birthday was coming up in October, but I didn't want to mention that I knew that he should be the one thinking of making a bucket list. "What about you? What are you doing after the season is over?"

"I haven't decided," he answered in a low voice. "It all depends on a few things."

A single thought entered my head. "Is your contract only for this season?"

I couldn't remember hearing anything about the length of his employment, and the idea that he'd be leaving in a little over a month made my stomach churn.

"I only agreed to this season with the Pipers."

There was one thing I knew: Kulti didn't like coaching. He'd said so himself.

Why would he want to stay and coach again?

Jesus Christ, the idea of him going back to his flat in London made me so sad that the excitement from the whole shoe-buying thing, crumbled under its weight.

At the same time, that made me feel like a selfish dick. Who was I to be sad over someone, especially a friend, doing something that made them happy when I knew damn well something else didn't? I knew I was in no position to give anyone a guilt-trip over anything, but the idea of him leaving sucked.

I swallowed the sadness away and forced a smile on my face even though I wasn't looking at him. "I see."

He was going to leave Houston. Blah.

He might have turned his head, but I wasn't positive, and I didn't want to talk about it any longer. "So... are you hungry?"

* * *

AT THE NEXT soccer camp four days later, Kulti showed up with two more people. The first guy I recognized was an American goalie who had played for the national team in every major tournament the last six years right along with my brother. The second one was a pleasant surprise.

"Franz!" I walked toward the older man, bypassing Kulti, to give him a hug. "I didn't know you were coming!"

He hugged me in return, two quick taps to my spine. "My business in Los Angeles didn't take as long as I had anticipated."

"Well, thank you so much for coming back," I told him.

Someone made a grumpy noise. "Sal."

Franz let out a short laugh as he let go of me, stepping back. His face was tipped down, open and easy, as he whispered, "Someone is territorial, hmm?"

I turned to look at the man whose gaze was burning a hole into my skull. Pretzel face territorial? I highly doubted it, but I found myself way too pleased by his scowl.

"Are you going to introduce me?" I asked, gesturing toward the popular goalie.

"No." He kept that damn insolent look on his face, his arms extending wide in a universal gesture I was becoming familiar with.

Curling my lips over my teeth, I raised my eyebrows at him. God, someone was in a freaking mood and it put me into an excellent one. The smile on my face grew even bigger.

He flicked his own eyebrows up at me. Those dark brown, thick slashes went up and back down, silently telling me that he wasn't going to introduce me until he got what he wanted.

For one second, I thought about ignoring him and just introducing myself, but...

Kulti liked to play games, and I liked to win them.

Somehow I managed not to smile as I stepped forward and hugged him, silently worrying that he would make me look like an idiot if he didn't actually go through with it and hug me back. I mean, it wouldn't be the first time he acted like I had cooties. I just hugged him and I hugged him tight.

Completely catching me off-guard, Kulti, my freaking German with supposedly no conscience, pressed his cheek to the top of my head and wrapped himself around me. He hugged me back. His body was hard and tense as he did it, but it was different. It wasn't an angry hug; it was something else. It was like when I was a kid and would hug the crap out of my dog because I loved him so much.

Like that—but not.

When he finally pulled away, I glanced up. I didn't take it personally that he wasn't smiling down at me. He was just glaring, well really more like glowering, but whatever. I gave him another hug, and felt the weight of his arm settle over my shoulder.

It stayed there.

The other man was a goalie named Michael Kimmons. He was taller than Kulti and just a little older than me.

"Hey, it's nice to meet you. Thanks for coming." I thrust my hand out at him when I felt the German's arm clamp down the instant I introduced myself.

"Mike Kimmons," he said with a hard shake.

"Sal Casillas."

"I know your brother Eric," he threw in. "We play together."

I nodded at him and smiled.

"You mentioned to me he plays, too. Where?" Franz asked in a curious tone.

"He's on loan to Madrid right now," I explained.

"I had no idea." The second German nodded with a slight frown. Before he'd retired, he'd played for Madrid's top opponent, Barcelona. "Do your parents play?"

"Oh no. My dad has asthma and my mom," the gigantic bicep surrounding my neck like a boa constrictor bulged, "isn't exactly a fan."

For one stinking moment, I had the fear that Kulti would say something about who my mom's dad was. One brief, painful moment I imagined him spilling the beans because it was something impressive to say in front of people who would think it was interesting. I really thought he might.

He didn't.

He steered the conversation away. "We'll split up into two groups," he ordered and I let him, because it had become evident to me that he was starting to enjoy these days playing with the kids. It almost made me feel a little bad that there was only one camp left after today.

The day went fine. Mike Kimmons was a little too serious for the kids, but some of them recognized him and it made up for him not playing around with them much. Kulti offered to be paired up with him for some reason, and I tackled the other group with Franz.

Once the three hours had passed and most of the kids had left, Franz pulled me aside while Kulti continued taking pictures with a few straggling participants and their parents.

The older German gave me a serious look. "I overheard something while I was in Los Angeles, and I need to tell you."

Fuck. Preparing someone for news was never a good thing. My Big Girl Socks went on. "Okay."

He cast a glance in Kulti's direction before hurrying

through what he felt the need to tell me. "There's a rumor you will be traded to New York at the end of this season."

My ears started ringing. My stomach churned.

New York? With Amber? If that wasn't bad enough, the team already had a solid popular starting line-up. I would never get to play.

Most importantly, I didn't want to go to fucking New York.

Franz touched my shoulder. "I recruit for NL," he was referring to the Newcastle Lions, one of the top men's teams in the United Kingdom, "Think about what I told you the last time. If you decide you'd like to try something different—" he shot me a look, "something better, I can help. I don't understand how you've gotten buried in the system here, but between Reiner and I, there isn't much we can't do with our connections."

Fully aware that this wasn't the time to lose it, I pulled my Big Girl Socks on higher than ever and forced myself to nod at the man who had told me news he didn't have to share. Could he have been lying? I didn't see why he would, so I wasn't going to be narcissistic about it.

*Why* bounced around in my head over and over again.

Everyone knew I loved playing in Houston. The WPL wasn't big enough for people to be forced to play where they absolutely didn't want to. Most of the time, players were willing to go wherever they were sent. When I'd first gotten drafted, I'd been allowed to choose the top three teams I wanted to play for. Obviously, Houston had been at the top of my list with stars by it, followed by California, since it was close to my brother, and then the Phoenix Novas, who had since moved to St. Louis.

I was the top scorer for the Pipers. I worked hard and didn't give them much hell besides what had been going on these last few months, and I helped out my teammates as much as possible. Somehow this was how they were repaying me?

Gardner's warning, Cordero's dislike and the things my teammates had been doing recently swirled in my head.

I felt betrayed. Cheated on. And I couldn't decide whether to be sad or take a key to Cordero's car.

*Okay*. That was a little extreme. Sort of. *Patience. Patience.*

There was only one person who could have been behind this possible move. That spiteful, little asshole.

"Thank you for telling me," I somehow managed to tell Franz, even though my insides were ready for anarchy.

"Don't waste your potential, *ja?*"

I nodded at him, feeling this huge surge of emotion climb up my chest, and it wasn't good. It made the smile on my face feel short of the braveness I wanted to portray. "I'll figure something out."

"Call me, email me, whatever you need," he said sincerely.

"Thank you, Franz. I really appreciate it." I did, even if the news made me want to cry.

Going to play with freaking Amber and her minions?

Apparently my thoughts were written all over my face. He gave me a sad smile that made me feel even worse.

A soft touch at the small of my back had me straightening up my shoulders. "Franz is spending the night. Have dinner with us," Kulti said, stopping at my side.

Bile pinched my throat, and I had to keep my gaze away from his. "I need to go home. Thank you, though."

He ignored me. "I'll ride with you. Franz, take my car."

"Rey, I want to go home," I told him firmly.

"I want you to come over," he replied, already turning around. "Where are your things?" Kulti didn't even wait for me to say anything else before he started walking in the direction of my bag. Damn it.

"Rey," I called out, following after him.

He glanced over his shoulder but didn't stop walking. "You don't have anything else to do. Stop being difficult."

"Umm, I do have things to do. I have to go for my run later, or I might do some yoga." Or cry, or scream... the usual.

The German waved me off.

I was going to kill him."*Reyyyyy*!"

Nothing.

Son of a bitch.

"He's difficult, isn't he?"

"That's the understatement of a lifetime," I told Franz. "What a pain in the ass. I really don't know how someone hasn't killed him in cold blood yet."

The other man barked out a laugh.

From across the field, I spotted the Kulti in the process of throwing my bag over his shoulder. "There's no point in even trying to argue with him, is there?" I asked Franz.

"*Nein*."

"He's such a pain in the ass."

Franz snickered. "He is."

I sighed. I could leave after a little while. Hopefully.

I met Kulti at my car where he had apparently already gone through my bag to get my keys. He tossed them over the roof and we got in, waving at Franz as he slipped into the Audi parked next to mine. As soon as we were inside, I shot him a look. "You could have let Franz ride with me instead of making him ride alone."

He gave me that annoyingly even look. "He will survive by himself."

I glared at him for a beat before shaking my head. "You're being rude."

"I don't care."

Not a surprise. I turned on the ignition and pulled out of the lot before I finally thought about it. "Why didn't you invite Mike?"

"I don't like him."

Seriously, I would never understand men. "Then why did you invite him today?"

"He owed me a favor," was his simple response. Then he added, "And his plane ticket was reasonable."

Wait a second. "You—" I couldn't get the words out. I had to swallow and process what he'd said. "You paid for their tickets here?"

Kulti didn't even bother looking at me; his attention was directed out the window. "Yes."

I dropped my head against the steering wheel and took a deep breath. This was all too much for one afternoon. Way too much. Everything seemed to pile on top of me. "How do you expect me to ever pay you back?"

"I don't," he answered, turning to face me. "The light is green."

Sitting up, I kept my gaze forward. I couldn't look at him. If I did, I wasn't sure what the hell I would do. "I didn't even think about how they made it here. I'm such an idiot. I'm sorry for not thanking you more."

Nothing.

I clutched the steering wheel and kept my mouth closed the entire drive back.

I was getting traded.

Half of my teammates thought I was a tramp.

The idiot next to me had been paying for people's plane tickets to come to my youth camps, my free camps.

I was at least a little bit in l-o-v-e with the same idiot, but realistically it was more like a lot. My childhood feelings had come back in full force, more real than ever. Plus I knew myself, and I didn't tend to half-ass anything.

And said idiot was leaving at the end of the season.

What the hell was I doing with my life? Everything I'd worked up to, worked for, suddenly seemed to be repelled by me.

What was I going to do?

My nose tickled in response.

We arrived at his house and parked, but still I couldn't get myself to say anything. I wanted to cry. I really wanted to cry, and I sure as hell didn't want to do it anywhere near here.

I kept my gaze down and followed the German up to his door where Franz was already waiting. We'd barely gone inside when I felt a choking cough in my throat. I knew I needed to get away from them. "Where's your bathroom?" I asked him in a voice that sounded even weird to me.

"Up the stairs, first door," he answered, his voice distant enough to let me know he wasn't standing that close.

"I'll be right back," I lied, already hauling my butt up the stairs, desperate to get away.

Two swipes at my leaky nose later with the back of my hand, and I was inside. I didn't even bother turning on the light before I was plopping onto the porcelain rim of a tub I could appreciate when my life wasn't falling apart.

I was getting traded because I was friends with someone.

My throat convulsed and I hiccupped. *Don't cry, don't cry, don't cry. Don't do it, Sal. Don't you fucking do it.*

I managed to hold out thirty seconds before the next hiccup wrecked my upper body. It was followed by another and then another. By the fifth one, I hunched over and pressed my palms to my eye sockets. I didn't cry hardly ever. When I was upset, I did other things to get my mind off of whatever was bothering me. There were very few things in life worth crying over, my mom had told me once.

Sitting on that tub, I really tried to tell myself that getting traded wasn't the end of the world. I tried to convince myself I shouldn't take it personally. It was just business and it happened, sometimes, to other people.

That only made me cry harder.

I was an idiot. A stupid fucking *idiot*.

When I thought about Kulti cashing in favors to get players

to come to my camp and buying kids' shoes and how he'd given me a freaking hug, it only made things worse.

I cried like a baby, a big silent baby that didn't want anyone to hear her.

"*Schnecke,* did you—" Kulti's voice abruptly cut off.

In hindsight I would realize that I didn't hear him come in because he didn't knock. He just barged right in, sticking his big fat head in the room like there wasn't a chance that I was on the toilet doing something he wouldn't want to see. I was so caught off guard, I couldn't muffle the next sob or bother to try and hide it.

I missed the horrified look on Kulti's face before he came inside and shut the door behind him. I didn't see him drop to his knees or put his hands on my own, lowering his head so that his forehead pressed to mine.

"*Schnecke*," he said in the softest, most affectionate tone I'd ever heard. "What is it?"

"Nothing," I managed to blabber out. I was shaking and my upper body was convulsing with soundless cries.

"Stop with your lies and tell me why you're crying," he ordered even as he scooted forward and stroked a big hand down my spine.

"I'm not crying."

"You are the worst liar I have ever met." He moved to rub my shoulder. "Why are you upset?"

Every time he asked, I somehow managed to cry harder, my body shaking more; there were actual noises coming out of me. "It's stupid."

"More than likely, but tell me anyway," he said in a gentle voice.

I couldn't catch my breath. "They're... going... to... trade... me," I bawled to my freaking humiliation.

The hand on my shoulder didn't let up its comforting circles. "Who told you?"

"Franz," I said, but it really sounded like more *Franzzzz-agh.*

Something quick and vicious-sounding in German shot out of his mouth: a spit, a curse on top of a curse.

"He's not lying, is he?" I asked his shirt collar.

Kulti sighed into the top of my head. "No. He wouldn't say something unless he was sure," he confirmed.

My heart and my head were both well aware that the signs had been there.

"Gardner warned me, but I didn't listen," I told him. "This is so stupid. I'm sorry. I know it's not the end of the world and this is embarrassing, but I can't stop crying."

The big German I'd been in love with since I was a kid, put his arms all around me. And he shushed me. Literally, he said, "Shush." Then he held me a little closer and said into my ear, "You're better than this. Stop crying."

"I can't," I whined for probably the first time in at least ten years.

"You can and you will," he said tenderly. "I can't imagine how you're feeling right now—"

Of course he couldn't. He'd never been traded against his will and if he had, it had to have been for a better position and more money. For me, it was like getting dumped. Violated. Thrown away.

"—but you're better than this. In two years you'll be thanking them for being so stupid—"

His pep talk wasn't helping. "I gave them the best years of my life," I might have wailed, but hoped I didn't.

"You have not. You haven't even reached the peak of your career."

I was inconsolable. Reiner Kulti was telling me I still had better years ahead of me, and it wasn't making me feel better.

"Taco. Stop. Stop this instant," he demanded in a grave voice.

I couldn't. All I could keep thinking was that Houston was where I wanted to be. It's the place I had made my home. If they had asked me first if I wanted to go somewhere else, it would be one thing, but these under-the-table deals were for the players you tried to get rid of so that they wouldn't blow a gasket.

There was snot running down my nose and it made the German huff in exasperation and tighten his hold around me, his arms like a shield against the world. "I know this is my fault, and I swear I'll make it up to you," he murmured in that thick accent I wanted to wrap myself in.

"It's not your fault," I said muffled against him before changing my mind. "I don't regret it at all. This is their fault for being so damn dumb. I've always done whatever they wanted me to do. I'm a team player. I don't completely suck. I get to practice early and stay late, and this is how they repay me? By trying to send me to fucking New York? Where I'll probably never get to play again?"

I sat up, not caring in the least that I had to look like a giant mess and sniffled at my friend. I was feeling the weight of a hundred galaxies on my shoulders, feeling my dreams on the cusp of slipping away. I knew I was being overdramatic, but it was all too much. "What am I going to do?" I asked him, like he had all the answers.

Kulti palmed my knees again. That handsome face that had aged gracefully was solemn, but he looked me dead in the eye as he spoke. "You're going to keep playing. I promise you, Sal. I would never put your career at risk."

I sniffled and made a watery noise in my throat, my shoulders shaking and warning of another round of tears.

The German shook his head. "No. No more. I won't let you down; now stop crying. It makes me nauseous."

That was almost funny. I wiped at my face with the back of my hand and he scowled, reaching back to pull a few pieces of toilet paper off the roll before handing them to me. "Control yourself," he ordered.

I almost laughed. I sniffled and wiped at my face with the tissue he gave me. "You can't tell me to 'control myself,' it doesn't work that way."

"You're supposed to do what I say," he said, snatching the tissue away from me and dabbing at my cheeks a little more forcefully than necessary with a frown.

That made me crack a small, pitiful smile. "Who said that?"

He met my eyes. "I did."

I pressed my lips together. "That's convenient."

Kulti reached back and grabbed more toilet paper. "You're a mess," he said, continuing his cleanup process. "I didn't take you to be a crybaby."

"I'm not." I tried to snatch the tissue away from him, but he held his hand out of reach. I stretched and he easily pulled his hand away further out of my grasp. "I can wipe my own face off."

He smacked my hand away. "I don't do anything I don't want to," he grumbled, returning to dabbing at me.

"You know, the world doesn't revolve around what you do or don't want to do," I said as he rubbed a little too hard under my nose, making me wince.

"Sorry," he apologized. "I'm not used to this."

"You've never had to clean off a girl's face before?"

He pulled back to observe his work. "Never."

I let out a deep sigh, eased by his admission. "In that case, thank you for the honor."

Kulti didn't say anything; instead he put a hand on each cheek and tipped my head back. I had never been more aware of not having make-up on or looking like hell than I did right then. The man, who had dated supermodels, actresses and probably a whole bunch of women with perfect bodies, didn't comment on my freckles, the bags under my eyes or the scars I had.

He finally dropped his hands and gave my thighs a pat with a long, deep exhale. "Let's go downstairs."

"I'll meet you in a minute," I said.

An exasperated breath later, he'd taken hold of my hands and pulled me up to my feet. "No. You're fine."

"Rey, seriously, give me a minute." I buckled my knees so that he couldn't drag me along.

With one yank, he pulled me forward. "So that you can cry more? No. Come. I have the coffee you like."

I sniffled and he gave me a dirty look in return. Why did I even bother? "You're a bossy bitch, you know that?" I asked him even as I let him lead me out of the darkened bathroom.

"You're a pain in my ass, do you know that?" he shot back.

I snorted as we went down the stairs one after the other. "I used those exact same words to describe you to Franz, buddy."

The German turned to peek at me over his shoulder. "Another thing we have in common."

"Ha. You wish."

A snicker came out of his mouth, but he didn't argue anymore. We found Franz in the kitchen sitting on a stool, looking at his phone. He glanced up and immediately frowned.

"I'm fine," I said before he said anything. "I really am; I'm just being a baby." Even saying it as an excuse did nothing to lessen the bolt of disappointment that shot straight through my heart. *They are going to trade me.*

But in the back of my head, Kulti's voice reminded me that it was only if I let them.

Fuck me.

"I didn't mean to make you upset," Franz interjected quickly. "Please forgive me."

"No, no way. There's nothing to forgive. Thank you for telling me. I'm just feeling a little overwhelmed. I guess I don't handle getting the shaft well." They both looked at me over my word choice. "I don't like to lose and I feel like I'm losing," I explained.

They both finally nodded in understanding.

Kulti bumped my shoulder, talking to Franz over me. "Make a list of the women's teams you know of."

"Wait. I don't even know what I'm going to do," I said, suddenly panicking again at the thought of going somewhere even farther away than New York.

Jesus Christ.

Europe? Was I really thinking about it? I was kicking up a fit about New York, but considering going to freaking Europe?

"You want to stay here with these people?" Kulti asked, just shy of sounding incredulous. "Not everyone deserves your loyalty."

He was right, of course, in a selfish way.

"I still have a year left in my contract."

"Too much can happen in a year, Sal. You could tear your ACL again, break a leg going down the stairs… anything."

Kulti 2, Sal 0. He was right again. Anything could happen. In eight months I would be twenty-eight and if I was really lucky and my body held out on me, I might have three or four years left in my career. *Maybe* more. Maybe. I didn't want to put too much hope into longer than that; my knee and my ankle would be the ones making the decision, and there wasn't much I could do to change their mind when they decided they'd had enough.

So.

Europe? New York was closer. Then again, New York was a decision being taken out of my hands and I was not a fan of that, not a fan at all. I didn't want to go to there and it was mainly just to spite Cordero. Who the hell did I know in Europe, anyway?

Was I really using not knowing someone as an excuse to

stay in the U.S. when that choice would have me playing under a woman that would make it impossible for me to do well? Was there even a choice, really?

Indecision filled my chest and shamed me. Was I going to let fear get the best of me and keep me somewhere I wasn't going to be happy? Keep me with an organization that obviously didn't want me anymore because I was friends with my coach? How fucking stupid would that be? If twenty-two-year-old career driven Sal Casillas could hear me now, she would kick my twenty-seven-year-old ass for being a pussy.

A tiny part of me realized that I didn't need to rush into a decision yet. There were still four games left in the season, and if we moved on to the playoffs—*when* we moved on to the playoffs—there would be more games. I had time, not much but some.

Big Girl Socks on, I thought about it.

Screw it. There wasn't a decision to make. I'd be an idiot if I stayed in the WPL and gave someone, who didn't have my best intentions in mind, a key to my future. Wasn't I? What would my dad or Eric tell me?

It only took a second for me to decide what they would say: get the hell out.

"You're right," I said and straightened my spine. "I have nothing to lose even if things don't work out."

I didn't see Kulti roll his eyes. "Make a list of the teams you're familiar with," he said to Franz.

The demand got me thinking instantly.

"Hold on. I don't want to get on a team because you ask someone for a favor. Tell me the names of the teams you think I could be a good fit for, and I'll talk to my agent about seeing what she can do."

I didn't miss the look they shot each other.

"I'm serious. I don't need this to haunt me down the road. I want to go somewhere where I'm needed, or at least wanted."

Because it was the truth. I hadn't gotten to where I was by taking advantage of who my grandfather was, or who my brother was. I had worked too hard to avoid getting screwed over, like I was now, and I didn't plan on letting it happen again.

They exchanged another look.

"I'm not joking. You especially, Pumpernickel, promise me you won't pay someone to take me." I cringed, realizing what I'd said and gave Franz an apologetic smile. "It's a joke, I swear. I have nothing against Germans."

"No offense taken."

Kulti agreed to nothing.

I elbowed him in the ribs. "Rey, promise me."

That time I did catch him rolling his eyes. "Fine."

"That doesn't sound like a promise to me."

"I promise, *schnecke*," he grumbled.

I totally caught the small smile that crossed Franz's face as he heard the nickname Kulti called me. It was the first time he'd used that term in front of someone, and Franz's smile said that it couldn't have meant a bad thing. At least that's what I was pretty sure of.

"You're positive this is what you want to do?" the German asked seriously, a gentle reminder of how he'd lost his crap when I first mentioned Franz's idea of me playing overseas. Now, he was totally focused and calm. He looked ready to kill someone.

I'd be lying if I said I wasn't at least a little bit terrified. The fact was, I could either let my fear of the unknown make me a victim, or take control of my career.

There wasn't really a choice in the matter.

You don't get to live your dreams by waiting around for someone to hand them to you.

Or at the very least, you hold on to them for dear life when others try and take them away.

I nodded at my friend, determined. "I'm positive."

* * *

I WAS YAWNING every two minutes by the time Kulti finally glared at me from across the table where we were all playing poker. I hadn't laughed when he busted out the cards and asked if we wanted to play, but I'd wanted to.

"Stop giving me that look. I'm going home now before I fall asleep," I said, pushing the chair away from the table.

"Call a taxi."

"No. I can drive home. I live close enough, it'll be fine." Before he could argue with me I leaned over and gave Franz, the man who had won both games we'd played, a hug. "Thank you for coming to camp today and thank you for all your help with the other stuff, too."

"Let me know as soon as you hear back from a team. I can help you narrow it down," he said, giving me an affectionate pat on the back. "You still have my information?"

"Yes." I pulled away from him. "I'll definitely let you know if I hear from anyone."

"You're an idiot. You will," the bratwurst interjected, getting up.

"I don't know how I've lived my entire life without you and your kind, encouraging words. Really. It's a miracle I've survived this long."

Kulti was doing his usual scowl-thing, but the corners of his mouth were tipped up as he grabbed the back of my neck with his broad palm and swung me around to face the doorway. "I have never met anyone that needed me less than you do."

The way he said it, I wasn't sure whether it was a compliment or not, so I didn't comment on it. I just bumped my shoulder against his. "Thanks for inviting me tonight."

He nodded as we walked out the path leading toward my car. When we stopped by the driver side door, he put one hand on it and the other on my upper arm. "I'll make this up to you."

"You don't have to make anything up to me. This isn't your fault. I knew what I was doing. As long as you don't forget I exist after the season is over, there won't be anything to regret, all right?" I said, even though on the inside a small part of me was still frustrated and a bit depressed about all of this.

Kulti cocked his head. "You think I could forget about you?"

"No... well, I don't know. You haven't known me that long. I'm sure you have—" I almost said 'tons of friends,' but at what point had this guy given me the idea that he had a lot of friends? Never. Not once. "I'm sure that you have plenty of distractions back home. I didn't mean it in a negative way. I just know life gets in the way sometimes."

"I don't waste my time on things, Sal. Do you understand what I mean?"

The hairs on the back of my neck prickled up, and hoarsely I answered. "Sort of." He wouldn't waste his time doing things with me if he didn't like me and didn't want to be my friend, I knew that much.

He opened his mouth and closed it. He wanted to say something; it was evident on his face. The German swallowed hard and an even look crossed his features, making me incredibly aware of everything: of the sticky summer night, the darkened sky missing its stars, the way his skin let off the barest hint of something sweet smelling. His fingers tightened over me, his thumbs digging into that groove where my shoulder met my collarbone.

I'd seen his face hundreds of times, and it seemed to never be enough. After I had gotten over my infatuation with him, I'd envisioned myself with someone who worked for himself: a go-getter maybe, good with his hands, quiet, honest and nice. Possibly a mechanic. I had wanted someone who would come home, a little dirty, a little sweaty and capable of fixing things. I pictured a steady, reliable type of guy. I wasn't sure where I'd gotten that fantasy from, but it had stuck with me. Adam, my ex, had been that way, mostly. He'd been a general contractor straight out of a romance novel—incredibly good-looking and sweet. I hadn't thought he was real at first.

Now facing Kulti, so much taller than me, older than me, serious, sneaky, temperamental and having only mowed a lawn once in his life... I couldn't find it in me to be disappointed that this was where my dumbass heart had taken me. I was an idiot, of course. What the hell was I doing having feelings for this jackass again? Unrequited love and I had known each other once, and I didn't want to be up close and personal with it again. So what was I going to do? I had no clue, but I was worried my heart would get stomped to death.

Hope for the best? Blah.

I missed the glance he took at my mouth. Missed the way he fisted his hand as he pried it off my shoulder. I didn't see the look on his face when he stared at mine for a brief second.

"Good," he finally said, easing his hand off the car door and tearing me away from thinking about how I was going to get over this whole being-in-love-with-the-wrong-person-crap. "Call when you get home."

I couldn't help the smile that crossed my face. Maybe he wasn't in love with me, and maybe I wasn't really the best friend he'd ever had, but he cared about me. Most of his actions made it loud and clear, even when he was being a bit of a gruff, emotionless dick. I could have done worse.

All right, that wasn't true. I couldn't have loved anyone else, definitely not anyone worse. I wouldn't have done something so stupid.

Not that having feelings for him wasn't completely fucking dumb, because it was, but... whatever. This was so hard.

"I'll send you a text when I get home," I agreed, opening the door and getting in. Once the car was on, I rolled down the window and watched him standing just a few feet away. "You know, even if you didn't get Mike, Alejandro and Franz to come to the camp, and bought shoes for the kids, I would still think you were kind of great… most of the time, right?"

The lights outside of his house caught him looking up at the sky. "Go home."

To my great pride, I only felt determination in his silence on the way back to my place.

What was the saying? When one door closes, another one opens. I might just have to do a little breaking and entering to get the right one for me.

# 23

In the month that followed Franz's admission, life seemed to strap a jetpack to itself and take off in every direction, both the good and the bad.

Pipers practice went on as normal, or at least as relatively normal as possible. Going back after I found out what Cordero was planning was tough, really tough. I was a horrible liar with an itty bitty temper that desperately wanted to make an appearance. How could I face these people like nothing was wrong? How could I make it seem like I wasn't dying a little inside while planning my escape?

It was hard. We had advanced to the first round of the playoffs. I was resentful and angry, and my emotions hadn't wavered at all. The worst aspect of being so bitter was the part of me that held my ego above winning. Pride told me I shouldn't give a single crap how the rest of the season went. The reasonable half of me that didn't get sappy right before my period, said that I had no business thinking that way. I needed the Pipers to do well.

Everything was wrapped up together now. I'd spoken with my agent and asked her to discreetly see if we could find a spot for me somewhere else in Europe—specifically the teams Kulti and Franz had suggested that afternoon at his house. She'd been more excited than I could have imagined, and within two weeks sent me an email telling me there were three teams interested in speaking with me.

I talked to my parents on the phone and told them everything. The first thing out of my dad's mouth before he told me he had plenty of airline miles to visit Europe was, "*Este cabron.*" This bitch, referring to Cordero. After that, I called my brother where he proceeded to chew me out for being friends with the German, and then offered to help me find a place to live, followed by a passing "fuck them," referring to the WPL. We ended the conversation with me critiquing his latest game.

Then there were the emails, the phone calls and the reporters.

Why people even cared about the pictures that popped up of Kulti and I during the youth camp blew my mind. Four youth camps worth of cell phone pictures taken by parents, teachers and students, flooded both gossip and Kulti fan sites. Shots of us smiling, laughing, a few with his arm around me or with blurred faces of kids between us, were being sent to me by my dad who thought it was the coolest freaking thing ever. I on the other hand, was only slightly horrified by the attention.

'A LOVE AFFAIR ON THE FIELD,' was the last headline he'd sent me with stars in the subject.

Before that had been, 'KULTI'S EX WANTS HIM BACK' and, 'KULTI CAUGHT WITH PLAYER.'

"How long have you been dating?" became the question I dreaded hearing the most in the world.

Honestly, it was only thinking about my dad and knowing he was probably egging on the rumors in his circle of friends that kept me from actually commenting. I could die tomorrow knowing I hadn't done a single thing wrong. There wasn't anything to weigh down my conscience.

I stopped talking to members of the media who asked. I stopped checking my email nearly all together once I received a message in Italian along the lines of *you're an ugly bitch and I hope you die.* I also only answered calls from numbers saved in my phone.

I didn't say anything to the German, because what was the point? No one was threatening to kill me. I was also partially concerned he would overreact and blow it out of proportion.

Overall things were fine.

Until they weren't.

* * *

We were in Florida for the first playoff game when it happened.

I was standing near the Jacksonville Shields' goal with a few other players from both teams, crowded together to wait out the winner of a battle for the ball, when Grace managed to steal it away. We were tied zero to zero and well into the second half. Someone needed to score.

I waited and waited. I watched the veteran Piper move the ball around and kept up my vigilance to see who stood close enough to accept a pass at a moment's notice. I'd been playing with Grace long enough to recognize her body language and what she wanted to do. There was an opening between us but the distance was a problem. Obviously there was only one thing to do, and I was ready.

She kicked the ball up high. I braced for it and watched it fly right at me.

It was going to be a header, definitely. Head meet ball, ball meet another player with a better shot at the goal. It was one of my favorite moves.

I went for it; I jumped straight into the air as a version of my lifelong friend and enemy, the ball, continued its trajectory toward me. Someone elbowed me right in the boob, but I ignored the pain. I could sense people moving around nearby.

I was going to get it. I was going to get it.

Later on, I would realize that I didn't get it.

The last thing I was aware of was the sharp pain that cracked the back of my head.

....

....

*Sal!*

*Casillas!*

*Schnecke!*

*Goddamnit!*

*Schnecke!*

*SCHNECKE!*

....

....

I didn't even know I'd gotten knocked out until I opened my eyes and found myself on my back, staring up at Kulti's face, whose eyes were maybe two inches above mine.

Kulti's breath washed over my mouth, ragged and uneven. His face full of an expression I wasn't remotely familiar with. And his eyes....

"Move back! Move!" someone yelled from nearby, and I found myself blinking, trying to remember what the hell happened.

A second before Kulti was pushed away by two paramedics, he squeezed my hand. I hadn't even realized he'd been holding it.

* * *

"OVERNIGHT?"

The doctor smiled at me. "Yes, overnight. We just want to be on the safe side with your medical history."

This wasn't my first or my second concussion. It also didn't help that the player who had elbowed the daylights out of me, was twice my size and had an arm that would have given a professional bodybuilder a boner. If I was going to get knocked out, at least it had been by a girl like Melanie Matthews, the second most aggressive defender in the WPL after Harlow. My concussion was practically a badge of honor.

"All right." I didn't sigh because it would have made me move half an inch and that was more than I wanted to. She really had knocked the shit out of me.

"Excellent. The nurse will be in here to check on you. The call button is to your left if you need anything."

Unfortunately or fortunately, however you wanted to look at it, this wasn't my first stay in the hospital. Knee surgeries, ankle surgeries and that one time I got pneumonia had all landed me an overnight stay. It wasn't the end of the world.

"Your team rep is outside, I'll let her in," the doctor said.

"Thank you," I called out to his retreating figure loud enough that it made my head buzz with pain.

By some miracle, they had given me a room to myself. My best guess was that it was the Pipers insurance that provided it, so I wasn't going to complain at all.

A knock came at the door, but it didn't open until I called out. Sheena's head popped through the door before she swung it open and came in. "Sal, how are you feeling?" she asked, a small plant in her hands. She'd been the one who had ridden over in the ambulance with me after they'd carried me off the field like I'd broken my spine.

"I'm all right," I told her. "I feel like I've been beaten with a sledgehammer, but it's okay."

She smiled and set the plant on the rolling table next to the bed. "I'm happy to hear that. What did the doctor say?"

"It's a concussion, but since it isn't my first one they want to keep me overnight to be on the safe side."

Sheena let out a slow whistle. "You gave us a scare. That's for sure. Is there anything I can get you?"

"I'm fine, but do you think you can have someone bring me my bag or at least ask Jenny if she can keep it for me? It's in the locker room."

"Sure, Sal. No problem," she agreed.

Then I asked her the question I'd been wondering about for the last two hours. "Do you know if we won?"

"We did. Genevieve scored in the last three minutes."

Well at least this crap hadn't been in vain. "That's great," I said.

"It sure is. She's the next generation, isn't she?"

The next generation. She was only five years younger than me, for the love of crap. It wasn't like I was about to croak or needed to invest in a wheelchair anytime soon, jeez.

"Yeah, she is," I gritted out, annoyed. I wondered if she knew what Cordero was planning.

We looked at each other awkwardly, at a loss for what else to say.

She smiled and glanced at the door. "Well, if there's not anything else, I should head back now. I wanted to make sure you were fine."

"I'm all right, thanks."

"I'll leave my number on the pad over here in case you need me, and I'll make sure your bag gets picked up," she assured.

I somehow smiled using only the minimal amount of facial muscles. "Thanks, Sheena."

She left, and I sat there in the quiet room alone, finally letting myself think about how much this concussion sucked ass. I knew what was going to happen. They were going to make me sit out of practice, and at least one game depending on what the doctor suggested and what the Pipers' trainer decided.

I would have hung my head low except I knew it would be

painful. Sure I didn't want to die; I understood how important it was to put my health first. But when it came down to it, this was the last thing I freaking needed. *Shit*. Shit, shit, shit, shit, shit. *Ugh*.

One minute of wallowing was what I usually allowed myself. I made the most of it.

As soon as the sixty seconds were over, I took a deep breath and reminded myself that I was lucky my injury wasn't worse. I could have died, right? In the end, this concussion wasn't the end of the world.

Then I reached over and grabbed the phone next to the bed, even though it made me a little dizzy; I dialed my mom's number first. When she didn't answer, I left her a voicemail, and then called my dad who I knew would have been watching the game at home. Dad could have been in church and still found a way to watch my game. He always did.

"Hello?" he practically shouted into the phone.

"Dad, it's me, Sal."

That time he did yell, away from the phone at least, saying something that sounded like "It's her!" in Spanish. "Are you okay?" he asked in that worried tone only fathers were capable of.

"Yeah, I'm okay. It's just a concussion," I assured him.

He spat out some more curse words in Spanish, and I could faintly hear my mom in the background telling him to control himself. "I almost fainted, you can ask your mom," he exaggerated. "You're really okay? No brain damage?"

"No brain damage, I promise I'm all right. I wanted to call and tell you before you booked a plane ticket here. I'll survive."

Dad let out an audible exhale. "*Gracias a Dios*. You get that hardhead from your mother—"

Mom screeched something in the background, and I had to fight the urge to laugh.

"Save your jokes for tomorrow. I don't have my phone on

me, but I'll make sure to call you as soon as I get my things back. If you need anything, I'm staying at the..." I looked around and gave him the name of the hospital printed on the whiteboard in front of the bed. "I really am okay though, so don't worry, and tell Mom I tried to call her but she didn't answer."

"*Si, esta bien*. Call me as soon as they release you. I love you. If you need me, I'll be there as soon as I can."

I smiled on the other end. "Thanks, Dad. Love you. Bye."

My dad said goodbye in return and we hung up.

With nothing else to do, I turned on the television and watched what was left of a movie about house-sized tarantulas. About an hour later, a few knocks tapped at the door before I heard who could only be Harlow and Jenny arguing on the other side. They, and by 'they' I meant Harlow, didn't wait for me to welcome them inside. The defender pushed the door open and strolled in the room, followed by Jenny and three of my other teammates.

Har looked around the room. "This is fancy."

"Hi, Har, Jenny." I greeted the other girls that came along with them too.

Jenny came to sit on the bed with big bright eyes. "You scared the devil out of me." She grabbed my hand gently. "I thought you were dead."

Harlow chuffed as she sat by my feet and let the other girls take the chairs. "I knew you were fine."

"They told us you have a concussion," one of the girls said.

"A moderate one," I told them.

The wince was visible around the room. They all knew what it meant and none of them tried to feed me kind words. The situation sucked.

"Yeah, it blows." I sighed. "I'm not even going to bother asking if I'm playing the next game, it'll just piss me off when they tell me, 'no' to my face."

Jenny squeezed my hand. "What matters is that you're okay. Did they make sure you don't have any hemorrhaging?"

How could you not smile at that?

The girls stayed for almost an hour, making me smile and fight back laughs as we joked around about random things that had nothing to do with the Pipers. They finally promised to see me the next day, if I was on time for the flight, and Jenny assured me she had taken my things back to our room. As they got up and started to head out, Harlow leaned in and whispered, "You want me to do something about Mel?"

Oh dear God.

I patted her cheek and totally lost it. "No, Har. It's all right. Thank you."

She eyed me. "If you're sure..."

"I'm sure. Thanks though, I really do appreciate it."

Harlow eyed me suspiciously as she walked out, as if expecting me to change my mind and ask her to exact vengeance on my behalf. I suddenly realized I wouldn't just be leaving the Pipers. For the first time since I'd decided I didn't have any choice but to go somewhere else, the reality of leaving two of my closest friends for the last few years really got to me.

Having to make new friends and get in well with new teammates wasn't that daunting. I'd done it over and over again throughout my life, but if I stayed with the WPL, I wouldn't get to play with them anymore anyway, would I?

I swallowed the melancholy down and reminded myself that I needed to do what was best for me. Right.

"Knock, knock," Gardner called out in the middle of pushing the door open.

"Come in," I called out.

His graying head was the first thing I noticed. He was still wearing the same suit and tie from the game.

I kept an eye on the door expecting Kulti to come in after him, but there was no one there. Well, that was disappointing.

"I'm happy to see your head is still attached," he said gently, taking a seat.

I smiled at him, only halfway feeling it. Since the Franz thing, I hadn't been sure how to act around Gardner. I doubted he knew, and I especially doubted that he had anything to do with their decision to trade me, but there was no way to know for sure. "Hey, thanks for coming."

"I had to come check on you, kid. Phyllis and everyone else send their best wishes." But they hadn't wanted to come. Okay. It wasn't like I wanted them to visit anyway. "How are you feeling?"

I shrugged my shoulders lightly. "Fine. A little frustrated, but it's okay."

"I wouldn't expect any different from you." He grinned.

"Tell me how the game went," I asked.

Gardner only stayed for a bit. He kept eyeing his watch until he finally sat up straight. "I need to get going, there's a few things I need to do before we leave tomorrow. The hospital staff knows to give me a ring once they know for sure when you're getting released, but give me a call too so that we have someone here to pick you up."

"Write your number down for me, will you? Jenny has my cell."

He jotted it down on the same paper Sheena had used earlier. "Feel better. I'll see you tomorrow."

He left, and I was alone again.

I didn't let myself think of Kulti, and why he hadn't come to check on me yet.

I watched a little more television, grateful I actually could without my heading hurting worse, had a visit from a nurse, and finally gave up hope that the German was coming to check on me around eight o'clock. I mean, we were just friends. He wasn't my boyfriend or anything. Plus, I'm sure he'd found out from someone else that I was fine.

I got off the bed and headed to the bathroom where I showered, put on the same underwear and scrubs they'd let me wear since I'd declined a gown, and went back out. The instant the bathroom door opened, I knew someone else was in the room. I could see the green and black running shoes on the mattress.

Sure enough, in the chair closest to the bed, was a surly scowling German with his feet propped up, a fruit bouquet on his lap and remote on the armrest. The television was set to the Sports Network. Kulti's head, the hair still as closely cut as always, turned slowly in my direction. "Taco," he greeted me.

"Berlin." I rounded the chair and went to sit on the edge of the bed, facing him. Kulti's lids were low as he regarded my face, plucking a piece of star-shaped pineapple from the big bouquet on his lap. He didn't look amused or particularly happy to see me either. "What's your problem?" I asked him when he continued staring.

He crossed one foot over the other, put a strawberry in his mouth, and kept right on scrutinizing me.

All right. I eyed what was left of the fruit. "Did you bring that for me?"

Those green-brown eyes stayed steady as he took a piece of kale, put it between his lips and chewed.

When I stuck my hand out to pluck a chocolate-covered strawberry, he moved the bouquet out of my reach.

"Seriously?"

He blinked.

"What's up your butt?" I asked.

He swallowed the kale in his mouth and kept his face even. "I called you."

It was my turn to blink. "I was too busy being carted out on a stretcher to drop by the locker room and grab my phone," I deadpanned.

"I see." He put a piece of pineapple in his mouth.

"Is that why you're mad?"

"I'm not mad."

"You're mad."

"I'm not mad."

"Rey, I'm not blind. You're pissed off. Just tell me what you're mad about. The team won."

Kulti turned, set the arrangement on the table behind him, and sat back sniffling drily. His eyes flicked up to the television screen, and his nostrils flared as he tipped his chin up. "Look."

I had to turn my entire body toward the television mounted up on the wall. The two familiar anchors for *Sports Room* were going through their highlights of the day. I caught the end of number four: an amazing double play during a baseball game.

"*Number three today is from a Women's Professional League game. Sal Casillas, of the Houston Pipers took the term 'header' to a different level during a second round playoff game.*"

The clip began with me jumping, surrounded by three opposing players. It showed Melanie, the girl who had elbowed me, circling around at the last minute and jumping up high too. Then it happened.

Holy crap, my head hurt at the replay of her arm shooting back and my head snapping forward, followed by the shot of me crumbling to the ground like I was dead.

"*Oooh,*" one of the anchor's disembodied voice filled in the action. "*That hurt me.*"

The footage kept going, showing Melanie being shoved away by Harlow as a referee ran up to see what was happening. Out of the corner of the screen, two male bodies were seen running onto the field, one overpowering the other in less than a second, long legs pumping faster and faster in a sprint that could have set a world record. The man slid to his knees across the turf, hunching over the body—me—on the ground.

"*Now you know it's bad when Reiner Kulti is on the field checking on his player,*" the other anchor said in a mocking voice.

The scene changed to another clip just as the camera

zoomed in on Kulti grabbing my hand, placing his free palm right next to my head. His mouth opened, and his face was distressed...

That warm fuzzy feeling I associated with the German when he was at his nicest, pulsed through my veins.

"Don't you ever pass out on the goddamn field again."

I turned my body back to face Kulti, who was sitting there looking unbelievably uncomfortable. "You *were* worried about me." I pressed my lips together. It wasn't the right time to smile, so I wouldn't.

Part of me expected him to explode, but the creepy controlled tone he used was even worse than the vicious temper hidden in that fantastic body. "Don't sound so surprised."

"You were the last one to come visit me," I told him in a low voice.

His head jerked back, a scowl on his face. "I made myself go for a run to calm down enough so I wouldn't show up here and yell at you. I wanted to wring your neck, Sal."

"I didn't even do anything." I wasn't sure whether to think this was funny, sweet or annoying because it seemed like he was pretty much blaming me for being in Melanie's way. "I thought you'd be proud of me for surviving getting hit by a player that size."

Then he went for it, and I just sat there and took it. "You scared the hell out of me!"

An image of a lion with a thorn in his paw flicked through my head and by some miracle I didn't smile. "You're yelling," I stated very calmly, eating up his reaction.

"Of course I'm yelling! I was yelling at you when you were pretending to be dead on the field, taking ten years off my life," he snapped, his face going red at the cheeks. "I thought—" he shot me a sharp look that almost alarmed me. "Don't ever do that to me again. I'm too young to die of a heart attack."

Holy crap, he'd really been worried. I loved it. I loved it so much I snorted despite the sharp pain that spiked through my head. "I would say claiming you're too young is a bit debatable, don't you think?"

The German tilted his head up and cursed something low and long in German. "You were brought to this planet to give me an ulcer, weren't you?"

Oh my God. That made me burst out laughing which hurt like hell because my poor head felt so tender, but I couldn't stop and I didn't want to.

"Why are you laughing? I'm not making a joke."

My whole body was shaking as I laughed, but somehow I managed to wheeze out, "You make it sound like I was sent from an alien planet to ruin your life. Jesus, Rey. Don't say stuff like that right now, my head hurts too much."

"Stop that," he demanded. "You're going to make it worse."

I pinched the bridge of my nose and made myself calm down. It took longer than necessary for me to get it together, but I managed. Eventually. Finally sobered up, I smiled at him, coughing with the laughter left over in me. "It really means the world to me that you got all riled up worrying over me. " I couldn't stop smiling.

And he noticed. "This isn't meant to be funny. Why are you smiling?"

"Because."

"What?"

I rolled my lips over my teeth and gave him an even look. "I watched this one game where your teammate, Keller, got tackled and had four of his vertebrae dislocated. The camera zoomed in on you, and you were retying your cleats or something. I don't know why I just remembered that. Two of my favorite things about you were that you never gave a single shit what happened to anyone else on the field, and that you never missed games unless you couldn't walk. It's impressive, really. It makes me feel really special that you care about me."

"I care about things," he argued.

"Oh? Like what?"

"Winning."

I bit my lip to keep from laughing. "Okay."

"My fish."

His fish. Jesus Christ.

Kulti blinked slowly and didn't say anything for a long time even as I made sure to keep watching him with an expectant look on his face. When he finally answered, it caught me off-guard.

"You."

Me.

Wait. Me?

I'm pretty sure I was beaming down to my soul. The words just kind of came out of me, unrestrained and unblemished. "Your friendship means the world to me, too you know."

He didn't break eye contact as he reached back and grabbed the fruit arrangement, finally deciding to share. I took it from him and looked it over, taking a chocolate-covered strawberry off in the process of my inspection. "Did you get a discount on this?"

"No." He paused. "Why?"

I slanted a look at him before taking a bite of the berry. "Half of the fruit is missing."

He reached forward and took a grape that was being used as a flower-shaped pineapple's stigma. "Nothing is missing. I ate it."

This man. I squeezed my eyes shut to keep from laughing. He either didn't notice or didn't care.

An hour or so passed, and he still hadn't left by the time the next nurse came in to check on me. "Ms. Casillas, how are you—"

The poor lady shut her mouth, her eyes widening at the sight of the German sitting in the chair with his feet right next to mine. Her swallow was visible as she darted her eyes back and forth between the two of us.

"Oh, ah, I had no idea you had a visitor." She cleared her throat. "It is past visiting hours but," she cleared her throat again, her cheeks turning bright red. "I can keep a secret as long as you're quiet." In her early thirties, she was young and pretty. Her eyes kept switching back to him, suddenly jumping in place a little.

She left a few minutes later after doing a quick check to make sure I wasn't exhibiting any signs of imminent death. "If you're planning on taking an extended nap while you're here, that chair in the corner has a footrest that comes out and it reclines."

I waited until we were alone before asking, "Are you planning on staying?"

His answer was to toe off his sneakers, revealing bright white socks. I guess I could take that as a good sign. "Have you heard anything from your agent?"

"Nothing new. Someone is supposed to be giving me a call next week from a team in Sweden that seems interested." A flutter went through my belly. *Sweden*. I still hadn't wrapped my head around it.

"Which team?" he asked casually. I told him the name and he nodded. "That's a good one."

I didn't miss the fact that he'd done research on the teams or clubs, as they were called overseas. I sure as hell wasn't going to bring it up.

"What about France? Germany?"

"I know she heard back from two teams in Germany, but she hasn't said anything else about it, and France, I have no idea." I wiggled my toes beneath the thin blanket I'd used to cover myself up in the freezing cold room. I suddenly remembered what I'd told Franz about Amber. I'd yet to tell Kulti the story and it made me feel guilty. Here he was after worrying about me and apparently spending the night, and he didn't know the truth. "Rey?"

"Taco."

"Remember when you heard Amber calling me a whore, and I didn't want to tell you why?"

Kulti was still staring at the television when he answered. "I know why."

Say what? My head throbbed in response to his statement. "You do?"

"Yes, something about that woman with the horse teeth throwing a tantrum because her husband is a liar. You left the team." He glanced at me. "Now that we are on the topic I have to tell you how much of an idiot you were. That situation wasn't your fault, and the coach should have let her go instead of you. You're faster, you make better decisions, and your ball-handling is much better." He sounded so nonchalant through his speech; I couldn't wrap my head around everything he said. I was still hung up on the fact that he freaking knew.

"How did you find out?" It was supposed to be a secret, damn it.

He lifted a shoulder. "My manager knows everything."

Yeah, my mouth opened in disbelief. "She heard about it?"

"She makes an effort to know everything before convincing me to do something. She did her research on the team, and I'm assuming she found out then. Don't frown at me. Secrets don't exist for her; I wouldn't be surprised if she knew all the bad things every player on the team has ever done."

My cheeks went hot, and I tried to rationalize what he was implying.

"You could have asked me. I would have told you," I grumbled.

Refusing to look at me, he replied, "You were taking too long."

Dear God. I was going to murder him. "That's all you have to say?"

"Yes. I already said you were an idiot for not fighting them, but there is nothing I can do about it now. If someone ever did that to you now, I would feel differently about it. That will never happen again, understand?"

For some strange reason, his defense had me beaming. It didn't matter anymore. It was in the past and... well, he didn't think what I'd mistakenly been accused of was a big deal. Why should I? Maybe it was time to leave Amber and her idiot husband behind. Hopefully I'd have a fresh start.

I took a deep breath and took in his side profile, cute nose, perfectly proportionate chin and his beard stubble. "What about you? Made any decisions yet on what you're going to do?"

He swung those light-colored eyes over to me. "No. I haven't decided anything."

I watched him out of the corner of my eye. "Have the Pipers asked you to re-sign?"

"Yes." He glanced back over at me, smiling that baby grin. "Do you believe the term 'fuck off' would be an appropriate answer?"

I cracked a smile and reached over to squeeze his shin. "I think I like it."

* * *

HIS PHONE WAS RINGING AGAIN.

"If you don't answer it, I'm going to," I threatened him, not straying from keeping my eyes on the scenery outside.

"Neither of us is answering," he said what I had already come to assume after the fourth time his phone had rung since I'd gotten released from the hospital.

What seemed like every five minutes, the trauma had started all over. Beep, beep, beep. The most boring ringtone ever created had been on a constant loop.

"Who's calling?" I finally asked.

"My publicist. Cordero. Sheila."

Oh brother. "You mean Sheena?"

"Yes. Her."

"What do they want?" No one had called me. The only person I had spoken to was Gardner, to let him know that the doctor had come in that morning and said I was free to go. But it had taken hours to get discharged. Holy crap. The team had flown back without me, a van dropping my things off before heading to the airport. Gardner had said he'd let Kulti know what was happening since he apparently decided to miss the flight and catch the next one with me.

He sighed. "They don't want us to get on the same flight together."

That had me turning in the cab's old leather seat. "Why?"

He made a face that said how stupid he thought this all was. "The photographs."

The photographs if someone realized who he was. I wasn't anything special to look at, no one would recognize me, but he was a different story.

It was my turn to sigh. "I can sit by myself."

"Don't start, Sal," he grumbled, still not looking my way.

"What? I get it. It would be less crap for them to deal with."

That had him glancing over, his mouth set into a firm line. "This isn't 'crap' and I'm not going to pretend like we don't know each other. I'm not a child and neither are you."

Jumping to agree to their terms so quickly made me feel like a guilty asshole. I hated saying he was right, but it was the truth. What did I have to hide? I looked at the hazel-green orbs staring at me and remembered that this was the person that had spent the night in a chair too small for him, and woken up every time the nurse checked on me. That made me feel like that much more of an ass-wipe.

For one brief moment I asked myself what the hell had I gotten myself into. This was the equivalent of being scared of heights and getting a job window-washing skyscrapers.

But as I took in his thirty-nine-year-old face that had been such a huge aspect of my life when I was younger and had somehow become an ever larger figure now that I was a lot older, I accepted the fact that there wasn't much I wouldn't do for him. I wasn't positive whether to let that make me feel weak or to accept it for the gift it would have been if I let myself think of it that way.

I had a man I respected that respected me, and he didn't care if the world knew we meant something to each other. Our friendship hadn't been given to either one of us, we had worked at it. On top of that, I felt something for him even if he was an egotistical, arrogant, stubborn pain in the ass. He was my egotistical, arrogant, stubborn pain in the ass.

So, yeah, I wasn't about to let someone—anyone—cheapen our friendship. That person sure as hell wasn't going to be Cordero either.

"I'm sorry. You're right." The only thing I didn't want and wouldn't want, would be to get stared at. That was all. A thought entered my head. "Does your publicist hate us hanging out together?"

"My publicist hates most things, *schnecke*, don't worry about him."

That wasn't super reassuring but all right. I smiled at him. I guess his publicist could sign up on the long list of 'People Who Aren't Fans of Sal.' Someone had told me once that you couldn't make everyone happy, and I'd kept that close to my chest for a very long time. Once you reluctantly accepted that people were always going to judge you no matter what, it got a little easier to deal with having people dislike you.

A little.

"Why are you frowning? Is your head bothering you?" Kulti asked in a worried tone.

Yeah, there wasn't much I wouldn't do for him. Not that I would ever admit it out loud.

I repeated that to myself the instant the first person recognized Kulti at the airport. I kept repeating that to myself when a security officer was forced to lead us into a special room to wait until boarding began. When I became overwhelmed at the people craning their necks to get a good look at the German, I told myself that this was all part of it. My face got all red because he wouldn't let me walk ahead and pretend like I didn't know him. *This was all part of being friends with the German.*

But it definitely sucked and I wasn't a fan.

# 24

"Where do you want me to drop you off?" Marc asked.

Two weeks had passed since my concussion, and I was itching to start playing again. I hadn't been allowed to practice with the team, but I hadn't totally slacked off. I'd kept up running on my own and doing some easy ball-dribbling with the German in his backyard after giving my brain some time off to recuperate. He made sure to stay at least five feet away from me at all times so that he didn't accidentally hit me in the face.

"In the front, please."

He nodded as he turned on the street where the Pipers building was located. Marc hadn't been super-talkative the last week or so, and I knew it was my fault. After my parents and Eric, he'd been the next person I told about possibly going to play somewhere else. While he said he understood, he hadn't taken it as well as everyone else had despite my explanation that I'd probably be sent to another team regardless. Marc didn't even pretend to not be sad about it.

Then again, no one spent as much time with me as he did.

"Call if you change your mind and need a ride," he said as he eased his big truck to a stop.

I got ready to open the door but waited, facing him. "I will, but it's not a big deal for me to call a cab. I know you need to get to the next job."

The man who used to give me wet willies when I was little simply nodded, and it tore my insides up. I didn't know what to say to him. Nothing could possibly come out of my mouth that would make him feel any better. So I saved my words and instead, reached over to pat his knee. "I love you, dude. Thanks for the ride."

He puffed out a breath and tapped the top of my hand. "Anytime, Salamander. Good luck."

Short words were a guilt trip from him. Bah. I nodded and reminded myself for the twentieth time that I was doing the best thing for me by trying to find another team. Plus who said anyone would actually go through with everything and sign me? I'd spoken to three teams on the phone, and all the conversations had seemed pretty positive.

Except the whole 'What made you decide to leave the WPL?' question.

Any publicist would have wanted to murder me when I told the general managers the truth. Maybe lying would have been the smarter idea, but I couldn't do it though. I told them. "I've given the WPL the last four years. I don't want to play where I'm criticized for things that don't matter on the field. All I want is to play. I want to win a cup."

They'd either take me or they'd leave me, but at least I'd go somewhere on my own merits.

Surprisingly, none of them had questioned my friendship with Kulti.

I hoped things worked out. I really hoped things worked out, but with the Pipers heading into the semi-finals in three days, I knew I had to play better than my best.

The only thing holding me back was medical clearance from the team physician and trainer.

The doctor had done just that, that afternoon. I was healthy, fine. There wasn't a single reason why they shouldn't let me practice or play.

This was the reason why, three days later, I didn't understand what the hell happened.

* * *

I WAS aware something was wrong when I realized that Gardner was avoiding eye contact during our semi-final pregame practice, but I didn't know for sure until he started going over the strategy he wanted to take against the Arrows.

"We're going to make a few changes to the starting line-up for this game—"

Cue the screeching tire sounds in my head.

*I fucking knew it.* I knew down to the marrow of my bones what was about to come out of his mouth. My gaze shot over to the German, who was busy looking over Gardner's shoulder, a furrow creasing the skin between his eyebrows.

He rattled off the names of the players starting: Jenny, Harlow, Grace, another and another and another. They were all names that didn't belong to me. Disbelief made my face go hot when the only 'change' to the roster was my missing name, replaced by the same girl who was always competing with me when we did sprints.

"There's no reason we can't win this," Gardner said in a confident voice while I stood there, humiliated and nearly ready to commit murder.

I tried to tell myself while he stood there babbling encouraging words that I shouldn't take it personally. It wasn't like he hated me and didn't want me to play. I cared what Gardner thought about me, I really did. He'd always been more than simply a coach, he'd been my friend.

Jesus Christ, I needed to scream.

Someone else could have rationalized that he wasn't starting me because I hadn't practiced in two weeks, and I'd sat out the last two games, with the Pipers winning just fine. But I couldn't. I couldn't because I knew this decision had been made by someone else.

It was fine. It was totally fine, I reminded myself. Just because I wasn't starting didn't mean I wouldn't get to play.

Yeah, I couldn't believe that either, no matter how hard I tried. It was the freaking semi-finals, and I wasn't going to play.

*Big Girl Socks on.*

This wasn't the end of the world. This wasn't the end of the world.

I let out a shuddering breath as Gardner wrapped up his speech. From over his shoulder Kulti was staring at me. His face blank except for how prominent his jaw suddenly became. I knew what he was trying to convey with that look alone.

He was telling me not to be him.

He was telling me to keep it together.

I needed to cool it.

Breathe. Deep breath. *Big Girl Socks on.*

Wait, wait, *wait.*

It was Harlow who came up to me first as the team broke up to leave. She put a hand on my shoulder and tipped her head down. "Sally, this is horse shit," she said in that same volume she would have used if she were talking about the weather.

"It's fine, Har," I told her, even though it wasn't. It really fucking wasn't fine. The veins at my temples were throbbing, for crap's sake. I didn't even think I was capable of being so angry.

"Fuck that, it's not fine," she argued. "I'm gonna go say something to them—"

*Patience, patience, patience.* "No, don't do that. Don't bother, really." I reached down to grab my bag and stood, attempting to calm myself. Looking back at her face, I swallowed and couldn't help but smile at my buddy. She'd been there for me for so long. I put my arms around her and gave her a bear hug. "I want to tell you before everyone finds out, I heard they're trying to trade me."

She jerked back, her brown eyes wide in shock. "No fuckin' way."

"Yeah way. You see how they're treating me. I'm going to try and get out before it's too late," I explained, trying my best to not sound sad about it. "It's our secret. I have to tell Jenny—"

"Tell me what?"

No one else was around as she came up to stand in our triangle. Harlow was the one that answered. "The team is going to trade her."

Jenny's mouth dropped open. "What? Who told you that?"

I shrugged because it didn't matter.

Tears immediately welled up in her eyes. "What team?"

"New York."

Neither one of them said anything.

It was Harlow that asked, "What are you going to do?"

"Go to Europe, I hope," I explained. "Maybe. If someone wants me."

My poor Jenny's eyes filled up with tears. "You're really leaving us?"

Oh God. "I'm leaving this, not you guys. You know Cordero's never liked me. I'm not really surprised he finally decided to get rid of me, but I can't believe he'd try to pawn me off to New York of all places."

"They'd never let you play." Jenny shook her head.

A hand cupped my elbow before trailing a path all the way to the small of my back. The heat of a man's body seared my side. "You'll be fine," a male voice stated.

It took a second for my brain to register what was happening. Kulti was touching me in public, at practice no less, in front of my friends and whoever else was left in the locker room.

When his hand slid up my spine and settled on the shoulder furthest away from him, the tension drained from my lungs and shoulders. This was the end. He was my friend, nothing else. I had nothing to hide, nothing to be ashamed of.

Fuck it. I put my hand on top of his. "Hopefully someone will take me."

"They will," he stated with complete confidence.

I'm glad one of us was certain.

His gaze settled on me, like he didn't even realize there were other people there. "I need to talk to you."

I wanted to ask about what, but figured I should wait.

"See you later?" I asked Jenny and Harlow who were watching us closely.

"Yeah," they both agreed.

He didn't bother waiting until we got to my car. Kulti stopped me in the middle of the parking lot, an exceptionally serious look on his face. "They aren't going to put you in the game."

"I know."

"If we don't do anything and the team moves on to next round, they aren't going to let you play the final either."

Grief and anger were so similar it was difficult to distinguish which one was crushing my lungs. "I know."

Kulti took a step forward. He'd let his beard grow in the last couple of days, and it framed his face perfectly, really making his eyes pop. "Do you trust me?"

Did I trust him? My head jerked back a little and my eyebrows went up. I better be able to. "Yes."

His nostrils flared as his chin tipped down. He resembled the man I'd admired on the field for so long. "Let's talk to Cordero."

I had just told him I trusted him, but I still wanted to ask what the hell we were going to talk to that ass-wipe about. Trust, right? He wasn't going to screw me over. Kulti knew what was at stake.

I wanted to throw up, but instead I nodded.

* * *

"I'LL MEET YOU THERE," Kulti said before disappearing into the first restroom we came upon.

All right. I had no clue what the hell we were going to do, but I continued toward Cordero's office. His secretary was at her desk. She looked what you'd imagine an older secretary to look like, neat, white hair trimmed short, a button-up sweater layered over a shell-collared shirt. It was almost easy to believe she was nice.

She wasn't; at the very least she'd never been nice to me.

"Hi, Mrs. Brokawski. I wanted to see about talking to Mr. Cordero, please." Kill them with kindness, right?

The rude old bat looked away from her computer, summing me up and finding me lacking. "You need to schedule an appointment."

Someone was skipping the pleasantries. All right. "If I could just talk to him for five minutes? That's it. It's very important," I stressed and lied to deaf ears, which had turned away to focus again on the computer screen.

"I already explained, you need to schedule an appointment. He has an opening for Monday at eleven," she stated.

"There's no way for me to speak to him today?"

The lady rolled her eyes and wasn't discreet about it. "No."

Obviously she wasn't going to work with me. "Thank you anyway," I said before turning around. I started walking in the direction I'd come from, intending to find the German to let him know he was going to have to be the one to get the rabid badger to let us in. Before I even left her visual range, Kulti was there walking forward, frowning.

"She won't let me in to see him," I explained.

He blinked once then grabbed my hand, palm to palm, and walked with me back to the secretary's desk.

Kulti didn't bullshit around. "I need to speak to Cordero. Now."

Her slim wireless frames moved up to see who was speaking. Her entire face changed when she spotted the German. "Mr. Kulti, you should really schedule an appointment—"

"No. I need to see him now," he cut her off.

The old bat's eyes swung over to me, and I didn't miss the wrinkle on her nose. Well, the multiple wrinkles on her nose. "Let me get him for you."

Exactly fifteen seconds later Mr. Cordero's ancient guardian was standing at the doorframe, holding the door wide open and waving us forward. "He'll see you now."

The general manager of the Pipers was sitting behind his desk as we walked in, Kulti ahead of me, still holding my hand. I knew what it would look like, and I didn't find it in me to care. Not even a little. The German took the seat furthest away from the door. I took the other one, watching Cordero, who looked completely undisturbed.

"How can I help you?" the man asked with a distasteful expression.

"I'll take the job if you let her play the next two games," Kulti went right out and said it.

My head swung around to gape at him. What?

Apparently, I wasn't the only one surprised by his words. Cordero's eyes widened. "You will?"

"On two conditions. The first is that you let her start," he stated evenly.

The oldest man in the room seemed to think about it, almost stupefied. "That's your compromise?"

"One part of it."

He didn't want to take the job. He'd told me so. What in the hell was he doing?

"Rey," I whispered.

The German turned to give me another look; that look that reminded me I had promised to trust him.

Damn it.

"Yes or no?" he demanded from Cordero.

"I..." he stuttered. "I can't have you both on the field at the same time. There have been complaints from other players—"

The King raised a hand, shooting me a meaningful long look I wouldn't understand until after he finished speaking. "I'll sit out both games," he offered, watching me while he did it.

For that brief moment, time stopped.

Cordero had no idea what had just come out of Kulti's mouth. He heard the words, but he didn't understand the meaning behind them. I heard the words and understood, but ... but...

"No," I told him.

He didn't once break eye contact with me, confirming that he wanted me to really get what he was implying, what he wanted me to understand. "Yes."

"Rey. You don't know what you're doing."

The German gave me a hard look, his face both intense and serene at the same time. "I've never been more sure of anything."

Oh bloody freaking hell.

"*You* will sit out to let her play?" Cordero asked surprised, obviously not as oblivious as I had thought.

For Kulti to sit out a game...

With no hesitation and still staring directly at me, the pumpernickel said to the Pipers' general manager. "Yes. Do we have a deal?"

The other man seemed to only think about his answer for a

minute. "Okay. You've got a deal as long as your next demand isn't preposterous."

I couldn't help but stare at Kulti. My entire body was zeroed in on him, on his words, on his face and on that swell in my chest that wanted to squeeze my vocal pipes until they burst.

"Good. The other thing I want is for you to take a look at Sal's contract. I'm buying her out, and I need to know how much to write the check for," the bratwurst explained. Before I could argue, he made sure I knew he was talking to me and not the general manager. "Don't argue. You would do it for me."

"Just because I would—"

"I would do anything for you."

Ahh shit.

I flung up my common sense into the air and held my imaginary ovaries out in sacrifice. My heart was pit-pit-patting a beat it had never known before. I was going to have a heart attack at twenty-seven. Holy crap.

Kulti was going to sit out the last two games, and he wanted to buy out my contract for me.

*He doesn't know what he's saying. He doesn't know what he's doing,* I repeated to myself, trying my best not to lose it right then and there.

"Cordero, do we have a deal?"

Neither one of us was looking at the weasel, so we both missed his scoff and the incredulous look on his face. As much as this old idiot was essential to what was happening that moment, it didn't feel like it. This was me and Kulti, and Cordero was just background noise to get to where we were heading. "You want to buy out her contract?" Cordero's laugh had an edge to it. "You're more than welcome to."

If I wouldn't have been in such a daze over what Kulti had implied, I might have been offended at how easily this ass-wipe sold me off.

"*Not together*," Cordero mocked under his breath.

The thing I would realize later was that I could have argued with him and defended myself. I could have told him nothing ever happened between Kulti and I. At least before we went into his office, he'd never been anything but platonic toward me. Fatherly, brotherly, friendly, Kulti had been all of those things throughout the course of our friendship. But what was the point in trying to convince someone who would believe whatever he wanted to believe otherwise?

Most importantly by that point, I couldn't have cared any less what one mean little asshole thought about me.

Because Kulti had made one thing known in the minutes that transpired right before he offered to buy me out from the Pipers.

It was the most amazing, most unexpected, most surreal thing ever.

He lo—

I couldn't say it. I couldn't even think that he might have real feelings for me.

Holy shit.

Obviously, he was out of his mind and completely misguided. Yeah, he was insane. That was it.

I stared at him in the minutes that followed, only faintly listening to whatever was going back and forth between the two old farts in the room. What the hell was he doing? What was he *thinking*?

"I'll have legal contact you later, Ms. Casillas," Cordero's voice snapped me out of my trance.

I tried to think back about what he'd been saying before I zoned out, and I was pretty sure he was going to have the legal department call me to sign the contract that would free me from the Pipers.

I didn't even have a team waiting for me with open arms yet.

Oh jeez. I'd figure it out. It would all work out.

"I'll be waiting for their call," I said absently, getting to my feet when the German did.

"I'm ecstatic you've decided to join us again next year," Cordero called out as we exited his office.

Kulti said nothing. It sent off warning signs in my head that I pushed away until we were in a place where I could ask him what in the hell he was thinking agreeing to sign another contract. Silence was our companion on the way out of the building. He didn't touch me. Didn't tell me how much he cared about me. He didn't even explicitly say he liked me.

But I guess he'd done enough already. Right?

We made it all the way to my car and got inside before I broke.

Turning carefully in the seat to face him, the side of my right thigh up against the back support, I gathered my words and sorted them as he watched me the entire time. When I was ready, I gave myself a pep talk and met his eyes. "Look, you're my best friend, and I am so thankful to have you in my life, but you don't..." I couldn't say it. I couldn't.

"I don't what?" he asked in a cool tone, those clear eyes locked.

"You know what."

He blinked. "No. Tell me."

Yeah, not happening. I couldn't even put the word in the same sentence with his name. "I know you care about me, but you don't have to do all this. I can figure something else out. It's too much."

The German crossed his arms over his chest, his expression unforgiving. "It isn't too much, not for you."

There we went again. Sweet Jesus. "Rey, please. Don't say stuff like that."

"Why?"

"Because it gives people the wrong impression."

Those jewel-like eyes narrowed into slits. "What impression

is that?"

"You know what impression it makes."

"I don't."

"You do." Dear God, if this friendship continued, I'd probably have premature hair loss in no time.

"It isn't an impression. I could care less what anyone else thinks when it's the truth."

Oh hell. "Rey, stop it. Just... stop."

"No." The expression on his face was determined. "You are the most honest, good thing I've ever had. I won't deny it to anyone."

Dear God. Panic flooded my belly. "I'm your friend." I sounded timid, borderline panicked.

His forehead was as smooth as ever. Kulti looked more calm and collected than I'd ever seen him. There was no trace of anger or frustration on him. He was somber and serious and terrifying. "No. You mean so much more to me, and you know it."

I opened my mouth and closed it, and suddenly I couldn't be in the tiny car with him any longer. I needed out. Out. Right then. That instant. I needed to get out. Fresh air, I needed fresh air.

So I did just that. I got the hell out of the car and slammed the door closed behind me. I crouched down on the ground with my head in my hands. I was on the verge of having either a panic attack or a shit attack; I couldn't decide which. My heart was hammering a mile a freaking second and I was just squatting, trying to convince myself not to die from a sudden heart attack at the age of twenty-seven.

This was like the best dream and the worst nightmare all wrapped into one beautiful package.

I hunched over more and pressed the heels of my hands into my eyes.

The sound of the passenger door opening and closing

warned me that my temporary peace was about to come to an end. Seconds later I felt the one and only man—the cause of why I was losing my mind—drop down in front of me. His knees hit mine as his hands came to rest on my shoulders, giving them a light squeeze.

"Why are you telling me this now all of a sudden?" I croaked.

His hands stroked down the line of my upper arms to stop at my elbows. "I won't be the reason your career is blemished," he explained.

The reason my career was blemished?

Oh. *Oh.* I'd been the one to say it from the very beginning: it didn't matter what anyone else thought as long as we both knew we hadn't done anything. I could go to my grave knowing I hadn't done any fraternizing with my coach. Oh my God.

"I wanted to wait until the season was over. I didn't want to rush you. A few months are nothing compared to the rest of my life, *schnecke.*" Kulti nodded, his eyebrows hitching up a quarter of an inch as recognition hit me. "You have no idea what the day of your concussion did to me."

His face tipped down as his expression turned grave. "I thought your neck was broken. It was the most frightening thing I have ever experienced. Franz called and asked how my *schnecke* was doing.

"*My schnecke.* My little snail, do you know that's what it means? It's a term of affection in my country. My love. My snail. I don't want to waste more time. I have nothing to hide and neither do you."

I tilted my head back, my throat completely exposed as I sighed in desperation. "Please don't say stuff like that."

"It's the truth."

"No, it's not. We're friends. You said I was your best friend, remember? You can love me but not be in—" I couldn't say it. I shut my mouth and gave him an exasperated look.

"I can and I am. When you love something you do whatever you need to do to protect it, isn't that right?" He tilted his face down, making sure our eyes were meeting.

All I could manage to do was stare and hyperventilate.

He nodded, his big hands kneading my arms. "You're supposed to say, 'Oh yes.'"

I could feel my lower lip trembling as his thumbs rubbed the tender part in the crook of my elbow. "You're delusional."

"I'm not." Kulti tipped his head down, eye to eye like he'd been with me when I'd woken up from my concussion. "Understand, I would wait for you however long you needed me to, but I hope you don't ask me to wait any longer than the end of this season."

Panic made my throat tighten. This was all too much. "I have a choice in this. I don't know—"

"You know, Sal. It's why we fight and make-up. Why we'll always fight and make-up. You were the one that said to me that you fight with the people you love the most, remember? You and I fight all the time, see?"

Those big hands left my thighs and before I could wonder where they were going, they landed on my cheeks. In a split second, he tilted my face just slightly down and we were eye to eye, his breath on my face. Those amazing hazel eyes were closer than they'd ever been.

Then he kissed me. Unexpectedly, out of the blue, sudden as a heart attack.

The dream of a teenage Sal and the dream of twenty-seven-year-old Sal, became one.

Reiner Kulti, my German, my pumpernickel, pressed his lips to mine. The same lips I'd kissed a minimum of fifty times on the posters that had once been on my wall. His mouth was warm and chaste, pressing, pecking, one, two, three, four times. He kissed one corner of my mouth, then the other.

Holy mother of God, I was a sucker for those corner kisses.

I opened my mouth just a little and kissed him back. Our kisses were a little more open-mouth than closed. Five, six, seven, eight times he let me press my lips to his. He let me be the one to kiss him back. Nine, ten, eleven times, right under his lips, on a chin that hadn't gotten the memo it had been shaved that morning.

His breath rattled in his chest as he pulled back, eyes closed, mouth firm and tight.

My heart ran and ran and ran. Without thinking about it, I put my hand on his chest and felt. I felt the furious pounding beneath all that muscle and bone, just like mine. Excited, racing, sprinting, trying to win like always.

I loved this man.

Sure, it made me an idiot and loving him didn't necessarily mean anything, especially when I wasn't positive that Kulti wasn't on drugs but...

Well hell. Life was about taking chances. Going for what you wanted so that you didn't get old and have pages of regrets. Sometimes you won and sometimes you lost, as much as I hated it.

His thumbs dug into the soft place between my jaw and ears, placing one more sweet simple kiss on my cheek that I felt under my skin. "Two more games."

Two more games.

The words had me jerking back. What was I doing? *What the hell was I doing in the freaking Pipers parking lot?*

Luckily, he decided to take a step back right then. His lips were pink, his eyes glassy. His nostrils flared as he watched me closely. "Let's go, yes? Every day this gets more difficult."

I nodded, trying to shake off the stupor that had taken over. *Get it together.*

We got into the car and I scrubbed my hands over my face before starting it.

Focus. What I needed to do was focus.

# 25

"Where's Coach Kulti?" I overheard one of the girls ask in the locker room that evening as we got ready to head to the field for the start of the semi-final game.

"No clue," someone else answered.

I kept my head down and continued stretching. Besides Gardner, I was the only one who probably had any idea that Kulti was sitting in the stands incognito. He had made the wise decision to ditch the beanie he wore all the time, and instead went for a white Corona cap I'd taken from my dad's truck years ago.

With a plain T-shirt, jeans and tennis shoes, I felt pretty confident no one would have any idea who he was. When we'd gotten to the stadium, he hadn't seemed worried about sitting alone, surrounded by people who would more than likely cause a riot if they knew who he was.

We'd taken his car and driver to the stadium at his insistence. He was supposed to be picking up a ticket that someone had gotten for him at the main gate. Right before I began walking toward the player's entrance he'd asked, "Will your parents be here?"

Like my dad would ever miss a semi-final game. Ha.

Once I made it to the locker room, Gardner looked around at the girls. "Listen up, quick change to the starting roster: Sal, you're in. Sandy, you're sitting this one out," he called out.

I didn't miss the ugly groan that made its way out of the other player's mouth. I sure as hell kept my face even, a talent I'd picked up from the master, Kulti. The truth was, I hadn't cooled down even a little bit.

These assholes were going to bench me for freaking 'political reasons'. Sure it sucked for Sandy who now wasn't going to play, but that sure as hell wasn't my problem. With the exception of the two times I'd been benched and the thing with my ribs and concussion, I'd played every single game from beginning to end. I had earned my spot. Plus, I wasn't the only forward's place Sandy could have taken. I had busted my ass to get what I had, on the field and off the field. On top of that, she was only twenty-two. There were a lot of things I'd let myself feel guilty for, but playing in a semi-final game instead of her wasn't one of them.

From across the locker room, I spotted Jenny looking in my direction, but I still didn't change my facial expression. Gardner went over some details and plays he wanted us to keep in mind as we went up against the New York Arrows.

One thought prevailed: I would rather do a dozen more press conferences and move to Brazil than be traded to New York.

They could even be press conferences like the one I had done at the beginning of the season.

Which finally made me wonder after all these months... Sheena had never said anything else about it or the video she'd planned on pulling together after the press conference from hell. What had happened with that? I'd worry about it later, for now my one and only subject of focus was the New York Arrows and their dumbass captain, Amber.

I hadn't even begun dreading seeing her with everything else going on. Even now that I finally remembered, I still didn't give a crap. If anything, it gave me that much more motivation to wipe the turf with her whiny black heart.

I could do this.

I closed my eyes and relaxed. Everyone had their own way of mentally preparing for games. Me, I had a gift for zoning things out and clearing my head. I didn't need music to get pumped up. I just visualized our game and calmed down.

"It's time, Sally," Harlow tapped my elbow.

I opened my eyes and grinned up at her, smacking what had to be one of the tightest butt-cheeks in the world, and walked alongside her all the way to the field.

"You gotta tell me later how you got back in," she whispered into my ear.

I smacked her butt once more, but it was more because I was so amazed at how muscular it was than for any other reason. "Magic."

Magic would be the best way to describe how the game went.

'Complete and total annihilation' would work too.

From the moment we stepped out on that field, I felt it in my veins and on my skin. I'd swear it was in the air. There were more people in the stands than there had ever been. Down the field was the New York team. We did some more last-minute stretching, Gardner called us for another quick pep talk, and we took the field.

Within the first five minutes, Grace scored a goal.

Three minutes later, with a wild header from one of the girls who hadn't said a word to me in over a month, I threw myself in the air and scissor-kicked the crap out of the ball, feet well over my head. It was Harlow barreling toward me that told me the ball made it in. As soon as I was standing, she had her arms wrapped around my knees and she was holding me up, jumping up and down.

I was still in her arms when I spotted them in the first row. They were on their feet screaming, the white Corona cap had a seat center field with a familiar-looking man wearing a jersey with my number on it right next to him. Next to that jersey was another one of mine, smaller and in a different color. Kulti, my dad and mom.

That second rush filled my chest. I wasn't sure how he'd done it—I definitely had no idea how he managed to score those seats, and part of me didn't want to know. But they were there together. Three of the people I loved most in the world, and they were acting like they'd won a billion dollars. Without a doubt in my mind, I knew Marc and Simon were also there somewhere cheering me on.

In the second half, New York scored one goal right from the top.

A Piper scored a goal after that, bringing the score 3-1. By some insane miracle, I snuck up the corner of the field and accepted a pass from Genevieve. I didn't even understand how the ball made it to me, but I nailed a kick as hard as I could. My anger was fueled by the shove and "slut" taunt Amber had given me a minute before. We were kicking ass, so she could call me whatever she wanted.

We finished the game with one more last-minute goal that had our fans out of their seats cheering like crazy. Sure the stadium wasn't packed like the men's games were, but it didn't matter. The fans we had were beyond dedicated and that more than made up for it.

The next hour went by in a blur of hugs and congratulations, and Gardner prattling about both the good and the bad in those ninety-five minutes. I showered and got out of there as quickly as I could, not in the mood for anyone but those three people in the audience.

I walked outside following high-fives and butt pats to some of the players on my way out, there were camera crews and journalists prepared, lights bright, microphones ready.

"Sal!"

"Sal!"

Big Girl Socks, on.

"Hi," I greeted them all with an anxious smile, taking a step back when four microphones were shoved in my face.

"Congratulations on your win, can you tell us how the Pipers managed to do it?"

I summed it up for them: teamwork, great defense and quick thinking.

There were more and more questions. What I thought about this and that.

And then... "Where was your assistant coach tonight?"

"I wasn't told," I replied.

"Are the rumors regarding an inappropriate relationship between the two of you affecting your game?" someone else asked.

I bristled on the inside but managed to smile. "I would be distracted if there was something for me to be distracted about, but my only focus this season, like every other season, has been winning. That's all."

"So you're denying that there's something going on with you and Kulti?"

I'm in love with him and he thinks he feels something for me, I thought to myself but instead said, "He's my best friend and he's my coach. That's the only thing I'm confirming."

All I got in return were blank faces from the people hoping for something more dramatic. If only they'd been around earlier when I'd received and given the sweetest little kisses in the world from the man in question.

"Thanks for coming," I said and made my exit, hustling past the other family members and fans who were waiting by the press. I shook some hands, gave a few hugs and waved at people I recognized.

It was that damned Corona cap I spotted first, as far away from the media as possible; next to him were my parents, Marc and Simon. It was my dad who saw me approaching first. He came rushing toward me, his face glowing. Dad grabbed me in a big hug and said the words that he used every time I made him exceptionally proud.

"You could have scored at least two more goals."

"Next time," I agreed, hugging him back.

My mom was next.

"You're not leaving yourself open as much. Good job."

Finally after my mom let me go, Kulti stepped forward before Marc or Simon could. He put a hand on my shoulder, his eyes holding mine steady and only the faintest hint of a smile on his mouth.

"Yes, oh wise one? What words of advice do you have for me?"

That small smile blossomed. "Your parents said it all."

* * *

"*Buenas noches, amores*," my mom said goodnight to both my dad and I before disappearing into my bedroom. My parents were spending the night.

Dad leaned back against the couch and sipped the beer he'd bought on our way home. Our group of six had all gone out to eat immediately following the game. He waited until the bedroom door clicked shut before saying, "Now can you tell me why Kulti wasn't coaching tonight?"

The fact he'd made it almost five hours until finally breaking down and asking why the German had sat in the stands was amazing. I had to give him credit for holding onto the question so long when it had to be eating him up inside. "Yes."

He exhaled, and I had to fight the urge to take the bottle from him and take a swig.

"He sat out today so that I could play. He's sitting out the final so I can play then too," I explained slowly. "The other girls have been complaining about how he's playing favorites, so..." The last month of my life suddenly came down on my shoulders again, and all I could do was shrug helplessly.

Dad stared and then stared a little more. One of his eyelids started fluttering a little. "Tell me what happened."

I did. I told him about how I'd been cleared to play, but how they'd initially said I was going to be benched.

Dad gulped down half the bottle in response. He looked about ready to pop. If anyone understood the magnitude of what Kulti's actions meant, he did. "Sal..."

"Yes?"

"What are you going to do?"

"I don't know."

He gave me a look. "You know what you need to do."

"I don't know."

"You know."

God, was this what talking to me was like? "Dad... I... I don't know. I don't even know what to think about all of it. We're in completely different leagues. I'm me; he's him. It would never work."

He nodded, seriously. "I know. You're too good for him, but I've taught you better than to be so conceited."

Oh God. Why did I bother? I started cracking up. "That's not what I meant and you know it. Jeez."

He smiled over and pressed the cool glass of the beer bottle to my knee. "Does he know about your little obsession?"

I gave him an 'are you kidding me' look that had him chuckling in response.

"I want to see them."

"See what?"

"Your chicken wings," he deadpanned.

I groaned.

He took it to another level when he started squawking.

"I've always known you were insane."

Dad snorted. "I thought you were a tiger, *hija mia*."

There he went. Leave it to my dad to bring up exactly what I'd been worried about. Had I really lost my guts? "I don't know how to tell him. I don't even know why he thinks he has feelings for me either, Dad. What am I supposed to do? He's doing all these things and saying stuff, when he's never even given me the idea that he thinks of me as anything more than a friend. What am I supposed to do?"

He gave me that look that said he wasn't impressed that I was asking for his opinion. "Do you really want me to tell you?"

I nodded.

"When I met your mom, I knew exactly who she was. Everyone knew who she was. I've told you before, I didn't talk to her first, she came up to me." Dad smiled gently at the memory. "I didn't have anything to offer her. I didn't even finish high school and your mom was *La Culebra*'s daughter. It didn't matter how many times I told her she could find someone better; she never left. If it didn't matter to her that we would never be rich, then why should I push her away? I loved her and she loved me, and when you have love, you find a way to make things work." He pressed the bottle to my knee again. "*You* can have anything you want in the world. Anything you've ever wanted, you've worked for, and I know that you know that. 'I can and I will,' remember?

"I'll tell you this, too. I knew something was going on when you showed up at the house with him. No man is going to go visit your family because he's bored. No one would spend so much time with you if he didn't want more, and my birthday was months ago, Salomé." He pointed at his heart. "Think with your heart, not your head. I've never known you to not take every opportunity you've ever been presented with. Don't start passing on them now."

# 26

"Where's Coach Kulti?"

"He's taking time off for the rest of the season," Gardner answered before walking off.

I stretched my arms up over my head to really get a good stretch into those shoulder muscles always nagging me. All the while pretending like I didn't hear the group talking twenty feet away.

"He's been here all season, and *now* he's decided to take time off?"

"I'm not surprised."

"I can't believe it."

"Really?"

"I bet Sal knows what's going on."

"Duh, she knows. I'm sure they spent last night together."

A couple of my teammates giggle-laughed. So funny.

"You know, I heard she went by Cordero's office and he gave her an ultimatum: Stop seeing him or he'd trade her."

"No way! What'd she say?"

"Oh, I have no idea, but I think that's why they were planning on benching her in the semi-final the other night. If that would have been me, and they told me I wasn't starting, I don't even know what I would've done. But not Sal, she just stood there. I didn't see her bat an eyelash."

"No shit. She's never upset; I don't think she feels anything. I know I've never seen her cry."

Yep, still not looking.

"Me neither. Her entire life revolves around playing. She's a robot or something."

And that was my cue to zone the group out. To zone every single girl I'd at one point or another helped, including Genevieve.

A robot. They thought I was a robot.

I took a breath.

Everything was fine.

I only had one more game to go. That was it. Five more practices to get through before the season was over.

What was that saying? When life gives you lemons, go to a taco stand.

* * *

WHEN I PULLED into the driveway that day, there was a mountain bike off to the side, and next to it was the German. The Audi was nowhere in sight.

"I didn't know you were here," I said, getting out. "I took a yoga class at the gym already; otherwise I would have come home and made you do some with me." I wasn't even joking either. His butt in downward dog... God help me. It seemed to be one of the only things that could cheer me up lately.

Kulti dusted off said bubble butt as he got to his feet. "I've only been here an hour."

From anyone else, the comment would have sounded like he was impatient, but he didn't look anxious at all. "Did you ride your bike all the way over?" I asked, eyeing the black mountain bike I'd never seen before.

"Yes," he said, taking my bag from me. "I bought it this morning."

I followed him up the stairs and handed him the keys to open the door. He left my bag in the exact same place I usually had it and set my dad's hat on the appropriate hook. My dad had said I wasn't allowed to ever wash that damn Corona hat.

"I'm going to hop in the shower. I'll be back out soon."

In no time, I was in and out. By the time I made it back, he was on the couch watching television. I grabbed a protein bar and took a seat on the other end.

Kulti tilted his head and raked his gaze from my face down, down, down to land on the white tank top I'd put on over a clean sports bra, and then kept right on burning a visual path to my thighs. He took a quick breath I almost missed. Those amber eyes slid back up to my face.

"What is it?" I scrunched up my face, expecting the worst.

"Do those freckles go everywhere?"

He was talking about the freckles on my chest and my stupid, stupid nipples reacted as if he were calling them to attention. "Umm..."

A tendon in his neck flexed, and Kulti gave me what could have been considered a grimace. "I'll behave." A shaky sigh made its way out of his chest and reached straight into mine. "I need to tell you what my lawyer said."

"Is it bad news?" With my luck lately, I shouldn't expect any different.

"No. She looked over your contract, drew up our own, and she'll be sending that to Cordero tomorrow with a check to buy you out."

There were so many keywords in one sentence. Leaving the Pipers was really happening. Jesus Christ. "That's all?"

"Yes."

It would all be over soon. The reminder that Kulti was paying to get me out of the Pipers made my stomach feel just the slightest bit weird. It was happening. Oh man. "I—"

"Don't say anything about your contract." He shot me an even look. "I had no idea how much it was worth, and frankly, it was insulting once she told me the number."

To him it would seem like chump change. Well, to most professional athletes it would definitely seem like nothing. What could you do? I enjoyed playing, and I made ends meet with what I did with Marc. It wasn't a big deal. I didn't need a luxury car, a massive house or name-brand things to make me happy. But it was the thing he said about how I would do it for him if the tables were turned, that kept me from kicking up a huge stink. He was right. I would buy him out if he were in my shoes, so I wasn't going to be a huge hypocrite about it. Maybe I could pay him back somehow later on.

"Has your agent heard back from any of the teams?" he wanted to know.

I shook my head. "No. She told me to be patient. Chances are, I won't get any offers until the season is over, so we'll see." I gave him a brave smile that I only partially felt. "I'm going to try not to worry about it. If it's meant to be, it's meant to be. If not, then... I'll figure something out. This isn't the end of the world."

"It isn't," he agreed.

I sighed and decided to change the subject. "Everyone was asking where you were today."

Kulti snickered. "I was very disappointed not to be there," he deadpanned, which made me laugh.

"Yeah, right. What did you do instead?"

"I bought my bike and went for a long ride," Kulti explained.

He triggered my memory, and I suddenly remembered what I'd been meaning to ask. "Hey I kept forgetting to bring it up, but where did you go those two days you missed practice? When I texted you and you didn't respond. Thank you for that, by the way."

"I was home." Kulti glanced up at the ceiling.

"So you were just ignoring my text messages?" The fact he didn't even try and bullshit me made me respect him a little more.

He lowered his gaze to side-eye me. "I was furious with you."

If I remembered correctly, I'd done the same thing when I'd been angry with him for being weird in front of Franz and Alejandro. Bah. I reached over and patted his knee. "Well like I told you in my text, I'm sorry for what I said that day. I was frustrated, and I didn't mean it."

"I know that now." He blinked. "You aren't a quitter, and I wouldn't let you give up anyway."

Talking about those nearly back-to-back conversations made my eye twitch. "Don't be a dick and accuse me of sleeping with your friend then."

Kulti made a face that was almost remorseful. Almost. "I was... agitated. I didn't like the idea of you spending time with him in secret. It bothered me."

I'm not sure why it took me so long to understand what had upset him, why Franz and I practicing bothered him so much. Was this real? If he wasn't full of crap about what he was saying, a lot of things finally made sense. Why he was so adamant about us not going on dates with other people when Sheena had suggested. The face he made when I'd told him about my ex.

"I don't like the idea of you being with another man."

*I will not smile. I will not smile.* "I wouldn't like the idea of you spending time with another woman and not telling me about it either." There, I said it. I just went right out and said it.

All right. I cleared my throat, bit both my lips at the same time and shrugged. "There isn't anything wrong with that. I thought you were just being an asshole about Franz. I sure as hell don't like thinking about you being with other women, or even being reminded of your ex-wife, if I'm even allowed to say that. I know I don't look like the women you're usually interested in, or dress like the women you used to date, but you know that and you're still here. That has to count for something," I told him honestly.

"I'm not going anywhere," he claimed.

"You can say that all you want, but you told me that you are the way you are and you're never going to change, so I'm going to tell you the same thing. I am the way I am, and I'm never going to change either. I wasn't built for a whole bunch of drama, Rey. Everything going on right now, this is it. I'm maxed out. I want a steady, stable life. When I commit to something, I'm in all the way. I don't share, or even play around with the idea of infidelity. You're my friend right now, but I don't want something to happen that makes me want to move on with my life. I don't want to be forced to pretend like these last few months haven't happened. You mean too much to me."

Maybe I was expecting him to get all smug about what I said, but he didn't. Instead, that intense expression that usually lived on his face reached a different level. He gave me one of those stares that made the hairs on my arms stand up. "You say that as if there were anyone else in this world I would want. You have no idea what I feel for you." He blinked and spat out something I never would have expected. "There is no gray area for me where you're concerned. I don't share, and I expect nothing less from you."

I... what in the hell do you say to that? What? What could you possibly say? It was psycho sure, but it didn't bother me. I'd been the teenager that drew mustaches on his ex-girlfriends' faces for months when their pictures would come up in magazines I looked through.

I swallowed and stared at that lightly lined face, at his crow's feet and the lines under his eyes. He was the most handsome man I'd ever seen. It was plain and simple.

"You never said or did anything to let me know you saw me as more than a friend," I explained, making sure we were eye-to-eye.

The German didn't look exactly appeased by my observation. He licked his lips and leaned back against the couch, eyeing me with an expression that was part aggravation and part something else. "What would you have done if I'd said something?"

The hell? "Not believed you." Why would I? We'd been so hot and cold; I never understood what the hell was going through his head.

He raised his eyebrows and nodded. "That's your reason. What would I gain from telling you the first moment I realized you were meant to be mine? Nothing. You're supposed to protect what you love, Sal. You taught me that. I didn't wake up one day and know I didn't want to live without your horrible temper. I saw so much of me in you at first, but you aren't like me at all. You're you, and I will go to my grave before I let anyone change any part of you. I know that without a doubt in my mind. *This*," he pointed between us. "This is what matters. You are my gift, my second chance, and I will cherish you and your dream. I will protect both of you.

"I've been waiting, and I will keep on waiting until the time is right. You are my equal, my partner, my teammate, my best friend. I've done so many stupid things that you've made me regret—things I hope you will forgive me for and look beyond — but *this*, waiting a little longer for the love of my life, I can do.

"You are the most honest, warm, loving person I know. Your loyalty and friendship amazes me every day. I have never wanted anything more in my life than I want your love, and I don't want to share that with anyone. I haven't done a single thing in my life to deserve you, *schnecke,* but I will never give up on you, and I won't let you give up on me."

And wasn't that the shit of it?

Someone could tell you that they loved you every day, but still lie and cheat. Or they could never say those three words, but be there for you every day and be more than you ever wanted or dreamed. He wasn't warm or cuddly, quiet or particularly nice to others, but he was nice to me, and in my heart I knew he would stand by me every time I needed him.

When he left a little later, I lay in my bed and cried two tears. That was it; because it all seemed too good to be true and there were things I hadn't told him that could change how he felt about me.

What would I do if he changed his mind?

* * *

THE PIPERS final game against the Ohio Blazers had finally arrived, and I had the jitters.

"You're going to win, stop worrying."

I blew out a loud breath from my side of the car. He'd offered to have his driver take us to the stadium that afternoon. He didn't have to leave early, the doors didn't open for at least another hour; but Kulti did what Kulti wanted to do and for some reason, he wanted to go at the same time I did.

*You're going to win.*

I was so lucky someone cared about my career so much. Most girls could only wish to be this lucky.

That was the problem though.

As the days counted down toward the big final game, I became more and more nervous. Kulti hadn't acted any differently. He hadn't tried kissing me since that afternoon outside of my car. When he'd come over to my place, we'd do what we always did and in the middle of his visit, he'd ask me how practice went. Twice we went outside and volleyed the ball back and forth, but that had been it. Except for that one night when he said things to me I never could have dreamed up, he'd been the close-mouthed man I was used to spending time with. Before he'd left, he'd promised to give me time and space to think and focus on what was the most important: the final game.

I still couldn't help but ask myself what was going to happen after the game.

What if I didn't get on another team? What if I was injured today? What if I blew my knee out in the off-season? Or the next season?

What would I do then?

The logical part of me knew that I was freaking out about nothing. It wasn't totally unusual. When I was anxious in situations like these, my mind made up a bunch of other crap to stress about too. Of course this thing between Kulti and I was at the top of my list.

It all weighed on my chest like a ticking time bomb.

What if.

What if.

What if.

He nudged my thigh playfully with the back of his balled up hand. "Stop worrying."

"I'm not worried, I'm just thinking about stuff."

"Lies."

I shot him a look and leaned against the seat, thinking and stressing.

He let out a deep sigh. "Tell me what's wrong."

I bit my lips and took in that soft crease between his eyebrows, the color of his eyes, the way the lines that bracketed his mouth deepened in worry. How could I go back to my life if this thing between us didn't work out? I'd been young and angry when I'd had a huge crush on the man I only knew on paper and television. It hadn't been real. But this was real. This Rey was real and kind when he wasn't a major pain in the ass.

I couldn't get rid of the apprehensive knot taking a poop in my stomach. This wasn't a 'what if' I wanted to deal with. So screw it. Maybe the best thing to do would be for me to get this worry over with before the game.

"What's going to happen when I can't play anymore?" I asked him, shoving my hands between my thighs so he couldn't see them shaking.

I heard him shift in his seat. The leather creaked and then continued creaking as he settled in. "What are you babbling about?"

"What are you going to do when I can't play anymore? My knee might only have a few more years left in it. What will happen then?" I asked, eyes going to the roof of the car because there was no way I could handle his face in that moment.

"That's what's stressing you out?" His voice was low and too calm.

"Yeah. Mostly. On top of everything else."

"Sal, look at me." I let my head drop to the side so I could look at him as he spoke. In a plain white T-shirt with a check mark on it, fitted faded jeans and his favorite pair of black and green shoes, he was almost surreal. It just made what I was asking worse.

I was sitting in the backseat of a car with Reiner 'The King' Kulti on the way to the WPL final game, asking him if he was still going to love me once I couldn't play anymore. Good God.

Was I really bringing this crap up now? I changed my mind. I didn't want to know yet.

I didn't want to ever know where our limits stood.

"Sal."

The car slowed to a stop. Behind Kulti's head, the window showed the outline of the entrance I was supposed to be walking through.

"I'm stressed, I'm sorry. We'll talk later, all right?"

He looked at me for what felt like a long time but was more than likely just a few seconds before finally giving me a grave nod, excusing me from the hole I'd dug for myself.

I couldn't breathe, and I needed to focus. My hands were still shaking, and I was more nervous than I'd been since I was a teenager playing in my first U-17 game. Life would still go on regardless of what happened, I reminded myself. Swallowing hard, I smiled at the German. "Wish me luck."

"You don't need it," he responded, his face still ultra-serious.

*Get it together, Sal.* Focus, focus, focus. "Find me after the game?" I asked.

"Yes." He said a word in German I thought meant 'always' but I didn't want to really think about it.

I flashed him a smile and got out of the car. Just as I was about to slam it closed, Kulti piped up, "Focus!"

* * *

THERE ARE some games that I'll sit back and recall like I was a fan in the stands watching the action.

The first half went slow and no one scored. There was nothing memorable about it.

In the second half, a light was burning under both teams' asses. Defense and offense, both teams were on it. The game took a turn for the vicious by the time the fourth yellow card was thrown up; one was Harlow's and one was mine. We hustled, we sweat. We ran and we fought against the Blazers.

And in the last fifteen minutes of the second half, a team scored.

It wasn't us.

We couldn't manage to get a solid hold on the ball at any point afterward.

And we lost. It was that simple.

We freaking lost.

It was like having your dog eat your homework. Losing reminded me of when you're typing something in a document and then your computer restarts on its own. Or baking a cake and it doesn't rise.

Using the word 'crushing' might have been a little extreme, but it was the truth. For me, at least. I was crushed.

Watching the other team yelling and cheering, hugging each other...

Honestly, I wanted to punch each of them in the face and follow that up with a good cry. You don't always win and that's the truth with everything ever, but...

*We lost.*

* * *

I PRESSED my closed fists to the bones above my eyebrows after time had ended. I looked up into the stands; the disappointment was apparent on so many people's faces. I had to look away, watching our fans was chewing up my stomach. Pipers were scattered around the field, looking just as dazed as I felt. No one could believe what had just happened. I definitely couldn't.

I swallowed and realized that this was the last time I'd be on this field.

I choked up.

I'd lost. We'd lost.

My family was in the audience. Marc and Simon were in the crowd someplace. My German was too.

Pressure squeezed my lungs as I made my feet move. They took me away from the opposing players celebrating, oblivious to the inner hell I was going through. The loss was bitter in my mouth and definitely in my soul. I shook a few hands, gave a couple of the girls on the Ohio team a hug and congratulated them on their win.

But Jesus, it was hard.

Everyone deals with loss differently. Some people need consolation, some people get angry, and others want to be left the hell alone. I was the type that needed some space.

If only I'd been faster, or gotten where I was needed instead of being busy taking my frustration out on a player that had tripped me...

I spotted Harlow with her hands clasped behind her head, cursing under her breath. She was still in the same place she'd been when the clock had run out. Jenny was even further away, hugging another Piper who looked like she was crying.

*We'd lost.*

And that loss bubbled in my throat.

"Sal!"

I scratched my cheek and turned around to see one of the opposing players walking toward me. She was a younger girl who had been all over me during the game, quick and creative with her feet. I mustered a smile for her, slowing my retreat into all-out mourning.

"Hey, would you mind trading jerseys with me?" she asked with a sweet grin.

Yeah I was a sore loser, but I wasn't a turd. "Sure, sure," I said, pulling mine up over my head.

"I hope this doesn't make me sound like a total dork," she said, taking her jersey off. "But I love you."

I had just finished taking the sweaty top off when she said it, and I couldn't help but grin a little.

The other player had her hands up over her head, the material around her wrists when she stopped moving. "That came out all wrong. You're a big inspiration for me. I just wanted to let you know. I've been following your career since you were on the U-17 team."

This girl was younger than me, but she didn't look like a teenager either. Hearing that I inspired her… well, it made me feel good. I wasn't any less frustrated or disappointed that we'd lost, but I guess it made it a little bit more bearable.

A little.

"Thank you so much." I handed her my Pipers jersey. "Hey, you've got great footwork, don't think I didn't notice."

She flushed and handed over her red and black top. "Thanks." Someone yelled something and she glanced back, holding up a hand in a 'give me a minute' sign. "I need to get going but really, great game. I'll see you next season."

Next season. Blah. "Yeah, good game. Take care."

Melancholy hit me hard, really hard. *Don't cry. Don't cry. Don't cry.*

I wasn't going to cry, damn it. I never cried when we lost, at least not since I'd been a little kid.

"Sal!" My dad's voice cut through a hundred others.

Two quick looks around, several more "to the right!" shouts from him and I spotted my family. Dad's upper body was hanging over the barrier, hands planted to keep him from falling onto the field as he yelled while my mom and sister stood behind him. Ceci looked embarrassed.

I sniffed and made my way over, scrounging up a smile that could only be meant for them. There were other people yelling out my name and I waved, but I walked as fast as I could toward my family, needing to get off the field before the presentation of the championship trophy began.

Grabbing the first rungs of the barrier, I hoisted myself up to plant my feet on the concrete foundation and stood up, getting wrapped in a hug the instant I was standing. "You couldn't have done any better," Dad said in Spanish, straight into my ear.

*Don't cry.*

"Thanks, *Pa.*"

"You're always my MVP," he added as he pulled away, hands on my shoulders. His smile was sad for a moment before he squeezed my shoulders and made a face. "Have you been working out more? Your shoulders are bigger than mine."

That only made me want to cry even more, and the noise that came out of my mouth let him know how hard this moment was for me.

My mom finally pushed my dad to the side with a huff. "You played so well," she said in Spanish, kissing my cheek. Her eyes were watery, and I couldn't begin to imagine what was going through her head. She never said anything, but I knew big games like this were always hard on her. Things with my grandpa were an open wound that I wasn't sure would ever heal.

"*Gracias, mami.*" I kissed her cheek in return.

She patted my face and took a step back.

My little sister on the other hand just stood there with her usual smart-ass smirk on her face, shrugging her thin shoulders. "Sorry you lost."

From her, I would take what I could get. "Thanks for coming, Ceci." I gave her the best smile I could while I tried dealing with how I'd let everyone down.

The noises on the field were getting louder, and I knew I needed to get off the field as soon as possible. "I should go before they start. I'll see you tomorrow, okay?"

They knew me well enough to know that I needed the night

to decompress and get over this. One night. I'd give myself a night to be angry.

Dad agreed and gave me another hug before I dropped back onto the field and hustled toward the exit leading to the locker rooms. A few of the Pipers were standing around the doorway. Some of them were crying, some comforting each other, but they were the girls that had been talking about me the last few weeks. Not in the mood to deal with my teammates' crap, I kept walking past them, ignoring their looks as much as they had ignored me lately.

"What did I tell you? A fucking robot, man," Genevieve's voice carried through the concrete walls.

We'd fucking lost and I didn't have any feelings. Fantastic.

*Don't cry.*

Security guards and other personnel dotted the hallway. I shook a few of their hands and let them give me pats on the back. I sniffled to myself, letting the disappointment flare through me again. I knew I'd be fine. This wasn't the first big game I'd lost. Unfortunately, it was one that had taken months to work toward with so many obstacles along the way, and with Kulti so predominant in the process, it seemed so much more painful than usual.

If only I'd done better. Been the player everyone expected me to be.

"*Schnecke.*"

I jerked to a stop and glanced up. Making his way toward me from the opposite end of the hall was the tall lean figure that I wasn't sure I wanted to see yet. There were other players walking ahead of me, and he ignored them as they tried to speak to him. He didn't even pay them a second glance, which was unbelievably rude, but it made me shake my head when I was fighting for my dignity. I couldn't even wrestle up my Big Girl Socks.

Kulti stopped the second he was about a foot away. His big

body was solid and unmoving, and his face that perfect mask of careful control that didn't give me a hint of what was going on in his big German head. It only made me feel more awkward, more uncertain, more frustrated that we hadn't won.

Setting his hands on his hips, pulling his shirt tight against his pectoral muscles, he blinked. "You have two options," he explained, sizing me up. "Would you like to break something or would you like a hug?" he asked in a completely serious tone.

I blinked at him and then licked my lips before pressing them together. We'd lost and here he was asking me if I needed to break something or if I needed a stinking hug. Tears pooled in my eyes, and I blinked more and more as my throat clogged up. "Both?"

His facial expression still didn't change. "I don't have anything for you to break right now, but when we leave..."

It was the 'we' that got me.

The 'we' that convinced me to throw my arms around his waist and hug him so close later on I'd wonder how he managed to breathe. He didn't even hesitate wrapping his arms around the tops of my shoulders, his head tipping down so that his mouth was right by my ear. "Don't cry."

The tears just poured out. My frustration, my disappointment, my embarrassment all went right for it. Every insecurity was present. "I'm sorry," I told him in a watery voice.

"For what?"

Oh my God, my nose was running faster than I was capable of keeping up with. My heartbreak right there on display. "For disappointing you," I forced myself to say. My shoulders were shaking with suppressed hiccups.

His head moved, his mouth edging closer toward my ear. Those big muscular arms tightened around me. "You could never disappoint me." Did his voice sound strange or was I imagining it? "Not in this life, Sal."

Yeah, that didn't help at all. Jesus Christ. My nose turned

into a running faucet. "Is this real? Are you real? Am I going to wake up tomorrow and see that the season hasn't even started and these last four months have been a dream?" I asked him.

"It's very real," he said in that same strange voice.

What a wonderful thing and a very sad thing at the same time.

I could hear footsteps getting louder around us as they echoed in the hallway, but I couldn't find it in me to give a single microscopic shit who was approaching and what they would think.

"I really wanted to win."

His answer was to rub my back, his fingers sliding beneath the thick straps of my sports bra.

"I hate losing," I told him like he didn't completely understand, pressing my face deeper between his pecs. "And they think I don't care that we lost. Why would someone think I'm a robot?"

Kulti just kept right on rubbing, his fingers cool and rough on my damp skin.

I sniffed. "And now you're stuck here, and I didn't even win. I'm so sorry, Rey."

His fingers burrowed even deeper under my sports bra, the seams popping in protest of what he was doing as his palm lay flush against my skin. "You aren't going anywhere without me."

Say what? I reared my head back enough to look at his face, indifferent to how much of a wreck I had to be. "But you told—"

Kulti's face was gentle. His eyes were brighter than ever. "I have so much to teach you, Taco," he said with a flick of his eyebrow. "Unless you have something in writing, there would never be proof of an agreement to begin with."

This ruthless shit. I should have been shocked that he lied to Cordero, but I wasn't. Not at all. I laughed but it was one of those laughs that you let out so you didn't keep crying. "You're such an asshole." But I loved him anyway.

His mouth tipped up, just barely. "Ready to leave?"

I nodded, cleared my drowning throat and took a step back. "Let me get my things first. I don't want to be here anymore."

I hesitated for one second as we turned and spotted some of the girls staring. They must have been the group that just passed us. This hard ball of resolve formed in my belly, and I slipped my fingers through Kulti's.

Screw it. The season was over. I was done, tapped out.

I grabbed his hand, and he smiled.

We'd taken maybe eight steps when he asked, "Who called you a robot?" in such a sweet, sincere voice it was easy to believe it was a casual question.

But I knew him too well, and by that point, I didn't even care. "It doesn't matter."

"It matters," he replied in that same tone. "Was it the same player that told Cordero about you calling me a bratwurst?"

I stopped walking so abruptly it took him a step to realize it. "You know who told him?"

"The nosey one. Gwenivere," he replied.

"Genevieve?" I coughed.

"Her."

My eye. My eye twitched. Freaking Genevieve? "Your manager told you?"

He nodded.

I swallowed. Unbelievable. What a backstabbing bitch. Holy shit.

"Your face says enough," he said, tugging me back to continue walking. "I'll wait for you out here."

I smiled at the small group and gave his palm a quick squeeze before disappearing into the mostly empty locker room. I should have stayed, listened to Gardner talk about the season, but I couldn't. I grabbed all of my things, stuffed them into my duffel bag and left. Tomorrow I would go back and return what wasn't mine. I could also see Jenny and Harlow before they left to go home.

I found Kulti standing against a wall giving Genevieve and the other girls standing by the door a look that could have boiled someone's flesh right off. I wasn't going to ask. I raised my eyebrows at him, and just before we took off, I smiled over at the women, choosing one word and one word only: "Bye."

*Have a good life*, I added in my head. I had high hopes I would.

"Come on," Kulti murmured, leading me through the group of reporters crowding the exit.

He shouldered them out of the way, and I kept walking, not giving a crap that I should have said something to them. It seemed to take a year to make it to his car.

I slid in first, watching as he followed after me, pressing that long, muscular build against mine. His arm slipped over my shoulder as he angled into me, smothering me with his broad chest. That was all he did. He didn't tell me not to keep being disappointed or angry. Kulti didn't tell me everything would be fine. Kulti just kept on holding me until we made it to my garage apartment.

Wordlessly, we went up the stairs and he unlocked the door. He dumped my bag in its usual spot. I told him I was going to shower. The next few minutes all seemed like a blurry dream, and I took a lot longer than usual. By the time I finished, I was proud of myself for not crying more than I had. I mean, grown men cried in football when they lost, it would have been fine for me to bawl too...

If I was a baby.

I'd cried enough at the stadium.

It wasn't the end of the world. It really wasn't. I would keep telling myself that until I got over it.

Kulti was waiting in the kitchen when I finally ambled out

of my bathroom. He shot me a look over his shoulder as he scraped something out of a skillet and onto two plates. "Sit."

Taking a seat at one of the two barstools at the counter, he slid a plate of mixed veggies, sliced sausage and rice to me. Neither one of us said much as we sat together eating. I felt somber and a bit depressed, and I figured he was just giving me space to mope a bit. I'd have to ask him another day how he dealt with these things.

When we finished, he took our dishes and set them in the sink with a small, tight smile. He went and sat on the couch, leaving me alone in the kitchen. I'm not sure how long I sat there but after feeling pretty miserable, I finally got up and made my way to the living room to see him sitting in the middle, going through one of my dollar-store Sudoku books. As soon as he saw me, he set it aside.

Kulti pulled me onto his lap.

It happened so quickly I couldn't really focus on anything. His mouth dropped to mine, which had already parted in anticipation.

That split second of anticipation was nothing compared to the actual deed. His mouth was warm and supple, willing and demanding as he dragged his tongue across my bottom lip. I did what any other sane person would have done; I opened my mouth. His tongue tasted faintly like the spearmint he chewed on sometimes as it brushed against mine: once, twice, over and over again, thirsty and needy. He was crushing me to his body as our kisses got deeper, rougher, almost bruising. They were devouring.

Holy crap, I loved it.

The game and the loss became a memory and a worry for another time.

My hands reached for his sides, stroking his ribs before drifting to his waist. His hands had a mind of their own, one going straight for the back of my head, burying deep into the thick, wet hair I'd thrown up into a knot. His other hand reached for my jaw, cradling it. I took the time to suck his tongue into my mouth, greedy and selfish. It was too much and not enough.

I wasn't the only one who thought it. Kulti used his arms to hold me to him. His grip was desperate, like he wanted to crawl inside of me. Something big and hard brushed against my hip as he held me. Oh my God. Oh my God.

Years had passed since the last time I'd had a boyfriend. It had been many, many years since I'd put relationships on hold to focus on my career. So this was… I didn't even think twice before dipping my fingers under the hem of his shirt, my thumbs brushing the soft skin there.

What did he do? He jerked away from me, just an inch, only an inch, pulling his shirt over his head and putting my hands back at his sides. I ran them up his ribs, over his back and shoulders, feeling, feeling, feeling. God, he was so muscular, his laterals rippled under my touch.

"You smell like oatmeal, clean and sweet…" he rumbled, sucking my earlobe into his mouth.

It didn't matter that he was still technically my coach until what? Midnight? Or that he was a celebrity of sorts and that I got rude emails from his fans. All that mattered was that he was my friend above all else, and he made my blood boil like no other person in the world ever had. I couldn't get enough.

Kulti pressed his chest to mine with a savage growl, his fingers pinching the thin material of my tank top in frustration. In one move that I really didn't want to think about because it was so effortless, Kulti yanked my shirt and sports bra over my head, tossing them aside.

Oh jeez. Oh jeez. I managed to kiss his throat and that soft place where his shoulder met his neck before he pulled back enough to look at my breasts. His breathing became even more ragged than before, which said something for a man who used to sprint up and down a soccer field for a living. He swallowed, his lips parted, and I could have sworn the bulge at my hip jumped.

The German shifted me with those big hands, pulling me across to straddle his hips as his mouth dipped down to catch a nipple between his lips. He gave the flesh a suck. Good lord, he sucked hard. I moaned. I moaned and arched into him, rubbing at the hard, thick shaft nestled between my legs.

He cursed in his low German accent before pulling away far enough to kiss the freckles that ended right above my nipples. I couldn't stop looking. I couldn't. It was so *hot*. I was panting, he was panting. His hands tried to circle my waist, to pull me up even closer to his mouth.

Something insane and deceptive and tempting streaked through my body, and I went for it. Fuck it. My fingers fumbled at his waist, at the button of his jeans, wanting him now. I'd spent most of my life trying to be a good girl, accepting that I wasn't made for anything that wasn't worthwhile. As I dug my knees into the cushions of the couch on either side of his hips, trying to get him to help me out so that I could unzip his jeans, he groaned and thrust his hips up. Down they went, the broad dome of his erection peeking out from beneath the elastic band of his underwear.

The groan that broke through Kulti's mouth, mixed with my own wild beg. My "Please" that sounded like a cry, was a predecessor for him wrapping his arms around me and pulling me in close. The short hairs on his chest rubbed my nipples.

"Please," I begged him again.

His answer was to pull back once more and dip his head down low enough so that he could take as much of a breast into his mouth as he could. His hand slipped into the back of my shorts and underwear, skin to skin, palm to cheek. Long fingers trailed down and over the cleft of my ass, lightly brushing over a spot that had me jumping in place before he even reached where I wanted him. His fingertips swept over the two damp lips, and I made an awful, wonderful noise in my throat.

"What do you need, *schnecke*?" he asked, rubbing a finger in the crease between my cleft and thigh. "You are so wet. Do you want my fingers in you?"

I was going to freaking die.

"Tell me. Do you want my fingers in your warm pussy?" he asked me, eyeing me with wide, bright eyes that lingered over my face as he touched the sensitive skin.

I begged him twice before he finally slipped a finger inside of me.

He dipped so slowly, I thought I would pass out before he pulled back. I started moaning, rolling my hips as his pace increased steadily. His other arm wrapped low around my back to keep me close, our mouths finding each other's. We kissed and kissed, and he moved his fingers over and over again.

It was the single most sensual thing I'd ever experienced. All I could feel was the warmth of his chest on mine, his arm around me, his mouth pressed to mine, his finger inside. I rocked my hips and then rocked them faster, my breath splintering, chopping itself into pieces, building me higher and higher.

Pulling his mouth away from mine, he trailed wet kisses across my jaw. His lips were at my ear, his thumb circling my clit. "You belong to me."

A shiver up my spine was the only warning I got from the orgasm coming.

I came. I came and I came and I came.

My legs trembled and my stomach muscles jumped. The entire time, the German kissed my shoulders and my neck. He held me, kissed me and he rubbed his hand over the small of my back.

What felt like half an hour later but was more than likely only a couple of minutes, I slowly settled down to rest my bottom on Kulti's lap, taking a couple of deep, steadying breaths. His hand had slipped out of my panties and at some point, he'd started cupping my ass. I slumped forward and pressed my forehead to his neck, feeling his pulse thundering away. I gripped his sides and let my thumbs rub up and down his ribs, his proud erection nestled right between us, a purple head staring straight at me, weeping.

I slid one hand down and across the rippled muscles in his abdomen, and with the backs of my fingers, ran a line down the underside of his shaft over the cotton material of his boxer briefs. He took in a quick intake of breath, his hips bucking beneath mine. I looked at his face as I did it again, this time up and down, the muscle jumping beneath my touch. Kulti's mouth was parted, a deep flush over his cheeks and neck.

I jerked the waistband of his underwear toward me and slipped a hand inside, wrapping my fingers around the hot flesh. What I got in return was a groan, and Kulti tipping his head back as he made just about the sexiest face to ever register on the sexy scale. I leaned forward and bit the part of his throat between his Adam's apple and chin, the German making a hoarse, erotic noise in his throat.

He was thicker than I expected, longer than I would have imagined. Smooth, hard and hot. Kulti was perfect in my hand. Beyond perfect. And I moved my hand up and down the length staring me right in the face from two feet below. I squeezed as I jerked him off.

It was more visual memory from the hundreds of soft-core porn movies I'd occasionally caught on late night cable that reminded me what to do.

"Does this feel good?" I asked him, sliding my bottom back on his legs a little further away.

"You have no idea," he grunted, neck straining as I tightened my grip at the base of him.

I mean, I sort of did, but whatever. Now wasn't the time to argue.

With my heart pounding in my throat, I kept one hand around him while I slid down his legs. He watched me with those heavy-lidded amber eyes, his breathing getting heavier and heavier until he gasped when I wrapped my mouth around the pinkish-purple tip of his head.

"Sal!" he shouted.

One pointed tongue on his frenulum and one more swift suck, and Kulti was letting out a deep, ravaging groan that I'd remember forever, pouring himself down my throat.

Holy shit.

I sat up completely, wrapping an arm around my breasts as I sat there, taking in his breathless, handsome face almost twenty years after I'd first fallen in love with it. The sun, time and life had made him classier.

The thought weighed my conscience down.

Kulti stroked my arm with one hand. "It's been a long time," he apologized, tracing a pattern only he saw on my skin. "And you're too beautiful for your own good."

I screwed up my face and snorted a little, not letting myself think of all the gorgeous women he'd been with over the years.

He slid his index finger straight up between my collarbones, a thoughtful look on his features that didn't make me feel any better. Was he remembering all of the amazing boobs he'd seen in his life? Gross.

"What are you thinking?" he asked, his fingertip curving over bones, tendons and scars.

"About all the boobs you've seen before," I told him honestly, my throat clogging up in anger I had no right to feel.

He glanced up quicker than I thought was possible, his mouth tight at the corners in a frown.

"I know I don't have a right to say anything about things that happened before we met, but it's a little hard for me. If something isn't to par, think about my scissor kick. I've heard some guys tell me it's boner-worthy," I offered with a smile.

The frown on his face melted right off. "Sal."

"I'm just kidding. Mostly." I sighed and shrugged my shoulders. What was I doing? I needed to tell him the truth.

With a sigh, I stood up and pulled my bra on.

Fingers touched my lower back. "What's wrong?"

What was wrong? Bah. Why hadn't I told him yet? He needed to know. It made me feel like a fake after everything that had happened. "I need to tell you something."

"What?"

I started to reach for my shirt when he swung his legs off the couch and stopped me with a hand to my arm.

Sitting up straight, I tucked my hands between my thighs, elbows tight to my sides and focused my gaze on my knees. I tried to think of the words I'd planned since my dad had accused me of being a chicken. Not sounding like a stalker was a lot harder than it seemed, especially when I could still taste him in my mouth.

What if—

No what-ifs. I just needed to do it. I really did.

"I used to have a huge crush on you when I was a kid," I started, warming him up. "Up until I was about seventeen, there were posters of you all over my room. " In for a penny, in for a pound. All right. I could do this. Honesty mattered. "I was in love with you. I told everyone I was going to marry you someday.

"You were my idol, Rey. I kept playing soccer because of you."

I rubbed my hand over my eyebrow, still keeping my gaze forward on the coffee table. It wasn't like I was telling him something crazy. Every girl I'd ever known had crushed on a celebrity at some point, but... I'd just had his penis in my mouth. I should have told him earlier. I should have told him a long time ago.

Pressing down on my eyebrow, I kept going. "I should have told you before but I didn't want to. It took me long enough to talk to you, and by the time I could do it like a normal person and not like a fan-girl, I didn't want to. I didn't want you to look at me differently. I *don't* want you to. I'm sorry. It was a long time ago and I'd been just a kid back then."

There was silence. Total silence.

And I thought to myself, *this is over.* Our friendship was done. Any hope I had of... well, that was done with too. But what could I do? Nothing. I couldn't take it back. When I was a kid, I had no idea I'd ever meet Reiner Kulti, much less become friends with him. I definitely had no idea that I would ever fall in love with the human version of him, the real man. Unfortunately, you can't turn back time and change the past.

Then again, would I want to? I'd gotten to where I was because I'd idolized him, because I had wanted to be him. What the hell else would I be doing if it hadn't been for him and that damn Altus Cup when I was seven?

Goosebumps rose up on my arms as I sat straight and lunged for my shirt again, pulling it on as the German shifted in his seat right next to me.

I had just tugged it down over my stomach when he shoved his cell phone into my hand with a single order. "Look."

Big Girl Socks on, I cast a single glance at his face but he had that same blank expression, the cool one. I looked down at what he was showing me on the screen. It was a picture of something.

"Take a closer look."

I took the phone from him and brought it up to my face, enlarging the image to see what he wanted to show me. It was a picture of a picture. Well, of a drawing to be exact. It was an orange sheet of construction paper with big, black words written in a little kid's handwriting.

Wait a second.

I looked even closer, blowing up the image more.

It was the little kid version of my handwriting.

**Dear Mr. Kulti,**

**You are my favorite player. I play soccer 2 butt I'm not good like you are. Not yet. I practice all the time so 1 day I can be just like you or beter. I watch all of ur games so don't mess up.**

**Ur #1 fan,**

**Sal**

**<3 <3 <3**

**P.S. Do u have a girl friend?**

**P.P.S. Why don't u cut ur hair?**

"I was nineteen when that showed up to the club's offices. It was my third fan letter ever and the other two were topless pictures," he said in his low, steady voice. "That letter stayed in every locker I used for the next ten years. It was the first thing I looked at before my games, and the first thing I saw after I played. I framed it and put it in my house in Meissen once it started to wear out. It's still there on the wall of my bedroom."

Oh my God.

"You didn't put a return address on the envelope, you know. It only had your street's name and Texas on it. I was never able to write you back because it wouldn't have made it, but I would have, Sal," he said.

Looking at the picture reminded me so clearly of writing it, so many years ago.

He had kept it.

"I still have the three others you sent me."

If I was someone who swooned, or whatever kind of crap happened to people when they were in shock, I would have been doing it. This was... there was no word for what this was.

"Did you know it was me when you took the position here?" I asked, still looking at the picture.

"No. I didn't realize it until you introduced yourself in Gardner's office. I couldn't believe it. I knew your last name from the videos of your playing but I didn't know your first name," he explained. "I only remembered your first name from your letters."

Good grief.

"So you've always known?" My voice cracked a little at the last word.

"Did I know you'd been my number one fan once?" he asked, nudging my rib enough so that I looked up at him. A gentle look replaced his harsh, usually brooding features. "Yes, I knew. If I would have paid attention the first day of practice, I would have figured it out sooner. And then you cussed me out—"

"I did not cuss you out."

"—and I understood that you'd grown up." Kulti rubbed my lower back. "I take so much pride in knowing you've become the player you are because you looked up to me, Sal. It's the greatest compliment I've ever been paid."

Bah.

He kept right on going, oblivious to my heart shooting off fireworks. "I've met enough people in my life that I can recognize who wants to know me for the right reason and for the wrong reason. I have trust issues, you know that. It took me time to figure out that you were someone I could trust, but it didn't take that long. I know *you*. I know that someone who will defend her father and risk losing her career is someone I can trust, someone that I can respect. Loyalty is one of the most precious things I've ever encountered. You don't know the things people would do to get ahead, and I would bet my life you would never turn your back on anyone that needed you.

"Every single thing that has ever happened in my life has

led me here, Sal. Destiny is a ladder, a series of steps that takes you where you're supposed to go. I am the man that I am, and I have done the things that I've done, to get me to you."

What do you say to that? To a man that kept your childhood letter for half a lifetime and mentioned you and destiny in the same sentence?

I bit the inside of my cheek and leveled a look at him. "Are you sure you don't care? I used to kiss your posters. Now that I think about it, I'm really surprised no one in my family spilled the beans and said something."

Rey palmed my face. "Not at all."

## 27

"I was really sad to hear you ladies lost last night," the front desk employee said as he handed me a visitor's pass.

I'd have to give myself a pat on the back later for not even wincing at the reminder. Somehow I managed to shrug, pinning the pass to the bottom of my T-shirt. That damn Pipers and Wreckers mural above the desk taunted me. "Me too."

"I'm sure y'all will get 'em next year, don't you worry about it," the nice man suggested as I put my bag over my shoulder to go through security and up the elevator.

"Hope so. Thanks," I told him before giving him another smile and continuing up the stairs.

Really, I did hope the Pipers would win next season. It would be great for them.

All right, I'd be fine if they didn't, but I wouldn't be mad if they did.

I'd been doing a lot of thinking since talking to Rey the night before, and even though I wanted to vomit at the insecure point my life was in, I realized I really was doing the best thing for me by leaving the WPL. If it were up to Cordero and the rest of the coaches who hadn't given me a second thought, I would never play for another Altus Cup.

Or screw it, for a gold medal. Why not?

If I moved, played somewhere else and got my nationality...

*Why not?*

*If* I moved. But I wasn't going to worry or psych myself out too much. Things happened if they were meant to happen and if they didn't, I'd figure out something else.

What I was doing now was moving on with this stage in my life, and I was surprisingly more than okay with it.

I found the equipment manager's office halfway down the hall on the Pipers floor. She was inside and looked a little surprised to see me, but she took my things and said she'd see me later. So apparently, the news hadn't gotten around that I was out.

This was all was totally fine. There was only one other person I'd want to see before I left, and his office was two doors down. It sure as hell wasn't Cordero either. I had no interest in seeing that miserable man ever again. Plus I wasn't sure if he was aware Rey had lied about rejoining the team or not, and I didn't want to hear about it. His part with me was done. The German had already assured me once more that I didn't have to worry about him. His money gave him a great legal team, so he said.

Legal team. Jesus. That's what I'd gotten myself into. He didn't just have a lawyer, but a whole legal team. God.

You only live once, right?

Gardner was in his office with the door open when I stopped by. I knocked twice. He looked only slightly frazzled as he typed away on his keyboard, frowning when he saw it was me. "Sal. Come in," he waved me forward. "Shut the door."

I closed the door behind me and took a seat across from him, hands on my knees.

"Where were you last night?" he asked first thing.

"I left right after the game. Sorry. I just wasn't in the mood," I explained truthfully, taking in his tired features. "Are you all right?"

He rolled his eyes. "Same old hell as usual from Cordero, it's nothing I wasn't expecting. You? Hold on, what are you doing here?"

I gave him a small smile. "I came to drop off my things with the EM, and to tell you bye."

Gardner leaned forward. "Where are you going?"

This was the whole reason I was here. I really did like Gardner, but I didn't want to be a blubbering mess. "I'm leaving the team. My contract was bought out a few days ago. As of midnight, I'm a free agent."

The man, who had coached me for the last four years and ninety-eight percent of the time been fair and understanding, looked like I punched him in the gut. Sure he'd tried to bench me in the semi-final, but I knew that was Cordero's doing. I wouldn't forget four years of friendship with Gardner for one moment. "I don't understand. You had a year left with us. Are you that angry about the semi that you bought your contract out?"

He knew damn well I couldn't afford to buy my contract out.

"I'm not leaving because of you, G. I swear." I'd already decided not to tell him about Cordero trying to trade me because really, what was the point? It didn't matter. "It's just time for a change of pace. Cordero hates my guts more than ever and half the girls on the team..." The word robot bounced around in my head for a second before I thought of this new opportunity in my life with green-brown eyes. "It hasn't been easy for a little while. I can't stay when they don't respect me."

"Fuck, Sal." His hands went to rest flat on his desk. "You're not kidding?"

"Nope."

It took him a long time to finally say something else. "Do you know what you're going to do now?"

I would have loved to have told him I'd already gotten signed with another team. I really would have. The fact was I hadn't. I had no solid clue what I was doing. "I'm not sure yet, but this isn't the end. I just wanted to drop by and tell you thank you for everything. Keep in touch. Good luck. I've loved working with you, and I think you're great." I raised my shoulders up and let them drop. "Promise to email me even if it's just to complain about the girls?"

Later on I'd realize that Gardner took it about as well as Marc had: plain shitty. That's how well he took the news. He took it really shitty.

He promised to keep in touch and wished me the best as always. That was the last thing we said to each other before I left his office.

I made ten feet before a feminine voice called out, "Sal!" and Sheena came barreling out of the assistant coach's office she'd been in a second before.

"Hey, Sheena," I greeted her.

"Hey, hi. Sorry to come running out, but I wanted to talk to you before you left. You are leaving, right?" I nodded, unsure whether she was talking about leaving the team or leaving the office. "I won't take your time then, but these pictures popped up last night of you and Mr. Kulti after the game. They aren't good—"

"I'm sorry, Sheena. I don't mean to cut you off but," I gave her a tight grin, "it doesn't matter. The pictures don't matter."

"They look bad, Sal. I know the league, and they're going to be giving Cordero a call to complain pretty soon if they haven't already," she explained. "They're more than likely going to want a statement from you apologizing—"

Apologizing? I shook my head. "No. I'm not doing it and they can't make me."

"But—"

"No." Dear God, I sounded like Rey. "I'm not going to." She'd find out soon enough why. In the meantime... "I have a question for you real quick. Whatever happened to that video of the press conference you were going to release? You never said anything to me about it again."

From her facial expression, it looked like she wanted to keep going on about the pictures of Rey and I, but decided to answer my question instead. "We didn't release it. Mr. Kulti had final approval and he demanded we shelve it. He said we would be humiliating you and he didn't want to do that. I thought you knew? He bought the footage from the news stations so no one could do anything with them."

# 28

**Snippet of the Transcript of the Press Conference (Back in April)**

KCNB REPORTER: Miss Casillas, how do you feel about having a player like Reiner Kulti coaching your team this season?

CASILLAS: I think it's great. He's the best soccer player in the world. His ball handling is fantastic, his on-the-spot play-making is unbelievable, the power behind his striking is incomparable and he's a great penetrator. We have a lot of girls on the team that could... did I just use the word penetrator?

KSXN REPORTER: You did.

CASILLAS: [silence] Is that even allowed on television? That word? Can I say that?

KCNB REPORTER: I don't believe we can use it.

CASILLAS: I'm so sorry. Really. I don't think I've ever used that word in my life. I guess I've taken too many balls to my face... fuck my life, did I just... Oh God. I used the 'F' word and I said I've taken a lot of balls to my face in one sentence. I don't...

GARDNER: [cracking up] Sal...
CASILLAS: I'm just going to shut up now.

# 29

"We'll have breakfast in the morning?" Dad asked. We'd just had a late dinner out, following an afternoon spent at my apartment.

I nodded. "Yes. I promise."

Dad eyed me critically. "You'll call me if you hear anything from your agent?"

It was ten o'clock at night. I highly doubted she was going to call me before the next morning, but I kept my mouth closed. My dad seemed more nervous than I was about everything now that the season was over, and I didn't want to fuel the fire. One of us with indigestion was bad enough. "Promise."

"Okay." He smiled over at me. "I'll see you in the morning then." One more hug and he whistled over to where Rey stood next to their car, talking to my mom while Ceci sat inside, the glow from her cell illuminating her face. "*Amor, estas lista?*"

Mom had to have rolled her eyes considering she was the one who'd been standing by the car waiting for him for the last five minutes. "*Ya vamonos. Salomé, dame un abrazo.*"

Snorting under my breath, I walked back and gave her the hug she just demanded, knocking on the window to wave at

Ceci. I could see Mom and Dad arguing inside and a second later, the driver side window rolled down possibly an inch. I'm pretty sure the words, "Bye, Kulti," were mumbled out a second before the window was rolled back up and my dad pulled the car away and out of the lot.

"I'm pretty sure my dad told you bye," I laughed.

The German had a small smile on his face. "I believe so."

Dad hadn't said a word to him during dinner, using me as a workaround to ask him questions. He was a freaking lunatic. "At this rate it'll be six months before he shakes your hand and a year before he asks you how you're doing."

"I'm in no rush," he said, giving me a nudge.

I nudged him back. "*Listo?*" I asked him in Spanish if he was ready. His Audi was parked two rows down.

"*Si*," he nodded, grabbing my hand.

Him speaking Spanish... Dear God. It would never get old.

We made our way to the car and got into the back. The driver must have turned it on when we'd walked out of the restaurant because the inside was nice and cool. Rey slid in after me, draping an arm over my shoulder. I tipped my head up to whisper, "I'm curious, when can you apply to get your license back?"

"In two months," he replied, looking down at me.

"Are you going to get a new one?"

Rey raised a single shoulder. "If we're here."

*If we're here*. The togetherness of his statement sent a chill down my spine. Two weeks ago, I would have laughed if someone told me I'd be sitting in the back of Rey's Audi with his arm around me, talking about him following me to a different country. Yet here we were, and it made me feel so lame that I couldn't find it in me to put up more of a fight. "You really will come with me?" I asked. "Even if I end up in Poland?"

"You won't end up in Poland but if you did, then yes, I would still go with you." He nudged me.

"What are you going to do? I don't want you to get bored or hate me—"

"I can do whatever I want. I've enjoyed my career and nothing would make me happier than to see you enjoy yours. Understand?" Rey raised his thick, brown eyebrows at me, as his hand slid all the way down until he reached my bare thigh. "I don't see how I could get bored when I'll have to keep you out of starting fights all the time."

"Oh please." I laughed.

"You're a troublemaker, *schnecke*." He grinned, the rough calluses on his fingertips brushed over my kneecaps as he shifted in his seat to get a better reach.

Rolling my eyes, I shook my head. "Whatever. I just want you to be happy. I think I can handle your circus—"

"You can and you will," he cut me off, trailing a line down my shin with his fingertips. His entire body was angled toward mine.

I barely restrained myself from rolling my eyes. "But I want to make sure you can handle mine."

Those swamp-colored eyes seemed to swallow me whole. His fingers went over my calf, squeezing the muscle lightly. His big hand kneaded my calf again. "There is nothing I'm not willing to do for you."

I was suddenly so thankful I'd put on one of my nicer dressy shorts instead of jeans. I shivered, arching my back without even realizing it. He was the one that made my chest tighten. The person whose face both seemed to be able to make me scream in anger, and within days make me feel like I was living a dream.

"Sal," he drawled in a low rumble, sucking me out of my quiet admiration. His hand crawled back up my leg and onto my thigh, slowly slinking up the material of my shorts to caress the skin there. Kulti squeezed the meaty, muscular part of my hamstring before shifting me forward on the seat so that his fingers could slide even deeper into the confines of my bottoms.

I hissed when the tips of his fingers grazed my bare ass, dipping under the damp cotton of my underwear. "Rey, wait."

"No," he said, toying with the band. "I've waited long enough."

"Your driver can hear us," I whispered, way too self-conscious about the man sitting three feet away.

He let out a grunt that I took as acceptance until his mouth covered mine, a deep groan rattled in his chest. Hot wet lips grazed over my parted ones as he gripped my leg tightly. It was endless. His full mouth was the Pacific Ocean; it was huge and dark and wide and so, so easy to get lost in. The little pleased noises he was making sucked me out into his ocean even deeper.

He pulled away for a minute, swiping his hot tongue over my lip. He moved his hand to grip the width of my thigh, pulling my legs apart. "He has headphones in," he said against my skin, pressing those perfect, straight white teeth into my skin. Kulti dragged his teeth over the curve of my jaw and the column of my throat, where he paused and bit gently.

I sucked in a breath and jerked away just a little, conscious of the driver who seemed to be minding his own business, but… "Rey, I showered early this morning. I probably smell."

Rey took a quick inhale that had me break out in a shiver, the tip of his nose a brush on my neck. "You don't." I would have sworn the tip of his tongue touched my skin.

Oh my.

My hips shifted forward in the seat on their own, searching for his hand, for his groin, anything and everything, while he moved down to bite where my neck and shoulder met. "I need you, Sal."

Jesus Christ. Jesus freaking Christ. I couldn't help but eye the driver.

Rey nipped at my earlobe. “He can't hear.” The hand that had been on top of my thigh slid up and under my shorts so fast, I didn't even get a chance to mentally prepare myself for the thumb brushing over the seam of my body through my underwear. His mouth covered mine again, sucking my bottom lip between his as his finger grazed over the material covering my clit. Rey made a noise in his throat as he slipped one of his fingers under my panties to graze against my lips with the back of his digit. He did it once, twice, three times. I knew I was turned on, really turned on despite being self-conscious about our location.

He brushed over my lower lips one last time, sliding his finger out of my underwear. Gaze on mine, Rey brought his fingers to his mouth. Those brown-green eyes were locked on me as he licked his index and middle finger slowly. A smile crept across his face. “I'm going to need another taste.” He licked his fingers once more.

I was going to go into cardiac arrest.

The car pulled into my driveway, and the second it was in park, Rey put my clothes back into place right before he linked his fingers through mine and pulled me out of the car. My keys were handed over for him to unlock the door. We'd barely gone inside when he leaned down to fuse his soft lips to mine, kissing me gently. He towered over me. His hands gripped my hips loosely, thumbs pressing into my bones.

“I want you,” he murmured against my mouth. “More than I have ever wanted anything...” He kissed the edge of my lips. “Are you sure you want this?” he asked, pressing his lips to my neck again.

Was I sure I was a woman? Or that I liked sunny days and chocolate-covered strawberries?

I arched against him. “I'm positive.”

“Yes? You understand what you're getting yourself into?” He gave my neck a light bite that had me shaking in his arms.

Did I understand that nothing would ever be the same? That I was probably giving up my privacy and life as I knew it if this—us—didn't burst into flames?

Yeah, I knew. But I knew that I loved him, and I didn't give my heart away willingly. Like he'd said, life had worked to bring us to this point. Why should I start counting down the days now?

Most importantly I knew he'd done all the things I would ever want from someone I loved. He protected me, supported me, he was giving, and he worked hard. He was loyal. You don't throw away something like that even if it isn't perfect and effortless. As cheesy as it was, the best things in life aren't easy or cheap. I didn't eat fast food because I knew I could go home and make a nutritious meal instead. I could have used cardio as my only exercise, but I wanted my body to be in the best shape possible, so I did a variety of different exercises. Why wouldn't love be the same way?

"I know, Rey," I said, wrapping my arms around his shoulders.

He straightened up and gave me the most intense look I would ever witness. "This is not temporary."

Oh hell.

Some people don't find possessiveness attractive. My last boyfriend had been the most trusting, even-tempered guy I would ever meet. But the words coming out of Rey's mouth... It was like I was signing part of myself away to this man who claimed everything and nothing.

In what felt like a heartbeat later, we were in my room and he was pulling my shirt up over my head.

"Let me shower first," I told him.

He shook his head, already dragging his tongue and teeth over the swells of my breasts. He sucked my nipples over the soft material of the normal bra I'd put on as his hand jerked my shorts and panties down to my knees. Rey palmed me between my legs, groaning deeply as he undid the clasp of my bra and let it gape, exposing my breasts.

"You're so wet." His fingers grazed over my lower lips before spreading them gently. Rey groaned, walking us over to the big chair I had in the corner of the room. He sat down first before sitting me on his lap with my back to his chest. He kicked my bottoms the rest of the way off, tossing each of my legs over his own spread knees. Kisses peppered my neck, alternating between brushes of his tongue. "My Sal," he murmured, smoothing his rough hands over the inside of my thighs. Each pass was longer, slower, reminding me that I was spread wide open to the cool air conditioning. The simple, easy motions of his hands alone turned me on so much and left me panting with anticipation. The fact he wasn't rushing this was like straight electricity to my veins.

My voice was a million miles away, lost in a galaxy that hadn't been discovered yet.

Rey made a soft noise against my ear as he swept his palms over and over my thighs, once, twice, each pass alternating between getting closer and further away from where I wanted him the most. Then he did it. With a high pass of his right hand, he detoured to slide the meaty part of his palm over that sensitive button of nerves between my legs and slipped his middle finger deep inside of me.

"Rey!"

His answer was a groan right into my ear, hot breath fanning over the side of my face. That finger moved in and out of me slowly, letting his palm press tightly against me on each downward stroke. His lips suckled the thin skin on my neck, making my hips buck. His finger curled inside, and I whimpered.

Rey slid another finger in to join the first, pressing as deep as they could go. He curled his fingers again and touched something that made my legs tremble. "Feel good?"

"Yes, yes." My hips were squirming to meet with his movement. It was too much, but I still wanted more, and from the sounds he was making, he did too.

"You're dripping down my fingers, Sal. Soaking my pants," he groaned.

I tried to move my hips away, but he quickly wrapped an arm around my waist and held me to him, his proud, impressive erection a log against my bottom and back.

"No, stay. I love it." His pelvis bucked against me, telling me just how much he liked it. After a few more slow passes, his hand started jerking in me quickly, his fingers pressed into that one magical spot so tightly I was gasping for air. "Just like that. I want you like that."

"Oh my God!"

"Good?" he asked, earning a tiny nod. The wet sound of him moving in and out of me quickly filled the room. Rey grunted, moving his fingers even faster, making me cry out even louder at the strange, euphoric feeling starting in the center of my body. "I want you all over my hand. I know you can do it," he said, sucking on my earlobe.

I couldn't catch my breath. I'd been running miles and miles every day since I was a kid. My stamina was something to brag about, but with his fingering and the way he pressed on my g-spot, I couldn't even think of whether this was heaven or not. When the tingling heightened, I arched against him and gasped.

Out of nowhere, the most explosive, hot orgasm of my life took over, blinding me, making me cry hoarsely something that was blasphemous in a dozen religions.

Rey was groaning behind me, grinding his lean hips into me. He cooed something in German, sweet, sweet, sweet, as he nuzzled my neck.

I was panting, my insides throbbing almost violently

around his fingers. My freaking abs were contracting and cramping. "Oh!"

He made a humming noise in his throat before closing his legs and mine in one movement. His fingers slipped out of me before shifting my body so that I was boneless and sideways across his lap. I could hear him breathing loudly as his mouth dropped down to mine, kissing me sweetly on the lips. His tongue gently explored past my lips and into my mouth. His hand cupped my shoulder before he snuck his fingers under the loose strap of my bra, our kisses only breaking apart long enough for him to pull the entire thing off.

Our slow, deep kisses of tongue on tongue ate up the time. Unrushed and tender, they went on and on, his hands stroking and painting lazy circles on my bare spine. Right around the same time his breathing calmed, his mouth pulled away from mine. Those heavy beautiful eyes were on me, searching my face, my neck and then down to my chest, stomach and bare hips. Rey shook his head while licking his lips. His hand caressed my shoulder before making its way to my breast and nipple. He hummed, brushing the back of his fingers over my nipple again. "I've been waiting for this forever."

"I love you very much." The words were out of my mouth, steady and determined. And true. They were so, so true.

I felt my face heat up under his intense scrutiny. His words were like gold, and I didn't mind that he didn't say anything in return. Instead his eyes were lasers, scanning over every inch of my exposed skin—everything. His hands were gentle and slow as they caressed me, brushing over the many, tiny and nearly invisible scars I had on my thighs and knees from years of soccer and from just being a kid.

He must have known that because he rubbed over me more reverently, squeezing my thighs in his big hands, thoughtless words in his mother language slipping out of his mouth. He slid his hands up my quads and over my hip bone. He brushed his fingers over my stomach, my belly button. His palm moved up to cup my breast, bringing it up to his face, and in a heartbeat his lips were sucking my nipple roughly again. His other hand kneaded my hip.

It all kind of went up in flames right then. I started grinding my pelvis into his hard thigh, and at some point he picked me up effortlessly and dropped me onto the middle of my queen-sized bed. He laid on top of me as I pulled his shirt off roughly and tossed it to the side. Reiner Kulti shirtless was probably the most magnificent thing I'd ever seen, but Reiner Kulti shirtless and covering me should have made me start spontaneously ovulating. His skin was tight and hot as I smoothed my palms over his pecs while he nipped at my neck. My hands were moving as if they'd unbuckled and unbuttoned a hundred belts in the past.

In the blink of an eye, we'd pushed his pants off his hips, and I was cupping his huge hard-on through the thin material of his jade-green boxer briefs. Rey's wet mouth kissed a line down my chest as he kicked his underwear off his legs.

His long cock bobbed in the air as he kneeled over me, a deep fascinating shade of pink and red and purple. In his full glory, Rey was lines of muscle, a hard, thick cock and strong, muscular thighs that told me a story about what his secret had been when becoming one of the best players in the world.

He was perfect.

"You're on birth control, yes?" he whispered after dropping down to his elbows to cage me between his bunched biceps.

I pressed my mouth against his, sucking on that full bottom lip I'd eyed countless times in the past. "Yes."

He groaned, kissing me with vigor, moving his mouth a moment later to suck on my earlobe. His erection was heavy on the inside of my leg, that blunt, damp head prodding against my lower lips. "I've been abstinent since I stopped drinking," he said softly.

A year? I was a deeply possessive person. I didn't want to think about him being with anyone, ever, but I guess I couldn't complain about his inactivity. I guess. But a year? It was almost hard to believe—almost. If this was anyone else telling me something like that I might have a hard time believing them, but I knew Rey wouldn't lie to me.

I also knew what he was telling me. We'd all been tested for everything under the sun when the season started, coaches included. Plus, God knows there was nothing for him to worry about.

His hips surged upward, rubbing his length over the seam of my cleft and I arched too, loving the feel of his hot, soft skin. Wrapping my legs loosely around his thighs must have been enough of an answer because he was smiling, dropping those narrows hips between mine.

Rey kissed me deep, his tongue against mine as he aligned himself. Inch by inch he pressed in, his thick cock stretching his path forward. He groaned louder than I did, having to work himself deep into me. "Sal, Christ," he grunted, looking down at where we were connected.

I couldn't help but look down at us too. The dark thatch of hair, a shade darker than what he had on his head, clashed against me; dark to smooth, the thick base of his shaft barely noticeable as he made his way inside of me. Rey rocked forward, kissing me softly as he slid in to the hilt. I groaned into his mouth as he pulled out completely before pushing in deep again.

His hand cupped my cheek, palming it just shy of being too rough. Those brown-green eyes were filled with something I couldn't recognize. His hips rolled heavy, his weight pressing him hard against me, pounding, filling; the sound of our skin slapping together was the most erotic sound in the world. Rey's eyes were locked on mine constantly, his jaw clenched with each thrust.

Those unpolished, desperate strokes of him inside of me went on and on, faster and faster. Hard meat slapping wet flesh. He started sweating, his back damp under my fingers. I ran my hands over his back and the butt I'd been obsessing over forever, squeezing it, grabbing it and pulling him in even when there wasn't any more room for him to move. His pubic hair was dewy against me as he circled his hips, making me cry out.

I wanted him all. Every inch long, every inch wide, his girth and his heat. I wanted each powerful stroke that tried to tunnel him into me.

Then I was coming. I groaned so loudly I'm sure if anyone had been standing outside, they would have heard me. Rey was biting his lip and groaning as an orgasm rushed through my spine and lower body, milking his long length.

"I need to come," he panted.

Who was I to argue? I arched up and kissed him, and I kept right on kissing him as his thrusts turned frantic and shallow before he finally pushed in to the hilt and stayed there, pulsing and groaning loud against my mouth.

We stayed like that forever, him on top, inside of me, his body hot, sweaty and perfect. It took me forever to catch my breath, but I rubbed all over those sleek, honed muscles in the meantime. I pressed my lips to the parts of his shoulders I could reach and kneaded his back. When his breathing evened out, I'd be lying if I said I didn't get a huge kick out of how worn-out he was, I wrapped my arms around him and gave him a hug. He lifted his head enough to give me a few pecks on my mouth and cheek, but it wasn't until he pulled back even further that my heart soared. He was smiling the biggest smile I'd ever seen, and it reached deep into my existence.

My poor heart didn't know it could love so much. I wasn't going to let my fears get the best of me. I had this one life, and if I didn't make the best of it, then what was the point? I'd been given plenty of good things to be appreciative of, and I wasn't going to let this newest gift go to waste. I had never considered myself to be unappreciative.

So I said to him the three words that felt more real than anything while I palmed the small of his back, repeating the words I'd said moments before. "I love you, Reindeer."

That smile the size of the solar system stayed strong but the emotion in his eyes quadrupled. "I know."

The arrogant ass. "You do?"

He kissed the corner of my mouth. "*Ja*." Rey kissed the other side. "You always have."

I snorted. "I don't know about *always*—"

"No. Always," he insisted.

"You haven't always cared for me, and I can live with that."

"You're a better person than I am, and I haven't loved anything the way that I love you, *schnecke*. I would say we're tied," he argued. His smile was gentle, his skin bright and flushed. "I've been waiting every day of my life for you. Your honesty, your loyalty," he punctuated each of my traits with a kiss to a different part of my face that had me grinning like a freaking fool. "Your competitiveness, your fierceness, your kindness and this body... I would do anything for you. Lie, cheat and steal. There is nothing I wouldn't do. Understand?"

I didn't, not completely at least. I didn't have a lot of self-esteem issues, I was good with myself but that wasn't necessarily a bad thing, I figured. I never wanted to become a cocky asshole.

I could love one, but I didn't want to be one.

"Sort of," I answered him honestly. "Are you really not staying on with the Pipers next season?"

"Absolutely not. I'm staying with you."

"But I don't even know where I'm going," I reminded him again with the least amount of panic I could muster.

"It doesn't matter. You'll go somewhere, and you aren't going alone," he assured me.

I blew out a deep breath and scrunched up my toes against his leg hair, making him jerk. "What about your house here?"

Rey dropped another kiss, ignoring what I was doing. "I'll sell it."

I let out a shaky exhale I couldn't hide into his neck. "I'm a little scared."

"Don't be."

"I can't help it."

"Remember that idiotic question you asked me in the car? About what would happen when you can't play soccer any longer?" He didn't wait for any acknowledgment. "Nothing would happen. We would have a different adventure to go on. You are my best friend, my love, my playmate and my teammate. You'll have a team with me wherever we are, with whatever we are playing."

For a man who didn't talk much, he really went for the knockout when he tried. Jesus Christ. Tears came into my eyes, and I couldn't even bother blinking them away. "I guess we'll figure out everything, right?"

He nodded. "I won't let you give up."

I smiled at him right before pulling at his leg hair again, earning a grunt that time. "I've never given up on anything. I'm not about to start now."

# EPILOGUE

## KULTI ANNOUNCES RETIREMENT

Soccer forward Salomé Casillas Kulti announced her retirement on Wednesday. Following six seasons in the European Women's Football League, three EWFL championships and one Altus Cup win with Germany, the captain and forward for CS Frankfurt will be officially hanging up her cleats.

"It's time," the thirty-four-year-old expatriate explained. "I've done what I wanted to do, and I'm ready for this next step in my life."

Speculation over her possible retirement was high following CS Frankfurt's last championship win, when she was spotted limping off the field. Her injuries have been well-documented over her career, but a comeback was managed each previous time. Before joining the EWFL, she played for the U.S. Women's National Team and spent four years with the U.S. WPL's Houston Pipers, bringing the team to one championship.

Casillas Kulti has been just as well known for her soccer skills as for her relationship with retired international soccer icon Reiner Kulti. Married five years, the couple has made no secret of their support of each other. 'The King' has been noted for his perfect attendance at her games and has been spotted wearing her jersey without fail. This is the second marriage for Reiner Kulti and the first for Casillas Kulti.

We wish the two nothing but the best with their plans in starting a family.

## ABOUT THE AUTHOR

Mariana Zapata lives in a small town in Colorado with her husband and two oversized children—her beloved Great Danes, Dorian and Kaiser. When she's not writing, she's reading, spending time outside, forcing kisses on her boys, or pretending to write. Or burning experiments in the kitchen.

MarianaZapata.com

Twitter: twitter.com/marianazapata_

Facebook: facebook.com/marianazapatawrites

Book Store: marianazapata.bigcartel.com

Merchandise Store: marianazapata.threadless.com

## ALSO BY MARIANA ZAPATA

Lingus

Under Locke

Rhythm, Chord & Malykhin

The Wall of Winnipeg and Me

Wait for It

Dear Aaron

From Lukov with Love

Luna and the Lie

The Best Thing

Hands Down

All Rhodes Lead Here

CPSIA information can be obtained
at www.ICGtesting.com
Printed in the USA
LVHW041910160822
726100LV00001B/13